"A BLOODIER ROSE"

being the second book of

THE SAUDER DIARIES

the continuing affairs of

airship pirate and gentleman

Hans Sauder

aboard the legendary airship

"THE BLOODY ROSE"

during its further exploits

in the skies above Europe

MICHEL R. VAILLANCOURT

The Sauder Diaries
"A Bloodier Rose"

By Michel R. Vaillancourt

~~~***~~~

Independently Published by Avenger Press Services

At Amazon.com CreateSpace

~~~***~~~

~~~***~~~

DEDICATION

To the international Steampunk Community, as diverse and varied as we are. This is a book about the collective experience we share in our music, our art, our costumes, and of course, in our literature. Without you, there is nothing to write about.

To the dedicated fans and readers of the first "Sauder Diary", your support, encouragement and kind words made this book possible.

To my "hit team" of editors and test readers, your work and dedication to the cause is invaluable.

I just write this stuff. All of you make it real.

Thank-you.

~~~***~~~

Table of Contents

"New Expendable Best Friends"

Diary Entry for 27th June, 1888

My name is Hans Sauder, of Bremen, Germany. I was born in August of 1866.

Yesterday I once again became an airship pirate. It can be rather amusing where life leads you.

As a result of this unexpected turn of events, I have decided to start a diary so that I can document my journeys aboard the pirate airship Bloody Rose either for my family or myself, depending on the whim of Fate.

I wish it understood from the outset that I am not being coerced into cooperation in any fashion. I am a free man, acting of his free will. Should I be taken captive or killed as a result of my actions, please have the mercy to mail this text to my mother.

My accomplishments thus far on my first two days in my new life are: getting my left ear pierced; a clandestine meeting with Camilla Williams of British Intelligence, discussing our possible courses of action with Blackheart and key officers, blacking Piet Aldebert's eye, and making ready for our voyage to America.

The meeting with Camilla added a particular depth to our working relationship that I must note will prove very valuable in the future. She is an *interesting woman with an aggressive sense of achievement.*

It has been a busy and satisfying couple of days.

*****

Hans gritted his teeth to suppress a sound of pain as Alexi Koblinski dabbed at his ear with the antiseptic. He was sitting on one of the examination tables in the sickbay. Annika was leaning against a wall and watching the two of them with her arms folded across her chest.

"There you are, Pan Sauder. That is the third of the three," he said swirling a sizable needle in a bottle of antiseptic with a set of grips.

"*Dankeshön, Herr Döktor.* That was more painful than I had expected," Hans said examining the neat row of three holes in his left earlobe with a hand mirror.

"Which would be why I suggested the topical anesthetic you insisted you did not need," Koblinski replied amusedly.

"Ready for these, Hans?" Annika asked, holding out her hand.

"Yes ... care to put them in for me?" he asked. She nodded wordlessly and moved over to where he was sitting. Alexi found something that needed rearranging at the other end of the modest-sized sickbay.

"I must say, Hans, I was surprised about this," she said quietly.

He smiled at her. "In for a penny, in for a pound" he said with a shrug.

"Why three?"

"One for my Right Of Passage when I first joined the crew and one for my return to the ship and my chosen life here," he said as she clicked the second of the three small silver-and-gem hoops closed.

"And the third?"

"For having met you."

She stopped and blinked at him. "Really?" she said hesitantly.

"Really. No matter what the future holds, Annika, I cannot ignore the effect you have had on my life thus far."

The door to the sickbay opened and MacIssac stuck his head in and grinned at Hans. "Ahoy there, Mister Sauder. Ye've some blond and stacked lass on the dock asking' fer ye by name. Ye've a fine taste in wenches if she's as nasty with her clothes off as on."

Annika put a hand on her hip and looked at Hans questioningly. Hans looked at the Scotsman, clearly puzzled. "What?" he asked.

"Aye, Fenelton got a touch frisky with 'er an' she laid 'im out with her parasol. 'e will nae be 'earin' the end o' tha' for a while," MacIssac laughed.

Hans rolled his eyes and looked at Annika. "It is just Camilla. 'Our Lady Whitehall', as it were. I will go and see what she wants ... we are strictly business she and I."

"Uh-huh," Annika said with a grin at him. "Same rule applies with Camilla as with Arietta!" she laughed. MacIssac and Koblinski looked completely baffled as to what she might mean.

*****

"You want us to what?" Hans asked Camilla.

She nodded at him. "You heard me correctly, my handsome pirate; America. England is willing to pay the *Bloody Rose* very well to undertake this task for us."

Hans scratched the back of his neck as he shook his head. "A most interesting choice of attire, *Fräulein*," he commented, changing the topic for a moment to give himself a chance to think. "Feeling inspired by the meeting place, were you?"

They were behind a set of tool sheds, essentially out of sight of almost anyone. The air was filled to bursting by so much noise from the various workers and machines that there was no practical way anyone might overhear them. However, they were still meeting in what amounted to a public place. She had yet again an entirely different clothing-personae adopted for this meeting. He wondered what her closet looked like.

She was dressed, quite truthfully, like one of the prostitutes that were to be found within a stone's throw of the dockyard gates after the regular work day was over. Her blond hair was tousled and teased with bits of ribbon, small bells and semi-precious stones on strings laced through it. She was wearing a saucy white shirt, largely unbuttoned, over a much smaller red one that left a fair amount of both her breasts and midriff on display. She wore three loose skirts of increasing length and different colours of blue. Each skirt was slit vertically in five places, so that as she moved there was always a scandalous collage of hues, calf and thigh to be seen.

She was a distractingly attractive woman, in spite of the fact he knew she was a spy working for British Intelligence. Fenelton could likely be forgiven for trying to pay for her services. Refusing to accept a twice-repeated "no", on the other hand, is what got his collar-bone broken. The bamboo shaft of her parasol, she had explained, was in fact filled with lead. It was a very pretty club in the hands of a very dangerous woman.

She struck a saucy pose with one hip and knee cocked, with her left hand on her hip and her right index finger tracing her lip. She gave him a bawdy wink. "I do so enjoy getting to play dress-up as part of my job, Hans. The only better part is undress-up later." She blew him a kiss and he blushed slightly.   She was obviously somewhat surprised. "My, my ... A modest pirate. Well, how very interesting."

"As usual, *Fräulein*," he continued, deciding the original line of conversation was much more in his favour, "I will deliver your message to *Kapitän* Blackheart.   He will decide. Is there a provisioning rendezvous as part of this deal?" Hans asked.

She shook her head and then paused.   "Well, actually, sort of. When you reach the Azores, they will have been informed by Marconi wireless to provide you with whatever fuel, water, food, and munitions you need. The tube contains a bank note for the first third of what you are offered to undertake this. You will get the rest when you reach our man in America."

Hans nodded. "Very good. I know that there were other operational plans for the next couple of months, but this is rather intriguing," he said.

"Do I understand correctly, Hans, that you are now a Commissioned Officer aboard the *Bloody Rose*?" she enquired quietly, while she sidled up to him and draped an arm over one of his shoulders.

"*Ja, Fräulein*. That is correct," he said putting his hands at her hips.

"What rank?" she asked in a similarly low tone.

"Officially a lieutenant."

"Of?"

"Officially the Advanced Weapons Officer," he replied, trying to ignore the whiff of her perfume he had just gotten. "But in practice I am standing engineering watches if we are out of battle. When the bells and whistles sound, then I am with the *Kapitän*."

"Both a man of intellect and a man of action. I like that. We are of similar rank, then. That is good to know. When we last met, you said you had a sweetheart aboard your ship?"

"Yes. That has a been a bit of a surprise, but it can be rather amusing where life leads you."

Camilla eyed him for a moment. "You are very lucky, Hans, being able to work with your lover," she said quietly. "My husband is a naval Captain. If we are lucky, we see each other every couple of months, between his travels and mine."

Hans lofted an eye-brow and regarded the attractive woman dressed as a street-girl, currently pressed against him. "Husband? What ever happened to being able to court you?" he asked, rather amused.

She chuckled. "I am a spy, Hans. Really ... if letting you chase me, take me out to dinner, and kiss me once in a while meant that you would have looser lips around me whenever you were in port ... well, how do I lose in that arrangement?"

He laughed softly. "My life is suddenly filled with beautiful, dangerous and cunning women. I am hardly protesting, I assure you, but it is taking some getting used to. And what does your husband think of you having a gaggle of bedazzled men willing to take you out to dinner?"

She moved sensuously against him, hooking a leg around his before she answered. "We have an understanding, he and I. I know he becomes lonely in his travels, so I do not begrudge him seeking solace from time to time. Likewise, he understands that my job involves using my body one way or another to achieve my objectives. We are hardly wanton trollops, he and I, but there are realities of the modern world that need to be acknowledged." She paused and then regarded him for a moment.

"What is on your mind, *Fräulein*?" he asked.

"Firstly, stop calling me that. You are Hans, and I am Camilla. We are both using each other and we both know that. I am using you as a way of achieving some of my given objectives. You are using me as a way of ensuring your worth to your Captain, both in terms of money and adventure."

"I will concede you that, Camilla," he nodded. He would have liked to argue with her, but if he was honest with himself, she was right.

"Do you trust me, Hans?"

"Not entirely, no. You have your orders to follow, for the benefits of your country. I am a pirate and if your husband was an airship captain instead of oceanship, he and I would be inclined to kill each other if we met professionally. Realities of the modern world, as you say."

"That is something I like about you, Hans. Something I like a great deal. You are a smart man with a quick grasp of situations."

"Thank you," he replied. "So, do you trust me, Camilla?"

"Not entirely," she chuckled against his throat in a fashion he found rather arousing for some reason. She shifted her stance against him, and he leaned them back against a shed wall. To any passerby, it would have looked like a typical moment between an airshipman and his paid girl.

"You are a pirate, Hans," she continued. "At the end of the day, you have no loyalties, save perhaps to your ship, your captain and your pay share. And your sweetheart, I should think. While I suspect that you are largely an honorable man, I also know that the ship you crew has a reputation for never wearing gloves when it comes to a fight. As such, I expect there will be times that you and I will be working at cross purposes, Hans."

"That is entirely likely, Camilla. The question I have is why we are discussing any of this at all?"

"You and I are uniquely positioned to make each other very successful in our given worlds, Hans. I just want to know if you understand things well enough that we can work together in a long-term way. I can have you as my pawn, my rook, or as my king."

"I do very poorly as a pawn in anyone's games, Camilla. I tend to find ways to upset the gambit."

"Pirates do that I have noticed," she chuckled and then nibbled at his neck. "And I personally think you would be a waste as anything less than a King. But do understand that ultimately, we are both pieces on the board in the hands of players who are willing to sacrifice us."

"So what does this all mean, Camilla?" he questioned, trying to ignore the distracting state of arousal she was inspiring. He needed to be able to think clearly, and she was impairing that with her physicality. He considered simply pushing her away, but at the same time, there was something that was akin to a challenge here and he was not yet going to change the game because she was playing her advantage.

"If I spy for you, will you spy for me?" she asked in a sultry voice that was more suited to an offer of sex than espionage.

"Pardon?" he asked, clearing his throat.

"Both of us discover interesting things in our jobs, Hans. That book, for example. You brought it to me first, not to anyone else. That made me look very good to my superiors. You were well paid for it, but its value to the Empire goes beyond what you were paid. If you happen upon any other items or news of that sort, please do bring them to my attention. I'll make it well worth your while," she whispered in his ear, and then traced the edge of his lobe with the tip of her tongue.

He roughly grabbed her by a handful of the hair at the back of her head and harshly bent her neck back away from him. She gasped in surprise, going rigid against him, but otherwise not resisting him. He looked at her with a pointed mixture of intolerance and arousal. "Will you really?" he said irritably. "You had best be offering something more than this, Camilla dear, because I can get this nine times over aboard the *Bloody Rose*. And since that is the case, you might as well give this a rest for now." He released his grip on her hair and she ran her fingers through it and then gave him a frosty glare.

"Suit yourself," she said coolly, leaning against him again and putting her arms around his neck. There was an icy silence and then she resumed speaking at him in a low-toned hiss. "I was not offering to sleep with you like a common whore to settle accounts on behalf of my country, Hans. You are an attractive man and it is hardly difficult to play at my cover with you, but please understand I can have my pick of attractive men."

"Perhaps cutting to the quick of the matter would be beneficial to both of us? We stay in touch, I trade you information that might be valuable to you and you, in return, would offer what beyond money?"

"Would a cache of Tesla rifles and a Hertz Wave Cannon be of interest to you?" she said with a noticeably insincere sweetness in her voice.

"Pardon?" he asked, clearing his throat.

"Much more your style of dirty talk, is it, Hans?" she said with black snicker. She reached inside her shirt over her left breast and pulled out a small brass sleeve tucked there for safe-keeping. The metallic cover protected a repeatedly folded piece of paper. She passed it to him. The warmth of her body lingered in the metal and he noticed it in an annoyingly visceral way. He tucked it into his pocket for now.

"Sitting on an airship dock ready for pickup, are they?" he asked caustically.

"Oh, do not be foolish Hans. That would be boring for you. No, these are in a ruined laboratory under New Slains Castle, on Cruden Bay in Aberdeenshire, Scotland. The most recent owner of the place got out of hand with some of his experiments and the British Army moved in and has had the place under lock and key now for about three years."

"The British Army?" Hans said skeptically. "The Russian Air Navy did not give us enough of a working over, so now you are shipping us off against the British Army?"

"Please, Hans. It is not like it is an entire regiment of rocketeers. It is a dozen men who are all there because they have annoyed someone or another and gotten a stint out there for six months of bad food, cold tents and lousy weather. You know what Scotland is like," she said with a delicate shudder. "You sneak in, take the toys and leave," she said with a mild wave.

She then tossed her wrist to her brow and feigned a dramatic swoon. "Oh dear, you naughty pirates have been naughty, but you are on your way to America to do our dirty work, so I suppose we will just have to forgive you."

Hans chucked at her. "And we have tacit permission to do this?"

She snorted and cuddled against him. "Of course not. In fact, if my bosses were to find out I have given that information to you, they would literally hang me. However we have been sitting on that stuff for three years now for want of any idea what to do with it. If it helps you bunch of rogues out on your little excursion to America, then it is better in your hands than rusting in a Scottish cellar."

"That is quite a risk you are taking, Camilla. Thank you. If you keep finding me gems like this, I will be more than happy to return the favour as I can. Now, I think it is time I headed back to the ship. I have much to discuss with *mein Kapitän*."

"Very good, Hans. Now ... when we get around the corner into the more public view again ... do me the favour of giving me a slap on the rump and a rough kiss, then shove a Mark or two into my skirt and make some lewd remark, would you? We do so need to keep up appearances," she said primly.

*****

"So do I understand you correctly at this juncture, Mister Sauder? Not only did your pretty English spy have another two-thousand Pound errand for us, you found a brass sleeve 'on the ground' containing the location of a cache of advanced infantry weapons in Scotland?" Blackheart looked as skeptical as he sounded. He sat back in his chair and shook his head at the German's news.

"*Ja, Herr Kapitän. Das ist* correct," Hans replied with a chuckle and did his best to look innocent. It was clear from the faces of everyone else that they were not buying what he was selling.

"I think I might be jealous, Hans," Annika said with a laugh. "All the way to Tesla weapons on the third date?"

Arietta snorted her coffee, resulting in a round of laughter from everyone.

"Some women are just more loose in their moral fibre than others, Annika," Hans said with as much continued bland innocence as he could muster.

"Captain-Gunner, please do not shoot the Captain-Rockets," Blackheart said with a laugh. "I am short of talented crew as it is."

"Oh, if you insist," she replied with a long-suffering sigh.

Arietta was nearly doubled over with laughter at this point.

"Once the Chief Engineer regains her composure, I would like your opinions on this. According to the papers from Our Lady Whitehall, they essentially want us to drop everything and undertake this tasking immediately. That will mean that our refit will be delayed by at least a month. It will also complicate re-crewing. We are short nearly a third of our compliment, which directly means we will be compromised in our combat abilities."

"I say we take it on," Annika stated firmly. "It is low risk, pays well, gives us some great guns, and allows us to visit the Allied trough in the Azores for quality supplies we cannot otherwise get. It also means we are not baking on a dock in Persia for July and August."

"While I do need to work on my tan," Arietta said with a chuckle, "I will agree that Persia for July and August is ugly. I understand that the graving cradles are all empty and thus the work rates are best then, but really, it is a miserable time of year. We can use the money we make on this little errand to offset the costs of moving our refit and upgrade work back to the fall of the year. And, as Annika says, being able to refuel on Imperial-grade kerosene and other stores is worth a huge amount. The Spitz's have taken such a beating that they guzzle kerosene like pirates do rum."

Blackheart nodded and glanced at Hans. "Your thoughts, Captain-Rockets?"

"I say we undertake it, but not so much for the profit as the positioning. We have just made significant nuisances of ourselves in Russia. Our Lady Whitehall made it clear that while we were not the only ones paid to go privateering, we were one of the few to return to collect the remaining balance of bounties. If I were the Russian Air Navy Grand Marshal, I might be inclined to have my friends south of the Scorchlands keep an eye out for us, in case the opportunity arose to settle accounts. A trip across the Pond might well be a very wise idea now," he suggested thoughtfully.

"An interesting point of view, Mister Sauder," Blackheart countered, "but do not forget we are essentially being paid to cause the Russians more problems that cannot be directly blamed on the Allied Empires. If we are looking to allow things to cool between us and the Russians, this is likely not the route to take."

Annika snorted in derision. "I refuse to live in fear of the long arm of the Tzar. If they send someone to deal with us, we will just add them to the list of recently looted. Guns and money is all the reason I need for this trip."

*****

Night had long since fallen over the waters of Cruden Bay. The North Sea crashed against the steep sea cliffs, with an ages-old pulse that seemed to have the waves reaching for the shining moon above. Seagulls wheeled and cried their weather's lament. Below, on the landward side of the bulk of New Slains Castle, was a group of huts and sod-wall shacks. A Union Jack fluttered in the night's sea breeze, lit by the campfire burning in the midst of the tiny settlement.

Three fences of barbed wire encompassed both the castle and the settlement, plus another pistol-shot width of ground. The fencing started at one point on the coast and ran around in a semi-circle to touch the sea again. A trio of soldiers, dressed in the uniforms of the British Army, were awake and on duty. Two walked together, tracing a circuit that followed the inside loop of the fence, and then along the coast to return to the start of their march.

Hans and Annika watched the two soldiers approaching slowly towards them. The men moved with the disinterested gait of men that were used to walking a patrol that nothing ever happened on. Hans found some wry amusement in the knowledge that in a mere handful of minutes, he would be the most interesting thing to have happened around here in recent history.

The third soldier sat at the fire, keeping it burning with a low glow. His primary job, however, was to maintain a watchful eye on the progress of the soldiers on foot patrol with a quintocular mounted on a tripod. Essentially, it was five low-power and wide-lensed telescopes mounted together in a battery that all fed their image through a singular viewing lens. This allowed the soldier at the camp to survey the surrounding area in the moonlit darkness as though it were only early dusk.

After an earlier period of observing the modest base, Hans had decided that the soldier at the nightscope was the most dangerous man of the trio. Attacking the guards on patrol, even incapacitating them instantly, would do nothing to stop the third soldier from rousing the entire garrison. If there was one scenario Hans wanted to avoid at all costs, it was starting a shooting war with the British Army. As Annika had pointed out, it didn't matter if they were all of the Army's misfits, twenty to thirty men with rifles were bound to kill something on every volley.

Beside Hans, Annika carefully uncoiled a weapon she called a *boleadora*. It was three arm-length pieces of thin metal wire joined together at a central point. Each line ended in a small weight. It was spun and thrown at a target and, according to the Russian brunette, capable of silently dropping a man in his tracks. The Spanish deck-officer Amram Nando, of all people, had taught her how to use it some time ago.

Right now, somewhere in the darkness of the camp, Arietta was supposed to be sneaking up on the man at the nightscope so that he could not raise the alarm when Hans and Annika attacked the two soldiers on foot patrol. With the overwatchman removed from the equation, no one would be the wiser about what was about to befall these two poor chaps.

Of course, if the Chief Engineer failed, in a few moments the trio of pirates would find themselves in the unenviable position of having kicked the hornets' nest, with nothing in the world that might resemble a fly swatter to defend themselves. The Italian-Ethiope had never failed on one of these sorts of tasks, according to her. Hans decided he would simply have to trust in that.

"I do not bloody understand this," the taller of the two groused to his mutton-chopped companion. His words were clearly audible to the two pirates they were walking towards. "We have been guarding this abandoned castle now for three years. On watch against 'looters and vagrants', they tell us. Why in the Scotch-coast Hell would a 'vagrant' come all the way out here?"

"No idea, my chum," the shorter solider replied. "They have more than twenty of the finest screw-ups in Her Majesty's Army up here ... soldiers, sergeants and officers. All of us are rotated through here in groups of four every three months. I am done up here next week, thank God. I cannot bloody wait to get out of here. It is boring as piss."

"One of the lads was telling me that they have not had a single intruder in the whole three years so far. Nary a shot fired. Waste of bloody time, if ... WOT THE HELL?," the first soldier barked in surprise as Hans leapt like a crouching tiger onto the man beside him. The German pirate drove his victim face-first into a mass of stonework.

Annika let fly the spinning weapon in the hand over her head, even as the first soldier unslung his rifle, intent on using it to club Hans. Before the remaining soldier could strike, the whirling boleadora wrapped around both the man's helmet and rifle. The metal of the rifle barrel slammed back into the soldier's face with a messy crunch, his eyes crossed, and he dropped with a quiet grunt, the rifle still tied to his head.

"Could you have been any louder, Hans? What happened to 'not a peep, Annika'?" she teased.

*****

With the three soldiers bound and gagged and their socks and boots tossed into a thistle patch, Annika gave a thumbs up. "So our man Campfire gave you no troubles?" she asked the assassin-turned-engineer.

"None at all," Arietta answered with a musical chuckle. "I thought he was going to faint on me when he turned around and saw me standing right behind him."

"I imagine that by firelight, in the dark and by surprise, you must be an awesome figure to behold, Chief," Hans grinned.

"Even better with the armour off, or so I am told," she said with a bawdy chuckle.

"A bit less pose and a bit more prowl?" Annika growled. "We need to find that cache and get it to the surface as quick as we can. We have at best thirty minutes we can count on before someone gets up to visit a latrine or the kitchen tent and all hell breaks loose." Annika glanced around and cocked the hammers on her two pistols.

Hans nodded at her. "Lead on, Ladies. I am the one least skilled at this sort of thing."

They made their way into the castle. The door had been spiked shut, but Arietta made short work of that with a pair of paste-tubes. When a portion of their contents were smeared in combination over the hinges, they simply rusted away in a matter of a minute or two. The trio moved the door aside quietly.

Arietta took a device she called a "Ghost Lantern" from a waist pouch and opened the shutters on it. It immediately produced a soft green glow that was equivalent to the light of a pair of candles. Arietta lead them along, while Annika moved behind them, covering their movement with her pair of pistols. They kept Hans between them as they moved.

As they paused at a staircase leading down, he looked back and forth at the two of them. "Why am I here?" he asked. "I am just slowing you two down."

"Firstly," Annika replied quietly, "this was your idea, so you get to be part of the fun. Secondly, you are a smart man with a sharp sense of perception — you may see something we do not. Thirdly, you need to learn how this is done."

"And fourth," Arietta finished, "you are an excellent fighter, so if this goes wrong, we know that we can fight our way out of this if we have to."

"Okay. I feel a bit better about my involvement in this. I think," he said dubiously.

"Come on," Annika hissed. "We do not have the time right now to be soothing your threatened male ego."

They made their way down the stairs, with all of the trio glancing around nervously. They made their way along a couple of dark corridors mostly on instinct until they came to a shattered door that led into a much larger room.

"Stop," Hans said suddenly. The two women did and looked at him. "Annika," he said quietly, "how would your *Ahtyets* protect his lab if he was to go on vacation?"

"On vacation?" she blinked at him. "He did not take ..."

Hans put his finger over her lips. "Listen," he whispered. A very faint sound, like groups of small metal hammers tapping on stone, reached their ears from the darkness ahead. Annika blinked and did not even protest at being shushed as she had been. Fear was visible in her eyes. "What?" Hans asked.

"Irondogs," she whispered. "He would have used Irondogs. Which is exactly what that sounds like."

"Irondogs? What are they?" Arietta asked. Hans was equally as puzzled.

"It is a mastiff-sized automaton that runs on electricity and is shaped like a hulking dog. They are made of metal, right down to leather-shredding claws. They weigh twice as much as the real animal, so if it knocks you down it can kill you just by jumping on your chest. The metal bodies are usually tough enough to ignore pistols and swords."

"So how do you kill one?" Hans asked.

"With a Tesla ray," she said sourly. "They are run by electricity, so they are very susceptible to Tesla weapons."

"Well," Arietta said with a sigh, "I supposed that makes this easier to plan."

"How so?" Hans asked in a hushed voice.

"I will throw a signal flare into the room to illuminate it. I will then shoot every dog I see with my revolvers and spend the next thirty seconds of my life remembering every bit of acrobatic training I have ever learned. You will have that thirty seconds to find a loaded Tesla rifle and start killing Irondogs."

"And if the guns are not there? Or discharged?" Annika asked.

Arietta took a flare out and ripped the ignition strip on it. It began to smoke. "Then I will die about thirty-two seconds from now, and your lives will not be much longer."

She hurled the flare into the room and dove in after it before either Hans or Annika had a chance to protest. There was a dulled whoosh of ignition and then light flooded through the open door from the room beyond. The sounds of a pair of rapidly firing revolvers reached the pair left outside the room.

Hans cursed in gutter-German, jerked the LeMatt from its holster and dove into the room as Annika had taught him just a few days ago. He came up from the shoulder roll with the big revolver levelled, to see what was inarguably a laboratory for electrical experiments. Work benches, equipment racks, powerful generators, man-sized capacitors, blackened transformers and fist-thick electrical cables littered the place. The ceiling was two heights of a man along the walls, arching up to three or four heights of a man in the middle. It was as wide as it was tall, and probably twice as long.

He glimpsed Arietta as she was leaping over a table with three of the mechanical monsters pursuing her. They were huge and Hans swallowed fear back at the notion of her fate if she faltered for even an instant.

"Get it in GEAR, Sauder!," Annika shouted at him. Together they ran to a set of cabinets and pulled them open, to find them empty. Annika roughly shoved him towards a set of doors while she ran to an *armoire*. He jerked the doors open when he reached them, trying to ignore the sounds of the steel claws on stone and the noises of Arietta's best efforts to touch the floor as little as possible.

"Hans!" Arietta shouted.

"Not yet!" he cried back as he started dumping the contents of the revealed chest of drawers to the floor.

"Hans! Behind you!" Arietta shouted in warning.

He did not even turn to look. He dove to a side into a shoulder roll. He spotted the fiend charging him, took a steady aim in a double-handed grip and fired the shotgun barrel loaded with a solid slug into the onrushing automaton. There was a spark of ricochet off the monster's metal hide and the beast staggered like a drunken sailor. He switched the hammer to the revolver barrel and fired nine times as fast as he could squeeze the trigger. The rapport of the big gun echoed in a sustained roll of thunder off the stone walls of the laboratory chamber. Sparks flew from every impact on the monster's head, leaving it reeling with each blow. The hammer fell on a now-empty cylinder, the Irondog shook its head again, steadied itself and turned towards Hans.

It would be the Judo throw of his life, he decided. No matter it was a quarter-ton metal monster; the principle was the same.

"Let it commit itself to action," he breathed to himself as he readied for the monster's attack. "Once it is firmly in the grip of Newton's Laws, I can redirect it as I please. I have thrown Blauchuk around, I can throw an Irondog."

Three blue-white sizzling balls of electricity cracked past him and hit the Irondog as it coiled to spring at him. It collapsed into a spastic heap of flailing limbs, tail and head and then was still. The scent of scorched air and ozone reached his nose even as he heard more shots behind him. He whirled around to see Annika standing on a table with what was apparently a Tesla rifle at her shoulder. She was coolly firing at the dogs that had quite nearly run Arietta down, as fast as the weapon would recharge.

The Russian Captain-Gunner fired at each of the three automatons in turn, giving the Italian-Ethiopian some breathing room as each shot impaired the machines more and more. Halfway through she simply dropped the rifle she held and grabbed the second she had slung around her and resumed firing. Silence descended on the underground laboratory as she finished the job.

Annika turned and then shot each of the inert automatons one more time. She nodded. "Found the guns," she commented.

"Thank heavens," Arietta breathed from where she was hanging upside down from an overhead suspension cable. "They were a bit faster than I would have guessed," she said.

*****

"*Schnell*!" Hans hissed as they strained to hustle the substantial bulk of the cannon up the stairs and along the corridor.

"Oh, shut up, Hans," Annika hissed back as they moved. "We are almost there."

"*Che è sufficiente, i bambini,*" Arietta scolded them both.

They got the nasty looking device out the front door beside the four cases of rifles. Hans and Arietta worked quickly to wrap a cargo net around the cannon and then clip the corners of the net to a balloon system they had taken from one of the Sargasso mines.

"Brilliant idea this was, Hans," Arietta said as they worked. "Okay ... ready?"

"Ready," Hans nodded.

"Ready," Annika affirmed from where she stood beside the now-netted rifles.

Arietta took a hand-dynamo out of a small equipment bag they had brought with them and clipped the wire leads to it. She cranked the handle as fast as she could and there were three thudding detonations as the chemical candles in each balloon package lit. Within a few seconds the balloons had inflated enough that they were floating upwards, but still without enough lift to heft their payloads. There was a few tense moments and then the rifle case began to lift off the ground.

Annika held onto a guide rope keeping it from immediately drifting into a wall or other obstruction. Likewise, Hans and Arietta worked to similarly control the two balloons lifting the cannon. They gave sharp tugs on their ropes which tore the ignition strips on flares attached to the load, allowing the airborne cargo to be spotted for miles.

"Okay," said Hans with a note of excitement. "Let us get out of here. The entire coast of Scotland is going to see those things floating into the air above the castle. I do not wish to get into a gunfight with the British Army just now."

They ran for the coast, and then headed along it as fast as they could manage. Overhead, they could hear the engines of the *Bloody Rose* growing louder in the night.

*****

"Excellent work to you all," Blackheart said, raising a glass to them as they and the rest of the officers sat together for a late-evening nightcap and debrief of how the sneak-and-grab had gone. "That is the quite story, I must say. Irondogs, no less. No wonder that the British Army had been sitting on that cache of equipment. I am unsure if they would have deemed it worth the aggravation to try and retrieve them." He chortled and had a sip of his glass of rum.

"Hans did an excellent job of planning the entire thing. Not a shot fired, and beyond some bruised noses and egos, no injuries on either side," Arietta said, sipping her glass of wine.

Aldebert snorted. "Of course no one was hurt and of course it took five times longer than it should have. Sauder planned it," he said derisively. "We could have done this much more easily and swiftly by just landing the Gunner-

Marines a mile away and over-running the camp at dusk. After the first two or three of them kissed the dirt, the rest would have run like mice. Then we could have landed the ship and loaded everything we wanted aboard. Instead of that foolishness of chasing cargo-nets dangling from balloons in the middle of the night."

Blackheart glanced between Hans and Piet but said nothing. Hans turned to look at the other man.

"We cannot afford to lose any more crew to misadventures and British marksmen," Hans replied levelly. "We barely have the manpower we need now."

The Dutchman waved dismissively at the German. "You are just unwilling to have any blood on your hands, Sauder. You are a weak and faint-hearted mother's boy that has already gone running home once to your ..." Aldebert's sentence was cut short by Hans' fist driving into his face, sending him sprawling out of his chair and onto the floor.

Hans swiftly got up and unceremoniously slammed his boot heel down onto the reeling man's left wrist. Aldebert cried out in pain.

"If you so much as move, I will break your wrist in two places with a twist of my heel," Sauder snarled. "Shut up and listen, little man. You will leave discussions of my family and my personal life out of any future conversations you have with anyone. The nicest thing that will happen if you make this mistake again is that I will break your ribs and leave you in *Döktor* Koblinski's care."

"Captain?" the Dutchman pleaded.

"Bit off a bit more than you can chew, it looks like to me, Mister Aldebert," Blackheart replied conversationally, looking past the edge of the table. "Mister Sauder is a bit touchy about his personal life, as I think you now know. If I were you, I would likely find other things to chide him about." He paused for an unhurried moment and had a mouthful from his rum glass while the other officers all watched the unfolding events with some surprise. "I would likely also not say too much ill about the Captain-Gunner in his presence, either. I expect he would take that rather poorly as well." Blackheart contemplated the remaining contents of his glass and then said "Let him up, Sauder."

Hans made a guttural noise and took his weight off the Dutchman's wrist. It was already beginning to swell.

Alexi glanced over at the Dutchman and sighed. "Please do be more careful, Mister Aldebert," he admonished. "It can be rather surprising how people react to unwarranted criticism. Let us get you to sickbay and get that taped up so you can stand your Steering House watch later."

"The Not-So Big Easy"

Diary Entry For July 4th, 1888

It has been a busy and tumultuous week. Annika and I are now lovers, so worth the wait. The ship has crossed the Atlantic Ocean, something that the Bloody Rose had never done before. We visited the city of New Orleans and met "Our Man Louisiana" there, to gain more information about whatever this is all about. I cannot disclose what it was we found out, but it is rather shocking. I tested my first man in a Right of Passage and will smugly note that I will be another ten percent richer every pay.

Crossing the Atlantic Ocean was done in three steps. We flew south by southwestward from Scotland over the Irish Sea and then straight south to Spain. From there we veered southwestward to the Azores Islands, which the British use as a combined way-point and base for oceanship and airship traffic. We did not stay long, save to refuel and rearm, and we were hardly made to feel welcome.

From there we flew to the American city of New York, which took us a day and a half. We then turned southwest without pause and flew overland to the city of New Orleans, which took us nearly another day of high altitude flight over the Appalachian Mountains. The sight of the

Mississippi River below us, and the huge delta lands that it poured through to reach the ocean, was impressive in its scope.

When we reached New Orleans, we spent a day quietly snooping about and recruiting new hands to fill our ranks. Two new Officers — Jeremy Grumman and Sarah Redsands — have joined us, as well as six general crew including an engineer, Tavish O'Ferral. Blackheart requested that I be one of those to test Mister Grumman in his Right of Passage. He did not fare well. Annika tells me that Redsands only fared marginally better.

The next day we met our contact person with British Intelligence. Kapitän Blackheart is using Annika and I as his "voice and reach" so that he is not exposed directly in this. While I do consider that prudent of him, I must also acknowledge that it means that Annika and I are "standing into danger" as we say in navigation.

I will not record the name or occupation for "Our Man Louisiana", lest this text fall into the wrong hands. However, it was an enlightening visit and he, a gentlemanly host. Annika, being the lover of guns that she is, managed to arrange the purchase of a pair of American-made multi-barrel weapons designed by a Döktor Gatling. She had thought they might be a good way of sweeping the deck of another ship, should we face a marine boarding like the battle with the Severnyĭ Volk.

While we were in New Orleans, Annika and I spent a night aground waiting to be relayed to our next in-line destination. We stayed together at a hotel, our cover ostensibly being a husband and wife team checking American ports for a place to begin an airship service and repair company. At one point in the night, we allowed ourselves to be carried away in the moment and she and I made love together for the first time. It was a most incredible experience; words cannot do it justice and so I will leave them unsaid. She is my woman, I am her man. We have an understanding between us about the "realities of the modern world that need to be acknowledged", to quote our Lady Whitehall.

*****

The airship cruised out of the morning clouds, five hundred feet above the coast of Spain, as she headed out over the Atlantic Ocean on a westward course. She was a little longer than a hundred feet, and was proportioned for speed. She was clearly rigged as a brigantine sailer, yet oddly the masts on her port and starboard sides had been unstepped and laid back flat against her hull. Her sail cloth was tightly bundled and furled, and her rigging tightened in. Instead, her flight was powered from a pair of propeller pods that extended below her keel from her stern area. Under their constant drive, she made her way smartly at a bit more than seventy knots. To anyone happening upon her, she might have looked like any other merchantman, perhaps heading to lucrative trade in the West Indies or America.

She suddenly showed her true colours as her concealed gun doors opened and her two rows of cannon per ship side were run out for action. She pitched and turned sharply, suddenly taking her course to the north, and then reversing her direction to the south in a surprisingly small radius. The guns were brought in, the doors closed, and she turned westward once more. A few minutes passed and then she repeated the previous drill, honing the skills of her crew. Across her stern, gold on red, was written her name; *HMAFS Bloody Rose*.

Inside, the pulsing drone of the two operational electric motors reverberated through the Propulsion Room. Michael O'Raedy, the infamous Captain Blackheart of the *Bloody Rose*, climbed carefully down the ladder leading from the weather deck into Chief Arietta Itala's domain. Both she and Hans Sauder, her anointed second-in-command as well as the Advanced Weapons Officer, stopped the discussion they were having at the other end of the cramped engineering space and looked at him in surprise.

"*Signore Captiano*, what brings you down here?" Arietta asked, her tone mirroring her features. "I cannot remember the last time you came down that ladder."

"Neither can I, Chief," Blackheart said gruffly. He made his way over to where Hans and Arietta were standing in front of two square yards of bulkhead that had been covered in paper which in turn had then been covered in technical notes. "Which is why I figured it was time I got off my arse and came down to reacquaint myself with one of the most important parts of my ship."

Arietta laughed in her musical lilt and nodded. "Hans and I have some dubious news," she said with a sigh.

"I heard as I came down. You cannot make the Hertz Wave Cannon operational. Why not?" he asked, looking up at the much taller woman. At nearly six foot of height and statuesque of build, she was a rather impressive sight. Her richly dark skin and pearl smile spoke of her Ethiopian heritage, while her social graces, education and language gave clear indication of her modern Italian upbringing.

"It would take the *Bloody Rose* twenty minutes at maximum power to generate enough electricity to fire it once," Hans explained gesturing at a set of numbers on the papered wall. "Or more than forty minutes if we tried to have some semblance of a normal life while we waited."

Hans was somewhat shorter than Arietta but distinctly taller than Blackheart. While the young German was tall and lean of build, the English pirate captain was stocky and powerful.

"Except that our Plante packs do not hold nearly that much power. Six or seven minutes, yes?" Blackheart asked.

"Well," Chief Itala answered, "when they were new, we could hold about the equivalent of eight minutes power. These days, with the beating we have taken and the lack of service on them, we are down to closer to four or five minutes. That is marginally enough to satisfy the maw of the EMIPALE during a fight and a bit of hurried damage control after."

"And we cannot use the weapon at a lower power setting?" the Englishman asked.

Hans shook his head and then answered. "We looked at it. It has more reach and hits harder than any other gun either she or I have ever seen. But it was built to very fine electrical specifications to do that. This is a gun for a base, not a ship, *Herr Kapitän*. Neither she nor I have the skill to modify it without risk of a cascade failure of some kind when we turn it on."

O'Raedy sighed irritably. "Fine. We will sell the blasted thing to the Americans, then. I am sure that Edison chap will want to see what his European peers are up to these days."

From there, Itala and O'Raedy spent the next hour together as she gave him a thorough briefing and tour around the Propulsion Room. They exclusively talked about the work list that awaited the first opportunity in a graving cradle. Hans listened in passing as he sat in Watch Keeper's Chair. Cruising as they were with no plans for taking prey meant that in general there was very little excitement to be had. Eventually the Captain and the Chief Engineer were back by where he sat. Not long after, Hans realized Blackheart was studying him rather interestedly.

"*Ja, Herr Kapitän? Was ist das?*" the German queried, looking back at the Englishman.

"I do not recall you having a blade scar on your cheek before, Mister Sauder," Blackheart said amusedly. "Rather neatly done, I might add. Jaw to left ear, much as both of mine are. However did that happen?"

"My brother and I got carried away in a bit of sport on my return visit home," Hans said.

"You let him win, did you?" Blackheart asked, as though the answer were a foregone conclusion.

"*Ja, Herr Kapitän, das habe ich,*" Hans admitted, rubbing at it absently.

"It ages you somewhat, Mister Sauder. A bit less boyish, hmm? I am sure the Captain-Gunner appreciates that. Very good then, try not make it a pair. I do not wish people confusing us," he said with a light wave. He chuckled to himself and then made his way up the ladder and out of the Propulsion Room.

" ... Because we have so many other similarities." Hans said with a roll of his eyes.

Arietta snorted, but said nothing.

*****

The *Bloody Rose* flew into one of the most heavily defended places in the world without issue. She was challenged by a frigate while she was thirty miles away from the Azores, but the new code books given to her by the British Air Admiralty were good and the reply was proper. She had flown "Jack over Roger" since day break, so the Allied frigate opted to escort her in to the sprawling base that covered most of the primary island. They docked without incident, but tension was high aboard the ship. Anti-airship guns dotted the place, easily visible. Likewise, Blackheart pointed out several land-based versions of the Cudahawk airship-to-airship rockets they carried, sitting in sets of four to a launcher, ready to go.

As Camilla had said, the base was expecting them for a replenishment stop. It would take a full day to refuel and resupply, plus bring aboard reloads for the Cudahawk launcher and Sargasso balloon-mine racks. They would leave the next day at noon.

An invitation arrived from the Base Commandant for the officers of the *Bloody Rose* to come to the "O-Room" for a social after supper. There was a personal assurance that the Allied Officers would be ordered to be on their best behaviour towards their guests.

Annika approached Hans shortly later in the Propulsion Room as he worked on a troublesome valve assembly. "Michael has requested I be his date for his excursion to the O-Room this evening," she said.

"Ah," he said sourly. "He has noted you are Russian, yes? And this is a room full of British, French, Spaniards and Germans? I thought you said he always picks his date based on the nationality of the host?"

She laughed. "Oh, Hans, please do not be like that. I expect he wants me with him exactly because I am Russian. This is just his way of grinding the salt. Michael has had very little use for the Allied Air Navies ever since he took leave of them. He will likely be chortling most of the night at their realization that the Commodore has ordered them all to be nice to a Pirate and his Russian escort. Besides, while he can take care of himself, really, I am the strongest head-on fighter in the crew. If something becomes unpleasant, having me at his side is good insurance."

"I suppose," he replied coolly as he scowled at the piece of equipment he was working on.

She looked at him with a combination of surprise and amusement. "You, Captain-Rockets, are jealous. *Da?*" she accused. He simply scowled at her and went back to what he was working on without reply. She chuckled and poked him in the shoulder. "You are! Why, Hans ... that is not something I would have expected of you."

He abruptly stood up and turned to face her, wiping his hands on a rag. "Of course I am jealous ... I was looking forward to spending the evening dancing and carousing with you!"

She reached up and kissed him lightly on the lips. She then gently laid a finger where her lips had been to quiet him. "Turn about is fair play. Ask Arietta," she suggested. "I am sure she would love the chance to spend some time with you outside of the ship. And as I am sure you have guessed, Michael has a soft spot for her. If he is trying to yank your lanyard, you are allowed to tug back. If he is just trying to annoy the Allies, then having Arietta on your arm looking like a million Stirling will not be a wasted evening. Just remember the rule!" she laughed.

He scoffed at her. "Sauce and ganders," he challenged.

"What?"

"You heard me," he teased. "If you are insisting on reserving the right to be my first, then I am insisting on reserving the right to be your next."

"Very good then, Captain-Rockets. I consider your terms of engagement acceptable. Just try not to have either of us wait too much longer," she said with a cheeky laugh as she turned on her heel to leave.

*****

Whatever the Allied Air Navy Officers had been expecting, it was rather clear that the group that arrived at "O-Room" for the evening social was not it. It was also quite clear that Captain Michael O'Raedy was playing to the audience; he had insisted on all of his officers dressing in their "best Governor's kit". All of them were wearing their usual evening meal ensemble of a white shirt, dark pants, and low boots. In addition, a small red lace ruff was at throat and cuff, with a knee-length blue-trimmed grey flight-coat, and similar coloured tricorn cap. The only difference was Blackheart; instead, it was a gold-trimmed black greatcoat and tricorn that he wore.

The pirates entered as a group, being announced formally by the "Duty President" as "Captain Michael O'Raedy and the Officers of Her Majesty's Privateer *Bloody Rose*". Someone muttered something about a "rose by any other name" and there was a round of laughter. That mirth suddenly died as the Commodore, a sharp-cut Frenchman with greying hair and goatee, crossed the floor to plant himself directly in front of Blackheart. The two men stared at each other levelly for a long moment and Hans was quite certain he would have heard a pin drop, let alone a blade pulled in the room.

"*Vous êtes terriblement sacrément courageux pour venir ici*," the Commodore commented scathingly, looking down the end of his nose at the shorter Englishman.

"*C'est la faute de la Reine. Lui reprocher*," the Pirate captain replied in stilted French, resulting in more than just a bit of offence in the room. Another long and tense moment passed between the two men. "*Vous savez, je pense que tout le monde ici s'attend à une lutte*," Blackheart said pointedly.

The two men stared at each other another second or two, and then could not hold the charade any longer. The two burst out laughing and clapping each other on the shoulders like old friends. Hans blinked at Arietta, who was on his arm. She grinned at him.

"I will explain later," she said with a cheery laugh. "These two are from 'way back', as the saying goes."

Everyone in the room collectively relaxed and things were somewhat more friendly. There was a predictable reaction to Annika's introduction which quelled rapidly when the Commodore suavely kissed her knuckle and made a gentlemanly comment about the quality of Russian exports. There was another bit of a stir when word got out that the Abyssinian beauty ostensibly here as the Advanced Weapons Officer's escort was in fact the ship's Chief Engineer. In short order, Arietta was all but holding court with about a dozen officers, all men save two, who were more than interested to talk shop with the striking and intelligent woman. Hans was feeling somewhat of a fifth wheel in the matter, but took the opportunity to study the dynamic of the room.

There seemed to be a general rule of "no more fun than the most senior officer present," he noted. In each of the groups that had formed throughout the room, it was generally the most senior officer of the group that was doing the talking, with only small interjections by the others. By contrast, there was no concern at all by any of the pirates about rank, speaking equally in turn and to anyone and everyone.

An hour or so after they had arrived, Hans was making his way to the bar to get replenishments for himself and Arietta. The Chief Engineer was currently involved in a technical debate about the finer points of using electric motors as the future of airship propulsion, so Hans opted to be the one to go to the bar for them. As he waited for the bartender to pour, Hans found himself being stared at rather intently by a French officer.

"You ... You are not Privateers. You are Pirates. A tiger does not change his stripes based on who feeds him," the French officer accused.

"*Vous avez raison, monsieur*," Hans replied in his best French, trying to judge what was afoot. Disagreeing with the man was going to provoke an argument, of that he was sure.

"My brother," the man announced without his gaze wavering from Hans, "was the Gunnery Officer of the *Triomphe*."

Hans felt his blood go cold. He vividly remembered that pitched battle in the frigid April skies over France. Hans was uncertain what was safe to say to the man; there were so many ways this conversation could go very, very badly.

"I am sorry for your loss, Sir," he said carefully, trying to sound as sincere as he could.

"Are you?" the Frenchman sneered, getting off his barstool and moving to stand in front of Hans. His demeanour was unmistakably confrontational. "I expect you are actually rather smug at what you have done," the Frenchman accused, gesturing at Hans aggressively.

Things were rapidly falling to silence in the O-Room, and a quick glance confirmed that both Blackheart and the

Commodore were eyeing the "discussion" at the bar between Hans and the French officer with some interest. One of the Frenchman's fellows quietly told him in French to "*le laisser passer*"; let it pass.

"*Mais non*," the Frenchman replied loudly. "I want to hear what this good ... gentleman ... has to say about it." Both the pause and voice were full of contempt. Hans was peripherally aware that Annika was slowly making her way towards him. He doubted any good would come of anything she might consider a calming influence on the situation.

His mind raced for a moment and then he nodded. "Allow me the chance to tell you, then," Hans said carefully. He slowly reached into his pocket and took out a fistful of money and dropped it on the bar.

"Bartender ... that should be about three Pounds there. Until it runs out, the French drink on me. I have never had the pleasure of crossing lines with a more skilled and determined airship crew before or since the battle with the *Triomphe*. The *Bloody Rose* has been all over Allied Europe and to north of Warsaw. We have battled the best the RIAN could throw at us. They were kittens by comparison to what the men and women of the *Triomphe* were made of. She took us by surprise with excellent cunning and ship-handling, and had us for Rights in no time."

Hans looked around, realizing that it seemed everyone in the room was hanging on what he had to say. He raised his voice to carry further. "Nothing more than Lady Luck determined us as the victor of that battle when she took us to swords and pistols, Sir. Her crew fought like the tigers you spoke of. By God as my witness I tell you, Sir, they all gave as good as they got. If that is the stuff of French marines, airshipmen and their Officers, Sir, then I tip my hat to you and I will happily toast you all."

"Mister Sauder, take your damn money off the bar," Blackheart said gruffly. Both he and the Commodore were now standing beside the two men. There was a bit of shocked murmur that went around the room at O'Raedy's command.

"But *Herr Kapitän* ..." Hans began.

"That is not a suggestion, Mister Sauder. There is no damn way that three Pounds Stirling is enough to make proper memory of the beating those boys gave us. Bartender, ring the bell; the *Bloody Rose* is buying."

The Commodore all but stamped a foot when he spoke. "*Halte là, capitaine. Je ne permettrai pas ça*," he scowled. "Absolutely not! You will not put a Franc, Shilling, Mark, or anything else on that bar. *Non!*"

"And why not, Commodore?" Blackheart asked sharply.

"Because I will not be outdone in my own Officer's Lounge by a bloody Pirate! I will pay for the drinks myself, *Mon Dieu!*"

*****

"Very well handled, Mister Sauder," Blackheart commented on the carriage ride back to their berth. O'Raedy, Nadezhda, Sauder and Itala were all sitting together in the one carriage. "Very well handled indeed. That chap was spoiling for any reason to challenge you to pistols, I expect. By giving him praise and a salute, there was not a damn way he could claim insult without it looking for what it was."

"I thought you were trying to get me killed when you told me to take the money off the bar," Hans laughed.

Blackheart chortled and the two women laughed along as well. "And Commodore Anton, God Bless the old warbird, closed the whole thing off in a way that none of his men could dare naysay. That man is a gifted diplomat."

"How do you know him, *Kapitan*?" Annika asked curiously.

O'Raedy looked out the coach window, looking wistful as he answered. "He was my commanding officer when I was a midshipman."

*****

They left the Allied Azores as planned and set off west by northwestwards, motoring on two propellers. They were blessed with good weather, allowing them to cruise at a comfortable six hundred feet the entire time. Hans and Annika decided to resume their morning sparring practices, something they had not done in a while.

On the second morning over breakfast, Sauder and Koblinski were chatting as they waited at the galley window for one of Chief Bridge's staff to pass them their meal plates. While the evening meals were served by a duty Steward in the Captain's Mess, the morning and noon meals were only brought as far as the window. It made sense to Hans; it kept those meals quicker, more flexible and much less formal.

"You know, Hans, you are looking far more relaxed these days than I can easily think of prior to our departure from London," the Polish doctor commented in passing.

"Thank-you, Alexi. I certainly feel much more at ease. Everything is just making more sense to me these days," the young German replied.

"Life," Alexi concluded with a chuckle, "is much more comfortable when you stop fighting with its fit."

It was mid-evening that day when the lookouts gave cry that land was ahead. They fixed their position in short order to be off the coast of the American city of New York. From there, they took a more southwesterly heading. They steadily increased altitude to between three and four thousand feet above sea level to cross the low but wide expanse of the Appalachian Mountain range that was under their bow for most of the remaining trip.

Once they were over the western foothills of the mountains, they began a slow decent down to their preferred altitude of between five hundred and a thousand feet. They steered slightly more southwards and were cruising into the airship docks of New Orleans well before dusk.

"I have been told, Mister Sauder," Nando commented as the two men worked together to bring the ship into the docks, "that New Orleans is the 'Paris of America'. I am thus far unconvinced."

For a city the size of New Orleans, Hans would have expected a more extensive airship dockyard. Instead, it seemed to have been a literal afterthought, built as part of the oceanship dockyard area. The American continent was largely safe for rail travel, Blackheart had explained when Hans asked about it. The disastrous events of the Crimean War which forced the dependence on airship travel in Europe were not reflected here. Instead, the Americans had a love of trains, building extensive railways. The Civil War had simply persuaded them to build rail-rolling battlewagons for travel through the more dangerous parts of the country.

There was much to be done once the *Bloody Rose* was secured at her berth, and the agenda of affairs was part of the discussion during the evening meal for the officers. The priorities were taking on at least a dozen crew, the ongoing repairs, making contact with the British spy here in New Orleans, and then beginning their investigation in earnest.

"Now, Captain-Gunner and Captain-Rockets ... you two are going to be my representatives in this matter," Blackheart said as he sliced some of his pork steak. "I need to be clearly visible conducting the affairs of the ship with

Chief Bridges. If I am personally skulking about the town talking to people I have no clear reason to be visiting, that will just attract attention to our errand. You two, of course, have any number of reasons to be traipsing around a town like New Orleans."

Annika and Hans looked at each other and then nodded to their Captain. "We have a description and an address, *Da*?" the Russian brunette asked.

"*Da*," Blackheart answered as he contemplated a forkful of peas. "So you should have little issue in making contact. From there, I am sure there will be a bit of hoop-jumping involved, just to ensure that affairs are being conducted out of the sight of the Tzar. It should be a fine bit of amusement for you."

*****

Hans leaned over the Quarter Deck railing just before supper of the next day, looking down on the activity on the main deck. There was always work to be done on an airship of any kind, let alone one that flew and fought as aggressively as the *Bloody Rose*. Normally at this hour things would be winding down, but Nando and Annika were pushing the crew hard, trying to get the last details done. He noted a few new faces below; recruiting from earlier in the day in and around the meagre airship docks had been a proportionate success.

He himself had spent most of the day working with Arietta and Visivald in the Propulsion Room on repairs and maintenance. It had been intense and focused work, of the sort that leaves the body restless but the mind weary.

"Busy, busy, aye, Mister Sauder?" Blackheart said, coming to a stop beside him.

"*Ja, Herr Kapitän*. Busy is good," Hans replied.

"Do you see the tall and broad shouldered chap down there ... square cut hair, salt and pepper, wearing a

Confederate flight coat?" the Englishman asked causally. The German nodded, spotting the man easily. "New officer ... a Watch Officer, in fact. The name is Grumman. He claims to be quite good. I am not entirely convinced, though. You might want to have a word with him about if he really does have what it takes to be part of a crew like ours, Mister Sauder. I am sure you do not want any laggards aboard any more than I do."

Hans turned his head to O'Raedy, looking a bit puzzled as to what sort of questions Hans would ask a seasoned airship officer. Blackheart cracked his knuckles, smirked, gestured in invitation towards the new officer and then strolled off. Hans looked at his receding back for a moment and then understanding dawned on him. So that was how it was done, was it?

"In for a Penny, in for a Pound," he said with a note of amusement in his voice. He made his way down the ladder, realizing that the Deck Officer, Amram Nando, and one of the Watch Officers, Doretta Tillie, had fallen in behind him as he made his way over to the American. "Excuse me, *Herr* Grumman," Hans said politely.

Grumman turned around from what he had been doing and glanced at Hans and the other two officers and nodded. "What can I do for you?"

"I am Hans Sauder, the Captain-Rockets. This attractive lass is Watch Officer Doretta Tillie. And the Spaniard is the Deck Officer, Amram Nando. We understand you are new to the Crew, aye?"

Grumman nodded coolly. "Aye. I have been a Watch Officer on the Confederate Airship *Raze* as well as the *USAS Indomitable*. I presume you are all here to offer me coffee and cake?" he said in a tone of voice that made it clear he very much expected the opposite.

Hans and the other two laughed. Nando spoke up, his tone of voice dismissive. "They cannot have been that great of ships ... I have never heard of them. What about you Sauder?"

"Not at all. Tillie?"

She shook her head and looked squarely at the American. "Not much of a pedigree as a pirate, if no one has ever heard of your ships. I do not think you have got what it takes to be a member of the scullery crew of the *Bloody Rose*, let aside the notion of an officer."

Grumman looked unimpressed. "Well, they let you on board, so the standards cannot be that high," he said with a laugh. Things on the weather deck were coming to a halt as the crew realized a Right of Passage was in the brewing.

"Well, we will see who winds up owing who ten percent of their shares in a few minutes. I will even be nice and not break your nose. You have not got much by way of looks as it is," Tillie said with a toothy grin.

Grumman undid a length of inch-link chain he had wrapped twice around his waist and chuckled. "It is going to be a pleasure to beat your ass to the deck, bitch. Shall we dance?"

The fight was effectively over in one hit. When Tillie stepped forward, Grumman swung the chain in a scything arc at shoulder level and she gracefully ducked under it. Before he could recover the moment, she summarily rugby-kicked him in the crotch hard enough that she lifted him to his tip-toes. He gave a short bark of agony and tumbled to his knees, clearly trying not to vomit. To add insult to injury, she then backhanded him like a school mistress with a truant child, sending him sprawling.

The assembled crew cheered and hooted as she stepped back dusting her hands off. "That is ten percent, my boy.

Learn to fight like a real Pirate," she laughed as the downed man struggled to regain his footing.

Nando scowled at her. "Oh, come on, Doretta. I will never get a decent fight out of him like this. He is too busy trying to get his stones out of his windpipe to put up a worthy scrap," he said in mock irritation.

"I have got more than enough for the likes of you. First California, next *Bloody Rose*," Grumman said gamely with a cough as he adjusted his grip on his fighting chain. The two men squared off. Nando fought barehanded in a light-footed, whirling style that very much gave the impression of how Hans thought a bullfighter might move. Grumman, even in tremendous pain as he was, fought an aggressive and powerful style, using the chain to threaten his opponent, force their movements and dictate the pace of battle. In a smaller space, where there would be less room to get away from the chain, he would have been murderous, Hans thought. But here, on the open weather deck of the Mediterranean Menace, Nando easily whirled, spun and dodged out of the way of the bigger man's arcing blows.

The crew shouted and cheered, egging both men on. There were more than a few that would have liked to see Nando get his comeuppance at the hands of the American. The Spaniard kept himself aloof and emotionally separate from the crew in a fashion that did not endear him to the men. Hans had no issue with him, but from meals in the Captain's Mess with him, it was clear that Amram was obviously lower aristocracy by birth and considered even most of the officers beneath him.

The two men had both traded several solid blows to this point, and Hans noted Blackheart was watching the fight from the Quarterdeck with some interest. Nando was bleeding from a bloodied nose where he had nearly gotten a mouthful of chain-link. There was another indecisive exchange and then Grumman over-extended with a swing of his chain. Nando whirled in, striking him three times in rapid succession, the last of which was an elbow that smashed into the other man's jaw dropping him in a stunned heap.

Nando looked down at him in disdain. "You forgot that it took two armies to get us out of California, Sir. You do not manage to approach representing one. Your history lesson just cost you ten percent of your shares." The haughty Spaniard punctuated his declaration by giving the American a swift kick in the buttocks as the he tried to stand, knocking him down again.

"You do not seem to be having a very good day, Mister Grumman. Do you wish to call this a wash, spare yourself the beating and just concede the match?" Hans asked him.

"That is quite all right, Mister Sauder. I did not join the *Bloody Rose* to quit because of a couple of setbacks. Let us see who is the better man."

"The answer to that, Sir, was known before your ink was dry. But we do have make it official. On your guard!" Hans laughed.

Grumman gave a snarled cry and stepped forward, lashing out with the chain. Hans was a bit surprised at how much faster that arc of metallic pain seemed to be when he was standing in front of it. They circled and feinted, struck and blocked. The crew around them was cheering, shouting, and stomping their feet on the deck. Bets were called and coins crossed palms.

Grumman was good, Hans knew ... the chain was snaking at him in ways that forced him to abandon an attack or change his movement. If he gave him enough time, the American would eventually land a telling blow. As it was, the other man had already added a few new bruises to Hans' collection.

Hans waited for the next swing, then stepped forward quickly and grabbed him by the leading wrist. He jerked hard, pulling Grumman off balance into a stumble. Hans' left fist connected with the other man's jaw halfway through his travel, snapping his head back violently. The American collapsed to the timber with a hefty thud and did not move. The rest of the crew cheered and hooted as Hans swept a bow. Nando pointed at a couple of the men and directed them to get the unconscious officer down to the attention of Doctor Koblinski.

*****

The next morning, Hans and Annika headed aground dressed in clothing typical for the day for a couple of travelling passengers. They each had a bit of light baggage with them to allow the option of remaining away from the ship for a night or two, if needed.

Predictably, it had taken a bit of effort to persuade Annika to borrow a modest blouse, skirt and bustle from the Irish Watch Officer, Onora Lynch. Fortunately the two women were of similar build and size and the attire essentially fit her, at least physically. Annika scowled at Hans when he wolf-whistled at her, once they were a short distance from the docking tower. He knew better than to do that within hearing of the crew; she would have felt obligated to beat him senseless.

They spent the morning acting like a couple of tourists, strolling about the more popular and fashionable parts of town, arm in arm. They had lunch at a very busy bistro that introduced the two of them to the zesty style of local cuisine. The food was surprisingly good in spite of a requirement for somewhat more drink than they anticipated.

From there, they made their way by carriage to the banking district of the town. They sat close together, his arm around her and her head against his shoulder.

"This feels vaguely normal," he chuckled quietly.

"A novel feeling, *Da*?" she said in a nearly disparaging tone. "So, 'Our Man Louisiana' is a Cobbler, servicing the wealthy business men of the city, *Da*?" she asked in verification.

"*Ja*," Hans said with a nod. "He knows someone is coming, but not who or when, apparently. We have a sign and counter-sign to exchange with him. From there, I expect we will retire somewhere more private than a store-front."

"Much as with our London armour maker," she replied.

*****

Less than an hour later they were being led along a hidden passage. It connected from the back of the Cobbler's shop to a small safe room where everyone involved could speak freely.

"I am Jeffrey Bellingham," their contact said as he sketched a polite bow. "At your service, lady and gentleman. Welcome to the city of New Orleans. How may I be of assistance to you?" Their contact was a tall and somewhat wiry man, with affected muttonchops and a receding hairline. He had a noticeable English accent and was well dressed, as might be expected of any London businessman.

Annika passed him a piece of paper. "That coded note should explain everything to you. Read it and we can continue from there," she said.

Bellingham sat down with a pen and a small slide-rule-like device. "I will be a few minutes, then. The cabinet over there has a bit of food and drink in it. Help yourselves."

It took the English spy less than a quarter hour to decode the message the pirates had delivered him. The spy chuckled as he took a sip from his glass. The trio were sitting with glasses of wine, plus small plates of cheese and bread before them. "Well, well. You lot have really managed to stumble into quite a thicket, it would seem."

"Oh? How so?" Hans asked carefully.

"Do either of you know anything about the Serpentis Combine or Egyptian mythology?" the other man asked.

Annika spoke up. "I am a tremendous fan of all things Egyptian, actually. Why?"

"So you might know of the God Min, then?" Bellingham asked. Hans glanced at Annika.

"Yes," she nodded. "Minor God, in charge of weather ... rain, specifically. Regularly unemployed," she laughed. The two men chuckled and the spy continued speaking.

"The book you pulled off that Russian courier ship turns out to have been a historical account by a very old cult-like organization called the Serpentis Combine. Snake-god-worshipping end-of-times sorts. Not a very cheery lot at parties, I am afraid."

"Do tell," Hans said dryly.

"It seems that once upon a time, and by that I mean just before Moses mucked things up for them, Egypt was a bit of a bread-basket," Bellingham said after a sip of his wine. "Farms, green fields and even small forests."

"How?" Hans asked. "The place is an arid desert by nature, save for what the Nile sustains."

"Ah, that would be the rub. That book describes a source of 'magic' within a great temple to Min that allowed the priests to summon nourishing rain and cooling clouds. However, the Temple of Min was swallowed up in an earthquake around 1400 BC, and the region slowly reverted to what we see today."

Annika frowned for a moment and played with the rim of her glass with a finger tip. "So, you are telling me that the British Government is worried about a 'magic' weather controller in a 'lost' temple from an old book held onto by a group of mad-as-hatters cultists?" she asked pointedly. "And they are tying up a hired gunboat, two or three spies and tossing a horse-cart of money around? It seems a bit silly to me."

Hans lofted a brow. "When you put it that way, Annika, it certainly sounds a bit far fetched does it not? Tell us, Mister Bellingham, what reason does the Admiralty have for risking such a huge waste of time, money and resources on what really does sound like a bit of a wild goose chase?"

The mutton-chopped Englishman looked at the pair. "I cannot go into full details," he began carefully. "What I can tell you is of two points. Firstly, the Serpentis Combine is well known to British Intelligence as being very credible in these matters; if they think it works, it likely does ... at least at some capacity. Secondly and most importantly, the Russians are taking it very seriously ... if there is even the remotest of odds that this might be real, the Empire cannot sit on its hands."

"Of course," Hans said with dawning understanding. "the worry is that the Russians know at least this much as well, if not more, since we got the Book from them. If they find the Temple and this turns out to even be partially true, then they can essentially do as they please with the weather of the country. They could derive a government that will suit their needs just by promising favourable weather to one faction or another. That would completely re-write the map of the region ... and set the stage for another rematch over Crimea and into the old Ottoman Empire."

"Yes, exactly, my good man. Which is an outcome that Allied Europe simply cannot allow to come to pass," Bellingham stated as he took a bite of strong cheese.

"So what does New Orleans have to do with this?" Annika asked. "Why did they not just tell us this in the Azores and send us packing off directly to Egypt?"

"Egypt is a big place, even by airship. We need to pin down the location of the Temple before we can do anything. The Serpentis Combine has mostly buggered off out of Europe; the Russian War was such a dreary affair for everyone involved. They largely relocated their organization here, in New Orleans. The place has a bit of a reputation for Voodoo, Candle Magic, things that go bump in the night out in the Bayou, and such ... a gaggle of doom-saying Cultists are pretty much invisible around here."

"And since it was their Book the Russians had, you expect that they know the most about it?" Annika asked.

"Spot on, madam. Spot on, indeed," Bellingham said with a nod.

Annika looked like she was nearly salivating. "Does the book reveal the location of the lost Temple?" she asked.

The British spy nodded in affirmation. "Well, nearly," he said, correcting himself. "So much has changed and the Book is in such a cipher that we barely know the neighbourhood, and certainly not the postman's box."

"The notion," he continued with a gesture, "is that I am going to have a few of my lads do some skulking around this afternoon and overnight and see if we cannot scare you up a lead that will get you a slightly better address for the Temple than 'Triple Nought, Leftmost Sand Dune, Back Right Desolation, Egypt'."

The trio had a good chuckle. "Very good then, Mister Bellingham. How can we help?" Hans asked.

The English spy thought about that for a moment or two. "Hmm. Honestly, old chap, I would suggest just staying quietly anonymous until we have had a chance to do our jobs. We really do not want to arouse too much suspicion. We knew that Ivan had been nosing about lately, we just were not sure why. I am reasonably sure we now know what it was he was after. The Americans are a bit wary of old Ivan, so I do not know how much progress he would have actually made, however."

Annika frowned. "Well, I think going back to the ship would be a poor idea. If we are supposed to be anonymous, then traipsing back and forth from a newly arrived British privateer will not help our cause."

Bellingham nodded. He wrote something down on a piece of paper and passed it to Hans. "That is a very good hotel here in town. Book a room there and I will be able to send you word of the arrangements for the morning." Hans and Annika passed a look between them and Hans hoped what he was thinking was not clearly written on his face.

"Excellent, Mister Bellingham," Annika said, carefully using the English honorific instead of her habitual Russian version. "One last thing, if you can ... and perhaps this will help to conceal the true purpose of the *Bloody Rose* being in town ... We are looking to purchase a pair of Gatling guns. Quietly of course ... with about fifty thousand rounds of ammunition for them. We would be paying cash. Can you arrange that?"

The two men blinked at her in some surprise. "Pardon?" the German and the Englishman both said at once.

"You heard me," she replied. "Two Gatling's, preferably the Model 1877s chambered in .45-70, with fifty thousand rounds ... ten sticks per gun, pre-packed, and the rest as loose. Cash on inspection; we can pay in either European or American script, or in gold bar."

Bellingham lofted a brow. "You certainly know your guns, Madam ..." he said as Annika gave the two of them a smug look with her arms folded across her chest. "I cannot guarantee anything, but I will make some ... enquiries ... That is enough ammunition to re-fight part of the Civil War. I will send word to the hotel to let you know if I am successful."

*****

"There is a vague feeling of *déjà vu* about this scene," Hans commented as he sipped at his glass of port. They were seated in the very well appointed and serviced dining room for the hotel which Bellingham had recommended to them.

"Beyond the part where I am not dressed like a man, you mean?" Annika replied in amusement.

"... and the part where I actually tried to explain who you were to the Hotel Manager and the *Maitre de Salon*, yes."

She snickered. "Really, Hans? Your wife? Klaus and Isobelle Dornier?"

"We might be in America, this might be a 'French' flavour of city, but I still expect that using our own names and getting a single room together would have caused some stir," he pointed out to her.

"Motorwell bats," she suggested in a tone of mock daintiness. Hans nearly snorted his port.

"You might well not care what anyone thinks of the morality of it, but I was more worried about running a bloody big target up a staff by telling the truth. I certainly do not wish Ivan paying us a visit later."

"Uncle Ivan is a sweetheart. I am sure he would knock," she countered with a chuckle.

"With a coach gun, aye," Hans retorted.

The two of them shared a laugh until the waiter came to their table with an offer of desserts and coffee. They each made their selections and waited until he had left.

"You do know there is only one bed in the room, yes, Hans?" she asked him carefully, her voice low and with a forced neutrality.

"Yes."

"And you do know that I will likely find it difficult to allow you to leave that bed a virgin, yes?" she questioned in the same tone.

"Yes."

"Are you going to have as much trouble as I am in not hurrying through dessert?" she asked with a small laugh.

"Yes," he grinned at her.

"I want you," she whispered in a husky voice.

"Good," he replied as he took a leisurely sip from his port glass.

*****

Hans closed the door behind them as they entered their room. They had been up here earlier, before supper. They had dropped off their over-night bags and then each taken an airshipman-speed birdbath. They had then departed immediately for supper. Neither of them had mentioned the velvet-draped, four-poster elephant in the room up until a half-hour ago at the end of supper. Annika turned to face him after he had turned the locks on the door.

"Are you nervous?" she asked quietly.

"Very," he admitted with a chuckle. She took him by the hand and led him to the bedside.

"So am I, actually." She gave an uncharacteristic giggle. "I think this will be the first time in ... well, years ... that I have actually been looking for more than just an itch scratched."

"Annika ..." he began uncertainly.

"Oh, shut up, Hans," she said, pressing herself against him and tangling her fingers in his hair to pull his lips to hers. For a clear moment, he recalled the first time she had kissed him like this, at that moonlit lake near Brussels. The same fire coursed through his body, and he knew what he wanted.

They hungrily devoured each others' mouths and necks for several heady, pulse-racing moments now, as they had back then. They explored each other through their clothes for an impatiently delicious time, until Annika broke off their current frenzied kiss. They were both breathless in their desire, and it was all she could do to whisper "undress me". He nodded to her and licked his lips.

The last of her clothing was soon after cast to a chair a distance away from the bed, and she stood before him with a defiant lustiness in her eyes. He had seen her nude before on a couple of occasions swimming together, but for some reason the sight of her like this now was electric to him. He pulled her against him almost roughly and she made a feral sound of appreciation. His hands explored her bare skin, and she shamelessly guided a hand to her slight breasts, and then encouraged him to explore her further.

"Let me show you something," she suggested between fevered kisses. "Like this ... and here ... oh, yes ..." She gasped something in her native Russian as his hands moved over her and he sensed her desire. She eased away from him, with a furnace in her eyes as she spoke. "You are over-dressed for the occasion," she said with an impish heat. "It is my turn to undress you."

He watched her as she cast his clothing carelessly over a shoulder. He was hers in this moment, and that knowledge gave her power and fire. That was reflected in her movements, her actions. It was intoxicating to him. It was not long before she had divested him of every stitch of clothing. She explored him as he had done with her, with a confidence that he wished he shared. She looked up at him and stopped the hungry drift of her hands over his skin.

"I saw that ... what is wrong, Hans?"

"I was just wishing I was nearly as skilled as you seem to be ..." he started. She silenced him with her lips upon his.

"You will not disappoint me. Fear nothing right now. Relish what we share," she said encouragingly. They were soon in a tangled and heated embrace upon the bed. She teased and tasted him everywhere she could, until he was sure he might go mad with his need for release. The musky smell of her arousal was like an inhaled fire.

*****

He woke some languid time later. She was awake, and gently brushed a lock of hair from his eyes. He wrapped his arms around her and held her tightly. He felt like the Universe had shifted around him in some imperceptible way. One way or another, he knew that his relationship with the feisty Russian brunette had changed.

After he had released her from his embrace, she propped herself up on her elbows and looked down at him. She seemed a touch smug for a moment and then slowly kissed him again. "So ... was that what you expected?" she questioned. He shook his head slowly, looking up at her. "Oh? In what way was it different?" she asked, curiously.

Hans turned crimson and said nothing until she cajoled him to answer her. "Ah ... I was ... warned ... that you tended to be somewhat more hurried and brusque in your affairs."

She blinked at him and then burst out laughing. She rolled off of him to lay flat on her back beside him, still laughing aloud. Whatever reaction Hans had been expecting, this was rather much not it.

"Hans Sauder, you cad ... have you been gossiping about me with the boys?" she accused, grinning from ear to ear. She seemed delighted at the prospect.

"Ah ... well ... your name came up as a topic of conversation once on a run aground, yes," he said sheepishly. "The truth be told, Pirates gossip like milk-girls," he laughed, relaxing as it was still apparent she found the entire notion flattering. "I did not ask ... a couple of the lads volunteered some ... 'advice' for me should I have the opportunity to bed you."

She rolled onto her side, resting her chin on his chest while she spoke. She shook her head, evidently amused. "Well ... It is dated advice, then. I have avoided sleeping with anyone in the crew for the past six months or so, other than Michael, of course. None of them are terribly interesting to me, really, and for some reason the few I did use as a scratching post for a night or two seemed to think that gave them some sort of benefit aboard the ship. It just caused problems."

She curled up against him and made a sound of contentment. He ran his fingers through her short hair, wondering what she would look like with a longer style. She nuzzled at his neck and kissed him there.

"They are right, though," she said, resuming the prior conversation. "Normally I do not take such leisure time with whomever I have chosen to bed."

"Oh? Why not?" Hans asked, curious. "Is it more exciting for you that way?"

"No, its because usually I am just being selfish. I want sex, I want to unlock the stress, I want to feel good, and whoever I am tangled up with is just a vehicle for that. I may like my toys attractive and well built, but I am only playing with them for my enjoyment, not theirs."

Hans looked somewhat shocked at her matter-of-fact declaration. He had no idea that a woman might think that way. A frown crossed his features as a thought crossed his mind. "So, am I just a conquest then, Annika? Another toy?"

"No, Hans, not at all. Back in Egypt, yes, that is all I was interested in. Good candy, as it were ... and you, Hans Sauder, are very good candy," she said with a bawdy chuckle that dwindled to a thoughtful pause. "Somewhere between then and now, however, my heart got involved," she mused softly. She traced a finger over his chest. "I wanted to be sure your first time was memorable."

He kissed at her bare skin, relishing its salted heat and taste. His kissed her again and smiled. "It was very much so. Can I interest you in immediately ensuring my second is equally good?"

"Spies, Guns and Deviltry"

Diary Entry For July 5th, 1888

Yesterday morning we were transported to a farmstead outside of the town to meet "Our Man Louisiana". Once there, we were given a more complete explanation of what is going on, what is at stake, and where we needed to go next. As trite as it sounds, it seems that the Fate of the Allied Empires is now at least partially in the hands of the Bloody Rose and her crew.

We were attacked at the farmhouse by a contingent of mercenaries led by a handful of Russian agents. It was a terrible battle that nearly went very badly, save for the appearance of the Bloody Rose which used her guns to end the stand-off. We pirates gave some medical attention to the injured and ensured that the attackers were truly driven off. At the same time, we took aboard the two Gatling guns and the wagon-load of bullets required to feed them.

We had no sooner departed the farmhouse than we were beset by a squad of Russian-built aerofighters. We took a bit of a drubbing, being nowhere as fast nor agile as the Russian aircraft. Eventually, after some spectacular heroics on the part of the Gunner-Marines and the Pilotage Team, we were able to down enough of them that the others chose discretion as their watch-word.

Thus does the Bloody Rose continue to demonstrate to the world that she has a horseshoe nailed to her keel somewhere.

Tomorrow morning will have finished our rapid repairs and set course for Cuba to steal a map in the possession of a wealthy collector. We will hopefully manage that with a bit of forethought and planning, and then be on our way to Egypt.

*****

They woke with the dawn and as soon as they had freshened up from the night's sleep, and then fell back into each others arms on the luxurious bed at her urging. Afterwards, they bathed themselves and then dressed at a leisurely pace. They then made their way down to the restaurant in search of breakfast in the same attire and guise as the previous day.

Once the waiter had departed with their sizable order, Annika hid a yawn with her hand. "Sex and battle have similar effects ... improved interest in both breakfast and laziness," she chuckled. Hans was obliged to agree with her.

The waiter returned after a while with their meals and then departed. Annika lofted a brow at something.

"What is it, my dear?" Hans queried.

She tugged a folded piece of brown paper, itself folded inside a piece of waxed paper, from between two slices of her toast. She carefully unfolded both pieces and read the writing on the brown piece. She nibbled on her toast and slid the message across the table so Hans might be able to read it. Hans in turn lofted a brow and then nodded. The note gave them a time about an hour or so hence and the number of a cab that would be waiting for them outside the hotel. The note explained that the cab would take them to a farm house outside of town where the guns could be purchased and information acquired over night could be discussed.

After breakfast, they returned to their room and packed their things to depart. Hans took a few minutes to write a note using a pre-agreed upon code. He sealed it in an envelope and paid one of the Hotel runners to ensure it was delivered to the *Bloody Rose* as quickly as possible. A short time later, Annika and Hans got into the expected cab and set off to their meeting house.

A quarter hour into the trip Annika looked up at him. She was sitting close beside him, her head on his shoulder as she liked to do, and they were holding hands.

"Yes, Annika?" Hans asked.

"About last night ..." she began slowly.

"... and this morning?"

"Mmm, yes, and this morning."

"What is on your mind, my little Russian witch?"

She grinned at him for a moment and then her features turned more serious. "Just so we are clear, Hans ... I have never been exclusive with anyone in my life. I even had three stuffed toys from which I chose a different one every night when I was a little girl. Fair is fair; if I cannot be exclusive to you, then I do not demand or expect it from you in return."

Hans looked at her for a long moment and then nodded slowly but said nothing.

She studied the expression on his face for a short time before she spoke again. "It is not that I do not care, Hans. I do. More oft than not, you will be who I seek to spend my idle time or pillow time with. Just do not be crushed if it is not always that way."

"Well," he said after a moment of thought, "we made no pledges or promises before we shared ourselves together. I suppose that it makes little sense to presume any were implied, particularly between a couple of pirates."

"But?" she prompted, sitting up more straight to look more evenly at him.

"It will just take a bit of time to get used to, Annika ... old emotional habits, as it were."

"We are both too young to be restricted, I think, Hans. You may think me a fine lover, but what is your basis for comparison?"

"An interesting point," he said with a thoughtful chuckle. "You are so modern in your thinking ... you are always such a challenge to me," he said with a teasing smile.

She kissed him soundly. "Get used to it. I intend to be a challenge to you for some time to come, Captain-Rockets."

*****

The horse-drawn cab came to a rest at a beautiful farm house outside the city. Swaying fields of flax and cotton surrounded the place, glowing in the morning sunlight. A small woodland provided shade and a windbreak on the western side of the buildings.

A warm breeze swept up a symphony of early summer scents that washed over them as they stepped down from the carriage. The farm house was done in a crisp white with green trim, and copper-roofed. Surrounding it was a small collection of outbuildings associated with the various needs of the farm, all done in a like colour scheme. Perhaps a dozen workers were around the place, all at various stages of the morning's work for the farm. None of them were paying very much attention at all to the well-dressed and newly arrived couple.

As Hans and Annika looked around momentarily, the front door to the two-story farm house opened, and Bellingham appeared. "Good morning to you both," he said cheerily. "Come in, please, do come in! The tea and biscuits are just ready now. We have some interesting news for you." The two lovers glanced at each other and Hans gestured for her to precede him.

They went inside, setting their bags down in the comfortably appointed sitting room. Just as their British host had said, fresh tea and hot biscuits were being set down on a serving buffet by a Negro servant girl. As well, coffee, preserves, and some just-picked fruits were available. While Annika made pleasant chatter with Bellingham, Hans opened one of his two *portmanteaux* and discreetly switched on a device inside it.

"So, what do you have for us, Mister Bellingham?" Annika asked once she noted Hans was once again sitting up in his chair with a cup of coffee in hand.

"Hmm? Oh, well, some very fascinating news, to be sure. It seems the Serpentis Combine have been making quite a collection of the locations of lost temples and such. That in and of itself is likely some concern, given the predilections of this lot. However, it seems that they actually know exactly where the Temple of Min is to be found. One of their more senior members — a Cardinal, if you will — has a map of the area where the Temple can be found as well as some other information. Steal the map, and off you go."

"Excellent. Where do we find this chap and his map?" Hans asked.

"A very expensive and likely well guarded tobacco plantation outside of Havana, Cuba. Not a terribly long jaunt by airship, I should think. The Serpentis Combine types all seem to have some sort of Evil Villain complex, so they keep all their odds and sods associated with their Cult activities usually in a hidden room in their basement. They are also not terribly fond of burglars, so do expect them to be poor hosts if you get caught."

"Outstanding work, Mister Bellingham. You and your boys have taken a tremendous amount of guess-work out of this for us!" Annika said, very clearly pleased with this news.

"Now, things are bit more of concern than we originally thought," the Englishman said as he nodded graciously to the Russian brunette.

"How so?" asked Hans, sounding curious.

"The 'Magic' of the Temple has quite a reach ... the records we were able to obtain from the Serpentis Combine last night indicate that the Priests of the Temple used it as a weapon a couple of times. All the way into what is now the Syrian extents of Persia."

Hans and Annika looked at each other in surprise and then back to their host.

"That is almost four hundred miles!" Annika exclaimed.

"Yes," the Englishman nodded gravely. "According to the information we were able to access, they were able to create quite a storm off the coast near Beirut ... convinced the aggressor of the day that perhaps it was a lousy day for sailing on the Med," Bellingham said with a touch of gallows humour. "I am sure you can immediately see the issue of concern here," he commented in a much more serious tone.

"Of course," Hans replied. "At the point it can be used as a weapon ... not only could the Russians change the climate of Egypt, and thus eventually change the map of the region through politics ... they could do it much faster just by creating weather catastrophes over almost a third of the region!"

"Correct. I will be alerting my superiors in England as soon as I can to the impending issue. But your mission is more imperative than ever. If the Russians could do as they pleased from Beirut to Cairo to the end of the Gulf of Suez ... there would be almost nothing the Allies could do to challenge them across most of the Holy Land," Bellingham said in a grave tone.

The English spy then passed a small leather and brass ledger to Hans. "That is a summary report of what we were able to dig up for you over night, including the latitude and longitude of the plantation. I hope it gives you what you ..." Bellingham stopped suddenly at the startling sound of a gunshot from outside. Before any of them in the room could comment, the sounds of dozens of shots filled the air and the sound of a ringing bell reached them.

"You have got to be joking," Annika exclaimed in clear surprise.

"Victoria's Virtue... who the Bloody Hell..?" the English spy cursed. One of the room's windows shattered with the unmistakable sound of a rifle shot and they all threw themselves to the floor. There was a pause followed by the booming sound of a firing cannon. It was almost immediately followed by a sharp detonation which blew all the remaining windows in the room inwards in a winnowing hail of glass shards. A fortunate happenstance of furniture protected them from harm.

"That was a four-pounder firing exploding ball," Annika said grimly. "Whoever they are, they came prepared to tear the place to firewood."

A panicked looking farmhand brandishing a pistol and wearing a wood-carver's heavy leather apron ran in. His left eye was already starting to swell shut, and the same side of his face had several cuts. "Mister Bellingham! Mister Bellingham, Sir! There are over thirty of them ... it looks like a group of mercenaries and a couple of Ivans, Sir!"

"Ivans? How the hell did they find us here? All right ... get all the men into the buildings or behind the cotton bales, quickly. Tell them to break out the carbines if they have not done so already, and give better than they get" Bellingham said, his frustration evident.

There was a ripping of fabric and the men turned to find Annika hacking her skirt off with a knife. "Oh, come on, gentlemen!" she hissed. "Keep your tongues in your mouth ... I am wearing pants under this ridiculous thing. I cannot fight wearing a skirt, petticoats, under-corset and a bustle! Get me a rifle and show me how to get to the second floor windows. We have to take care of that cannon!"

Bellingham recomposed himself, then nodded and quickly moved in a crouch to the buffet. He pulled out the long bottom drawer and reached into it, taking out a rifle and summarily tossing it to Annika. She caught it easily. It was a Waffenfabrik Mauser revolving rifle, similar to the Colt Model 1855. The principle difference was it was designed to fire metallic cartridges instead of the notoriously problematic paper ones. Outside, the sounds of gun battle were cut with the sound of another shot from the cannon.

"Bullets," she demanded. She was wordlessly thrown a small but heavy sack. She pointed at the farmhand. "You. Show me how to get upstairs," she ordered. The other man did as he was told and they left the room quickly.

Bellingham passed Hans a carbine and ammunition. "You know how to shoot, yes?" the British spy asked the German pirate.

Hans nodded. "Well enough for most things," he replied grimly.

The sound of moving furniture could be heard upstairs, over the staccato sounds of exchanged rifle fire. "I must say, its a rather odd time to be redecorating, do you not agree?" Bellingham chuckled as he crawled over to a window. He looked out the shattered window and fired at a distant figure.

Hans chuckled at him from where he had taken position beside another window. He glanced out and immediately took cover as he saw the flash and smoke from the field gun the attackers had brought with them. A moment later the farm house shook with the sound of a blast. From up stairs five shots rang out in rapid succession.

"That would be Annika convincing the gun's crew to chose a different career path for the duration of this engagement," Hans chortled.

"A forty-four calibre rifle bullet in the chest does tend to be rather a compelling argument," Bellingham commented sardonically. "Who is she, anyway?"

"The Captain of the Gunner-Marines of the *Bloody Rose*," Hans replied as he snapped a shot off at an advancing mercenary.

The English spy blinked at him. "You must be kidding? A woman keeps that rabble in check?" Bellingham asked as he crawled over to another set of cabinets and opened its bottom drawer. He pulled out what looked like a two-foot long periscope with a pair of lenses on top that merged to a singular eye-piece at the bottom. He also took out a small wood and brass box, about the size of two large books stacked atop each other. He slowly crawled back to the window he was at originally.

Hans fired, swiftly worked the action on the carbine and fired again. He took cover as two or three shots came back at him in return. "Got the bloody bugger, I think," he said with a note of satisfaction. "... and no, I am not kidding.

The Chief Engineer and the Captain-Gunner are both very talented women. It is quite a crew," he chuckled. Five more shots rang out in as many seconds from the upstairs.

Bellingham had now attached a couple of leads from the box to the periscope and flipped a couple of switches on. A few tubes on the box glowed, as did two small lights on the periscope. He used it to look out the window he was beneath, scanning the cotton fields turned battle fields. He reached to the box with one hand, turned a knob on it slowly and then nodded.

"We are stalemated. They out number us and surround us, so we cannot leave. However, your Captain-Gunner has effectively removed their trump card from the game; there are six dead men out there around what I would think is a three-man gun. They cannot advance, because we hold the fortifications and have carbines."

"Which means?" Hans asked.

"Which means that they are either going to give up and leave ... or wait until dusk when we cannot see their advance and charge our buildings then," Bellingham said grimly.

"Actually," said Hans, "we have the trump card. At this very moment, the *Bloody Rose* is en route to this location, homing in on a Marconi Beacon I had stashed in one of my *portmanteau*. When we hear her engines, which should be any minute now, I need to fire a signal flare into the air. *Kapitän* Blackheart will likely either land the Gunner-Marines behind them, or simply pound them from the air. However ..." Hans trailed off for a moment.

"However?" Bellingham prompted.

"Well, if I do not launch that flare, the *Bloody Rose* will presume we were double-crossed and simply level this entire farm. That would do Ivan's job for him very neatly."

"Then we should get you out to the kitchen porch so you can hear her approach and launch your signal flare, Mister Sauder," the other man said with a clear sound of consternation in his voice. They both fired a couple of shots out their respective windows and they heard a pair of rapidly fired shots from above them. Hans crawled to one of his two *portmanteau*, pulled out the two barrelled flare gun and then loaded a pair of yellow flares into it. They nodded to each other and Bellingham beckoned Sauder to follow him. They both quickly moved in a low crouch towards the hall leading to the back of the building.

The sounds of sporadic gunfire surrounded them as they moved together through the large farmhouse. A bullet cracked over their heads, shattering a flower pot on a shelf, showering them with dirt and pottery. They entered the kitchen to find one of Bellingham's men sitting on the floor, leaning against a flour bin, holding a pistol in one hand and clenching a bloody bullet wound in his abdomen with the other. Fresh blood, bright crimson on the tan of the waxed wood floor, pooled around him. His breathing was shallow and laboured.

"Careful if you go out back, Sir ... there are at least two of them out there with rifles," he said, gritting his teeth against the pain. "It seems they are decent shots, too" he said, forcing a smile.

Bellingham pulled a medical kit from the bottom of a closet and made his way over to the badly wounded man. Hans took a moment to shove fresh cartridges into his carbine. The distinctive sound of an airship's motors under heavy load faintly reached their ears; the *Bloody Rose* was approaching, running with one motor in reverse to make as much noise as possible to herald her arrival. The Englishman and the German knew that time was beginning to run out.

"Go, Sir," the shot man said. "I will be okay for a few more minutes."

"If you die on me, Jeremy, I will be very cross with you," Bellingham admonished. The other man grinned and nodded weakly in reply.

The English Spy and the German Pirate looked at each other, nodded once, and darted out onto the kitchen porch together, rifles at the ready. Both of them immediately dove and took cover in opposite directions. Rifle shots cracked through the air where they had been only a moment before, thudding into the house. Bellingham rose in a kneeling crouch and fired, ducked, reloaded, rose and fired again. As he dropped flat behind the heavy wooden barrel he was using for cover, rifle shots rang out. One went over him, while the second squarely struck the barrel, which began leaking what smelled to Hans like a weak vinegar mixture.

"Any time you are ready," Bellingham prompted casually.

Sauder nodded and set his carbine down beside him on the wooden deck of the porch. He cocked both the hammers on the flare gun he now had in his hands, pointed the twinned muzzles to the sky, and pulled both triggers. A single rapport marked the ascent of the two brilliant yellow stars. Almost immediately the sound of the engines of the *Bloody Rose* changed, becoming less resonant and more powerful. The flares had been seen and likely Blackheart was now running out the guns for action, Hans thought.

"That is it?" Bellingham asked.

"Oh, no. The show is only about to start," Hans replied. "Blackheart is a shrewd ship-handler and a brilliant tactician. I expect this will abruptly become an unpleasant morning for the Russians and their minions."

The *Bloody Rose* was barely clearing the trees on the west side of the farm when she roared in. Almost immediately she pitched to one side and then to the next, nearly quarter-rolls, so that the targets on the ground could be spotted from the Steering House. She then accelerated, and headed out over the golden fields. Sporadic rifle fire from the mercenaries sounded out. The airship heeled over, her down-angled side gun doors opened, the guns appeared and then there was a roar that sounded like the most ferocious crack of thunder Hans had ever heard. From this side of the muzzle, the entire focused fury of almost seventy-five pounds of grape-shot leaving the barrels was deafening.

The ground where the strike of over 2300 fifty-calibre projectiles landed seemed to erupt over a dozen feet into the air in a plume of dust and debris. The cloud lingered long enough to mercifully obscure what had befallen the men within it, hinted at only by a crimson tint. Another group of men panicked and ran, only to have the airship swing around, roll her unfired guns to bear, and obliterate them in another flash and roar of powder and iron. Hans swore he could feel the ground shake with each strike and he glanced over at Bellingham. The English spy blinked at him in horror about what he envisioned was happening beneath the *Mjolnir* of those broadsides.

The four-pounders began firing independently at anything they could see moving in the fields around the farm, while the heavier guns were rolled back behind their doors. The remaining mercenaries and their Russian masters ran for their lives as best as they could while the *Bloody Rose* rained an iron-shod, black-powder hell upon them.

In short order, the airship manoeuvred into an overwatch position above the carriage yard and rope ladders came tumbling down off both her sides. Soon after,

Gunner-Marines arrived on the ground, with rifles and cutlasses at the ready, fanning out around the buildings and ensuring there were no sneaks or stragglers.

Blackheart himself, an impressive sight with his Jacob's Sword and Tesla pistol at the ready, was part of the landing party. Bellingham seemed rather taken aback with actually meeting the legendary pirate captain when Hans introduced the two men. The talk was brusque and formal, both Englishmen knowing that with their respective crews watching that there was little real chance for anything but carefully maintained appearances.

Doctor Koblinski and Nurse Coline joined the landing party once the Privateers and Bellingham's able-bodied men were sure that the area around for a rifle-shot was secured. Annika kept a sharp watch with two others from the top windows of the farm house. Medical care as best as was able was given to the wounded of both sides, and the few prisoners were moved to a hidden room below the floor of the barn.

Two wagons of war materials were wheeled below the hovering airship. Additionally, a crate of hand-sized gold and silver bars was positioned beside the wagons destined for the *Bloody Rose*. Bellingham and Blackheart inspected both the contents of the wagons and the crates together, if somewhat frostily. Once they were both satisfied, the crated Gatling guns, the cases of bullets and the money were raised up with the airship's steam-powered winches.

Three hours after Hans and Annika had first arrived, Hans shook the English spy's hand in farewell. "It has been an rather exciting time working with you, Mister Bellingham," Hans chuckled.

"Indeed it has, Mister Sauder. I am somewhat sorry that the tea and biscuits got cold on us. Do stop by another time, sir, and I will be pleased to have breakfast with yourself and your Captain-Gunner."

"We shall. Good luck with dealing with Ivan and his chums around here."

*****

The *Bloody Rose* took a south-easterly heading at seventy knots, her motors thrumming steadily as she made way. She had been cruising at a thousand feet in the air for a little more than half an hour heading for their destination on the island of Cuba.

"Well, it sounds like we are well and truly on our way down the rabbit hole," Blackheart commented. He set his coffee mug down, looking at Hans and Annika who had just explained what they learned, as well as the nature of the ground attack to Captain O'Raedy and Chief Itala. They were in O'Raedy's Mess area. He was seated behind his desk in his well worn oak armchair, while the German and the Russian were seated before him. The Italian Ethiope was impishly perched on the corner of his desk, one foot lightly swinging back and forth.

"It would seem that way, *Ja, Herr Kapitän*," Hans replied.

"Well done, both of you. Any of that could have turned into a roaring disaster," Blackheart said with a nod to both of them.

"So what is our plan, *Signore Capitano*?" Arietta asked quietly.

"Firstly, we finish our coffee while flying to Cuba. Then we find the plantation and see about stealing that map. After that, all will be clear," Blackheart answered, swirling his coffee mug.

"Will it now?" Hans questioned as he folded his arms over his chest and leaned back in his chair.

"Of course, Hans," Annika replied. "If the map does exist, then it likely means there is enough truth to all of this that we need to follow it through to its end ..."

"... and if it does not, then it likely means the entire thing is a myth or at least not as near to the light of day as Whitehall thinks," Arietta concluded.

"I cannot decide," O'Raedy said thoughtfully, "which would be worse."

*****

Another hour and a half of flight found the *Bloody Rose* well over he azure waters of the Gulf of Mexico, when a keen-eyed look-out spotted a dozen black motes in the sky. They looked like nothing friendly he had ever seen, and he rang the alarm.

Hans had reached the Steering House as the onrushing craft attacked. They looked like bat-winged bi-planes, in a satin-sheen black that made them look perfectly devilish. The pilot was visible from just below the shoulders, inside a completely enclosing glass canopy at the very front of the aircraft. Rather unusually, they were a pusher-prop design, giving the entire aircraft a very front-heavy look, now more like a manta ray to Hans' eyes than a bat. The wings and tail were marked with the colours of the Russian Empire.

A total of eight of them streaked past in rapid succession at unbelievable speed, with a plume of black smoke marking their curving trajectories. They split away and arched upwards, evenly spaced around the compass with the *Bloody Rose* at the centre of this impressive piece of aeronautical display.

All eight aircraft turned as one, and plunged towards the *Bloody Rose*. Flashes of fire lit around the noses and belly of each of the aircraft much to the horror of the command crew in the Steering House of the now besieged pirate airship. Bursts of bullets tore into the planks and deckwork of the ship, followed by more than a dozen small explosions, tossing splinters into the air. The embattled airship veered sharply, and her cannons fired ineffectively at the attacking aerofighters, not marking a single hit.

"Rocket-propelled grenades launched from rocket-propelled aerofighters. Leave it to the Russians," Hans sighed from his post in the Steering House. "With state-of-the-art Maxim-style machine-guns just to add insult to the injury."

Annika cursed under her breath and then barked orders into a voicepipe. "They are using some sort of rocket motor when they attack," she announced, watching one with a spyglass. "I have never seen anything accelerate so sharply and fly so swiftly!" The facing guns of the *Bloody Rose* fired in rapid succession as another attacker literally rocketed past. Bullets and grenades pelted the privateer.

"Well, this is an interesting problem," Blackheart said as another fighter sailed past with its Maxim machine guns clattering away, pouring bullets into the upper deck timbers. "Using the rocket-assisted burst to attack us means we cannot use the ship's guns to catch them with grapeshot as they pass us. That is our usual solution for snobbish men in white scarves and aeroplanes. They cannot shoot us down, but at the same time they can certainly break enough things on the outers that a proper warship will find the job much easier. So, there is no ignoring them either. Rather sticky, do you not agree, Mister Sauder?"

Hans regarded Blackheart for a moment, somewhat taken aback by the conversational tone the Captain was taking. "*Ja, Herr Kapitän.* They are agile enough I will never hit one with a Sargasso or a Cudahawk, either."

"Hmm, rather unfortunate, yes. Well, think quickly, Mister Sauder, we have not got all day. You have the Action. Deal with this," he said with an airy wave.

Everyone in the Steering House looked at Hans in surprise. Hans looked at Blackheart blankly. "Pardon?" he said.

"I said you have the Action. You are in charge. The temporary captain. The man of the hour. The fearless leader. *Et cetera, et cetera.* Follow me?"

"I will argue with you about this later," Hans said after a moment of shock. He thought rapidly for a moment. "Make bells and whistles for heavy weather," he ordered.

"But there isn't a storm cloud in the sky," Annika questioned.

"Do as you are told, Captain-Gunner," Blackheart said from where he now leaned against the chart table, watching the rest of the Steering House crew. Annika shot both Sauder and O'Raedy a grumpy look and then did as Hans had said.

Hans turned to the Helmsman and Planesman. "You two ... the next fighter that passes us ... Follow it. I do not care what you have to do, just get us within two hundred yards of it. Captain-Gunner?"

"Sir?" she said clearly amused about something.

"Break out the Tesla rifles ... I need thirteen guns and twelve Gunner-Marines on the fo'c'sle as quick as you can. This will be just like shooting pheasant in a hurricane," he said blackly. He waited for her to pass those orders down her voicepipes. "Next ... unlimber the two Gatling guns. I want them on the stern; you, Dubé, Cortez and two other gunners. "

"Why?" she asked, bracing herself as the ship suddenly veered and plunged after one of the Russian aerofighters. The two crewmen at the flight controls were already all but shouting advice to each other about more left, steeper dive, sharper turn, harder roll.

"The fighters are vulnerable at two points ... when they try to come up behind us, they will be flying into our bullets from the Gatlings. As soon as they accelerate with the rocket boost, it looks as if they are ballistic ... it seems as if they fly a shallow arc until the pilot can regain control ... if the steering team can get us within a couple hundred yards before the pilot regains that control, then the Gunner-Marines firing *en-masse* with Tesla rifles from the bow will be able to down them ... the Gunner-Marines will be able to see the bolts from the guns, and correct their aim as a group."

Annika looked at him. "That is suicide. The aerofighters will just use their machine guns to strafe the gunners," she said.

"And if we do not give them gunners to shoot at they will eventually figure out that a couple of rocket-propelled grenades into our motor pods will cripple us! Do as you are ordered," he told her.

"You just killed me, Hans," she said harshly. "They will strafe the stern with those Maxims just to get rid of the tail guns we are firing."

"Do as you are ordered, Captain-Gunner," he said repeated, his tone turning cold.

They stared at each other for a long moment. She turned on her heel and left the Steering House without a word.

Hans turned to Blackheart. "Mister O'Raedy, you have the Action," he said as pulled his goggles down and his breather-mask up.

"Oh?" said Blackheart, lofting a heavy brow. "And where are you going?"

"To teach a bunch of Gunner-Marines how to shoot pheasant," he replied. "If the Russian pilots do not target the engines, they will eventually target the Steering House.

We need to bring them down. You know how to handle the ship in a dive-and-pursue better than I. I know how to shoot pheasant."

Blackheart looked at him. "You will die out there, Mister Sauder. At the speeds they fly, it is much easier for the fighters to target the bow than the stern. Particularly once they realize the Gatlings are firing at them."

"I know. But the Captain-Gunner does not yet realize that."

"Good luck, Mister Sauder," Blackheart said.

"*Dankeschön, Herr Kapitän*," he replied, and headed down the inside ladder into the lower part of the ship. He rapidly made his way along the interior corridor; bumping, jostling and lurching while the ship plunged, turned, climbed and veered. His stomach was churning as he opened the fo'c'sle hatch and climbed out into the eighty-mile-an-hour wind roaring across the decks of the *Bloody Rose*.

He fought the entire distance to get to the bow, using tethers on a metal safety cable. Hans moved to where the Gunner-Marines were hunkered down behind the wind-guards for protection, and joined them. Another fighter roared past, its engine noise audible over the sound of the wind.

"All right you scallywags ... who here has gone hunting pheasant, duck, goose or something of the like?" he shouted. A precious few hands went up. "All right, then. Group up! Two men who have not with one man that has. Give me the spare rifle!" he shouted. The extra gun was passed to him and he quickly figured out how to arm it for firing. The marines grouped up as he had ordered them to. "Now listen! As the next one goes past ... we all stand, aim and fire. You shoot until the wind knocks you down or you hear the next one coming! Watch where your shots fly and aim a bit ahead of the target; you will see what I mean! Any questions?" he shouted. The oncoming roar of the next fighter reached his ears, with the sound of it Maxims clattering away.

"Steady ... Steady ... NOW!" he shouted. The entire group rose as the fighter flashed past, crossing the bow in a dive, and then suddenly slowed down a hundred or so yards ahead and below.

It must have looked like a whale chasing a shark to the other Russian pilots. The *Bloody Rose* rolled hard to her starboard side, nearly a third-turn over, and then plunged nearly as sharply. She then lunged skyward, leaving her quarry directly ahead and high of the group of gunners at the bow.   There was no real volley ... every man was squeezing the trigger of his weapon as fast as the gun would recharge, which allowed each of them a shot roughly every two seconds.

The first fighter took a dozen hits in short order. The propeller motor died almost instantly, and smoke streamed from every hit as the blackened aluminium powder that coated the stretched canvas caught fire. Moments later, it exploded as its rocket fuel tank touched off. The pirates shouted and cheered.

"Take cover!" Hans screamed as the next fighter made its pass. The men dropped to the deck, as grenades landed around them, throwing splinters and shrapnel everywhere. "Come on, Annika ... quickly, woman ..." he said under his breath. Hans was the first to stand as the *Bloody Rose* gave pursuit to her latest assailant. The other pirates joined him, save one, who was face down on the deck.

The Russian pilot did not make the mistake of lazily flying straight and level after his attack run as the previous pilot had. Instead, he gunned his propeller motor for all it had, and climbed in a long arc up and to the port side. The steering crew gave their best pursuit, the ship shaking and protesting in every joint as it turned far tighter in a corkscrew ascent than she had ever been designed for.

The Tesla-gunners began firing, each experienced man shouting the correction to his two or three fellows to lead the target either more or less. The fighter made its escape, jinking and flying wildly as dozens of balls of electrical energy shot past it on all sides. The gunners threw themselves to the deck, waiting for the next attack. The next fighter aborted its run as the *Bloody Rose* suddenly touched off a volley of its challenge-and-reply smoke rockets, throwing a prismatic wall off her stern that obscured her position to her trailing attackers.

The next pilot was braver, bursting throughout the vertical coloured plumes on his rocket-assisted arc, only to discover two balloon mines drifting in his path ahead of him. The first one detonated too early, leaving the fighter unscathed. The second one detonated just after he passed it, shredding his left wings. The force of the wind tearing at the air frame at over four times the force of a gale did the rest, tearing the plane apart in a matter of seconds.

"Two down! We got two of them!" Hans shouted. "Get ready ... next one ... here he comes!"

The next pilot learned quickly, climbing high and then diving down, only committing to his rocket-powered pass when he was sure there were no new surprises in the offering. Bullets raked across the forecastle area and screams filled the air.

"Get up! Now! Get up you sons of bitches! Do not let your *Kapitän* down! Get up and shoot!" Hans shouted. They rose and fired, even the four now injured, blood covering their chests and legs, gamely blasting away. A fusillade of sizzling balls flashed through the sky filling the air around the Russian aerofighter. Its pilot was flying his plane to its limits; rolling, swerving, diving and climbing to ensure his escape. Hans had to grudgingly admit to the skill of the Russian pilots.

"We kill the bastard next time!" Hans shouted at them. "Take cover! Next attack!"

The sounds of the incoming rocket-fighter's Maxim guns was obscured by what sounded like a marching band's worth of snare-drums beating out a furious drum-roll. The fighter sailed past, black smoke and yellow-orange fire pouring out of its front. Hans swore he saw the pilot vainly pounding at the canopy release handle, unable to escape. The bullet-riddled aircraft rolled over and began a long, arcing spiral to the Gulf waters below. Hans cheered to himself mentally; Annika had the Gatlings set up on the stern and had scored their first kill.

Hans stood, bracing himself against the furious wind, his rifle in one hand while shaking his other fist. "The score is one for us, one for the *Kapitän*, and one for the Captain-Gunner, boys! If we bag more of these Russian bastards than they do, I will be buying the steak and rum at the next port! Come on! Ready ... Steady ... Steady ..."

The next fighter came roaring in, rocket-propelled grenades landing around the Steering House and its Maxims raking the ship from middle-deck across to her forecastle. Hans saw the line of gunfire tearing up the deck, reaching out to him in four rows of wood-splintering death. He froze in fear. Time hesitated as Hans realized he was going to die; there was no way to escape.

He was tackled roughly to the deck. Bullets raked over the huddled men, tearing into man and timber alike. Hans heard more screams. Warm blood splattered the exposed and chilled skin of his face. Someone was atop him and he shoved them aside as he struggled to stand. The remaining gunners were already firing away like men possessed. Hans turned to find Cemil laying on the deck with the front of his flight coat blood-soaked. His eyes were wide and glazed with shock behind his goggles. Cemil had been the man that had tackled Hans; the Arab had traded his life for the Englishman's.

Hans stared in stunned horror. His mind flashed to the day chumming around the Egyptian oasis port town with the one-eyed Arab and the times since that they had spent laughing, playing cards, talking about women or just causing trouble in runs aground. He steeled himself, choking back his emotions. This was no time for remorse. The men here depended on him.

The next attack did not come immediately. The remaining five Russians seemed to be trying to figure out how to best approach their suddenly very dangerous quarry. The *Bloody Rose* aggressively turned hard to the starboard side and began to climb. Her propellers screamed and the electrical thrum of the EMIPALE's magnetic drums intensified. The hunted was now hunting back, turning to take the fighters head-on, climbing towards them at their higher altitude.

"We are going after them boys! Get ready ... Steady! ... Steady! ... Two of them! Port and Starboard!" Hans shouted, desperately trying to seem remorseless and courageous before the men up here with him. Half the Gunner-Marines that had come up here were no longer able to stand for one reason or another. The Devil's Share was going to be well counted, and this had been his idea. They could not see him falter.

The two fighters flashed past, striking the ship with their rocket-propelled grenades and machine guns. Bullets smashed into the ship and the band of men at her bow who valiantly defended her. Hans heard the all-too-familiar sound of one of the propeller pods tearing itself apart after a hit and the ship began to slow even as she came about tightly to give pursuit to the port-side attacker. Cries and wails of injured and dying men pierced the howl of the wind roaring over all of them.

Another wall of smoke rockets lifted into the air behind the *Bloody Rose*, forestalling an immediate follow-on attack. At same instant, the battered gunners at her bow struggled to their feet and opened fire on their quarry with a bitter vengeance. The handful of survivors had learned with every pass how to lead and adjust for range and profile. The steering team were likewise getting better at this bizarre dogfight-style of airship manoeuvring. There was a long moment where the relative motion of the *Bloody Rose* and her quarry seemed to leave the fighter lazily arcing up and away like it was on a Sunday stroll across an English Commons. A stream of sizzling balls of electricity smashed into it, setting it ablaze and stalling its motor.

"Hit him again! That is it, boys! We have got the Russian bastard! He is ours!" Hans shouted, even as he squeezed his own trigger again. The group fired two or three more times each and were rewarded with the sight of the bat-winged menace tumbling from the sky out of control, spewing smoke and flames behind it.

That was more than enough for the Russians. They all veered away and used their rocket motors to rapidly break out of range and retreat. The weary crew of the *Bloody Rose* was more than willing to let them go.

*****

"Cemil will live," Annika said to him as she stood beside him on the wind-sheltered stern of the ship a couple of hours later. "I know you were concerned about him."

"He saved my life. He threw himself atop me and took bullets that had my name on them," Hans replied heavily.

"Well, it cost him a lung. A .303 is an awfully big piece of metal and he took a pair of through his left side. Koblinski is not entirely certain how he survived," Annika said flatly.

"So ... down one eye and one lung now?"

"... and one kidney. He got stabbed in a boarding last fall," she said with a note of black humour in her voice.

"And the others that were up there with me?" Hans asked.

"Three others were wounded but will live; one missing a limb. Four are dead."

"I feel sick," Hans said. He stared out at the distant ocean horizon, now flushing red with the setting sun behind them. "I cannot believe I did that to them ... they are my crewmates ... I ..."

"Hans," Annika said sharply. "What you did was brilliant. Blackheart put you on the spot in a situation you have never even conceived, and you managed to figure out a way to have us bag half a squadron of state-of-the-art Russian rocket-fighters."

"But I ..."

"No but!" she said to him forcefully. "You cost us four men to potentially save the lives of the entire ship! Dammit, Hans, we lose more to a single cannon ball sometimes. The only thing you did wrong was putting yourself at risk!"

"What?" he said.

"You heard me," she fumed at him. "Damn you, Hans Sauder ... what were you thinking? If the world's most stubborn Arab had not decided to roll the dice again, you would be missing most of your entrails right now!"

"Annika, I was just ..."

"Oh, shut up, Hans! I know what you were doing. I figured it out as soon as I got onto the quarterdeck and realized how well protected we were back there. There was no way that the oncoming fighters were going to strafe the ass end of this bitch once we were spraying eight hundred rounds a minute of forty-five-seventy at them. That left the forecastle gunners and the Steering House as targets ... and you had neatly made sure I would be in neither place!"

"But ..."

"No 'but', you idiot!" she snarled, visibly angry with him. "I just found you ... do not dare to get yourself killed trying to spare me from harm! Damn you, Sauder ... if Cemil had been a typical pirate, you would be dead! What the hell good does a dead hero do me?"

*****

"Mmm," Annika said languidly against his chest not long later. She impishly kissed the patch of skin open at the neck. *"Vy vidite*? Much better as a live pirate than a dead hero, *Da*?" They were curled together on a pile of ropes and silks in the Rope Locker. They were both still more than half-dressed, having only unbuttoned or untied the minimum required to satisfy their hunger for each other.

Hans chuckled at her, playing with her short hair. "You do present a very convincing argument, *Fräulein*."

"I did not need to be protected before we met, Hans. You being in my life as my lover does not change that," she said quietly. "Focus on keeping yourself alive, and I will focus on me. And we will have many more days together like this. When you start trying to save everyone around you, then you just get yourself killed. That does no one any good."

"Fair enough, Annika. I will try to remember that."

"The Trans-Atlantic Bridge"

Diary Entry For July 9th, 1888

Today we have returned to Egypt. In some perverse movement of the calendar, the lifetime that has passed for me since the first day I laid eyes upon the oasis city of al-Myāh Wālsma has in fact been a scant quarter year. When I first came here, I was disappointed that I could not take leave of the Bloody Rose and her infamous crew. Now, I am here willingly, gladly and wholeheartedly.

I am wondering how my family is doing. Karl must be finding life as abruptly different as I am. One day, perhaps a "butylka vodki" and a fine cigar will be the way we catch up on the differences in our lives.

After our persistent interference from the Russians during our visit to America, we made to Cuba in search of the Map that our Man Louisiana directed us to. We found the plantation outside of Havana as he said we would. Kapitän Blackheart insisted that Chief Arietta go alone, using her formidable skills as an assassin-spy to carry her. She returned, injured and poisoned but Döktor Koblinski was able to yet again work his magic. She did succeed in her infiltration and cartographical theft, and we now know our ultimate destination.

We then made good speed across the Atlantic for Egypt. At supper two nights ago, after a heady discussion, it was decided that "Auntie Coline's" work aboard the Bloody Rose has more than earned her a chair at the officer's table. I was very pleased at this turn of events.

Tomorrow, we strike out into the desert in search of the Lost Temple of Min. We will be armed with little more than an old map, a light of hope bought from a merchant and our luck. God help us if the Russians get there first.

*****

Hans leaned against the stern railing, looking out into the starry darkness of the Caribbean night five hundred feet above the waters off the north coast of Cuba. He pulled his goggles up and breather mask down; his gestures were short and sharp. He exhaled through his nose irritably and then pulled out a battered pocket watch. He flipped it open, glanced at it and then flipped it closed. He paused, realizing he had no idea what it had said. He opened it again, forcing himself to read it. Arietta was now twenty minutes overdue.

Almost two and a half hours ago she had gone over the side with her steam-powered glider-plane, heading for the outskirts of the sizable tobacco plantation a dozen or so miles from the edge of Havana. The plan had been fairly straight forward; she would glider-drop to the edge of the plantation, hide the glider and then sneak into the main building under the combined cover of darkness and the lateness of the hour. She would then locate the map, steal it, and escape to the glider.

The glider had been fitted with one of the self-inflating balloons from the Sargasso mines. She would strap herself in, trigger the balloon to inflate, and then drift with the wind for fifteen minutes and light a flare to reveal her position. The *Bloody Rose* had been loitering in the area that predictions said Arietta and her balloon expedition would drift towards. If all had gone as expected she should have been here, even at worst, twenty minutes ago. Which left Hans with the sinking feeling that things had not gone as expected for his dear friend and mentor, Arietta Itala.

Hans drummed his fingers on the guardrail he leaned on. One of the Gunner-Marines on weather deck rounds stopped beside him with a modern, machine-made cigarette glowing between his lips.

"Any sign of anything else in the air around us?" Hans asked him.

"No, sir. There isn't anything as far as the eyes can see. A couple of the boys are awful sweet on the Chief, and they've been staring at the plantation with spy glasses for the past hour. They don't see any signs of fire, or smoke or anything big going on," the young Austrian said.

"*Danke*," Hans said with a nod. The other man gave him a nod in return and then continued on with his rounds. He drummed his fingers on the guardrail he once again leaned on.

The sudden eruption a few minutes later of the bells and whistles of the general call to action startled him to exclamation. The electric motors of the ship thrummed loudly in the silent star-lit Caribbean night sky and the sounds of the previously silent ship coming to life were almost raucous. Hans felt the ship bank to port and he headed to that side. In the distance, a bit above the ship, was the brilliant white light of a signal flare.

Hans took the steps of the outside ladder leading to the Steering House two at a time. He arrived inside to find Blackheart intently staring through his spyglass at the distant light. He leaned over the voicepipe for the Propulsion Room and bellowed down for as much speed as the *Bloody Rose* could manage in her injured condition. He looked over at Sauder.

"It looks like Chief Itala is on the glider, strapped in ... but she is not moving and her head is down. I expect she is injured. Go get Koblinski and both of you meet the glider recovery crew at the derrick on the port side. Move man. Now," Blackheart growled. Hans did not need to be told again.

*****

"Well?" Blackheart asked quietly, looking at Arietta's unconscious form on the middle bed of the Infirmary where both Koblinski and Coline worked swiftly and with few words between them. Hans looked over and concealed his surprise at the clear concern on the Englishman's face.

"Her right-hand arm blade is broken off. Both her revolvers are empty. Her air pistol is empty. She has a knife wound in her right leg, two near misses with bullets on her left side, and three finger-sized darts in her left forearm. Her lips and fingers are blue, but she is still breathing; *Herr Döktor* believes the darts were poisoned," Hans reply quietly.

The Englishman cursed under his breath and the German nodded in agreement before continuing to speak. "She found the map ... she was unconscious when she was brought aboard. She strapped herself in, inflated the balloon, jury-rigged a pressure trigger for the signal flare and passed out, or so it would seem. The flare self-ignited when she had drifted high enough."

"And what is our status, Mister Sauder?"

"Annika has the map and is setting course for Egypt. We are running doubled lookouts, as when we were north of the Scorchlands. I have both Visivald and O'Ferral working on jury-rigging repairs to the starboard motor pod, but right now we are running on sail again. In another hour we should be able to give you seventy knots to make way with."

Blackheart nodded, looking back towards the Italian-Ethiope. "Well done Mister Sauder. I want the guns manned at all times until we are twelve hours away from the American continent. Those Russian rocket aerofighters had to come from somewhere; I am disinterested in being surprised by a flying airbase or some such nonsense. You and the Captain-Gunner have the action for the next two hours; keep me informed of any decisions you make. I will be here."

"Aye-aye, *mein Kapitän*," Sauder replied.

*****

"Well, good evening, Chief," Hans said in greeting as the portly Chief Steward approached where he was standing at the stern of the *Bloody Rose*. "What brings you out here at this hour?" He was exhausted and weary from the events of the past two days, but tried to sound in good spirits.

It was well into the dark hours of the morning, with the night sky of the Caribbean showing the moon, the planets and the white silken veil of the Milky Way in a nearly numbing glory. It was a display such as Hans had never seen in Europe. The events of the day had made sleep a goal just beyond his reach, and so here he was at the stern of the pirate airship, watching the jewel and crystal strewn vista above.

"I cannot sleep," the Englishman replied somewhat gruffly. "I thought some warm milk, a good pipe and some fresh air just might aid that." He absently finger-combed his unruly carrot-toned hair, to no effect that was perceivable to the young German. He then pulled out a well loved pipe and gave it a tap on the stern railing to empty it.

"Yourself, sir?" the Chief Steward asked. "What has you here at this hour?"

There was a few further moments between the two men that only yielded the sound of the wind and thrumming of the electric motor pods. "I am not entirely happy with the results of my first command of an airship today", Sauder said finally. "I got a lot of people shot up. *Herr* Blackheart has said nothing to me of it, but I rather doubt he is happy with the cost of my solution to the problem this afternoon. I expect his concern for the health of the Chief Engineer is the only thing that has saved me his criticism."

"That is bloody rubbish and we both know it, sir," Bridges said affably as he squinted at the label on the package of loose tobacco. "You did a ruddy wizard job of dealing with those Russians and it did not cost us anything that Koblinski and some recruiting will not cover."

Hans looked over at Bridges with his jaw agape and a stunned look about him. "Wait ... what?" he finally managed.

Bridges carefully packed a wad of tobacco into his pipe with his thumb and looked up at Sauder as he spoke. "Just another extraordinary day aboard the *Bloody Rose*, sir. You get used to that sort of rot after awhile. Good job, I say. As for the Captain, he says if you keep that sort of thing up, you will be fit for your own ship soon enough, sir. If not the *Bloody Rose*, then one of your taking."

"He ... he said what?" Hans blinked, starting to feel as though the entire discussion had suddenly taken a very surreal turn.

"Oh, yes. You have certainly got the potential, Sir. I was the personal steward to the first Blackheart, I am the Chief Steward to the current one, and I served on two birds before all that. You might say I have seen the whole history of this old girl. I know what a smart officer looks like, sir. You fit the bill right nicely."

"The first Blackheart? You mean O'Raedy is not the first?" Hans asked quizzically.

"That is right, Mister Sauder. In the Lore and Traditions of Piracy, the name of the captain and his or her ship are unchanging. So it is that the Captain of the *Bloody Rose* is someone named in current Legend as 'Blackheart'. No matter the man or woman's real name, the captain is Blackheart," the Chief Steward said, focusing on the match he was trying to light his brass and ivory tobacco pipe with. "Mister O'Raedy is the second to wear the name."

"Who was the first?"

"A Russian air-captain by the name of Vasya Gena Lagunov," the red-headed Englishman replied puffing at his pipe, ensuring that the flick of flame in the bowl meant the tobacco had really caught. "Good man. Got sick of the waste he saw in the Russian war and decided he was having nothing more to do with governments and rulers. He had the *Bloody Rose* built, got himself a crew, and established the Legend. He said he was going to 'declare war on every nation'. At least he would be fighting for something he could be sure of that way."

"How old is the ship, then?" Hans asked, unscrewing the cap of his coffee flask.

"The old girl is about seven years old, which makes her one of the oldest ships in piratedom, actually," Bridges said as he exhaled a scented cloud that was lost in the slipstream of the ship. "Mister O'Raedy took command about ... oh, three years ago."

"*Kapitän* Lagunov signed it over to him and that was that?" Sauder questioned, having a mouthful from his flask.

"There is a bit more to it than that, Mister Sauder," the portly Chief Steward said jovially. "When a new captain steps up, he or she has to defend their claim against all comers aboard the ship. The crew does not always believe a given man or woman is the right person for the job, and sometimes you need to crack a few ribs and jaws to persuade them."

The two men stood leaning against the stern railing, looking out into the bejewelled night sky behind the speeding airship, with nothing but silence passing between them for a few minutes.

"And *Kapitän* O'Raedy is not upset with my performance, you say?" Hans asked cautiously.

"Not at all, sir. Quite happy with you, actually. He generally is," he said, stifling a mild yawn. "Well, that bodes well for my odds of sleep. I think I will stroll forward and then find my hammock. Good night, Sir."

"Good night, Chief. Thank you for the company."

"Quite welcome, sir. Oh ... and if I might offer some advice? Do not make the mistake of confusing Michael O'Raedy with Captain Blackheart. One is a man with faults and weaknesses, the other is an inherited legend that is supposed to know no bounds in fearlessness and ruthlessness."

Sauder watched the Chief Steward make his way along the port-size breezeway, leaving the very thoughtful young German alone in the Caribbean night.

*****

Supper time of the next day found them east-southeast of British Newfoundland, running on two motor pods. Watch Officer Onora had joked she was forgetting what sails looked like and was tiring of the smell of burnt kerosene. However, the urgency of their mission combined with flying over the North Atlantic meant that running with the wind was simply not a viable option.

"I have a request to make," Alexi said carefully as the officers sat down for their evening meal.

"Oh," said Blackheart. "And what would that be?"

"Would it be possible for Nurse Coline to join us for supper tomorrow evening?"

Blackheart frowned at the Polish doctor. The others at the table glanced at each other in mild surprise. "Why?" the pirate captain queried thoughtfully.

"Well, she works very hard and I wanted to allow her the chance to sample Chief Bridges excellent cuisine as a reward for her extraordinary efforts. Without having to be a serving staff for the evening, that is."

Blackheart looked unconvinced but said nothing for a moment. He then looked at the other officers. "Your thoughts?"

Amram Nando spoke up immediately. "I respect your sweetheart's work, Doctor," he said in a chiding tone, "but the rules are clear. This table is for officers only. If we make an exception for her, then we are obliged to make it for others. I am sure that we can arrange to have a plate of the Chief's excellent cooking delivered to her. That is a common reward for the gunners and lookouts. She is not allowed at this table unless she is an officer," the Spaniard concluded firmly.

Hans looked around the table surreptitiously. It was clear to him that no one liked the Deck Officer's answer but at the same time, everyone knew that was the rule. Even Grumman, the Confederate-American, did not seem content with the situation.

"I agree with Mister Nando," Hans announced. Everyone blinked at him, including Nando.

"Do you now, Mister Sauder?" Blackheart said amusedly. "And why is that?" It was clear that Blackheart was not taking the young German's words at their printed value.

"Mister Nando is quite correct. The Mess rules are very clear. So long as she is not an officer, she may not sit at this table," he said affably. "I will note, however, that her contributions to this crew are remarkable. Speaking frankly, about a third of the officers at the table here this evening would be dead without the skilled assistance she has brought *Döktor* Koblinski. I will offer for consideration the notion that a plate of better food one evening is hardly enough."

"Do you now, Mister Sauder?" Blackheart said with a grin. "And what would you consider sufficient?"

Sauder looked over at Koblinski. "You will agree with me that while she is a talented Nurse, she lacks the required education to be a proper doctor, yes?"

The bearded Pole lofted a brow, choosing his words carefully. "Your assessment is accurate. She was a field Nurse with the French Army for three years before transferring to the French Air Navy. She worked directly with the Medical Officer of the *Triomphe* for two years before she jumped the gunwale to join us. So while she has a tremendous breadth of experience and commensurate skills, she lacks the formal training of a proper medical physician."

Sauder looked over at O'Raedy. "I put forward that calling Gwendoline Coline 'Nurse' is rather like calling Arietta Itala 'Engineer'. It does not properly denote her skill or value to the crew of this ship. *Herr Kapitän*, I formally request that Nurse Coline be promoted effective as of tomorrow's Morning Quarters to Chief Nurse. Of course, that would make her an Officer of this vessel, with all attendant rights and responsibilities."

The pirate captain tilted his head from side to side in an exaggerated display of consideration of the request. Obviously playing to the moment, he looked over to the Polish doctor who was having difficulty keeping his mouth from tumbling open in astonishment at Sauder's request.

"Well, Alexi? Do you think she would accept? Or do you hazard she would not be interested in the promotion?" he asked after having a sip of his wine.

Koblinski blinked rapidly a few times. "Oh! I am sure she would very much appreciate the accolade and accept it," he stammered.

"Good, good. Now, do you agree? You are her superior, after all. I should not want to promote her against your wishes, naturally," Blackheart said feigning solicitude.

A ripple of amusement went around the table as the Pole nodded rapidly in agreement. "Oh, oh yes. I do think it is the smart thing to do. Yes, very much so."

"Very good then. You may have the pleasure of informing her, Doctor. Please ensure she is not late for supper tomorrow night; it would no doubt upset our dear Deck Officer."

*****

Supper the next evening saw the newly promoted and rather embarrassed Chief Nurse Coline being toasted by the ship's assembled officers. She in turn thanked the Captain and then the rest of the officers for their faith in her and the chance to be part of their crew.

"So, tell me, Miss Coline," Blackheart said after a sip of his wine. "What prompted you to jump that gunwale? It could not have been something you had ever anticipated doing."

"*Eh bien, mon capitaine,*" she said with a youthful giggle, "it was a silly childhood game I used to play with my brothers and their friends. I was always getting captured by the pirates! They always seemed to have more fun than I did. So when three young men came into the sickbay of the *Triomphe* brandishing swords and guns, I thought *'Mon Dieu! Pas encore*! I will join them instead!'"

Blackheart roared with laughter and soon everyone else at the table had joined in. Alexi nearly choked on his drink and Hans was laughing so hard he had to set his glass down.

Towards the end of the meal, when the cigars and cigarettes were lit and the port had been poured, Blackheart looked over at Hans. "It is a curious responsibility we bear, is it not, Mister Sauder?" he asked whimsically.

"What is that, *Herr Kapitän*? Saving the world from an ancient weather weapon?"

"No, living up to a legend. That is part of what we do, as pirates, you know? Boys and girls, and children of all ages," O'Raedy said with a nod to Gwendoline, "consider the life of a pirate to be synonymous with adventure, deviltry, and abandon. When a man or woman joins a pirate ship ... they may have innumerable motivations for doing so. I am sure you recall my comparison to France's *Légion étrangère*."

"Indeed I do," Hans nodded as he exhaled a thin cloud of smoke into the air.

"I think the reason they look for us or the Foreign Legion is the legend that goes with it," the Englishman waxed philosophically. "And when they wind up here, one way or another, they become part of that legend. Take your good friend Master-Gunner Dubé ... can you imagine what will happen when he returns home and the young lady says 'yes'? He ran away to Europe, made his fortune as pirate of the *Bloody Rose*, and returned to take up the life of a gentleman plantation owner. A curious responsibility, indeed."

*****

It was another full day of cruising before the cry of sighted land announced the Spanish coast. They saw a Spanish patrol frigate who challenged them immediately, in spite of running "Jack over Roger". They answered with a series of coloured smoke candles fired from the stern according to the sequence indicated in their code book.

There was a few tense moments as the Spanish ship drew along side them at a scant hundred yards, matching their speed. Blackheart had the ship readied for action, but ordered the gun doors kept closed and the four-pounders on the weather deck left unmanned for now. The main guns were loaded with cinderball behind their doors, and the upper deck gunners were all waiting at hatch doors to spring out and take up their positions and start firing.

A flashing light from the bridge of the Spanish frigate which they had identified as "*el Tiburón Nube*" conveyed a message in Morse Code. "*Vamos a jugar juntos un día más,*" Nando said after reading the message. "It means '*We will play together another day*'," he translated.

Blackheart lofted a brow.   "Oh really? Well, then ... please reply with 'God speed and God willing," he said with a caustic chuckle.

*****

The course of the *Bloody Rose* took her along the border of Portugal and Spain, and then past the cities of Saragossa and Barcelona. She then was out over the immortal waters of the Mediterranean ocean.

It was these very skies where she had earned her title and reputation as one of the most dangerous pirate airships of modern times. It almost seemed odd to Hans that now, in many respects, they were agents of the Allied Empires on a secret mission of international importance. He wondered if Fate had unalterably changed the course of the "Mediterranean Menace" and her crew; would they ever be pirates again? Or were the affairs of the tumultuous and modern era they lived in now sweeping them along before it, like a child's balloon in a breeze?

In a few more hours she had overflown Sardinia and Sicily and had turned south to fly along the life-giving band of blue known to the world as the Nile River. Once again, they followed the Nile south for nearly two hundred miles and then turned West for almost a similar distance.

*****

It was just before dawn when the *Bloody Rose* approached the newly opened Docking Tower 32 of the Egyptian oasis airship port of al-Myāh Wālsmā'. The eastern horizon was within moments of its regular morning eruption of ruby and gold over the desert. The pirate airship manoeuvred easily to approach the dock against the thinnest of zephyrs, in spite of being short-crewed. Her leading lines were cast to the docking tower swiftly, and then her mooring lines followed equally quickly. Her electric-powered propellers spun to a halt, then the motor pods slowly retracted into the hull and sets of folding doors closed over the motorwell openings.

Inside the Propulsion Room of the pirate turned privateer, Chief Arietta leaned against an upright set of pipe work. She applauded the work of the other three engineers.

"Well done, Mister Sauder. Flawless; you did an excellent job of getting us alongside. At this rate, I will be able to stay in my bunk with a book and let you run the show for things like this," she said with her characteristic musical laugh.

A ripple of laughter went around the three men that worked for the charming Chief Engineer. "Good to see we have managed to reach a standard of pleasant boredom for you, Chief," Hans replied, still chuckling. "Good to see you up and about again, as well. How are you feeling?"

"Better, Mister Sauder. The good Doctor tells me the poison I was shot with produced an effect similar to an intense malaria attack. So, I am on medicines that I take with meals and I am to do nothing more intense than to applaud for work well done, or curse mildly for slack effort."

"Oh, well then this is a fine opportunity for us to relax and avoid work," Visivald said with a hearty chortle. "You have cursed at me enough over the past year or so that a mild spate is of no consequence!"

She wordlessly pitched a spanner at him which narrowly missed the side of his head. Sauder and O'Ferral laughed while Visivald protested that she might be over-exerting herself.

*****

An hour later found Sauder, Itala, Nadezhda, Nando and O'Raedy clustered around the table in the Captain's Mess, regarding the ancient map that Arietta had made off with from the basement collection of the "Cardinal" of the Serpentis Combine in Havana. Beside it on the table was a modern map of Egypt; they marvelled at the differences.

"That Temple is quite a trick, if this map is to be believed. The entire area around where it used to be is a thirty mile diameter oasis on this map. On the modern one, its a desert canyon of no redeeming value," the pirate Captain said, shaking his head. "In fact, I am sure I have flown over that area at least once in the past three years and saw nothing that looked more interesting than a scorpion and some rocks."

"Well that would be why the Book called it magic, *Herr Kapitän*," Hans said dryly. "I will be fascinated to see this thing and find out how it works."

"As will I," Arietta said with an eager nod.

"Why? We are just going to blow it up," Annika said with a shrug.

"Pardon?" Hans said, startled.

"We are, Captain-Gunner?" Blackheart asked, amusedly. "Now why would we do a thing like that?"

"Primarily because there is no such thing as Good Guys in all of this. The Allies may be paying us, but the fact of the matter is that we are Pirates, they are the Authorities and this is a 'magic' weapon capable of winning a war for whomever owns it," she snarled.

She sighed for a moment. "I would love to spend a week or two snooping around, taking chalk rubbings of the carvings, pictures with the Kodak box, mapping out the entire floor plan and just sink myself into the wonder of being the first explorers in living memory to see the place. It would be any archaeologists' dream! You all know how much I love Egypt and its history. But we need to think a bit bigger than our own hobbies here," she concluded sourly.

She continued on, waving her arms as if to drive home the importance of her opinion. "If the Russian Empire owns it, they will abuse it. If the Allied Empires own it, they will abuse it. You may well expect that after they are done abusing each other with it, they will start abusing *us* with it. I say we find it, marvel at it, and leave it a smoking gash in the earth with the status quo well preserved," she concluded firmly, crossing her arms across her chest. Hans well knew by now that particular gesture meant that her mind was made up and there would be no convincing her of anything else.

"That is a very dangerous position for us to take, Captain-Gunner," the Spanish Deck Officer said quietly. "If we double cross them, the Allied Empires will likely be very reluctant to be so welcoming at the 'O-Room' at the Azores the next time we pass by."

"Shake your head," Annika snorted derisively. "You of all people should know that as soon as we are done being useful to them in this little hidden war, we will be its next casualty. There is no reason at all to give any of them the weapons to wipe us from the skies of the only neutral ports we can run to when we cause too much of a stir in Europe."

There was a stony silence where the Spaniard glared at the Russian. For a moment, Hans was wondering if Amram might make the mistake of actually taking a furied swing at Annika. He nearly sighed aloud in relief when Blackheart broke the tension.

"You both have raised valid points. I will remind you all, however, that I am the Captain of this ship and crew, and thus the final decision on what we do is mine," he pointedly stated. "For now, our first job is two-fold in its composition. We need to find out who owns that particular piece of sand, and we need to find out if 'Uncle Ivan' has been through here already. Tonight, we will split shares and let the crew head aground for some needed relaxation. We have been running at the ragged edge for two months straight now."

He looked around at each of them and then continued speaking. "Tomorrow morning, we look to recruit a few more crew. As well, we get manpower working on repairs to the damage done from those rocket-fighters. At the same time, Captain-Gunner and Captain-Rockets, you will spend the afternoon and evening spending money and loosening tongues as you please, to find out what you can about our next destination and any potential surprises. Are we all understood?"

Everyone nodded in forced agreement. It was clear that no one was particularly happy with any of this, save

Blackheart himself who seemed curiously pleased at the lack of contentment amongst his officers.

*****

"So what do you think the old airshark is up to?" Hans asked Annika. They were curled up together in the Rope Locker, sipping coffee and dodging responsibilities for a few minutes before they got to the list of work that needed to be done.

"I do not know," she said sourly. "He is hardly a dull man. He must have already thought of everything I have said. I cannot imagine that he intends to actually turn the Temple and the Weapon over to the Allies."

Hans chuckled blackly. "Perhaps he intends to retire on the earnings and thus does not care if the Allies have a weapon that would keep us from ever again practising a 'Moses Reverse'?"

Annika made a rather unlady-like noise that clearly indicated her opinion of that notion. Once Hans was done howling with laughter, she spoke. "O'Raedy could have retired a wealthy man five times over in the time that I have known him. He is about as likely to retire voluntarily as I am," she growled and then had a mouthful of the coffee in the flask they passed between them. "I really do wish you would quit ruining a good coffee with the makings of a woman's tea; milk and sugar are for old maids," she grumbled.

"It is the only way I am sure you will not drink the entire thing yourself," he chided. She punched him in the shoulder.

*****

The engineering repairs to the ship started immediately. With one motor pod badly damaged, they had only a short time to try and get it working again. The last time they had been at the oasis port, it had taken them almost eight days to repair a destroyed motor. Hans was fervently hoping that the rocket-propelled grenade hit to this one proved to not be as severe as the destructive power of four pounds of grapeshot had been the last time.

Time would tell; the immediate job was disassembling the fairing and enclosure around the damaged motor. Once that was done, they would be able to properly assess the damage. With everything that had gone on thus far, it was something they had not had time to do.

On the upper decks, the usual amount of ship's husbandry was underway. Where they had taken no Prey thus far on the trip, there was no cargo to unload and deliver aground. A few of the crew grumbled under their breaths that their shares had best not suffer for want of "honest pirating" or there would be trouble.

However, the results of their gas lamp gathering on the weather deck early that evening put that particular line of complaint to rest, at least for a time. With the Devil having taken his shares, comparatively little over-all damage to repair thus far, and fourteen hundred pounds Stirling in bullion aboard, the shares were counted at slightly more than a respectable four pounds Stirling each.

That netted Hans a very comfortable 28 pounds and a handful of guineas. In addition, there were his "Duties" to be collected from MacIssac, Cemil and Grumman.

"Chief," he thoughtfully asked the senior Steward, "how long do 'Duties' last?"

"Oh, well sir, by the Tradition and Code, a 'year and a pay' after the Right of Passage. We all figure that if they have not learned anything from you by then, they are not going to," the portly, red-bearded Bridges said with a chuckle.

As he had before, he just passed that money along quietly to his good friend and Master Gunner, André Dubé.

They had discussed the matter at length one evening over most of a bottle of rum, and decided that Hans' contributions were shares in the Maple sugar farm that the Franco-Brit planned to retire to. They had even written up – somewhat sloppily, as a result of the influence of the rum – a "memorandum of understanding" between them explaining what percentage of the profits Hans was entitled to, when he should pass by Montréal to collect it.

Hans rather doubted he would ever see Montréal in British North America once, let alone stop by yearly. Then again, six months ago he would not have envisioned himself as an airship pirate, either.

*****

A pirate and his money are soon parted as the saying went and this particular evening was no different. The ship had been abuzz with talk of a night of "Pay and Party" in one of the crew's favourite ports.

Annika and the rest of the "Ladies of the Rose", excepting Arietta, were off together to raise Cain at a women's-only establishment in the "Pirate Quarter" of the town. Hans found the notion of a cabaret or public house that banned male patrons rather unusual.

The opposite was quite common, of course. There were numerous "Gentlemen Only" institutions catering to almost every social caste and possible life-interest. Some of those were international in presence, in some cases going so far as to duplicate even the layouts of the stair cases and the wood used in the flooring of all their establishments around the world. Membership was exclusive, and travel was the preview of the male aristocrat.

The only "Ladies Only" establishment he had ever heard of was the so-called "Ladies' Institute" in London, which had closed little more than a half-dozen years after it had opened. Hans amusedly reflected that, given the natures of the various "Ladies of the Rose", he rather much doubted they were out to a social evening of tea, scones and cribbage.

Jabbar Cemil was still recovering in the Medical Bay from his Russian-inflicted machine-gun wounds. Hans stopped in to check on him.

"Ahoy, you half-blind, shallow-breathed scallywag," Hans said with a good-natured laugh as he entered the Medical Bay. "Not dead yet?"

"Oh, Hell no," the Arab laughed. "The English, French and Germans have not yet managed to quell the bark of the son of the desert jackals, so the Russians most certainly cannot be expected to," he said, trying to puff up his chest. He groaned and rubbed at the bandages around his mid-section.

"Easy, *mein Freund*," the German admonished. "We will need you whole and in good health in the next couple of days. Both as a fighter and a translator, I expect."

Cemil nodded. "Be sure to have an extra bottle for me while you are aground tonight, *Saahibi*. This will be the first time being in al-Myāh Wālsmā' as a pirate where I will be unable to sample the cultural joys of this fine town. A tragic milestone," he said with a shake of his head and a laugh.

"There will be ample time in a few weeks, Cemil ... once this amusement with the Russians and the Allies is done, we are bound for the Graving Docks in Persia for repairs and refit. Make it that far, *mein Freund*, and I will buy the first bottle we artfully demolish."

"You have a deal, Sauder. Enjoy your run aground."

*****

A couple of hours later, Hans was prowling the streets of the Pirate Quarter, marvelling again much as he had the first time at the cacophonous kaleidoscope of the four open air markets and innumerable dens of iniquity which composed the Pirate Quarter. The crews of a dozen pirate airships made a raucous throng of shoppers and party-goers which in turn made the Quarter a busy place, even on a Sunday night. Now, as on his first visit, anything that anyone of any taste, appetite, morality or vice might desire was available as goods and services.

What he found much different was his reaction to the various sights, smells and sounds that reached him. He recalled having been rather shocked and in some cases appalled on his first night aground in the oasis port town. Now, he took it all in with a much more open mind.

He wondered if Annika would use the opportunity to indulge her vice for opium while she was here. She had told him she visited an Opium Den in Brussels when they passed through, and another in London. He remembered being scandalized that she indulged in the illicit vice, originally. This evening he felt himself being merely somewhat relieved that she was at least travelling with companions this time who were more than likely to ensure she did not wind up kidnapped in a stupor.

"... she is still not ready to retire to Beirut," he said to himself with a laugh. "And I am not ready for her to do that, either."

*****

Some time later, he found himself entering the "Desert Bizaare" looking for a particular petite red-head wearing a red silk sash and leather wrist cuffs. He had not been looking for more than five minutes when somewhat familiar voice addressed him from over his shoulder while a set of fingernails traced down his spine.

"Hello, Pirate ... Whitehall said you might be in town."

Hans turned around, puzzled and found himself looking down at his "Wench" from his night of poker, liquor and bar fighting at the end of his last visit to the oasis port. He lofted a brow involuntarily and then schooled his features. He wordlessly took her by the wrist and led her off to a side, pulling her against him.

"Well, well, Tiger, I am happy to see you, too," she purred and trailed a finger down his chest, following its decent with a lusty look in her eyes. She was dressed much as you might expect of an airship mechanic, save for the lack of grime and the abundance of makeup, perfume and bare leg.

"Whitehall?" he asked quietly. Between the band, the patrons, the staff and the animals, Hans very much doubted that anyone would be able to snoop on their conversation. However, he also saw no point to lacking in caution. For all he knew, the staggering pirate beside him was working as an undercover detective for the Russian version of the Pinkertons.

"Aye, Whitehall. You forgot to mention you were a Queen's Man when you were here last time, Pirate ... I would have given you a free night on the house," she said with a bawdy wink and a suggestively feline stretch of her frame.

"I am hardly a 'Queen's Man'," he scoffed. "I am a pirate that has interesting choice in attractive women and that is all. I am being well paid for my contributions to the Imperial cause."

She stood on her toes while leaning her entire body against him and nibbled at his neck. She snorted. "Of course. The masterless rogue and lawless knave you are. I believe you. Really I do," she chuckled coyly.

He scowled at her in spite of trying to conceal his irritation with her. "So you are an agent for British Intelligence, then?" he asked her while sounding somewhat sceptical. She nodded at him as she curled herself against him and traced her fingers over his shirt in whimsical patterns.

"What is it you want, Wench?" he asked.

"Well, I was hoping you would be looking for another evening of poker, snogging, rum and bar-fighting. I have not had that much fun or made that much money in a single night before or since," she said with a husky laugh.

"Made off with my table earnings, did you?"

"Hell yes," she said with a wicked grin. "You paid me a pound and twenty and I scampered off with twice that again from the table."

He laughed aloud. "I had wondered if that is what had happened. Good on you."

"And what about you, Pirate? What are you here for? Rum and whores?"

He bristled perceptively. "Perhaps the former and hardly the latter; my sweetheart would be displeased. I was hoping to pay for the use of your sharp tongue, Wench."

She opportunistically and arousingly licked at the bare skin his shirt showed at his neck. "Mmm, let me know how low you want me to take that service."

"That is not what I meant and I suspect you know that."

She sighed with a note of disappointment. "All work and no play makes the Pirate a dull boy," she chided. "Go get a bottle of scotch and come up stairs with me, Pirate ... I will be sure to make it worth your while," she said with a wink.

*****

Hans sipped at glass of scotch in his hand and glanced at the slight woman stretched out against him. They were sprawled on pile of pillows in the corner of the room. There was a reasonably sumptuous looking bed in the room as well as a hammock, and what looked like swing. She had forcibly tugged him over to the pillows and pressed him down atop them before joining him. They had as of yet done nothing he would consider remarkable, beyond the part where she was the one to pour the scotch. Liberated women, indeed.

"Mmm ... good stuff," she sighed after having a mouthful from her glass. "Strong peaty fire."

"So something about you is a falsehood," he said amusedly. "I recall you giving me quite a menu for your services when first we met. How did you know I would not be ordering?"

She laughed at him. "Oh, Pirate. Really? If you had been a paying customer, I would done you as you pleased. You are a bit of a looker and if I have to shag a pirate once a night to keep my job, it might as well be a handsome one."

He blinked at her. "So you are a member of British Intelligence actively working as a prostitute to cover yourself?"

"More like the other way around," she said with a dirty giggle. "I wound up in this water-hole town as a result of lousy luck and sour siblings. I needed to eat and I need a safe place to sleep, so I started the life of a working girl. About a year ago a chap out of Cairo approached me about supplementing my income. I keep my eyes and ears open, write my dear 'Uncle Benjamin' in Cairo once a week, and I am well paid for the value of what I deliver. Some times they ask me questions or tell me what to look for."

"Do I understand that 'Uncle Benjamin' told you I might be passing through and why?" Hans asked.

"Sort of. I got a few sketches of you and some of your crewmates, the name of your ship, and got told to pay attention to any Russians in town. I have a little something I can add to their vodka to help them relax and be a touch loose-lipped, you see," she said with a wicked grin and a nasty sparkle in her eye.

"Oh really?"

"Aye, Pirate. Russians are like men the whole world over," she said with a cynical bark. "Talk dirty to them, get them drinking, feel them up a bit and they will tell you anything they think will get a curvy girl onto her back. It does not matter they are paying for the result, they want to feel important and powerful, and that their 'conquest' has been wowed by who they are."

"My, my. Quite the nasty piece of work, are you not?" he chuckled.

"I do not hear you arguing with me, Pirate," she snorted caustically. "Want to hear what they have told me?"

"Do I have to pay you and take you to bed?" he asked amusedly.

"Only if you want to. 'Uncle Benjamin' has already paid your stay; anything else you choose to give me is a tip of one kind or another," she said with a wink.

*****

"So the Russians have already been through here a few days ago? And a sizable number, you say, Mister Sauder?" Blackheart asked thoughtfully as he dabbed some tomato sauce from the corner of his mouth. They were sitting at breakfast, and Hans was telling everyone present what he had learned. He had opted to leave out from who and how.

"*Ja, Herr Kapitän*. They came over land, not by airship. There were a hundred or so that were here; drank up a storm, spent a lot of money on both supplies and parties, hired a few locals as guides and set off to the south-east."

"The south-east? Hmph. Not good. That is where we are heading. Hopefully whoever owns that piece of land is not easily paid in Russian gold or things may be doubly difficult for us."

"The Russians are not stupid," Annika said blearily over her coffee. She and Onora were doubtlessly hung over, which meant that Arietta was being particularly loud in her laughter and excessively jovial; Hans was finding that by-play rather amusing. "The reason they have a hundred men," she continued, rubbing at the side of her skull, "is likely the size of the treasury they are carrying with them that needs to be protected. They would be very happy to pay a Sheik's ransom and better to get access to the Temple, given what it will do for them."

"That makes sense," Aldebert replied, as he picked at his breakfast plate. He, too, was looking a bit worse for wear.

"Not good," Blackheart repeated with a sigh. "Well, Captain-Gunner and Captain-Rockets ... you know what you are about today. Find out what you can about the landlord of our intended sandbox. We let go fore and aft with the dawn tomorrow."

*****

"What a delightful change," Annika said as they strolled along the largely empty mid-morning streets of the Pirate Quarter.

"Oh? What is that?" Hans queried.

"You and I are out for a social occasion and I am not dressed as some ridiculous dollhouse prop," she said in a scathing tone.

Hans laughed aloud as they walked. It was a moment before he was able to answer. "While your fighting rig is rather fetching, my dear, you dress very well as a woman. Remarkably attractive, actually."

"You sound surprised, Sauder," she said with a glare.

"You have been an ongoing series of pleasing surprises, my dear Captain-Gunner," he said, with an air of mock innocence about him.

"I am suddenly wondering if the Captain's previous ban on shooting you has expired," she snarled playfully.

"I am very sure it has not. I mean, what are the odds of finding someone like me in a place like this? I would be dreadfully hard to replace, I am sure."

"Fine, fine," she said with a weary voice and a wave of her hand. "I suppose I will allow you to live, so long as you take me to a late dinner tonight at that bistro we had breakfast at and then make love to me on a rooftop under the stars later on," she finished with an imperious tone.

"Such demands!" he replied in mock dismay. "I suppose I have no choice but to capitulate. Woe is me."

"Ah ... here we are," she said, her voice and demeanour suddenly all business. "This storehouse is owned by a merchant that sells supplies for visiting airships and their crews. His men and camels travel most of Egypt as well as into Libya and the Sudan. He will likely know at least who it is that owns the area around the Ravine."

They entered the front of the storehouse and were immediately confronted by two hulking Abyssinian men who blocked their path. They waved and repeated in broken English that the place was closed and that Hans and Annika were to leave immediately. The ensuing few minutes of charades and louder and louder discussion eventually resulted in the owner himself coming to see what was going on.

He was a tall, well-kept, hawk-nosed man with keen eyes and a noble bearing. He was well dressed in fine clothes and impressive jewelry; he looked both refined and masculine as a result of his attire.

The two pirates introduced themselves, and Annika was summarily ignored. Hans could tell she was seething at the snub, but knew full well they needed this man's help more than he needed to be nice to them.

"What is it you want from me?" the owner, who had introduced himself as Habib Usman Naseer Abujamal.

"Information," Hans replied. "And we are pleased to pay for it."

"Very good, *Estad* Sauder," he replied in a rich laugh. "I do nothing with Pirates or Empires for free. What information do you seek?"

Hans took out a small map of the area that they would be travelling to. "We are travelling to this area, and we wish to know who it is that claims domain over this land so that we may pay our proper respects. As well, if you could tell us what sort of 'respects' he enjoys as a greeting, that would be most useful."

"What ship are you with, *Estad* Sauder?"

"The *Bloody Rose*, *Herr* Abujamal."

"The price of your information is the chance to fill your 'market list' before you leave port. Can you do this?"

"I will bring the Chief Steward here myself, if I have to. You have my word."

The Arab eyed the German for a long moment and then nodded. "You have my trust, *Estad* Sauder. The man you wish to meet is Amir al-Heshjukur. He is a supposed descendant of the Mamluk Sultans of Egypt from the time before the Ottomans and the Citadel Massacre. He is very proud of his heritage and has a great love of adventure and travel. Bring him rich foods from other countries and be prepared to tell stories of your travels. You will have his good will that way."

Hans blinked at Habib. "I am very sorry, what was the name again?"

"Amir al-Heshjukur," the Arab repeated amiably.

*****

"Well that simplifies everything," Hans said as they walked back to the ship.

"Oh? You mean he will be thrilled to meet a bunch of story-telling pirates with a world-class cook?" Annika countered.

"No. I have his sword."

"Sand, Swords, and Invitations"

Diary Entry For July 10th, 1888

The game is afoot, as they say. Today we flew to the castle of the Amir, al-Heshjukur, that owns the grounds that the Ravine containing the Temple of Min is to be found within. As Fate would have it, the sword I bought the first time I was in al-Myāh Wālsmā' was owned by this very Amir. Given the story the old blade merchant told me, and the Amir's apparent love of adventure stories, I guessed correctly that he would be very intrigued at the opportunity to hear what had become of the sword since he last saw it.

With Cemil acting as our translator initially, we were able to gain audience with the Amir. From there, things went swimmingly. It turns out that the Amir al-Heshjukur is a well educated and well traveled gentleman and spoke British very well, much to our surprise. We learned that the Russians had already come and gone, but had made no friend of the Amir nor his advisers and thus were led to chase goose in the desert.

We have decided that we cannot have a company of Russians at our back while trying to unlock the secrets of the Temple. Thus, tomorrow we will ambush them and rid ourselves of them.

It is a risky game Herr Blackheart has chosen to play, but it is better to fight them on our terms *and at a time of our choosing, than to face the Russian Army on theirs. I recall the boarding actions we have fought with Russian Marines, and I must confess to trepidation at tomorrow's battle.*

Things continue to go well between Annika and I, but the break-neck pace of events in this mere week have been such we have had little time to ourselves. Tonight, we are taking advantage of the Amir's offer that the officers stay at the castle as his guest. The room is sumptuous and the bath nearly a pond. The bed is more fit for royalty than pirates, but I can tell from the look in her eyes Annika plans to see it put to good use before sunrise.

*****

The *Bloody Rose* sailed along on the desert morning's warming breeze. She was all but silent in her passage two hundred feet in the air above the orange-gold Egyptian sands. By night fall, they expected to cover slightly more that the same distance that it would have taken the Russian Imperials the past few days to cover.

Blackheart had opted to run with the wind for reasons of silence. If they happened upon the Russian force on the ground, Sauder expected that O'Raedy would reprise the battle with the mercenaries outside of New Orleans. However, if they over-flew the Russians before spotting them, or the Russians heard them coming, the *Bloody Rose* would be in danger of any portable artillery that the Russians may have brought with them.

While everyone agreed that time was of the essence, "*wisely and slow, they stumble that run fast,*" Blackheart had said. Hans had been amused at the notion of a Pirate Captain quoting Shakespeare.

The desert sun was harsh as they flew. Even with a modest breeze across the deck, there was no real respite from the heat. Koblinski spoke with O'Raedy of the perils of arriving with a dehydrated crew and encountering the Russians. The Captain subsequently ordered the ship to minimum manning at all stations and the water rations were tripled. Once an hour, they pumped water across the upper decks for two minutes to try and cool the ship. Steam curled into the air, streaming behind them. While some water was lost over the side to flow down the scuppers and into the air, not a drop lasted long enough to reach the searing sand below.

While the *Bloody Rose* was fitted with pair of Perkins-Harrison ammonia and ether-cooled ice-makers, they still consumed water for the ice. As Arietta had told Hans early in his stay aboard the *Bloody Rose* as an engineer, few things would force a pirate vessel of any size to run for a safe port faster than a hole in her water tanks.

Even though their last port might have been built around an oasis, water taken aboard was hardly free. Even so, Blackheart was willing to sacrifice the crucial resource. After all, a heat-stroked crew of pirates would be no match for a company of Russian Imperial Army Regulars.

A few times during the day they over-flew groups of Bedouin. The nomads were either on the move across the relative desolation of the Great Sand Sea, or encamped and hunkered down against the heat of the sun. Hans marvelled that anyone might live at all in a place like this.

"Actually, Sauder," Piet Aldebert commented as they stood in the Steering House, "our little hidey-hole here in Egypt is not unique in any way. That oasis is relatively small in fact. The largest is the size of Denmark, did you know? The sand is like an ocean, and the oasis are like islands. The Bedouin are nomads travelling from island to island across the sea of sand. Of course, I suppose it is unreasonable of me to expect a rich German living in England to know anything about life of nomads in Egypt." Hans noted the snide tone in the Dutchman's voice, but opted to let it pass.

*****

"You are ill at ease, Mister Sauder," Blackheart commented as he dabbed sweat from his brow with a handkerchief. The sun was finally about to touch the Western horizon, and with it the air temperature had begun to descend from a point above halfway to boiling to somewhere around comfortable. In a few more hours, the night air would be cool enough to warrant putting greatcoats or sweaters back on when outside.

Hans nodded at O'Raedy. "*Ja, Herr Kapitän*. We have not seen the Russians, and by run-time we are less than thirty minutes from the Amir's castle. That either means the desert has swallowed up an entire company of the Russian Army ... "

"... Or they are already at the Amir's castle," Blackheart finished for him with a grim nod.

"*Ja*. Not a comforting thought," Sauder replied with an equally grim expression. "I doubt the Amir is interested in having a recreation of Crimea in his front yard."

*****

The *Bloody Rose* slowly came to a halt a scant hundred yards from the towered walls of the Amir's fortress. The sun hung low to her bow, illuminating the scene in crimson luminescence. The pirate ship hovered broadside-to, politely keeping her gunnery doors closed in spite of being keenly aware that there were at least a dozen bare muzzles aimed in her direction.

"Mister Nando!" O'Raedy barked.

"*Sí, mi capitán?*" the Spanish Deck officer queried.

"I want everyone but cooks, stewards and minimum manning on the upper decks. I do not care what work you give them to do, as long as they are on the upper decks, moving around and looking busy. I wish to give the illusion of a significant headcount and a tremendous amount of industry."

"To what end, *Herr Kapitän?*" Sauder asked, puzzled.

"First impressions are important, Mister Sauder. I do not wish to be seen to be under-manned or lazy of character."

Hans was impressed by the clear use of modern technology here. The area for two or three lengths of a football field in all directions from the fortress walls were green fields, with irrigation provided by wind-powered pumps. An outer ring of walls, flat-topped, and as wide and high as half the height of a man, encircled the irrigated area. An assortment of oasis plants were cultivated for food and material use. At regular intervals there was a sizable pond into which all the surrounding irrigated land drained. Hans thought he saw a fish jump as he looked at one pond with his spyglass. The towers had electric lights within them, and it looked like the lights around the main gate were also electric. He wondered how they produced the electricity.

The massive brass and oak doors in the wall opened, with clearly visible gouts of steam and fire powering their progress. An entourage of a dozen men on horseback, emerged in a neat square formation and rode about a fifth of the distance from the wall to the airship. As the group moved, they changed to a line-abreast in a precision piece of cavalry work that spoke volumes of their talent as horsemen.

The middle three riders then trotted forward another dozen paces and stopped. The middle rider of that group then trotted forward a similar distance. He then turned his horse sideways, giving a clear profile of the gorgeous white stallion he rode, the gleaming scales of brass and copper mail that protected both steed and rider and the rich tack, harness and tassells that made up the riding gear. Hans whistled under his breath, eyeing the rider with his spyglass from the guardrail of the upper deck.

"Impressive, aye, Mister Sauder? It looks like your friend is quite a showman. He is certainly not doing poorly for himself this year; the guns on the walls are all modern Turkish pieces. If they decide they do not like us, it will be a very painful exchange of unpleasantries," O'Raedy chuckled.

"So now what do we do?" Aldebert asked.

"We wait for him to speak," replied Jabbar Cemil. Sauder had insisted the Arab be present as translator and to ensure they made no social gaffes. "These are his lands, and it is up to him to welcome us. We are the intruder; it is not our place to speak until spoken to."

The Spanish Deck Officer snorted and the Dutch Watch Officer rolled his eyes. "Since when did aristocratic diplomacy become of concern to pirates?" Nando chuckled.

"Sauder's 'civilizing' influence," Aldebert snorted derisively.

"British Pirate ... why do you darken the skies of the lands of the great Mamluk Amir, the mighty al-Heshjukur? Know you that you are between the hammer of the power of the Amir and anvil of Allah's will! Your existence is solely permitted by your initially irenic actions and the continued mercy and benevolence of the Amir!" the white stallion's rider called, his sharp baritone carrying easily to the ears of the pirates. He spoke with a clear English, with a hint of a continental European accent.

"What?" Onora asked.

"He said that if we twitch they will blow us out of the sky and they have got the guns to do it," Blackheart chuckled. "... and they want to know what the hell we are doing within cannon shot of the castle. Well, Mister Sauder?"

Everyone looked at Sauder, who pulled his scimitar from the scabbard, and gripped it by the cross piece with the pommel upwards. He unscrewed the pommel and tucked it in a pocket of his flight coat. He tugged on the wire wrapped grip; instead of coming off of the tang, its outer piece lifted off, leaving a central core still holding the tang. Around the central core was a linen paper; Hans carefully unwrapped it and passed it to Cemil.

"Use the hailer. Read it as though your life depended on it, Cemil. You are on stage, and the fate of the world depends on you," Hans said whimsically. Aldebert snorted and Nando rolled his eyes. Grumman lofted a brow and looked at Onora, puzzle in his features. She shrugged back at the Confederate-American.

Cemil picked up the Electric Bell Megaphone and nodded to Sauder. He looked out at the group of faces looking at the ship and began to read from the small linen paper scroll in Arabic. By the time he was done, Hans thought the rider on the white stallion might well fall off his horse.

The rider shouted back in his native Arabic. Cemil shook his head, replied and pointed at Sauder. There was a pause and then the rider called back once again in Arabic in what sounded to Hans to be a fairly imperious tone.

"Well?" asked Blackheart. "Did that achieve what you expected?"

Cemil nodded, looking rather impressed. "Yes, Sir. Hans is welcome to go speak to the Amir, personally, as a respected guest."

"Pardon?" Grumman asked, sounding more and more baffled.

"Mister Sauder has the Amir's sword on loan. The scroll paper is something of a personal recommendation and invitation to tea and scones. He found it while trying to get rid of a rattle in the handle," Blackheart explained amusedly. "Always full of interesting surprises, our Captain-Rockets."

Aldebert was looking at Sauder in nearly open-mouthed disbelief. Hans smirked at him and shrugged. "I suppose it is unreasonable of me to expect a middle-class Dutchman to know much about the value of powerful acquaintances and letters of recommendation," Hans said in a mockingly sympathetic tone.

*****

A little more than a quarter hour later, Hans, Annika and Cemil walked from the radiance of the *Bloody Rose*'s electric spotlights that illuminated the area immediately under the ship. They met the rider of the stallion half-way between the ship and the gate.

"So you are the Keeper of the Sword?" he asked Hans.

"Yes," Hans nodded, ensuring he stuck to good English only.

"I am Rahim Abd-Allah Hakeem Yunus Ahmed, the *Qaa'ed* of the Amir's men... the 'Captain of the Guard', as you would say it," he said grandly as he dismounted and offered his hand to Hans to shake. As they shook hands, Rahim continued on. "The Amir will be very pleased to meet you. I hope you are a good story teller; he will expect to hear much of you. And who are these two?"

"Jabbar Cemil, my right hand man. He translated the Amir's words for me when I first found them. He is a good man, and I travel nowhere in Allah's lands without him."

Rahim nodded. "And the woman?" he said, gesturing to Annika.

"Annika Nadezhda," Hans replied before she had a chance to speak. "She is the '*Qaa'ed*' of the fighting men of the ship," Hans explained. "Do not make the mistake of judging her by her sex ... she has left a trail of widows that runs from Cairo to the north of Europe," Hans said pointedly.

Rahim and Annika eyed each other with steel in their gazes for a long moment. Before they had come down the ladder from the ship, Cemil had suggested that Annika be dressed and introduced as 'just' Hans' woman. There was no way that the might of the *Bloody Rose* would be taken seriously by the Amir and the other fighting men of Arabian descent at the idea they were led by a woman.

Hans had been obliged to physically step between the Russian and the one-eyed Arab. After some stubbornly heated discussion, they had agreed that the truth was the story they would tell, and they would let the dice fall as they may.

"Your woman?" Rahim asked Hans, still looking at Annika. She was dressed in her full battle gear, with her cutlass loosened in its scabbard.

"She stands as her own woman and earns her own way," Hans replied.

Rahim nodded, and glanced at the sword that Hans wore at his side and then back to Annika. "I would love to see your skill first-hand, Madam. Perhaps later, *Inshallah*?" Annika merely nodded; her narrowed eyes suggested to Hans that Rahim might be in for quite a demonstration.

*****

They walked as a group, with Rahim leading his horse, to the line of waiting cavalry. From up close, it was clear they were all seasoned fighters. Hans would not have been surprised to discover that some of them had spent most of their lives in those saddles. The cavalry wordlessly formed a group behind them, slowly following them into the Amir's fortress.

The inside of the fortress area showed the obvious guidance of a mind that believed in minimal waste, clear organization and simple structure. While beauty had not been cast aside entirely within the inner courtyard, it was plain that this was a castle meant to do battle and that this was an area meant to give violently unpleasant greetings to uninvited guests.

Dozens of people moved about, both men and women. Several gave plainly curious looks to the two Europeans and the Arab being accompanied in by the *Qaa'ed* and his men. Rush-bundle torch-lights provided a significant amount of the light in the courtyard, but key areas were lit with electric lights. The large egg-shaped courtyard contained a small village worth of buildings, and was dominated by the four-story central keep, with a two-story wing of otherwise equal dimensions to each of the left and right side. The keep sat in the midst of the 'bulge' of the oval, while the gate they entered was at its tip. The stone of all the buildings was carved and decorated, as well as dotted with patches of green vines growing down from what looked like planters built directly into the building stones.

The cavalry moved away, and one of Rahim's men took his steed to the stables. Rahim led them up the wide staircase to the second story, and across the wooden bridge that was somewhat longer than a horse and cart between the stone stairs and the entry way.

"The Amir is a clever siege engineer," Annika commented as they crossed the bridge.

"And why do you say that, Madam?" Rahim asked, his voice a mixture of tolerant amusement and curiosity.

"The entry is raised a full floor from the ground. The steps are stone, but the bridge is wood. There are tracks in the floor where doors can be slid across the entry, from where they are hidden in the walls, to secure it. The bridge is held in place on this end with wooden pegs and rope ties; they can be hacked or burned to drop the bridge away, making it very difficult for an attacker to reach the entry. The foyer here is shaped like funnel; twice as wide away from the doors as at them. That means a group of riflemen can easily hold the doors for as long as their ammunition and courage holds," she said, gesturing around.

Rahim's attempt at concealing his surprise at Annika's knowledge was unsuccessful. "You know something of the topic yourself, I see, Madam," he said politely.

"Of course. My job is usually getting in the door," she said in a forcedly polite voice. Hans noted to himself that he would have to remind her that killing the Amir's Captain of the Guard in a "demonstration" would likely be considered rude of her. Or at the very least, poor form. A glance at Cemil suggested to Hans that the one-eyed Arab was thinking something similar.

They entered a large room, which was both brilliantly lit and decorated. It was very much what Hans would expect of an Arab that claimed bloodline to some of the greatest warriors that the North of Africa had produced thus far in history. Rich carpets and wall hangings adorned most of the place. Paintings, frescoes and mosaics accounted for the rest. An assortment of plants in pots, some of them twice the diameter of a rum barrel, lent the appearance of an oasis to the place. A small fountain poured water down over artfully placed stones, creating a soothing sound that banished silence.

Chairs and piles of pillows were arranged around low round tables of polished woods making small areas where groups might sit together but still be part of the greater hall. At the far end were three steps leading to a raised dais that lifted the Amir above all else in the room.

He was a man that incontestably had a bearing and presence that commanded respect. He did not so much look at them as study them as they approached where he sat. He was apparently intrigued by what he saw.

He was, by any estimation, a strikingly handsome man. His features were chiseled and angular, giving a sense of both athleticism and nobility. His closely trimmed beard ran from his sideburns, defined his jaw sharply, and encompassed his moustache and chin. His eyes were dark and intense, much as Hans imagined looking into the eyes of a wolf might be like.

His clothes were of rich fabrics, but not cut in excess; Hans guessed that the Amir would likely be quite capable of fighting in his current attire with little difficulty. The *keffiyeh*, which is what Cemil had told him the traditional Arabic men's head cover was called, was a crisp white linen. The *akal* encircling it like the band of a crown was made of rich wooden beads and bejewelled befitting of royalty.

"Who have you brought before me, *Qaa'ed* Ahmed?" the Amir asked in startlingly impeccable Oxford English.

"This is Hans Sauder, officer of the English ship '*Bloody Rose*', Amir. He has the *Sword of the Restless Dunes*," Rahim replied.

There was a moment of dead silence while the Amir looked at Hans. "Do you truly?" he asked conversationally.

Hans was not entirely sure how to respond. If he drew the blade, he expected he might well find himself in hot water. Possibly literally. However, the Amir evidently wanted proof of possession. He thought for a moment and then unbuckled the sword belt from around his waist and bundled it up around the scabbard. Without a word, he tossed it to the Amir.

The Amir grabbed the scabbard bundle from the air, with an evident look of amusement at the European man's boldness. The Arab unsheathed the blade and smiled at it, watching the beauty of its Damascus steel glisten in the room's torch and electric lights.

"How long have you had it?" he asked as he inspected the edge of the weapon.

"Almost three months," Hans replied.

"Where did you find it?" the Amir asked, easily returning it to its scabbard in a single action.

"In the port of al-Myāh Wālsmā', Sir. In a bladesmith's shop, hanging on a wall like a magnificent work of art."

"You know why it was there?"

Hans nodded. "You wished its adventures would never cease and you knew your duties here to your people would spell the end of your own adventures. So you had your man-servant sell the blade where it might continue its travels, even if you could not accompany it."

The Amir stood from his chair and came down the three steps between he and Hans and stood directly before the young German. He passed the sword and belt back to Hans.

"Welcome, Brother. Any man that has both the means and the spirit to walk the world with the *Sword of the Restless Dunes* at his side is welcome in my home as though he were of my family," the Amir said warmly and clapped Hans on the shoulder. It was all Sauder could do to not stare with his jaw agape.

*****

"So, like the Russians then, you are here chasing after rumours in the desert winds of a lost Temple in a ravine?" the Amir asked casually.

It was three hours later in the evening after their initial meeting with the Amir. They had been treated like royalty; rich foods and sweet drinks had been provided. A messenger had been sent to invite Blackheart to join them, as the Captain of the visiting ship.

The discussion initially had been entirely on Hans answering questions and telling stories of his entire time with the crew of the *Bloody Rose*, how he came to possess the sword and where he and it had been and what they had done. As he had been told, the Amir was a great lover of stories and was a keen listener. He asked intelligent questions and had clear opinions. Hans found the man a rather daunting intellect.

Then the Amir had introduced himself at some length. His full name was Shahzad Gawdat Mahir al-Heshjukur and a true-blooded Mamluk, with the title of Amir having been in the family for two hundred years. Amir was taken to mean "commander" or "governor" in these modern times, but Shahzad assured Hans that there was truly a prince's blood within his veins. Hans had no cause to doubt the noble Arab.

Much as the story Hans had been told, Shahzad had been quite the wanderer in his late teens and early twenties. His father could "smell the turning of the world in the desert's dawn breezes", and decided that his son was to be properly educated by the finest schools of both the Ottoman and European empires. So in much the same way and for the same reasons that Hans had been sent abroad by his father for schooling, so it had been with Shahzad.

The young Amir-to-be had sent endless letters home to his father detailing the things he witnessed and participated in and all the cultures vast and different from his own. When he returned, he and his father spent most of the monies in the treasury modernizing the castle and the fighting men they had. Now, the "Scorpions of al-Heshjukur" were some of the most respected fighting men within three hundred miles, and they were often well paid to provide security or military power. As well, they invested heavily in technologies such as irrigation and the like to harness the full value of the oasis that was the hereditary home of the Emirate. They now produced far more food than they ate, selling to neighbours at generous prices; this restored wealth that the modernization had cost and cunningly bought good will.

He had continued his father's vision of a modern Emirate, even after his death. While the adventuring days of his youth were done, he now found tremendous satisfaction at the results of the achievements of his work as a ruler. He had two wives, who he claimed he loved with equal depth and devotion. Thus far, they had borne him three daughters; he hoped for a son in the future.

Eventually, the discussion had come around to Hans and his visit here. As Blackheart had revealed to the command crew on the quarterdeck of the *Bloody Rose*, Hans had found the linen paper scroll while servicing his beloved sword. That fateful discovery had been while they were in the murderous airspace of the Russian Empire. The message had been written in Arabic, and thus Hans had taken it to Cemil for translation.

Cemil had been rather excited by the message he read. Enough so that it took Hans two tries to get the Arab to actually tell him what it said in English. Hans had been utterly stunned at the notion that the original owner of the blade had invited him to come visit and they would trade stories of each other's adventures with the weapon. He had been further surprised when it seemed that the far-fetched story the bladesmith had told him was true. After some discussion, he and Cemil decided to keep the discovery to themselves until they could determine a what to do with the situation.

At the point that Fate had made converging lines of the Amir's invitation and the need to find the ravine on his lands, Hans had gone straight to Michael O'Raedy and explained the situation. They both agreed that it needed to be played to their advantage. Too much depended on their mission.

Hans had explained all of that to Shahzad, who agreed that it was the right thing to do on many levels and praised both Sauder and O'Raedy for their cunning. Cemil as well was now somewhat of a celebrity when the story of how he had recently saved Sauder's life was told. This in turn led to descriptions of the other fights where the stalwart Arab had been seriously injured. In each case, he had "robbed fate" in the Amir's words, by taking a wound that would have otherwise certainly killed a friend.

"Captain O'Raedy, you are man who has tamed jackals and in doing so given them the hearts of lions!" Shahzad exclaimed. A murmur of agreement went around the room. *Qaa'ed* Rahim and a dozen of his most senior men were sitting around the room with them. They were ostensibly talking amongst themselves, but were all obviously within hearing of the animated and spirited retellings of adventures bold and sieges perilous.

More sweet foods and sweet drinks were brought out as the discussions quieted with the hour. Eventually a lull in conversation had given way to Shahzad's most recent question. Hans glanced at Blackheart, Annika and Jabbar. He then turned to the Amir and nodded.

"That is correct," he said carefully. "We may be pirates, but if the Temple exists to this day, and its power remains potent, none of us wish to see that used upon countless innocent people as a weapon."

Shahzad nodded. "I have poor news for you, then, my Brother. The Russians have a full company of infantry, a pair of giant mechanized men that use cannons as rifles, and a team of scientists with them," the Amir explained. "They left from here for the location they have derived on their maps late this morning."

"This morning!" Hans exclaimed in dismay. "Then we are too late!"

"Unlikely," the Sultan said with an airy wave and a smug chuckle. "Their leader and his lieutenant were rather rude, you see. Somewhat patronizing, really. Thus, I neglected to inform them that their map was wrong. Upside down, in fact. Myself and my people know the hills and ravines in this area like an English child knows his playground. So, I expect that if you were to accept my help, you would likely find the Temple Ravine long before they did. They are on foot; you move by air. They would be heading the wrong way; you would be heading the right way."

"Your help?" Blackheart asked cautiously.

"Yes, my good Captain. My daughter is of age to taste the outside world. She can be your guide. Afterwards, I think it would do her good to see the English capital and then perhaps the German one. I remember them fondly. She can make her way home from there, I am sure."

"We cannot guarantee her safety," Hans began.

"I would rather you did not. That should be her responsibility," the Amir said pointedly.

"It is," a young woman said firmly as she entered the room from a door beside the raised dais.

"Captain and Officers of the *Bloody Rose*, allow me to introduce my eldest daughter, Khadija. From what Sauder has said, Captain-Gunner, she is very much of the same spirit you are," he said with a laugh. "She is my greatest blessing from Allah, as well as my greatest trial. I have no male heir, and thus I must accept that Khadija must be fit to rule. I will have her do no less than I would expect from any son of mine. So, it is time for her to travel as I did, to learn as I did, and to live as I did at her age."

Hans groaned inwardly. Khadija al-Heshjukur stood with an air of challenge and defiance beside where her father was seated. She was dressed head to toe in lush scarlet cloth that showed little more than the honeyed-almond skin around her eyes. She had clearly inherited her father's eyes as she looked to each of the European guests in turn.

Annika spoke first. "We are fighters and the life we lead is a brutal one, Khadija. There is nothing gentle about the ship we sail, nor is there mercy for the victims she takes. As a woman, you must fight harder and more savagely than the men you will be with. You are beautiful; that will make you a target or a prize to be taken. Are you ready to spill blood both on the ground and on your hands to make sure all understand you are a Lady of the Rose? We are killers, each and every one, and we will brook no weakness of you, ever."

"I will leave men standing and weeping in shame of themselves for having lost to a woman. I will use everything I know to bring no disgrace and weakness to your company. What I do not know, I will learn swiftly from whomever will teach me," she said with a steady and defiant tone.

Annika eyed the young woman and nodded. The Russian brunette looked squarely at the Amir. "She should be ready to travel, in men's clothes and with weapons, for tomorrow morning."

"I will be," Khadija said firmly.

Shahzad looked rather amusedly between the two women and then to Blackheart. O'Raedy, for his part, was looking quite visibly pained. "I believe, good Captain, that the women think they have out voted us," the Arab said to the Englishman.

"Aye, well. Look ... as much as I would love to tell you that we are having no part of taking your daughter on a tour of Europe, the fact of the matter is that I am short of crew, short of time and need all the help I can get from you. But I want you to understand, Amir, that there is better than good odds that you will not see her again in this life if she ships out with us."

"If that is the will of Allah, then so it will come to pass, be it aboard your ship or in her bedroom. I would rather that she see more of the world than the distance of a spyglass from her bedroom window in the meantime."

The two men eyed each other for a long moment, and then Blackheart nodded. "Very well. As the Captain-Gunner says, Khadija you had better be ready to travel in fighting rig when we leave in the morning."

"I will be," Khadija repeated in the same tone of voice as her previous declaration.

"Now, of the Russians," Hans said slowly.

"What of them?" Shahzad asked. "They expected two days of march to find the ravine. Thus it will be late tomorrow before they conclude there is something amiss. You have your airship, and can be at the ravine in an hour or two."

"The problem is that we cannot take the *Bloody Rose* into a ravine or canyon ... the air shifts around too much and we would be at risk of being swept into a wall. So we can fly most of the way there, but the actual descent and exploration will be done on foot, just like the Russians," Blackheart said thoughtfully.

"That leaves a sizable land force potentially catching up with us on the ground while we are in the ravine," Annika pointed out.

"I do not like the sound of that at all," Hans replied.

"If we do not wish to be on the defensive, then we must be on the offensive," O'Raedy mused aloud. "We will pick a place they must travel through and ambush them as they return from their fool's errand. Our attack will be with an eye to giving them enough of a beating they turn tail for Cairo. They outnumber us, to be sure, but that advantage can be negated with good planning."

"It takes a bold stroke to decapitate a cobra. The timid hesitate and so perish to it's fangs," Rahim said, approving of Blackheart's ideas.

"And you said they had two cannon-carrying mechanized men with them?" Blackheart asked.

"Yes, that is correct. Armoured, twice as tall as a man, and I believe steam powered," Shahzad replied.

"Chimera," Hans groaned. "They brought Chimera with them. Even the two-legged versions will cause us problems."

Blackheart nodded. "We will have a devil of a time hitting them from the air with solid ball and grapeshot will bounce off them. The guns they carry will hit hard enough to do serious damage to the ship. We will need to deal with them before we can use the ship to pound the infantry."

"There is no way we can move cannon with us to deal with the two Chimera they have. The carriages, the powder, the balls and everything weigh too much for a group our size. None of our crew know anything about moving and fighting with cannon in deserts," Annika replied, shaking her head. The men all looked at her with varying expressions at her pronouncement.

"The four-pounders will not hit hard enough to do what we need," she continued, "and the eight-pounders will need a horse train each to move everything needed to fight. Without them, however, we will be lambs to the slaughter if we do not have a way of destroying those two mechanized monsters," Annika finished flatly, folding her arms across her chest.

"So shoot the barrels at them," the Amir suggested with an amused look. "You must know of rocketry."

*****

A couple of hours later had the oasis fortress basking in the glory of a brilliant moon and jewel-strewn desert sky of blue-black velvet. Shahzad had offered Blackheart the courtesy of having his officers stay as his personal guests for the night. The *Bloody Rose* was brought to moor off one of the towers from her bow and swung with the moderate wind. A modest amount of trade and barter had gone on, but now all was quiet. Soldiers on watch patrolled the outer walls and only the electric lights remained on.

The Amir was leading Hans and Annika of a tour of the entire place. Annika said little, listening to the two men talk. Hans was somewhat surprised, but knew that while the fierce Russian Captain-Gunner was known for stubbornness, she was not known for stupidity. She might not like the social constraints here, but was apparently willing to go along with them for now.

"So it is obvious that you use electricity for lighting and many other things, to an impressive degree. How are you generating it? With boilers?" Hans asked.

"After a fashion," Shahzad replied. "Behind us, in the anterior courtyard, are a set of mirrors. They focus the sun onto a set of stone blocks, increasing the amount of heat the blocks gather in the day. Copper rods are driven into the stone, to conduct the heat into a special room in the ground floor of the castle." They stopped at window over looking a small terrace garden as the Arab continued explaining.

"A set of engines of the kind proposed by Robert Stirling are there. They take the heat from the copper rods on one side and are cooled on the other by water pumped by wind into reservoirs on the roof. The difference in temperatures between one side and the other causes a piston to turn. That then is used to crank a dynamo. We store the power in Schönbein fuel cells. The water, now heated, is used for baths, cooking and the like."

"Remarkably clever, Shahzad," Hans said. "Elegant in its simplicity and requires you to burn nothing like wood or kerosene."

"Correct. We normally make a quarter more as much electricity as we consume in a day, so that ensures that the batteries are always full. It also allows us to expand our use; we are considering a mechanism of using electricity passed through a wire fence along our outer wall to deter or injure intruders. However, this is something I have not had much time to explore; there are only three of us here with the education and training to work with the dynamos and fuel cells, and we all have more primary responsibilities."

"Well, Shahzad, when all of this is over, I will try and return and perhaps lend a hand. I am familiar with these systems. I can promise nothing, but with luck I might be able to advance a project or two," Hans said with a genuine smile.

"*Inshallah*. If Allah wills it, Brother, it would be a pleasure. I must admit, I am quite interested in seeing the systems of the *Bloody Rose*. I imagine she must be quite powerful and complex."

"The complexity comes from lack of extra space. She has a tremendous amount of systems crammed in a relatively small area," Hans explained. "I do apologize, Shahzad, but I think it is time the Captain-Gunner and I retire. Tomorrow promises to be a very long and tumultuous day. Fatigue is the last thing any of us needs to bring with us."

"Understandable, Brother. I hope you find the room you are staying in to your satisfaction."

"I am sure it will be more than that," Hans replied.

"Oh, before you retire, Hans," the Amir started thoughtfully. "The Russians have paid handsomely for safe passage through my lands, Brother. They will be quite upset, I should think, when they encounter you and your crew. When you see them tomorrow, do let them know that I will be happy to give them a refund should they come to ask for one politely."

"Fire, Sand and Blood"

Diary Entry For July 11th, 1888

The Russians have been routed, we have found the ravine that is said to conceal the lost Temple of Min, and everyone I care for is still alive. This is a far better position than I expected to be writing from this evening. The Bloody Rose's fabled horseshoe is evidently in good working order even to this day. Should it ever be determined where exactly it is, I am going to build an armored box around the thing.

The day started with Annika and Qaa'ed Rahim coming to an agreement as equals, regardless of her gender. It was a most peculiar thing to me; while she did not win the rather intense contest of swords between them, it is also clear to me that she did not lose, either. Indeed, the Amir has offered her a place as a tutor to his daughters should she wish it once she decides her life as a pirate is over. Cemil was astounded and said this was a very impressive compliment.

Once Annika had been inspected by Döktor Koblinski, we set course to a shallow valley that we intended to set our ambush for the Russians. Guessing the rough rate of advance of their force, we anticipated that we would be able to set our ambush without roasting in wait at the same time. The battle that ensued was a vicious and terrible *affair. If this is how armies clash normally, I will forever remain a man of the skies. Blackheart once again proved he is a shrewd tactician and motivator of men. I am reminded that he should never be underestimated in his cunning.*

We then turned our bow towards what we hope to be our last stop in this journey before its conclusion. After a short flight, our newest crew member – the Amir's daughter, Khadija – took us essentially directly to the door of the Temple in the ravine. She knew the place from local legend; it has never allowed a band of treasure seekers to emerge once they entered its depths. It is sitting in the middle of an incongruous little oasis; I expect it to be a result of the "left overs" from the Temple's 'magic'.

We have anchored the Bloody Rose two miles away at the entrance to the ravine. Tomorrow morning, myself and several others will hope to beat the grim odds of escape that history gives us.

*****

The early morning air was quiet and still in the hour or so immediately after sunrise. A bird of prey wheeled over the green irrigated fields of the al-Heshjukur Emirate's oasis. A few high clouds spoke of the torrential rains that would be falling either now or very soon on Arietta's ancestral homeland. Within a couple of months, the Nile's famous flood would have pushed its life-giving waters and silts all the way to the Mediterranean Ocean.

Here, hundreds of miles from the Nile, the waters of life flowed beneath the ground. They welled up naturally to give life to the core area of the oasis. The work of Shahzad and his father had increased the hold of life in this area with their wind-powered pumps, bricked terraces and careful arrangement of the land. Their accomplishments were both respected and envied.

Hans looked out over it all from his guest room window. He personally had a deep respect for the achievements of the man that now called him 'Brother'. For a moment he felt almost embarrassed; what had he built? He had left the life of building and improving to his brother Karl, while he had shipped out with pirates. He took, he did not add. Had it been the right choice?

"I am ready, Hans," Annika announced behind him. He turned towards her, put his self doubts aside for now and smiled at her. She was already in her battle gear, with a fire in her eyes that told him she was looking forward to the mayhem promised by the day's planned events. She walked aggressively straight to him, wrapped her arms around his neck and kissed him soundly.

"... and good morning to you, Captain-Gunner," Hans said with a chuckle once their lips had parted. "I am hoping Khadija is ready as she was told to be," he said with a sigh. "We really do not have the time to play nurse-maid to a spoiled princess."

"Piet Aldebert said the same thing about you," she chided. "You have mostly worked out well enough."

He had a moment of outrage until he realized she was baiting him. "Nasty Russian witch," he muttered. She laughed at him and tugged his hand to lead him towards the guest room door.

*****

A short time later, they were descending the stone stairs of the keep into the central courtyard. Khadija al-Heshjukur, the Amir's daughter, waited for them beside Rahim. *Qaa'ed* Rahim was dressed much as he was yesterday, ready for war at a moment's notice. Khadija was dressed very much differently than last evening.

She still wore a scarlet head scarf that covered her hair and face, save for her eyes. However, she now otherwise wore clothing normally found in an Arabian man's closet.

It was comprised of a simple robe-like garment, of a colour like the desert sand, that covered her from shoulders to ankles. Atop this was a striped knee-length coat-like affair which she had left open down the front. It was cinched against her with a belt carrying a few pouches, a curved dagger as well as a long and gently curved sword. Her outer most garment was a sleeveless wool coat of a grey-blue sky colour, with thin and vividly red stripes cutting it. It seemed to Hans that she had some sort of shoulder straps under the coat, but he could not discern what purpose they served. At her feet were two respectable shoulder bags and a twice-larger pack with back-straps.

Rahim nodded to them both politely and Khadija bowed. "Good morning to you both," Rahim said in his warm baritone.

"Good morning, *Qaa'ed*," Annika replied sounding a touch formal. She looked at Khadija critically. "You are ready to go, I trust?" she asked the Arab woman.

"I am," Khadija replied confidently.

"I do have a curiosity I would like satisfied, before the Amir's daughter takes leave of us, *Inshallah*" Rahim stated.

"Oh, what is that?" Annika challenged.

Rahim smiled at her. "If you actually are skilled enough to teach her something about fighting as men do," he stated with a carefully diplomatic tone.

Hans winced. Rahim might as well have slapped her for the expression on her face. The German eyed the Arab, noting that the lines in his face and the speckle of grey in his beard suggested that he was at least ten years Hans or Annika's senior. He wondered if that would be an advantage or not in what was likely to be a rapidly arranged contest of arms.

Annika dropped her hand to the hilt of her cutlass and gave Rahim a sharken grin. "Would you like first hand proof? I am sure it will not take me long," she replied in a forcedly polite voice.

Rahim grinned broadly at her and gestured for them to step away from the stairs to a more open area. It was clear at a glance around by Hans that several of the *Qaa'ed*'s men had been waiting for this, and were watching carefully. Annika drew her two tri-barrelled pistols and passed them to Hans. He ensured the hammers were not cocked and thrust them through his belt.

Rahim likewise passed a hefty looking revolver to one of his men that moved to stand beside Hans and Khadija. "First blood?" he asked charitably.

Annika shook her head. "That is not how a pirate fights, *Qaa'ed*," she replied sweetly. "The fight is done when one of us yields or can no longer stand to answer. I will leave no injury on you that will maim or kill. I will trust you have sufficient skill to make the same assurance?"

Rahim laughed. "Bold talk, Madam. I await your first blow," he said as he unsheathed the long, curved and thin-bladed weapon at his side. It was a beautiful blade, well cared for and well travelled. It reminded Hans of a French cavalry sabre in its styling.

Annika drew the heavy cutlass she carried and rested it on her shoulder, taking stock of her opponent. An amused smile played at her lips and then she sprang forward with a fierce cry in her native Russian. Whatever it was that Rahim was expecting, the initial flurry of blows she unleashed that concluded with the knuckles of her left fist grazing his jaw had doubtlessly not been it. He parried or deflected every blow, and spun out of the arc of her fist with what looked to Hans to be an effortless grace. However, the murmur of surprise from the watching men suggest to Hans that Rahim was likely more on the defensive than they were used to seeing.

Annika pressed forward, with a series of slashes, kicks towards the leg and punches to the body that forced her opponent backwards a few steps before he suddenly leapt forward, breaking her tempo. Suddenly the Russian brunette was on the defensive, as his sword opened a sleeve and then rattled across her armoured corset. He grabbed her by her left shoulder and spun them both around, shoving her to the ground with the momentum.

A smattering of applause and cheering that accompanied the action caused Hans to grate his teeth quietly. He very much wanted to step to her side and lend her aid, but he forced himself to remain still. This was not his challenge to answer; if he interfered, he would simply undermine her credibility. If one of the other Arabs did not beat him senseless for his interference, she most certainly would.

She rolled away and came up, punching her bell towards the incoming sword he swung at her. He locked weapons with her, only to suddenly have her completely give way to his downward pressure. As he stumbled forward slightly, she punched him square across the face, bloodying his lip. He barely stopped the backhanded judo chop aimed at the bridge of his nose. He pushed her away from him and they circled each other warily.

He wiped the blood from the corner of his mouth with the back of his hand, with a look of determination about him. They both lunged forward again, with the clash of steel, the meaty thud of fists on bodies and exhaled expressions of pain and effort carrying across the mesmerized courtyard. Hans glanced at Khadija; she was watching the battle with eyes widened in surprise. Hans could see that no one had expected Annika to have lasted this long.

The two fighters clashed again, and Annika went sprawling, blood streaming from her nose. Rahim closed as she regained her footing, pressing his advantage in both position and strength. Hans missed what happened in the next moment; there was a shriek of steel sliding on steel, Annika's cutlass went into the air over the *Qaa'ed*'s shoulder and then he gave a startled cry of pain.

Annika rolled away and came up in a side-long crouch, pointing Rahim's sword at him. In a moment, he had her cutlass in his hands from where it had landed on the ground. He rubbed at the bicep of his sword arm amusedly and gave her a grudging nod of acknowledgement. She did the same, after wiping blood from her nose.

They circled, clashed, parted, attacked, parried and darted. Drops of bright crimson blood mixed with grains of white sand upon the well-worn stones of the courtyard. Annika left a red streak on his left forearm. He replied in kind across her right thigh. Another heated exchange of sword play left the courtyard ringing with the sound of its fury, but advanced neither of their causes.

Annika stepped in for another attack and steel rang on steel once and then once again. Rahim rolled with the momentum of the third blow she gave, whirling in place like a dervish and then lashing out with pommel of the heavy cutlass he held as he finished his rotation. He caught the young Russian across the back of the head, laying her out flat on the ground with the accumulated power of his motion. Her weapon skittered from her grasp as she landed heavily. Before she could recover from the daze she was in, he forcefully planted his foot in the middle of her back, pinning her to the ground. Hans heard the breath knocked out of her from where he stood and he winced slightly.

"You are done, *Qaa'ed* Nadezhda," the Arab said to her sternly. "I can either break your spine or sever your head from your shoulders at this point. Yield," he commanded, breathing heavily. He wiped at the blood coming from his mouth, in a messy mix with sweat and saliva. Another punch in one of their last exchanges had left a nasty bruise on his jaw.

There was a frustrated moment where it was clear to Hans that Annika wanted any other answer. Rahim was right; there was nothing she could do. She deflated and nodded. "I yield," she said between ragged gasps for breath. "You win."

Hans had expected the courtyard to erupt in applause at the Russian's capitulation. Instead, everyone was looking at the frozen tableau in stunned silence. A single pair of hands started an earnest applause behind him, and Hans glanced over his shoulder. It was the Amir.

"*Qaa'ed* Ahmed, that was quite a battle. I am unaccustomed to seeing you so grievously treated, even by the best of your own men," Shahzad noted wryly.

Rahim offered his hand to Annika and helped her to her feet, much to the murmured surprise of those assembled. He passed her sword back to her with a genuinely respectful flourish. She saluted him with it, and returned the weapon to its scabbard.

Rahim then turned to the Amir and bowed. "She fights like a lioness, *Sidi*. It has been over ten years since I have had to use that spin to save my skin. I have never before had my sword taken from my grasp while awake." The Arab spoke with a respectful reverence. Hans understood from Rahim's tone that he considered himself a true master, and he knew he had just met his peer in battle for possibly the first time in years.

Annika blinked at the two men, dabbing at her bloodied nose. One of her eyes would likely be blacked by the end of the hour, if not partially closed. Hans could see she knew something was going on, but the gravity of it was eluding her.

"*Qaa'ed* Nadezhda," the Amir began, "when it is time for my daughter to make her travels from your ship to my home again, should you choose to accompany her, you are assured a position within my House as the respected personal trainer of my daughters. I have met no one else yet with such spirit and skill as a woman warrior. You would be a blessing here."

Both Hans and Khadija looked from each other to Shahzad in stunned amazement.

*****

"Well, *Panna* Annika, you seem to be in good health, given the drubbing you took. It seems that your renowncdly thick skull protected you from a concussion in spite of the force of the impact to the back of your head. The stitches there will leave a scar, but it is covered by your hair. Avoid shaving yourself bald and it should not affect your looks at all," Doctor Koblinski chuckled at her.

She glared at him but said nothing. Hans very carefully kept his features neutral while finding something of interest on a far wall to study.

"Your nose is bruised," the Polish doctor continued, "but not broken; much the same with your ribs and your left eye ridge. All in all, a reasonably artful beating. You opponent was quite kind to you." He scribbled something down on a folio and then passed her a small vial.

"What is this?" Annika asked, eying the vial warily.

"A mild pain killer mixed with a serum to aid your body's immune system," Koblinski explained. "Take a measure with breakfast and with supper. You did have sand in some of your wounds, and they do ride horses over that sand. While Pan Sauder may appreciate the ensuing silence, I am sure you would be most frustrated as Captain-Gunner with a bout of lock-jaw."

*****

"Remind me again, Captain-Rockets" Annika asked as they reached the Steering House, "why it is I have yet to beat that man senseless."

"Because, Captain-Gunner, you love him like a favourite uncle, and favourite uncles are tragically possessed of an ability to mock you publicly in an endearing fashion."

"Right. Thank-you," she said with a roll of her eyes.

"None the worse for wear, I see, Captain-Gunner," Blackheart said amusedly. "The word of your mighty battle against the local master at arms has carried throughout the ship. I understand your second place finish was considered more than acceptable by the assembled fighting men of the Amir?"

Annika scowled for a moment. "I hate losing," she snarled.

"You might have lost the battle, Miss Nadezhda, but from what I heard from the Amir, you handily won the war. Your opponent regularly fights two men at once to a standstill for his morning practice, you see. No one adorned with a head-cloth expected you to last more than a few seconds," Blackheart said with a chuckle. "Never you mind leaving him beaten within an inch of his life. Mister Nando tells me that he has heard both the Amir and the *Qaa'ed* quietly singing your praises as a swordswoman since you two parted ways an hour ago."

Annika blinked at him. She looked at Hans as though to confirm what she had heard.

"But ..." she began.

"Propulsion, ahead three-quarters on port and starboard," the Englishman began rattling off orders, apparently ignoring her protest. "Centre-line zeroed and raised. Planes, twenty degree up angle. Rudder, take port turn to one-six-five. Deck Officer, stow fore and aft lines and rig. Guns and Rockets?"

"*Ja, Herr Kapitän?*"

"*Da?*"

"Rig for ground support on all guns. I want grapeshot in the fours and eights, with the twelves loaded with cinderball."

"Pardon? Cinderball?" Annika asked, apparently puzzled at the request.

"Aye ... we are fighting an army, Captain-Gunner. We need to keep them frightened and confused. Exploding incendiaries that splatter a sticky, burning mess over everything within a dozen paces and then throws black smoke into the air should do that that nicely. Captain-Rockets?"

"*Ja, Herr Kapitän?*" Hans repeated, while Annika moved to a voicepipe to relay orders.

"I want you and your winger Dubé to figure out how to convert three of the replacement four-pounder barrels we have in stores into rocket-powered anvils. Make sure they work, because it will you two enterprising gentlemen that will be lighting the fuses," Blackheart chortled with a nasty grin.

"Pardon? Anvils?" Hans asked, looking perplexed.

Blackheart lofted a brow and glanced between the Russian and the German.

"I have no blessed clue what you two have been doing together in your personal time, but whatever it is, its leaving you both deaf as a post," O'Raedy snorted. A ripple of amusement went around the rest Steering House.

"Yes, man!" the Englishman continued with a shake of his head. "The Amir is a clever devil and I have been thinking about his idea since he suggested it. Over-pack those barrels with enough high velocity powder, and the damn things will fly. I have seen it happen by accident when a gun's carriage was not lashed down right. I am pretty sure a Chimera getting hit in the chest by one of those things will wind up on its mechanical backside. At that point, its a sitting duck for the main guns on the *Bloody Rose*."

Hans blinked at him and nodded. He moved over to a side position and started working with a slide-rule to figure out how much powder was going to be needed.

"Mister Grumman!" Blackheart barked.

"Sir!" the Confederate Watch Officer replied.

"Do you have our destination chosen yet?"

"Yes, sir. Let me show you where we will lead Ivan and his little lambs to the slaughter." Grumman tapped a spot on a chart of the region and gave an ugly chuckle.

*****

"So, what odds do you give us that these will not just explode and kill the pair of us?" André Dubé asked Hans.

Hans gave a few moments of thought to the question. "Of not exploding? About three in four," he said with a chuckle. He looked across the empty sands with his hand shielding his eyes from the sun. "The good news is that we only have three of them to fire."

They were in wide and shallow sandstone valley that was a mile or so in length and a quarter of that wide. At this time of day, it afforded shade on one side and was reasonably defensible. Grumman, the Confederate-American, had seen action in the desert areas of America stemming from the aftermath of the Civil War. He had explained that with the terrain in the area, the heat of the day, and the large shade area that the valley wall would provide, the Russians would almost certainly take a rest break there. Thus, the pirates had set their ambush there. They would wait until the Russians had committed to one action or another – stay or go – and then attack. The valley was shallow enough that the *Bloody Rose* would be able to remain a thirty or so feet above the valley edge and fire at what ever it wanted. All that they worried about were the Chimera and whatever portable artillery the Russians had.

"Well, the odds of the Russians not shooting us for being in their way as they return is essentially nought in four, so I am happy to take my odds with the rocket-cannons," Dubé laughed.

"I hope Grumman was right," Hans sighed, scanning the horizon. "If they take any other route but this one, we are going to be in a lot of trouble."

Dubé took a swig from his canteen and passed it to Sauder. The young German took a mouthful and gave it back. "*Tu a d'raison, mon ami,*" the Franco-Brit replied. "The Chimera worry me the most ... if I have to, I can kill a Russian soldier with quiet, darkness and a knife. With armoured walkers, there is nothing we can do if these little surprises do not work," he said patting the hot black metal of the four-pounder barrel beside him.

"It will be a miserable fight, and the *Bloody Rose* will take a beating she cannot afford trying to handle the Chimera and whatever else the Russians have with them," Hans said simply. "I will be pleased if we escape with our lives."

Dubé perked up, then patted Sauder on the shoulder and pointed to the far end of the valley entrance. Hans turned his gaze to the indicated direction and nodded. A military formation was beginning the descent down into the valley; it had to be the Russians.

Hans and André watched the group moving along together. The two Chimera were following behind the main group. Hans wished he had a spyglass; Grumman had advised against them. The desert sun had a habit of reflecting off the front lens like a signal flare at the worst times, drawing unwanted attention. So, no one on the ground had one at Blackheart's orders. Hans shielded his eyes against the sun, watching.

The Chimera were essentially as the Amir had described them. Twice as tall as the men they followed and made of metal, they lumbered in an awkward looking gait. Periodic puffs of smoke and steam trailed behind them. That was likely why they were bringing up the rear, Hans reasoned. After all, no one would want to walk for hours through hot steam and exhaust fumes in this environment.

The unit came to a halt almost exactly where the Confederate Watch Officer had said they would, and then broke formation. It was clear that they were going to take refuge in the shade and likely drink from their canteens. From where Sauder and Dubé were positioned, they could clearly see the army men, the group of scientists in their civilian desert clothes, a couple of horse-towed cannons and a couple of supply waggons with very wide wheels.

"Okay, *mon ami*," Dubé said without a trace of humour. "It is time. One rocket-cannon per Chimera, and if we have no misses, I will land the third near their two cannons, *d'accord*?" the Franco-Brit suggested.

"Yes. Ready? Very well, turning the Marconi Beacon on ... now ... let us light fuses!" The two men grabbed the first weapon and shifted it and the wooden guide-rail it was mounted on. André sighted it purely by eye and by hope, while Hans extended the two sets of small make-shift wings. André nodded to Hans step clear and cranked the hand-held dynamo.

The detonation of the rocket launch reached the ears of the Russians almost two full seconds before the weapon did. As most trained military men do, they dove for cover and grabbed weapons. The rocket flew straight over the top of its intended target, slamming into the valley wall above the Russians, showering them with dirt, sandstone and debris. A long black plume of smoke hung in the air, like a finger pointing back to Hans and André.

Immediately, the two Chimera turned and began moving faster than a running man towards where the smoke trail pointed. A second detonation signalled the launch of another rocket. It streaked across the valley like a black iron bolt of lightning. André's correction had been good and it slammed squarely into the chest of one of the Chimera. It staggered, lurched amid the sound of protesting gears and control rods, and then toppled over.

The Russian infantry immediately opened fire with their rifles, peppering the sand and rock rise that Hans and André were hiding behind. Sand, broken pieces of rock and ricocheting bullets filled the air around them as the two men worked feverishly under what little cover they had. The remaining Chimera was already halfway across the valley to them.

A staccato roar sounded from the valley edge above-left of them and the area around the Russian riflemen seemed to erupt. Annika and Cortez had been positioned up there with the two Gatling guns, hidden under cover. When they had heard the shooting begin, Hans knew they would have broken cover, run the guns up to the edge of the valley and looked for targets. Now they were pouring the sustained fire of more than two full rifle companies into the Russian ranks.

André fired the third and last rocket cannon at the advancing Chimera, audibly saying a prayer of some kind aloud in French. The ground exploded in front of them as the Chimera snapped off a shot with one of its cannons. The blast knocked them both backwards and left them stunned where they landed. They shook their heads to clear the ringing in their ears and crawled up to their firing position to peer over. They cheered and shook fists in victory at the sight of the second Chimera flat on its back with the rocket-cannon barrel embedded in its chest.

The *Bloody Rose* roared in from the same end of the valley as the Russians had marched. The constant sounds of rifle, Gatling and cannon fire had masked the sounds of her engines until it had been too late. She had been waiting a few miles away, hovering just above the ground, waiting for the signal of the Marconi Beacon that Hans had activated to indicate she should begin her attack run.

The valley thundered with the sound of her broadside and yet again, Hans was thankful for the mercy of the crimson-tainted dust raised over the remains of the victims. The *Bloody Rose* wheeled around, targeted the two damaged Chimera and obliterated them with pairs of eight and twelve pound solid shot each.

Within another minute, the fight was over. The last echoes of the last volley from the pirate airship still rang in the air. From where Hans peered past the safety of his hard cover, he very much doubted that any of the Russians had survived. The area they had taken refuge in from the sun was unrecognizable now compared to when Hans and

André had first scouted it out on foot. The *Bloody Rose* had mercilessly pulverized the landscape and the men hiding in it.

"Just as he said it would be," Dubé said with a satisfied nod. "The old man is a cunning bastard with an eye for ambush. I am glad I get to be on this side of his plans."

*****

They combed the grisly scene of carnage looking for survivors with the Doctor and Chief Nurse. A group of Gunner-Marines armed with pistols and swords escorted the medical team, ensuring that a vengeful Russian caused them no harm. It turned out to be an unwarranted precaution.

The maelstrom of grapeshot and automatic weapons fire that had torn apart the Russian contingent had left not a single victim whole. There was no way they could be given sufficient medical care aboard the pirate ship to save them in the long term. While Blackheart forbade directly shooting them as mercy, he also recognized that leaving them for the animals of the desert to finish off was a greater cruelty. The best they could do for the precious few souls left alive was administer them sufficient pain killer to make certain their final minutes would be painless and short. Hans felt sick to his stomach, and Koblinski had a haunted look in his eyes as he did the best he could.

Sarah Redsands, supervising the salvage operation of materials with a group of Gunner-Marines, made a worrisome discovery. "They had a Marconi-style communicator," she explained to them, showing them the hefty piece of equipment connected to a few batteries. "It was on when we found it, and the Morse signal key had been screwed down."

"Which means what?" Hans had asked.

"I think they were transmitting a distress, and when they saw the *Bloody Rose* show up, the radioman left the set transmitting a constant fixed clear tone," the sandy-haired woman of Indian-American descent explained. "With the set transmitting constantly for the past few minutes until we found it and unplugged it, it would have been trivial for anyone to triangulate the position of the transmitter."

Blackheart cursed in the fashion associated with lower deck English sailors. Hans blinked at him.

"So the local command base that the Russians were operating from knows they were attacked and lost, as well as where it happened," O'Raedy said, visibly unhappy. "We know they came overland, which likely means they arrived in Egypt by a ship from the Mediterranean. We have maybe two days before they message is relayed north and they bring airships here to hunt for who did this."

"We had best make haste then, *Kapitan*," Annika said with a nod. "With two modern long-barrel field guns, two Chimera and a hundred and forty men having 'disappeared', you may presume that the RIAN will be expecting a much bigger interference than one little pirate ship."

Blackheart looked around, frustration clear on his features. "Pile the bodies and everything we else cannot take at the foot of the valley ridge," he ordered. "Captain-Gunner, mine the top of the ridge and again about a third of the way down. We will detonate the mines as we depart and the landslide will bury the remains. I am not leaving the bodies of these poor sods here for the vultures and desert dogs. Work swiftly; time is less our friend than ever."

*****

"So what do you think of airships for travel thus far, Miss al-Heshjukur?" Blackheart asked quietly. Hans was with them, Annika and Amram in the Steering House as they flew swiftly across the desert at a scant hundred feet above the terrain. They were running with all three motor pods in operation now, barely managing seventy five knots. The damaged motor pod was throwing sparks and vibrating in a worrisome way, but Blackheart had ordered it run to partial power anyway.

Khadija had been called to the bridge from her new position in the Propulsion Room to provide her knowledge to expedite the flight to the ravine. She was not at all a dull girl, and with only a little explanation of how a modern aeronautical map worked was able to rapidly help them pin down where it was they needed to go. O'Raedy had told her to remain in the Steering House to answer questions as they developed.

Khadija looked toward him, for a moment before answering. "It is a very different experience, Sir. It would seem to me to render almost any other style of travel in the desert irrelevant. It will certainly be something I discuss with my father; there are so many ways that we could use one."

"And what do you think of the Propulsion Room?" he enquired.

"It is a most daunting and sophisticated sort of environment. There is so much to learn and I know very little. However, Chief Itala is a gifted and inspiring woman; I cannot help but wish to make her proud of me."

"That is part of the Chief's magic, Miss al-Heshjukur. She brings out the best in everyone around her, and she inspires the achievement of the impossible," Blackheart said, scanning the horizon ahead with his spyglass. "I think you should do very well working for her. Given your father's interest in modern technologies, I thought it would be a good place for you to earn your keep with us."

"Many thanks, Captain O'Raedy."

"What can you tell us of the ravine and the area we expect to find the Temple entrance, Khadija?" Annika asked, looking at the area map with the Spanish Deck Officer, Amram Nando.

"It is actually rather amusing to me that you seek the place," she said. "Most children within a week's ride of the place know of the ravine from ghost stories."

"Ghost stories?" Nando questioned with a note of concern.

The young Arab woman nodded. "Usually told to the boys, but we girls hear them eventually. The ravine is said to have old ruins in them from days before the Pharaohs. The ruins are cursed," she said with a quiet awe, "and none that have entered beyond the light of day have ever emerged again."

"Hardly encouraging odds," Blackheart said gruffly. "We are likely going to upset a lot of storytellers when they have to start adding '... except for that bunch of bloody pirates ...'".

Everyone chuckled lightly for a moment. "What else can you tell us about the place?" Annika prompted.

Khadija thought for a moment. "As you know, the ravine is in the area my father claims domain over. So, he has fighting men on horseback visit that area once a month or so," she said gesturing modestly as she spoke. "He does not wish bandits taking up residence there. I have heard the fighting men tell stories of what they have seen. The ruins are in the middle of a small oasis. Near the middle of the oasis is an open pond big enough to swim in. The water is said to glow with magic at night. Sometimes, lights have been seen moving around within the oasis. The next day, no evidence of anyone having been there could be found."

"What do you think of that, Mister Sauder?" Blackheart asked in a thoughtful tone.

Hans rubbed at his chin for a moment and then shrugged. "My first reaction would be something akin to phosphoretted hydrogen marsh gasses ... but that requires an awful lot of either rotting matter or another source of hydrogen and phosphors."

"I rather doubt we are dealing with Will-o'-the-wisps in a desert, Mister Sauder. However, you do raise an interesting idea. Something is evidently going on around there that is generating some source of energy, be it chemical or otherwise."

"*Capitán*," Nando interjected, "we should be within sight of the ravine in just a few minutes."

*****

"Well then," Blackheart said as they approached the blossom of green in the middle of the otherwise dusty ravine. "I suspect we have found the place," he commented sardonically. He pulled his Tesla pistol from its holster and pressed a button with his thumb. It began to hum quietly, and the core of the barrel glowed a soft blue. Following his lead, everyone else in the armed party made ready with their weapons. After a glance over his shoulder at them, Blackheart pressed onwards past the perimeter between desert and oasis.

Arietta was directly behind Blackheart, followed by Khadija, with Hans behind the Arabic woman and then Annika behind him. A half dozen more Gunner-Marines with Tesla rifles followed behind their Captain-Gunner.

"This oasis is very strange," Khadija commented.

"Oh? In what way?" Blackheart asked over his shoulder, keeping most of his attention forward.

"The grass goes from desert to knee deep and then waist deep in just a few paces. Normally it would be ten times that distance to become this lush," she said, looking around her cautiously.

"Fascinating ... so we have a small oasis with an unnatural lushness about it in which lights have been seen at night. Chief Itala, what do you make of that?" Blackheart questioned, keeping a slow but steady rate of advance towards the heart of the oasis.

"Well," Arietta started, then interrupted herself by squarely swatting a fly buzzing around her. "It strongly suggests that we are in the right place. Everything we know about the Temple suggests that this is the exact type of influence the Priests used to produce across a large part of Upper Egypt. Even the air within the oasis has a very different quality to it, as though it were of a completely different environment."

"A true micro-climate, then," Hans said.

"So it would appear," Blackheart agreed. "Captain-Gunner ... what do you not hear, compared to the past two oasis' we have visited?"

Annika took a few more steps, considering the question in silence. "Birds," she announced. "There is no sound of birds or even small herbivores."

"I concur," O'Raedy said, chopping a few man-high greens from his path with his Jacob's Ladder. It left a sharp and acrid smell in the air with each swing, and the further scent of seared vegetable matter. "Which means that either the rest of the ravine is sufficiently hostile to prevent anything from finding its way here, or the natural creatures of the earth can sense something amiss with the area and avoid it."

"That, *Herr Kapitän*, is a somewhat unsettling notion," Hans commented, using a machete to further clear the trail they were blazing.

"Indeed it is," the Italian-Ethiope answered. "My experiences are that those things that nature shuns yet man pursues result in tragic stories," she said wryly.

"We can hope that this story will involve a happy ending featuring a bucket of rum and another of gemstones," Annika chuckled.

"Rum?" Khadija asked.

"Something you likely should avoid for religious reasons," Arietta said with a laugh, "but given your looks, you may be sure that the lads aboard the ship will wish to see you drinking heavily of."

"It is a type of alcohol," Hans supplied.

"Oh," she said. "My father said there would be many places such as this where religious concerns would clash with more worldly experiences."

"Oh? And what did he suggest you do as a rule in such places?" Blackheart asked.

"My father has acquired a taste for French *Champagne*," she said with a laugh.

*****

A short time later found them standing on the edge of a brilliant blue pond that shimmered in the late afternoon sun. To one side, a third of the way around, was a set of alabaster colonnades, partially obscured by vegetation. A smallish structure of the same material was in the middle of the colonnades; it immediately put Hans in the mind of a medieval mausoleum like those he had seen in graveyards.

"Beautiful," Arietta breathed. The vegetation was a full canopy here, with towering palms, massive ferns, brilliant flowering vines, and host of other vegetation in a rainbow of colours. Shafts of sunlight danced a dappled waltz on the leaves and water.

"Well," Blackheart said, breaking the awed quiet. "It would seem we have found what we came searching for." He led them around the edge of the pond to the door of the alabaster structure. Annika immediately noted the hieroglyphs and pictograms on the outside walls. After a few minutes of examination, she pronounced that they indicated this was indeed part of a Temple of Min.

The door to the structure had long ago been bashed in and cast aside. Sunlight clearly showed a foyer with stairs that led into darkness below. At the edge of the glow of sunlight, a group of skeletons were ominously visible.

"Mister Sauder," Blackheart asked conversationally, "what do you note of interest about the skeletons?"

Hans peered at them from the top of the stairs and then shrugged his shoulders. "Dusty and clean; they have been there a long time ... beyond that, not much."

"Captain-Gunner?"

Annika was likewise at a loss for what Blackheart might be thinking of.

"They are all facing up the stairs, on their chests," Arietta interjected. "They all died leaving the Temple, not entering it ... and two of them have an arm out stretched as though the were struggling to make it this far."

Blackheart nodded to the Chief Engineer. "Exactly my thought. We go no further today. We will return to the ship for the night, and tomorrow we begin at dawn. I want a full day of daylight for our explorations so that we are not trying to depart in the dark in unknown circumstances."

"Afraid of ghosts, *Kapitan*?" Annika chided.

"No. Afraid of having to deal, in the dark, with things that kill expeditions within sight of doors, in unfamiliar places that give pause to seasoned warriors."

"The Temple of Min"

Diary Entry For the Morning of July 12th, 1888

I am writing this passage in my diary in the pre-dawn gloom of the Egyptian desert. I have a flask of hot coffee and a moment of peace. In little more than two hours, I will be at the threshold of an ancient temple that legend says has never allowed a visitor to leave. Yesterday afternoon, we found at least one grisly example of this. As such, I have no idea if this will be the last coffee and peace I savour before I am counted amongst the Devil's Shares.

Yesterday was perhaps the first time I can clearly recall something akin to fear in Michael O'Raedy's eyes. I have seen cunning, malice, anger, calculation, respect, and reservation. Not fear; I was beginning to doubt his capacity for it, in fact.

Now that we metaphorically stand on the threshold of what could be the most important expedition in modern history, I think that all of us sense the peril we are now in. The power of the Temple has been dormant for over two thousand years; why do we think we will be any different than those who have gone before us in seeking it's source?

The Bloody Rose and her crew have cheated Fate many, many times. We all must trust this will be another one of those harrowing times. The price of our failure will be measured beyond just our lives in the history books yet to be written.

*****

"Here we are again," Arietta chuckled as they reached the edge of the oasis pond.

"Aye. Alright; everyone pay careful attention. Chief Itala, start your timer ... now," Blackheart said. Both he and Arietta clicked the stub on their pocket chronometers together and then he nodded. "We have nine hours of daylight left. We will explore for four hours, and then return to the surface. That will give us a one hour margin of error. If we must, we will repeat again tomorrow. Understood?" he asked, looking at the assembled team of ten pirates. Everyone nodded. "Good. Let us go ... history awaits."

They carefully descended the stairs, pausing momentarily to examine skeletons they had discovered yesterday. A brief inspection gave no revelations as to how they might have died or how long they had been there, save for that all that was left were dried bones. They moved on, entering the gloom beyond the fallen.

They lit lanterns to shed light around them and made their way along carefully. After a short time, they emerged down another set of stairs into a large columned room. The light of their Fresnel-lensed lanterns showed the walls were covered with mosaics and paintings. The images seemed to depict people worshipping the black-skinned, flail-wielding god as he stood on a cloud. The cloud sat atop a blue and yellow pillar reaching up from an oasis.

"The primary temple," Annika said. "This area will be safe ... it was for public worship by the common people. Towards the back, we should find a passage used by the priests to come and go. It might be concealed, to make them seem more mysterious to the commoners."

"Been studying, have you, Miss Nadezhda?" Blackheart questioned amusedly.

"Ever since we found that damn book over Russia," she said with a laugh. "The Captain-Rockets has not been the only thing keeping me awake at night." Hans was very happy at the darkness, as it concealed the flush in his cheeks as the rest of the group had a bawdy chuckle at his expense.

They made their way to the back of the temple, finding a raised platform with an altar upon it and a sizable idol of the rain god. Arietta chuckled at one of its features.

"God-like endurance, I see," she joked. Khadija averted her eyes in apparent embarrassment at the remark.

"He is always represented that way. He was not only the God of the rains and good weather, but also of good harvests and male fertility, particularly in the Middle Kingdom period," Annika explained.

Arietta scowled at her. "Your scholarly pillow companion is killing your sense of humour, dear sister," she teased.

"We can debate humour after we find the door leading down, ladies," Blackheart suggested pointedly. They looked around for a short time and eventually found a piece of masonry concealing a trigger lever. A door slid open, exposing another small room with a corridor that led off one way, and a set of stairs leading further down.

"Down," Annika said firmly. "The corridor would be to the living quarters of the priests and such." Blackheart glanced at the Russian brunette for a moment and nodded.

Hans thought about that; Blackheart was trusting their lives to Annika's enthusiasm for a hobby without apparent question.   That was part of the magic of Blackheart, he reflected   He allowed individuals to shine in their moments, directing the collective capabilities of his crew with a clear confidence in them that allowed them to excel where perhaps they would have hesitated.   He inspired boldness, and praised it regardless of success or failure. Hans would have to think about that further he decided.

They had taken two or three flights of stairs downward, emerging to a small stone chamber. Large stone statues of a variety of creatures both real and mythological, were spaced across the walls.   At the far end was another corridor. A further look around with lantern light revealed skeletons on the floor at various places around the room.

"Stop," Arietta said.   She adjusted the hood of her lantern to more clearly spotlight one set of skeletons. She then shone the light on another set and another. It was visible to Hans that all of them were severed in two.

"That is bad," the dark-skinned Chief Engineer said.

"Trapped," Annika stated.   "They look like they all got hit in the upper body and split in two."

"Animals would not leave the bodies where they fell. Guards would have cleaned up. So yes, it is an automatic system of some kind," Blackheart said.   "If you look, the statues all have open mouths. The skeletons are all within a few feet of a line drawn between a left and right pair of statues."

"So the statues are the trap system," Hans reasoned aloud. "How can we make them safe?"

Arietta spoke up.   "First, we find out how they work. Once we know what they do, then we determine if we can avoid the triggers.   From there, we plan appropriately." She turned around and pointed at two of the Gunner-

Marines. "Come with me. We are going back up in search of a tree. Everyone else wait here, and for Heaven's sake, do not go forward a step until I return."

What Hans guessed was a quarter hour passed before Arietta and the two Gunner-Marines returned, carrying the trunks of two small palm trees between the three of them. Arietta also had a few fronds with her. She lashed the fronds together in make-shift broom and started to her work.

She slid the two trunks, each likely a dozen feet long, out on the floor ahead of her and rolled them to form a corridor about a foot to a side wider than she was. She then brushed the floor before her clean with the fronds and sat her lantern down before her, illuminating the 'corridor'. She slowly tapped at each floor stone with a hammer, listening carefully. Khadija watched her progress with clear curiosity, evidently trying to discern what the dark-skinned woman was doing.

The progress was painstaking as she moved along on her elbows and knees marking each stone she checked with a white chalk. Eventually, roughly between the first set of statues, she tapped one stone and then stopped and looked at it. She tapped around it and then nodded.

"As I thought. Trigger stones ... The whole row in front of the statues. Everyone make sure you are out of the room," she said.

She drew a line along the edge of the trunk beside her, marking where it had lain on the floor. She scuttled back most of its length, sat on her haunches, picked the trunk up awkwardly and the slammed the far end down on one of the suspect stones.

The was a distinctly electrical noise and a gout of dust expelled from the mouths of both of the adjacent statues. There was a hiss of something sailing through the air at great speed and then a spark of metal on stone flashed from near both statues. Hans directed his lantern at one of the spots.

What looked to be a triangle formation of curved blades was laying on the ground in front of the statue. In fact, Hans realized that the shape was somewhat similar to the propellers on the motor pods of the *Bloody Rose*. A cord, also apparently of metal, ran back to the mouth of the statue furthest from the blade.

After just a moment, the statue apparently began reeling the weapon on a string back into the launcher in its mouth. The light of other lanterns illuminated that the same process and weapon had been fired from the mouth of the other statue.

"That is amazing," Khadija said.

"Well," said Blackheart. "Excellent work, Chief."

Arietta nodded and grinned at him with her brilliant smile. She turned and repeated the impact on the stones twice more as the traps reset. It was only almost half a minute after the statutes had fully recovered the blades into their maw that they would fire again.

The group of pirates cautiously advanced across the room, staying in the "safe corridor" that the Assassin-turned-Engineer cleared for them. They swiftly repeated the process five more times, triggering each trap in turn and then crossing its firing line as it reloaded.

"You know," said Hans as they passed over the middle point of the room, "I would swear those sound electrical when they fire."

"They do," Chief Itala confirmed. "For want of any other explanation, I would say the are fired electromagnetically."

Blackheart looked at her skeptically. "Electromagnetic saw-blade launchers in a thirty century-old Egyptian temple?"

"As I said, Captain ... for want of any other explanation. I am open to theories beyond 'it is magic'," she said caustically.

*****

Once out of the blade-trap chamber, they continued along another ancient stone corridor. It doubled back on itself repeatedly, as well as had a gentle downward slope to it. The group of pirate-explorers kept sharp eye around themselves at all times with their lights, fearing another trap. The corridor eventually came to yet another set of stairs leading ever deeper into the earth.

"Sir?" Khadija piped up. "Look, sir ... the ceiling over the stairs ... it is wet."

Both Blackheart and Hans shone their lanterns at the sloping ceiling ahead of them. "Good eyes, lass," Blackheart chuckled. It was exactly as the Arabic engineer had said.

"Water? Does the roof leak from the small lake above?" Annika asked with a note of concern.

"I do not think so, Captain-Gunner," Arietta said thoughtfully. "I would expect to see minerals or stains on the rock from where the water had leaked ... perhaps even a crack. It just seems wet."

"Condensation, then?" Hans suggested.

"I suspect so," Chief Itala answered with a nod.

"So ... where is the source of evaporation, then?" Annika asked, skeptically.

"It must be below," Blackheart said with a thoughtful nod. "This is where the air coming up the stairs strikes a boundary of some kind and the water condenses on the stone."

"That must be quite a sizable amount of water to create a climate boundary," Hans said with a whistle.

"Let us press forward and find out!" Blackheart declared.

*****

The stairs led to another chamber which had a single corridor that exited it. The corridor led them after a short distance to something that left them stunned at its threshold.

It was a substantial underground cavern, possibly the better part of a mile across. The massive cavern had scores of what looked like carved obelisks anchored in the otherwise jagged ceiling. The obelisks hung, point down. All of them shimmered with a vesperous purple glow. The glow shed barely enough light to see detail in the cavern.

The bottom of the cavern was a lake. It was impossible to determine how deep it might be; the beam of a lantern's light gave the impression it was at least deeper than the height of a man. The corridor led out onto a bridge that was probably a full two stories in the air above the water, and at least that far below the tips of the obelisks. The bridge crossed the lake, leading to the far side of the cavern to another door.

"What in Mary's name ...?" Blackheart asked in low wonder.

Before anyone could respond a dull moan began to reverberate through the cavern. The pirates all immediately raised their weapons, looking around for the source of the sound.

"Look! Up there!" Annika exclaimed.

Strands of purple-pink energy, like some bizarrely coloured lightning storm, were arcing between a trio of the inverted obelisks on the ceiling. As the sound shifted in volume and intensity from a moan to a shrieking crackle, so did the intensity of the display of energy. A brilliant arc of power sparked down and touched the water's surface, dazzling and deafening the pirates for a few moments. Sheets and balls of energy flashed and leapt across the lake's surface, creating countless secondary cascades that brought the entire water's surface to life for what felt like minutes of display. Some of those cascades seemed to crawl up the sides of parts of the bridge, covering areas of its deck in sizzling power.

They collectively cleared their senses as the discharges faded, blinking and working their jaws. They peered around cautiously.

"Not the Virgin Mother, *Captaino*," Arietta said with quiet awe. "Just the opposite. Its a working Dante's Battery," she said.

"Dante's Battery?" Hans asked, sounding baffled.

"Pure water is an insulator, Hans ... mineralized water is a conductor. However, if you inject enough power into a body of pure water, it acts more like a capacitor. The problem is that you need huge amounts of energy, and huge amounts of water ... and the power slowly dissipates over time," Arietta explained. "I am going to go out on a very thin limb and say those structures at the ceiling are Aether Collectors ... and over time, they build up enough power to discharge and energize the lake below. But ... the lake is saturated, because the power of the Temple has been turned off for centuries. That is what causes the Wisps above us ... and why the oasis above us exists ... there is so much energy here that even with the switches 'off', it is probably arcing across the relays somewhere."

"Aether Collectors? Those are pure conjecture, Chief," Blackheart began. "No one even has a working ..."

"I am open to suggestions as to what else would cause that kind of a discharge over an area this vast," she said pointedly.

"What kind of power are we talking about, here?" Hans asked curiously. The Gunner-Marines were equally curious, as was Khadija.

"You could likely run Düsseldorf on what three of those obelisks produce," Chief Itala said flatly. A low whistle escaped the lips of one of the Gunner-Marines.

"How about we focus on the detail where this bridge is a death trap?" Annika suggested pointedly.

"Pardon?" Blackheart asked.

"When whatever those things are discharge, the ensuing cascade effect covers parts of the bridge," she explained. "I am pretty sure that getting caught in the middle of that would be fatal," she said as she shifted her sword belt.

Blackheart thought for a moment. He pulled out his spyglass and passed it to Annika. "Sauder, sit her on your shoulders so she has a bit more height. Captain-Gunner, take a look and see if there is any sort of way to tell if parts of the bridge are safe or not."

A few moments later, Annika had her legs hooked under his arms and was peering out over the bridge. "Well, *Kapitan* ... it looks like it is fairly easy to discern ... parts of the bridge are sooted and look as one would expect from periodic electrocution ... other parts are untouched. It seems to be a repeating pattern."

"Good. We know that it takes several seconds from the time we hear the moan begin to develop before the discharge. And then several more seconds from the discharge to before the cascade begins to engulf the bridge. We do not tarry crossing the danger areas, and run like madmen for the nearest safe area when we hear a discharge starting to happen," Blackheart said confidently.

"I will suggest we do not tarry crossing any areas of the bridge," Hans said wryly. "I am disinterested in forming new circuits for Aether Collector discharges."

"As my father would say, '*Always hope for Allah's Mercy*," Khadija laughed, "*but try not to give Him reason to consider if you need it*'."

They made sure their equipment was secured for fast movement and set out across the bridge at a brisk pace. They all knew that they had a good distance to cover and were all very conscious that being tired at the far end of the traverse could possibly prove fatal. As Annika had said, it was a regular pattern of safe and unsafe areas. It was very clear to everyone by sight and smell which ones were which.

As they moved as fast as prudence would allow, they all noted the periodic fountains of boiling water and steam that would gout up from the lake. Also, they could clearly hear and see seething spheres of ball lightning, some larger than rugby balls, sizzling across the lake's surface. Chief Itala told them this was consistent with what she understood of descriptions of a so-called Dante's Battery. It also meant that getting within a few feet of the lake's surface would result in what would most assuredly be a fatal electrical arc between the lake and the victim.

"So, no swimming then, ma'am?" one of the Gunner-Marines quipped.

They were about a third of the way across the bridge when the sound they had been fearing reached their ears. As poor fortune would have it, they were also in the middle of one of the hazard zones of the bridge.

"Run for your bloody lives!" Blackheart bellowed. Inexplicably, however, he stopped. He stood there waving and shouting at everyone to pass him. No one stopped to argue with him. As the last Gunner-Marine passed him, he threw a swift kick at the young man's backside and began following behind him at a dead run.

"Get your lard arse moving, Daniels! I am not safe until you are, and if you kill the pair of us with your snail's pace I will be yelling and swearing at you all the way to Hell, man! Move! Faster!" Blackheart bellowed in a voice that Hans rather much thought might convince the Devil to lock the doors and turn the pair of them around.

"Keep running! As far to the middle of the safe area as you can get!" Arietta shouted. "And then lay down and cover your eyes! If you stand, you might wind up getting hit anyway! Faster! Faster!"

Few things move faster than frightened pirates Hans reflected as the shrieking crackle of the Aether Collector discharge reached his ears. Annika tackled him to the ground from behind and the roar of what sounded like a cross between the wind in a North Sea storm and Jacob's Ladder gone berserk deafened him. He pulled Annika against him, eyes firmly closed and face against her shoulder. He had no idea if Daniels and O'Raedy had made it or not.

The air smelled of sulphur and something viciously acrid, and it felt like furnace's heat. The sound of the electrical cascade pouring over the bridge, like a surging ocean wave, was a deafening howl unlike anything he had ever heard produced by man or nature. He could feel the hair on his head, face and arms standing straight and he prayed that he and Annika were far enough away from the cascade to not be struck.

After what seemed like a very long time, the sound abated and he opened his eyes cautiously. Everyone else was doing the same, save Blackheart who was already standing a few feet past them all, lighting his pipe.

"Well, that was quite a show," he said with an impressed look. "Are we ready to press on?" he asked with an indifferent tone.

Arietta glared at him and said nothing.

They endured another discharge event around two thirds of the way across the bridge. It was just as intense an experience as the first, leaving everyone somewhat rattled. Even the supposedly unflappable Blackheart was putting on a brave front from what Hans could tell. He was a skilled actor, but ultimately Hans could tell he was acting.

"I am very curious as to how it is the energy cascades always cross the same parts of the bridge," Annika said as they continued on from the latest blast.

"It looks to me as though the stones do not have mortar between them on those sections," Hans said. He had been wondering the same thing and, during a moment of recovery after the last blast, he had scraped away some of the soot and oxide.

"It looks like a metal of some kind," he continued as they hurried along. "I am guessing the parts of the bridge arch, that are part of the way to the water, are likewise built. When a cascade reaches the bridge, those metal points are near enough to arc to. Then, once having found a path of lesser resistance than the air and water elsewhere, the energy exploits it until the cascade calms."

*****

They reached the far door without other incident and continued on a short distance, painfully aware that time was passing. The corridor was in a pattern similar to a "W", eventually coming to a heavy stone door that spun about a central axis. They cautiously passed through it after careful inspection, to find a second such door only a handful of yards ahead. It let them out into a foyer of another room that brought them up short with what they all saw.

It looked as though someone had planted a garden here. Average sized date-palm trees, wide leaved banana plants, huge ferns and lush grasses filled the place in a riot of green. A dull buzz of insects bespoke of the life teeming within the chamber.

The room was large, perhaps half a football field in size. The vaulted ceiling arched upwards to a central peak; perhaps ten times the height of a man at the centre and a third that at the sides. Columns were regularly spaced throughout the place, a few yards apart. At the central peak was what looked like stationary ball of lightning, casting a brilliant white luminescence over everything in the garden.

A set of mechanical fans at the far end of the right corner of the room turned slowly, blowing a low but steady breeze over a large pond. A pebble stone path wound a snake's course through the greenery, across a small bridge over the pond, to a platform which had a door to exit the room. The door was flanked by a pair of jackal-headed statues that were half-again as tall as Hans was, he guessed. Each one held a hefty looking polearm with a gleaming metal blade at a position of attention, silent watchers of the garden chamber.

"An indoor oasis?" Hans boggled.

"So it would seem, Captain-Rockets. Complete with fabricated sunlight," Blackheart marvelled, shielding his eyes as he peered upwards at the light.

"Keep your wits about you in here," the Captain-Gunner ordered. "With the dense foliage, we are vulnerable to an ambush as we walk the path." Everyone looked around with a renewed suspicion and kept their pistols and rifles at the ready.

They slowly made there way along the winding path, marvelling at the sights that met their eyes. A set of small bucket hoists lifted water from the pond at the far end of the chamber. Each bucket poured water into what were apparently irrigation runs that disappeared into the brush. A single metal axle joined all of the bucket hoists together. The axle protruded from the wall and turned with a slow and constant pace. Thick leaf-litter covered the ground and periodically it sounded as though small things moved around within it.

As they reached the stone bridge that led across the small pond, Annika raised her hand. "Stop," she said quietly, staring at the statues standing beside the door.

"What is it, Captain-Gunner?" Hans asked.

"The polearms that the statues are holding ... why would they be made with bronze staves and what look like steel blades if they are ornamental?" Annika asked.

Everyone blinked in surprise and looked again. "In fact," said Blackheart thoughtfully, "if you look carefully ... they are actually being 'held' by the statues hands ... the butts of the weapons are just sitting on the ground. As you might expect a Swiss halberdier to stand on guard."

"Sir?" one of the Gunner-Marines asked tentatively. "You are not suggesting those things are going actually swing those polearms at us, are you?"

"Actually Kenneth," Annika said with sigh, "that is exactly what I am saying. Come on boys, time to earn our pay."

"What exactly are you proposing to do, Captain-Gunner?" Blackheart asked, raising a hand to indicate everyone was to stay put.

"The group of us cross the bridge and see if those things do move. If they do, we fall back across the bridge firing Tesla rifles like madmen and you all make ready to do what you can," she replied.

"Chief Itala will ensure the bridge is clear of more conventional traps before any of you set foot on it. Then you may cross and move forward. For God's sake, Captain-Gunner, be careful," he said.

Arietta declared the bridge to be safe after a few minutes. She noted that it was an entirely separate piece, carved from a single block of stone and resting on the reinforced edges of both sides of the pond. The pond was only a few feet deep and flowed from an upwelling on the left to a grated level-drain on the right. The Chief Engineer retreated, took a double-handed grip of her pistol and set into a kneeling position beside a corner rail of the bridge. She nodded grimly to Annika who cocked the hammers of her two pistols and stepped onto the bridge.

Hans stood at the other side with the hefty Le Matt pistol in his hands. Blackheart moved beside him with his Tesla pistol thrumming at the ready. Khadija stood behind the Chief Engineer, shouldering one of the Tesla Rifles they had stolen from that Scottish Castle.

Annika and the five Gunner-Marines slowly walked across the bridge, with weapons aimed at the statues. No sooner had Annika stepped off the bridge than the gemmed eyes of the statues glowed brightly. The sound of what reminded Hans to be millstones turning together easily reached their ears. Dust tumbled off the statues and the heads turned to look towards Annika. Before anything else happened, she pulled the triggers of her two tri-barrels and then the other Gunner-Marines joined in.

The initial fusillade of gunfire, both solid and electrical, produced no visible change in the statues. It seemed as though the Tesla weapons were completely ignored, whereas the six bullets Annika unloaded as fast as she could fire at least tore a few small pieces out of her target. The statues walked forward resolutely and swung their massive weapons. The sound of metal slamming into stone resounded through the chamber as the group of Gunner-Marines scattered and dove out of the way.

"Back across the bridge! Move it!" Annika shouted as she shoved her emptied pistols into their holsters. "Do not even try parrying those monsters ... they are gouging stone!" Annika did a forward dive and shoulder-roll between the two guards and pulled out a pair of long-barrelled revolvers. She started firing in alternation hitting each statue in the back repeatedly. The two statues stopped and turned towards her while swinging their halberds at her. She narrowly dodged their swings as the other Gunner-Marines retreated across the bridge.

Hans flipped the lever on the Le Matt and slammed two bullets into one of the statues. It turned towards him and began moving in his direction.

"Everyone back up and stay on the path," Blackheart ordered. "They move slowly ... sling the Tesla rifles and pull your pistols!"

Arietta fired at the one still menacing Annika who was playing a desperate game of dodge and roll with it. As soon as the second bullet from the Italian-Ethiop's gun struck, it apparently forgot the Russian brunette and turned towards its most recent assailant.

"They chase the last person to hit it hard. Everyone keep your distance and alternate your targets to keep them confused!" Arietta shouted over the sounds of constant pistol fire.

"We are not hurting them!" Hans shouted in frustration. "We are just chipping pieces out of them!"

Annika, having been forgotten where she was, reloaded quickly and rapidly emptied both her tri-barrels and her second set of six-shooters into the back of one of the stone juggernauts which had just reached the end of the bridge furthest from her. Blackheart was staying ahead of the slowly retreating group, firing his Tesla pistol at the one still advancing towards them. He systematically shot the advancing invincible menace in every part of its body, clearly hoping for a weakness somewhere.

Hans fired four bullets into the back of the one that had just returned to attack Annika. It swung at her once, narrowly missing the athletic woman. It then turned and began advancing towards Hans.

"This is ridiculous!" Hans shouted. "We cannot just keep them strolling back and forth until we run out of bullets!"

Blackheart dodged aside from the one that was nearly atop him as it swung its polearm at him. He back pedalled a few steps and fired twice at the things face. There was a brief hesitation and the glow in the eyes flickered.

"The eyes!" Blackheart bellowed. "Aim for the eyes! Shatter the ..." his command was cut short by the metal haft of the weapon slamming into his chest with an ugly crunch. He was lifted into the air by the momentum and crashed into the foliage and brush a short distance off the path.

"Hans! Give me a step!" Arietta shouted and then ran towards the young German. He dropped the pistol at his feet, went down on one knee and laced his hands together. As she reached him, her next footstep was into the cup of his hands and he stood with as much muscle as he could muster. Between her momentum and jump, combined with his added power, the dark-skinned woman fairly flew through the air. She landed with a surprising dexterity on the shoulder of the one that had just struck Blackheart. The statue seemed confused as to what it should do for a moment, which was all the time that Arietta needed to swing around to its back. She pulled a pistol from her belt and fired it at point blank into the statue's closest eye.

The reaction was instant. The stone monster staggered clumsily and Arietta lost her grip, tumbling from its back. She landed dazedly in a graceless heap on the ground, and the statue turned towards her. It raised its massive weapon, preparing to strike.

Off to Hans' right, where O'Raedy had landed, there were sounds of mayhem. Khadija and one of the Gunner-Marines had gone to give aid and were now furiously hacking and chopping at something.

The sounds of pistol fire, cursing and shouting pirates and his own hammering heart rang in his ears. He emptied the revolver into the back of the juggernaut looming over Arietta, but it had already committed to its swing.

Kenneth, one of the Gunner-Marines, raced past him. He swung his cutlass upwards with all the strength he could muster at the the down-arcing blade, with a scream that was a mix of ferocity and terror. The collision of the two weapons resonated in the garden chamber and sparks flew at the point of meeting. The young Englishman was driven to his knees with the cutlass braced in both his hands over his head.

Improbably, both he and the Chief Engineer he protected were still alive. The statue raised its weapon again, aiming for the Gunner-Marine.

Annika opened fire with both her revolvers from where she stood on the bridge railing. She hammered the stone monster in the face with a dozen bullets in half as many seconds. Somewhere in that process, she shattered the other eye-gem. The statue jerked violently like a spastic clockwork coming apart at the gears, and then simply fell apart into a heap of stone.

From the other end of the chamber, near where they had entered, a cheer went up. Hans turned to see the remaining three gunners shaking their fists and pistols in the air with a similarly destroyed statue on the path before them. They had apparently led the thing on a chase the entire length of the room, and managed to shoot out both its eye-gems before it made mince of them.

"*Sayyid* Sauder! *Sayyid* Sauder! Come quickly! The Captain is injured!" Khadija shouted in clear consternation.

Hans drew his scimitar and swiftly slashed his way to where Khadija and the Gunner-Marine Daniels had rushed to aid Blackheart when he had been thrown by the statue. He was brought up short by what he saw.

Blackheart was sitting heavily against a tree, his chin on his chest and his eyes heavy. His left pant leg had been slashed open to the mid-calf and his right and left shirt sleeves had been hacked off. On all three limbs, Hans could see ugly raised bruises that were bleeding.

"He was bitten by snakes!" Khadija explained frantically. Around them were the chopped remains of what Hans guessed to be a dozen arm-long, devilish looking serpents. They even had horns over their eyes.

"He got knocked right on top a snake's nest, sir!" Daniels exclaimed. "He was already bit three or four times when we got here!"

"Arietta!" Hans bellowed.

"Oh, calm down, man," Blackheart said weakly. "Its just a fatal amount of venom ... nothing to be excited about."

Within moments, everyone had joined them and together they moved him away from the nest and onto the pathway. Arietta injected O'Raedy with two ampoule's of a substance, one in each arm. She was muttering in Italian the entire time with a desperate look in her eyes.

Annika had the Gunner-Marines guarding the doors leading in and out of the garden chamber. At least they were not hovering around as the Italian-Ethiope and the Russian did anything they could think of to save O'Raedy.

"Airy?" he asked faintly. They had pulled his greatcoat off him, and rolled it up to make a pillow for him.

"I am right here, Michael," she said, trying to sound brave. Her voice betrayed her.

"I am glad it was ... was not ... you," O'Raedy whispered. "Too bad ... I ... will not ... get to ... take you ... dancing ... again ..." The man that the world knew as the infamous Captain Blackheart, commander of the Mediterranean Menace herself, closed his eyes, and died.

Arietta cried. Her tears splashed onto the lifeless lips of the man she had called her captain and friend. Hans choked back his own tears, and he held Annika against him for a long moment. Even Khadija seemed to understand that she had just seen the passing of a king.

Annika regained her composure and shouted for the other Gunner-Marines to join them. They made their way over, a combination of uncertainty and shock in their eyes. None of the Gunner-Marines had ever known a *Bloody Rose* without Michael O'Raedy at its helm.

Eventually, Hans knelt beside the dead man and closed his sightless eyes. *"Auf Wiedersehen, Kapitän. Gott Geschwindigkeit und Dankeschön,"* he said quietly. "The world is now a much poorer place at your passing."

*****

Hans rose from beside the dead man and turned to face Annika and Arietta. He looked at the Engineering Chief. "You will be taking command, I presume, *Frau* Itala?" he asked in a formal voice.

She laughed grimly and wiped at her eyes. "Hell no. I have no interest in being in charge of that scow. I need my relative anonymity, Hans. Being *il Capitano* of the *Bloody Rose* would simply attract current members of my old life to visit on unfinished business."

"*Frau* Nadezhda?" he asked, looking at the Russian Captain-Gunner expectantly. To his surprise, she shook her head.

"*Nyet, Gospodin* Sauder," she said in the same formal tone he had used to address her. "I have no sense of ship handling, ship battles or business. I am very good at what I do, which is limited to terrorizing errant Gunner-Marines and merchantmen."

"Then who?" Hans demanded. "We need someone to lead us out of this mess, or the Russians will finish us! None of the watch officers have the charisma to take over the command of the ship. If we do not return with a clear command, that bunch of brigands will start squabbling in a ship-wide civil war."

"I think the short term matter of getting out of this cursed hole in the desert is a somewhat more pressing matter," Arietta noted dryly.

"And committees kill people," Annika snorted in clear derision. "So which one of us is going to do this, at least until we can get back to the ship and resolve this as the Traditions say?"

There was a heavy silence that lasted what seemed to Hans to be a very long time. "I do not bloody believe this," he breathed.

"What?" Khadija asked, acutely aware of the tension in the air around her.

Hans wordlessly knelt beside the still warm body of the man that had brought him so far in such a short time. He hesitated briefly and then slowly removed the black greatcoat from beneath the dead man's head. He stood with his back to those watching him, paused again as though convincing himself to continue. He pulled it on and fastened the middle two buttons, the way the previous Blackheart always wore it. It would need tailoring; it was almost a riding coat on Hans.

He turned around to meet the shocked gazes of Annika and almost everyone else. Only Arietta and Khadija did not look surprised. The Italian-Ethiopian had a pleased, if sad, smile and gave him a nod. The Egyptian woman seemed as though it had been a foregone conclusion to her.

"I am taking command of the expedition, effective now," he said as he pulled his revolver and scimitar from their respective keepers. "Do any of you wish to debate the matter?" he asked, cocking the hammer on the pistol.

There was a distinct silence in the ancient stone garden chamber.

"You know that if you intend to keep wearing the Black Coat, you will have to defend your claim against all comers aboard the *Bloody Rose* when we return to the ship, Hans?" Arietta asked him, adjusting her pistol belt.

"I guessed as much. My personal body count is well over three hundred at this point; a dozen or so more will not change the speed of my trip to Hell," he said in disgust. "I am hoping that one or two brutal demonstrations will keep things relatively quiet. That seemed to be the *modus operendi* of O'Raedy, and it seemed to work fine for him. So, for the immediate future at least ... it would seem that my new name is Blackheart. Are we all clear on this topic, or do I need to eviscerate someone to prove I am serious?"

"I am your Chief Engineer, *Captaino* Blackheart, for so long as this lasts" Arietta said with a genuine smile and a brief curtsy. Her eyes still held pain in them but she at least seemed hopeful.

"I am the safety of your back and the death of your enemies, *Kapitan* Blackheart," Annika said with a sharken grin. There was a ripple of affirmation from the other Gunner-Marines.

He pointed at two of the most junior Gunner-Marines. "You two. Carry the body. Treat him with respect. If you do not and the Captain-Gunner does not discuss it with you, I will," he said sharply. He looked around at everyone and then gave a curt nod. "Come on. We have the future of Allied Europe to save."

*****

They left the garden chamber via another pair of revolving doors identical in function to the pair by which they had entered. The outer door led them back into the inky darkness of another subterranean corridor. They re-lit their lanterns and slowly moved forward. Another "W" pattern corridor sloped ever deeper into the ground. They emerged into another large room, with a raised walkway wide enough for two around a central area. The walls were covered in pictograms with what seemed to be staff-sized bejewelled levers. It was the floor of the central area that captivated them.

It was what appeared to be a scale map of Egypt and its surroundings. They shone their lanterns around, trying to grasp its scale and scope. At least forty paces long and proportionately wide, it showed the Nile, the Mediterranean coast, the Red Sea, the deserts of Libya, the plateau of Ethiopia and more.

A flicker of purple light illuminated the ceiling of the room and they all shone their lights upward. Hanging from the ceiling was another obelisk similar to the ones over the lake. It, too, was surrounded by a vesperous purple glow. It seemed as much a mist of energy as a radiance of any kind.

"Bloody hell," Hans muttered. "How does this one work?"

"I think, *Signore* Captaino," Arietta said quietly, "that we have nothing to fear. I think this is the control room."

"Or firing room, yes," Annika agreed.

A barely visible arc of purple energy flashed to an object on the floor with a quiet pop. Hans stepped out onto the raised walkway tentatively, looking around. Everyone scanned around with their lamps. They slowly and cautiously explored the room from the walkway.

"So what do we have here," Hans asked, looking at everyone after they had regrouped at the door.

"This is it," Annika said. "There are no other doors that we can find. Air comes in as a breeze from up near the obelisk."

"The map on the floor is most assuredly Egypt and its neighbours," Khadija stated confidently. "What is most curious is that it shows towns and villages where there are either only ruins or sand today. In opposition, it does not show a few modern places."

"That makes sense," Arietta said with a thoughtful nod. "It is around three thousand years old. This map is what it looked like to the people that made it." She paused. "It looks like the levers are control mechanisms governing the use of the system. The pictograms seem to indicate what weather is produced by the lever in question, sometimes in combination with the others. It seems that at least three levers, each in a different area, need to be pulled to operate the system."

"That makes sense," Hans stated. "No one person can use the power of the Temple. It would prevent a single madman or saboteur from turning the 'Magic' against them as a weapon."

"The targeting system seems to be very straight-forward," Annika said. "As you and I saw, there is small version of an obelisk that a man might be able to move on the map. It is laying on its side; I would say that whatever befell the temple caused it to be knocked over.   The intermittent arcs from the ceiling are drawn to where the small obelisk is."

"And through some agency, that is what the 'Magic' of the Temple uses to determine what the weather requested from the levers will be centred on," Hans said, tugging at the waist belt of the greatcoat.

"So ... do we want to prove we understand it?" Annika asked.

"How, ma'am?" Kenneth asked.

"We turn it on," she replied.   "We know where the Temple is ... it is plainly marked on the map. We pick a spot an hour from here that Khadija knows to be empty of life, we drop the target obelisk on it, and then dial up a light rain. We then return to the ship, fly to it and look."

Hans shook his head. "We do not have the time. For all we know, the Russians will stroll in behind us and take the place over, with us having done all the work to get in here," he said with a snarl. "No. We target the Temple itself. There must be a way to manage the intensity of the weather the Temple creates."

Everyone blinked at him and Arietta nodded. "Sì," she she said slowly. "There is a lever that the pictogram seems to indicate would perform such a function. The further down, the more intense the weather."

Hans thought for a moment. "And if a rainstorm's worth of water came pouring into that Dante's Battery, what would happen?"

"It would poison it," she said firmly. "The water must be perfectly pure or it will not work.   Worse, it could potentially produce electrical events that would be unbelievably destructive."

Hans looked at the group of Gunner-Marines. "Go get the entire stone-pile from one of those statues. Bring the polearm, too. Be quick about it. We have a Temple to drown."

*****

"There," Arietta said. "That should do what you want. We pull this rope as we leave and that will yank the pin free. That will start the weights mechanism slowly increasing pressure on the lever until it begins to move. If we have guessed right ... over the course of an hour or more a drizzle will become a monsoon."

They had worked steadily for over the past hour, ignoring the warning ring of the chronometers partway through. They had each carried a rope and a couple of small blocks with them as part of their gear. They had made use of those items to build a system of rope and pulleys that would slowly lower a very heavy block of stone, thus pulling down the "throttle lever".

They had carefully identified the levers they presumed they would need to manipulate to generate a rain. They had examined every other part of the room to ensure they had left nothing unnoticed or to chance. All that remained was to set the Obelisk upright in the correct position and then raise the levers to the "firing position" as Annika called it.

They had stripped a couple of the levers that they would not use of their gems. Hans had a feeling they were going to need a sudden influx of cash at the end of this and selling thumbnail-sized gemstones would likely be a way to do that. They had figured out the rhythm of the small discharges from the overhead obelisk and Arietta was confident that she could jump down, set the receiver obelisk upright in the correct place and scramble back up to safety. Hans insisted she wear a safety line, just in case. As it turned out, she had been right.

"Everyone out into the corridor," Hans ordered. "Just Annika, Arietta and I stay here at the door. Move." He shook his head at the round of "Yes, Captain" that reached his ears. He was still having a hard time getting used to the idea he was Blackheart.

"We will not be able to move across the lake bridge fast enough carrying the body," Hans said stiffly. "Bring him back out to the Garden Chamber and place him in the centre path area," he ordered the Gunner-Marines. "It is the best we can do."

Arietta looked pained, but nodded at him. They would soon be arming a world-changing weapon and pointing it at themselves. They barely knew what that would really mean.

"Ready, Chief Engineer?" Hans questioned the Italian-Ethiope. She nodded silently.

"Ready, Captain-Gunner?" Hans asked the Russian brunette.

"*Da, Kapitan.* Let us do this and be on our way. The worst is not over yet."

They moved to the respective levers they needed to operate. Hans raised a hand, waited a moment and then chopped downwards. They all pulled their levers and turned to see what would happen.

There was a brief moment where nothing seemed to occur. Then, slowly, the mist around the ceiling obelisk began to glow brighter. Suddenly, other points in the ceiling illuminated with a similar light as the Garden Chamber, but not as intense. The entire obelisk was now aglow and energy was visibly crackling around its point, reaching out in thin arcing wisps towards the ground. The tip was now an intensely bright point and the sound of a potent energies held barely in check began to rise in the room. The first two or three complete arcs struck the tip of the receiving obelisk and lights around the entire map floor flickered to life.

A sharp crack like a Tesla rifle firing echoed in the room and a solid beam of energy leapt from the transmitter to the reliever. A deep vibration began to resonate in the room, like a colossally massive version of one of the *Bloody Rose*'s motor pods had begun to turn. All of the lights in the room were on, and every detail of the place was well lit. The power beam from the transmitter to the receiver was solid and constant. Ripples of power pulsed outwards a short distance around the receiver's base.

"I wish I had thought to bring the Kodak box," Hans sighed aloud. "Okay, everyone ... spike your lever and meet me at the door." They all drove iron spikes into the slot under the lever they had pulled, effectively jamming it in the "on" position. It would not be easy for anyone coming behind them to turn this off. They were committed.

Hans, Arietta and Annika sprinted for the door leading out of the so-called "firing room" and Hans grabbed the pull-rope for the pulley mechanism. He nodded to Annika and Arietta and then pulled the rope.

"Now we run like madmen and hope we have not just outsmarted ourselves."

"Black Coat, Blackheart"

Diary Entry For July 12th, 1888

Everything has changed since last I wrote. I barely recognize the world I live in. I am sitting in the relative quiet of the Captain's Cabin at a desk I have stood in front of many times. This is the first time I have sat at its chair. The greatcoat of a twice dead man who I now am, barely fits me. I wonder if this is not prophetic in a way.

We have likely crossed a Rubicon of sorts. The Temple of Min, one of the most amazing marvels of the ancient world, has been rendered inert after a most spectacular display of its power. I intend to tell the Allies that the Temple was a water-filled ruins when we found it and is of no danger or interest to anyone. Hopefully, they will accept that answer from us with little question.

I am now the Captain of the Bloody Rose. Micheal O'Raedy is dead, and the only thing that seemed to make sense at the time was for me to assume command. Piet Aldebert is dead and while I regret the barbarity of the demonstration that took his life, I do not regret his decision to volunteer. So, as of this afternoon, I am now known to the world at large as Blackheart of the Bloody Rose. I note with some sobriety that this is unlikely to be a development either my mother or father approves of. I can only guess at what Uncle Orel might think.

Once we were certain that the Temple would never be used as a weapon by anybody, we made for the Nile. We managed to finish off our centre-line motor pod in our race to the ravine yesterday and thus only were making seventy knots when we reached the delta. We were almost immediately attacked by a pair of Russian frigates that were loitering in the area, apparently looking for us.

It was a violent and brutal fight. I distinctly recalled Alexi's advice to me when I first joined the crew concerning my Right of Passage; show off. I chose that as my philosophy in this engagement. We blew one to scrap and I personally led the boarding of the second. Annika was later somewhat opinionated about my choice of actions, but I firmly believe that the crew now understands that it is business as usual for the Bloody Rose. The face may have changed, but Blackheart is still their Captain.

Unfortunately, during the battle we lost another motor pod. As such we are running on sail over the Mediterranean on a westerly course for the night to allow the engineers to make repairs. We will be in sore trouble if come the morning hours we are unable to make better than forty knots.

*****

Muddy water had already begun to trickle down the stairs as they passed the skeletons they had first seen last evening. Rain drops the size of a man's hand poured in sheets from the grey-black sky.

"This is just like a Caribbean fall storm," Arietta shouted over the roar of the rain.

Khadija was stunned at what she saw. She gaped a long moment before finally saying "I have never seen anything like this before."

"It would seem we miscalculated," Hans laughed as he gazed out at the curtain of rain before them.

"The timer probably worked fine ..." Annika shouted her reply. "What we did not allow for is that it took us four hours to get down there. Even twice as fast a return would have been two hours, not one."

"Well ... we are here now," Hans said wryly. "Let us go. It has been raining like this for at least an hour now. We have no idea how big this storm is, and I have no interest in being caught in the bottom of a ravine in a monsoon."

They slogged through the beating rain, having been soaked to the bone in a matter of a few moments. The sand had long ago become mud and the rain water was beginning to pool and form streams. The actual oasis pond had begun to overflow its basin as new rivers poured into it from all points of the compass.

Waterfalls streamed and cascaded down the ravine walls. Visibility was poor between the storm cloud and the time of day. They moved carefully in the increasing gloom, collectively disinterested in floundering face-first in mud.

"Captain! Look!" one of the Gunner-Marines shouted, pointing back the way they had come.

They looked back over their shoulders and were amazed to a momentary standstill. A distance behind the ruins, a streaming column of blue and yellow phosphorescence reached from the ground into the sky. The energy seemed to be pouring into the dense clouds overhead.

Hans wiped rivulets of rain water from his face and pushed his hair from his eyes. It seemed to him that the storm was consuming the energy being fed into it. He thought that he could see arcs of lightning, both electrical and aether, lancing through the cloud.

"Amazing," Hans said with a shake of his head. "I doubt I shall ever see the like again in my life."

Arietta nodded at him. "It is such pity that we were never in a position to see how those Aether Collectors worked ... that would be something that would change the world."

"The only good news," Annika said with a bitter laugh, "is that no one is going to believe a word of this, so we do not need to worry about being blamed." Everyone laughed in the sheeting rain for a moment and then moved on towards where they thought the pirate ship waited for them.

After what seemed to be a long time, they emerged from the storm. The rain tapered off suddenly and it felt like stepping through a curtain. They looked back behind them and then ahead. Hans looked up at the stars and then back in their direction of travel.

"About a mile or so left to travel, Captain-Gunner?" he asked.

Annika nodded at him, after tousling her drenched hair for a moment to dry it somewhat. "*Da*. About that."

"So the storm is about two miles wide, then ... relatively compact and very intense," Hans said thoughtfully. "If we had dialled the wind up to a fury to go along with it, I can see how that would ruin an afternoon of sailing on the Nile or the Mediterranean very handily."

"It is coming down at about an inch or so an hour in there," Annika said. "That is going to be an awful lot of water funnelling into the ravine."

Arietta nodded as they walked towards where the *Bloody Rose* would be waiting for their return. "Another hour or so and the water will be pouring like a rapids down the stairs. An hour or so after that, I expect the water will reach the Battery Lake and the minimum result we should see is the storm choke itself to death as the power runs out."

"If that is all that happens," Hans countered, "then I will be sending the Captain-Gunner with half the contents of our powder magazine to ensure that the entry passage as far as the spitting statue room is erased from existence."

*****

"So what is your plan when we get back to the ship, *Kapitan*?" Annika asked after a few minutes of walking in silence. Hans was aware that everyone was interested in his answer.

"Get us all into dry clothes and then immediately get the entire crew onto the weather deck and tell the truth," Hans said gruffly after a moment. "Michael O'Raedy died a hero's death battling stone automatons and that I am taking command unless anyone wishes to contest the matter."

"And if someone does? Like Nando or Aldebert?" Arietta asked pointedly.

"Then I beat them to the deck and leave them in a condition that requires Koblinski's care for a day or two," Hans said, trying to sound more sure of that answer than he felt.

"You have done an excellent job getting us out of that hole in the ground alive, Hans," Arietta said carefully.

"But?" Hans asked with a lofted brow.

She chuckled ruefully at his tone. "... but are you sure this is what you really want?"

"Why would it not be?" Khadija asked defensively.

"It is not the sort of job that you take or quit on impulse, Khadija," Annika said with a rough tone. "Once he gets aboard and the crew agrees that he is Blackheart, then he has lives and destinies that are his responsibility."

Hans stopped walking and turned around sharply. "Is the problem that you two do not believe I can do the job, then?" he demanded as everyone else came to a stop.

Annika and Arietta looked at each other and then back to Hans. "I know you have the ability to do as good a job as Michael O'Raedy did, in your own way, Hans. So did he," Arietta said flatly, setting her hands to her hips and looking rather stern in the starlit gloom. "The question is if you think you are ready for this burden? You are still a young man and relatively new to this way of life. If you tell me this is what you want with your heart and your soul and you are ready, I will not doubt you."

"... but I notice you have not actually done so," Annika said pointedly. Hans and his two friends stared at each other in the desert night. Khadija stood off to a side, not far from Hans; her bearing and stance gave indication of her discontent with the developing dissent. Daniels, Kenneth and the three other Gunner-Marines looked somewhat uncertain of what was unfolding.

"Listen to me, then. All of you ..." Hans said, anger clear in his features. "I did not throw aside my nicely planned life as the heir to the Sauder empire to stop half-way in my life as a pirate. This is who I am, this is the life I lead and unless any of you can give me one credible name aboard that scow that can do this job better than I can, then this is what I am going to do! I do not have to be the best gunner! I do not have to be the best engineer! I do not have to be the best navigator! I do not have to be the best ship handler!" he growled, pacing like an aggravated panther.

"I need to be able to get all of those people to believe in me! That is the job of Blackheart. I watched Michael O'Raedy for the past few months. I watched him like a hawk, trying to figure out what the bag-bleeding Hell it was that made people like you ... and me ... want to please him and feel like we had achieved something in his eyes."

"I figured it out. Today in fact," he continued, gesturing as paced. Everyone seemed taken aback by his intensity and were listening raptly. "He set a standard just above our reach and challenged us to go ahead and do it anyway. And then, it became such a habit for us all, that we would do it for him automatically! He just stood to the side, kept us pointed in the right direction, gave us praise and the odd veiled threat to keep us sharp, and let us go."

Hans pointed at Arietta. "When you were trying to figure out how those blade-thrower traps worked, Chief ... whose idea was that?"

"Mine," she admitted.

"What did O'Raedy do to help?"

"Nothing. He stayed out of my way and let me work," she said with a nod.

"And you, Captain-Gunner. Whose idea was it for you to take the Gunner-Marines ahead and find out if those two pole-arm statues were actually traps?" Hans demanded.

"Mine," she admitted.

"What did O'Raedy do to help?" he repeated.

"Nothing. He stayed out of my way and let me work," she said with a grin as she echoed Arietta's words. "Oh ... he told me to be careful. Like that was an option," Annika laughed.

"He let the right people with the right skills and the right encouragement get the job done and then praised you for it," Hans said, waving his arms grandly. "That is the Blackheart we respected. The man we would all fight to the death for. The man we would do the insane for ... think about it this absurd situation we are in! A bunch of bloody pirates hired as privateers by the English government to play secret agent games, battle the Russian Empire by proxy, conduct diplomacy with the local Amir, explore a three thousand year old Temple that the resources of two Empires had not yet found, weather its defences, unlock it secrets, and ensure the Russians do not get their hands on it ... think about that! For pirates? That is insane as a mission!"

He looked at them all, having stopped pacing and was now tapping his foot on the ground as though giving a lecture. "AND WE JUST DID IT," he roared at them, his voice echoing in the night. There was a long pause as they all stared at Hans and he looked at each of them in turn. "... so give me one ... just one name ... of anyone else on that scow that you think can do that job better than I can. If you cannot, then this is who I am, this is the life I lead and Blackheart is my name."

There was a long period of relative silence, with the only noise being the evening desert wind and the sound of the storm at their backs. Hans opened his mouth to speak as a dull rumble reached the edge of their hearing. The pirates started looking around as they sound grew louder.

"Captain!   Look!" Khadija shouted, pointing back towards the storm. They all looked where she pointed and their eyes went wide in horror.

The streaming column of blue and yellow phosphorescence that reached from the ground into the sky had become a violent torrent. The energy seemed to be tearing into the dense clouds overhead, which in turn seemed to be rife with destructive arcs of power. Secondary arcs of violent discharges leapt back to the ground, causing substantial explosions which were clearly visible through the storm. The rumble was now both audible and physical, with the ground beneath their feet trembling.

"The Battery Lake ... it is discharging all of its energy! Run! Get out of the ravine!" Arietta shouted.

"You heard her! Move!" Hans shouted. They ran for their lives. After only a few moments three pulsing shocks rippled through the ground. Hans looked over his shoulder to see an area greater than the width of the ravine erupt hundreds of feet straight into the air in a mammoth blast.

The shockwave hit them with the force of running headlong into a stone wall. They were all sent tumbling to the ground like pitched ragdolls. Hans heard shouts of surprise and cries of pain all around him. Slabs of rocks, sheets of hot sand, steaming globs of water, and shredded vegetation rained down around them. One of the Gunner-Marines gave a distant scream as a boulder landed beside him and then rebounded, striking his leg. The roaring violence surrounded them and filled their senses to excess for an eternity of seconds.

Hans forced himself to his feet as quickly as he could, looking around. "They must have felt that all the way to Cairo," Hans said, looking back towards where the oasis had been. The others stood and Hans directed them to help the injured man.

"It looks like God took a shovel and dug a hole," the injured man said, through gritted teeth. Hans had to agree. The detonation had pulled a cone-shaped chunk of the earth to the level of the underground lake and heaved it into the sky. The storm was still pouring rain, but was now fading quickly, bereft of the unnatural source of its origin. Hans noted that the ground around the edge of the crater was collapsing periodically as the earth settled from its upheaval. He was fairly certain they were far enough to be safe from that concern.

"That's broken," Arietta said grimly as she examined the injury left by the flying boulder the size of a harvest pumpkin. She pulled a pair of foot-long metal spikes from her gear and used them as splints as she worked to set the man's leg.

"What is your name, man?" Hans asked.

"Morgan White, Sir," the English Gunner-Marine replied gamely.

"We will get you back to the ship, *Hern* White. Your chums will help, and if they cannot do it, I will do it myself. *Döktor* Koblinski will have you back on your feet in no time."

"Thank-you, sir."

*****

It took them some time to finally reach the *Bloody Rose*. They got the broken-legged Gunner-Marine aboard via derrick, winch and sling and then Hans had him taken straight to the sickbay.

It took no time at all for the word to spread through the ship that the expedition had returned without Michael O'Raedy, and that Hans Sauder now wore the black greatcoat. Amram Nando, the Spanish Deck Officer, confronted him in his sleeping bay as he was getting changed.

"What happened, Sauder?" the Spaniard asked with a sharp look in his eyes, leaning in the doorway. While he did not seem outwardly confrontational, Hans noted that the other man was effectively blocking the door.

"I need you to trust me, Amram," Hans replied as he wiped the grime and dirt from his face with a cloth. He watched the other man in the mirror over the fold-away desk.

"Oh? And why is that, Sauder?"

"O'Raedy died in a battle with the Temple's defences. Someone needed to lead the expedition out of there, so I did it. In a few minutes, I am going to walk out of here and explain to the crew what has happened. I need you to get everyone onto the weather deck, just like O'Raedy used to do for announcing pay shares. The Traditions have to be respected, but we need to ensure that we are under control as quickly as possible. The Russians will make short work of us if we are fighting amongst ourselves."

"I see. I agree with your conclusion. I will muster the crew, as you ask," the aristocrat turned pirate said. He picked at something on his sleeve for a moment as Hans pulled a clean shirt on. "Do you intend to continue to wear the Coat?" Nando asked, tilting his head. Hans had no idea what was in those eyes as they gazed at each other via the mirror.

"Yes," Sauder said, as he turned to face the Spaniard, continuing to meet the other man's gaze. "I do. You are an irreplaceable asset to this crew, Amram ... I hope you will stay on with us."

"I will see you on the weather deck in a few minutes, *Capitán*," the Spaniard said as he pushed himself off the door frame and departed. Hans stared at the door for a few moments.

*****

Hans stood at the quarter deck railing, with the other officers. Gas lamps and electric lights illuminated the officers and the crew before them. The desert air was chill, enough so that periodically Hans could see a wisp of his breath. For now, he once again wore his grey greatcoat. The black greatcoat with gold trim of Blackheart was folded neatly behind them on a chair. He would don it again once the crew affirmed him, but for now, it risked giving offence to the very men and women he needed the support of.

The *Bloody Rose* had her masts and sails unfurled, with her motor pods retracted. She was running silent and lazy before the wind on westerly course. The planes and helm had been "locked and lashed" to keep her at a slow climb on this course while the crew met on her decks for a historic moment. All posts were abandoned and the entire crew were present.

It was clear to Sauder that there was a significant amount of unrest and concern amongst them. Their futures were at stake; O'Raedy had been a singularly exemplar instance of a successful pirate captain. His combination of personal charisma, hard-nosed cunning and ruthless leadership had made this one of the best ships to be upon and his crew knew it. Some of them had come from other crews, having jumped from another ship to the *Bloody Rose* at common ports of call when the opportunity presented itself.

Change brought uncertainty. The wrong man with the mantle of Blackheart could spell ruin for all of them. Too timid a captain would mean missed opportunities and reduced wealth. Too reckless would mean prison and death. O'Raedy had always managed to balance perfectly. Now, all of that was cast aside.

"Captain-Rockets, are you going to explain what happened?" the Captain-Gunner asked quietly.

"I think that should come from you or the Chief Engineer. I am, after all, one of the people who stands to profit most by O'Raedy's death. It will not come well from my mouth," Hans replied.

"I have this," Arietta said and stepped forward to the railing. She had donned her bladed bracers and heavy boots before she had come to the weather deck, Hans noted. In fact, all the officers were visibly armed, save Koblinski and Coline.

"*Bloody Rose*! Listen to me," the statuesque Italian-Ethiope commanded. The buzz on the weather deck from the crew fell silent from as she spoke. She was a commanding presence when she chose to be, Hans reflected, both in body and voice. "As you might have seen by that little flash in the sky earlier ... we have succeeded in what we came to do. Neither the Allies nor the Russians will never use that thing to start a war, or turn it on us!"

A shout went up and cheers and applause rippled through the crew. As it subsided, she continued speaking. "Our victory has cost us dearly, however," she faltered a moment and bit her lip. Hans could see the sadness in her normally bright eyes. Perhaps she and Michael O'Raedy had not been a couple as he and Annika were, but it was clear to the young German they had been close friends and this loss had struck her deeply.

"Our victory has cost us dearly," she repeated. "Captain Michael O'Raedy is dead. He died battling automatons of stone and technology, buying the rest of us time with his sacrifice to figure out how to best them." She paused a moment, letting the verification of what everyone had heard as rumour sink in. "He died a hero, *Bloody Rose*! We will drink to his memory once we are out of this mess!" she declared and a ripple of affirmation went through the crowd.

Annika stepped forward beside Arietta. "Michael O'Raedy's death leaves us with no *Kapitan*," she stated. "The Traditions and Lore say that any man or woman amongst us now may speak to claim that title. If you speak to claim the name of Blackheart, you must answer challenges from all that come forward," she said, loosening her cutlass in its scabbard. "Is there anyone here that would lay claim to the title of *Kapitan*, and the name of Blackheart of the *Bloody Rose*?"

*****

Hans stepped away from the officers he stood with and descended the stairs from the quarterdeck to the weather deck where the rest of the crew were gathered. He was keenly aware of the eyes of everyone upon him. A respectful space parted for him as he moved through the men and women assembled there, to stand at the guardrail.

"Listen to me!" Hans shouted at the assembled pirates. "Listen to me! Any man who wants to be Captain ... Our Traditions say that man must prove his claim to all challengers. I will do that ... Out there," he bellowed, pointing out past the guardrail to the mast and rigging where his smallsword had hung what seemed to be so long ago. He turned, took a few steps back, ran and leapt over the guardrail.

He landed in the rigging and swiftly climbed up and stood on the mast. He gripped the rigging with one hand and the other drew his scimitar. "HERE is where I first joined you. HERE is where I will have words with any of you that say you have better claim than I. I say that there is no man or woman among you that are better fit to lead, to fight and to be the legend that is Blackheart of the *Bloody Rose*! If you want to dispute that ..." he gave an ugly grin and flicked the blade. "I have killed a hundred men in the past few days. You will not add much to the Devil's tab."

There was a pause as the crew looked amongst each other and muttered. The Scotsman MacIssac stepped forward with his belaying pin on his left shoulder and his treacherous gap-toothed grin. He stared fixedly at Hans as he walked to the railing. He paused and they stared at each other for a long moment. It felt like a lifetime had passed to Hans since he fought with the rowdy Scotsman for his Right of Passage. Hans waited for the MacIssac to make his claim.

"A pirate captain has te be able te lead his boys an' girls te victory," MacIssac said, turning to face the crew. "... An' this man has dun tha'. A captain pirate has te be willin' te spill blood ... his, his crew's and his enemy's ... te git the job done. An' this man has dun tha'," he declared, walking back and forth in front of the guardrail, gesturing with the pin in his left hand at the crew. "A pirate captain has te be able te spit in the eye of Fate and git away with it. An' this man has dun tha'. A pirate captain has te be able te make another pirate stand taller, live bolder and fight harder. An' this man has dun tha'."

MacIssac pointed at Sauder with his bloody belaying pin. "This man showed mercy when he could a' killed. He's been generous with his crew mates when he could a' been greedy. He 'as lead and fought 'ard when he could a' left us. An' old chum of mine, Blauchuk, died defending this man 'cause he made that bull of a man believe even a damn Dragon was fair game for a pirate of the *Bloody Rose*. I say tha' man ... tha' man is my Captain. An' if ye wants to dispute that with him ... you'll bloody 'ave te get past me first!" he declared as he turned to face the assembled pirates. It was very clear to everyone that the Scotsman was deadly serious.

Annika stepped away from the other officers and made her way down the stairs. She cast a challenging look at the crew around her and they all seemed to take a step backwards. The corner of her lip curled in amusement and she walked directly towards MacIssac. They stared at each other, and there was an ugly break in the heavy silence as both of them drew swords.

"Listen to ME, now, *Bloody Rose*," Annika commanded, her gaze now beyond MacIssac and on Hans. She smirked, backed up two steps, and sheathed her sword, much to the Scotsman's relief. She turned to the crew. "Being the man the world calls *Kapitan* Blackheart of the *Bloody Rose* takes courage, cunning, brains and passion. I have seen the pirate we call Hans Sauder show all of those things. I say there is no one else I will call Blackheart so long as he lives. So if you wish to fight my *Kapitan*," she snarled as she again drew her sword, "before you get past MacIssac, you will have to get past me." She stood beside the Scotsman, facing the crew. Her eyes flashed a murderous challenge.

Arietta came down the stairs from the quarterdeck, still wearing her bladed bracers. She strode confidently to stand before MacIssac and Nadezhda looking at them both silently. She nodded to them each in turn in a visible sign of respect. Without a word, she then moved to stand beside Annika, facing the rest of the assembled crew. She folded her arms across her chest and her body gave a clear sense of challenge. The rest of the crew looked around at each other, clearly aware of the gauntlet before them.

Piet Aldebert walked out of the crowd with his cutlass and pistol drawn. He had come down the stairs at the opposite side of the quarterdeck and had made sure everyone got out of his way as he crossed the crowded deck. He stopped outside the easy range of any of Hans' avowed guardians.

"Step aside, ladies," the Dutchman ordered, looking at them contemptuously. "He has to defend himself. That is what the Traditions say. Pirates cannot afford to have that squalling rich brat a weeping heap of remorse every time he has to spill a bit of ..."

The Dutchman's head snapped backwards to the sound of thunder and blood spattered the deck. The body dropped to the deck like a puppet without strings. Everyone looked towards the sound of the gunshot. Hans stood with his arm straight and level, with a plume of gun smoke trailing from the shotgun barrel of his pistol.

"You will all notice I am not a weeping heap of remorse," he stated coldly, re-cocking the hammer on the revolver. "Is there anyone else who wishes to test my resolve? I am Blackheart. They will hurt you, to stop you from getting to me. I will kill you. Without hesitation." There was a pregnant silence.

"Alright, you scallywags ..." Hans barked. "Are we going to spend all night staring at each other, or are we going to go give the Russians everything they deserve for the hell we have been through so far? Who is with me?" He thrust his sword arm into the air, the blade clenched in his fist, glinting and glittering in the ship's lights.

Like a single, savage animal, the crew roared its approval.

*****

The *Bloody Rose* spent the next few hours under sail as her crew "Met the Captain", per the Lore and Traditions. Hans was taken through the entire ship by the officers and he spoke to every pirate aboard, regardless of rank. He heard grievances, both old and new; received suggestions, both insightful and amusing; and, was given a list of defects and requirements for the future, both real and imagined.

Afterwards, Chief Bridges unlocked the door to the Captain's Mess with his second spare key and gave it to Hans. "Well, Captain, I have already had the lads move your belongings here, Sir. I have already tidied up Mister O'Raedy's personal belongings, so you need not worry about that. I am sure the last thing you want right now is to be contending with his underwear drawer, as it were," the portly Chief Steward said with a laugh.

Hans could not help but chuckle. "Thank-you, Chief. Do you have a minute to speak with me?"

Bridges eyed the young German, now his Captain, with some clear amusement. "Sir, my job is to have a minute to speak with you. Consider me your extra set of hands and eyes. Tell me what you need and I will do my best to find it out, get it done, or tell you why you are off your bloody rocker, Sir."

Hans laughed aloud and nodded. "Fine then, Chief. Come in and close the door."

The two men went in and Hans unbuckled the poorly fitting greatcoat. He dropped it on the back of the chair at the desk. He looked around and shook his head.

"You are surprised, sir ... and I think you might find it amusing that I am not, nor would be Mister O'Raedy."

"Pardon?" Hans blinked, turning around to look at the Englishman.

"Aye, Sir. Mister O'Raedy had commented to me a few times he had woken up and the first thing he had thought was *'I wonder if this is the day Sauder will try and take it from me'*," Bridges said amiably.

Hans stared at the other man in shock for a few speechless seconds. "He ... really thought I would try and usurp him?" Hans said slowly.

"Mister Sauder ... in Pirate parlance, that is not called 'usurping' ... it is a 'self-promotion'. It is a perfectly reasonable part of the entire life of Piracy ... if the Captain cannot keep order then he or she ought not to be Captain."

Hans thought about that a moment. "What are the rules for self-promotion?"

Bridges chortled merrily. "Still sharp as a whip, Sir. I always did like that about you. Same idea as a Right of Passage, really, Sir ... make it clear you have an issue to discuss with the current Captain, or Captain-Gunner, or Chief-Engineer, or what have you, and then have it out with them. We would all prefer no one die in the process, but these things do happen. The winner gets or keeps the job. The loser keeps his or her yap shut until at least after the next Month and a Pay."

"I take it that cheating is frowned upon ... such as shooting the current Captain in the back?" Hans asked in a bit of gallows humour.

"Oh, aye sir. That sort of foolishness can get you strung off the starboard side mast for a run through some trees, unless the rest of the crew was thinking it needed doing anyway. That said ... no need to be less than vigilante. A proper pirate Captain needs to know what his crew is thinking and who is eyeing his job."

Sauder nodded, thinking for a moment. "Who do I need to worry about, Chief?"

"Well, you shot your number one problem ... a bit drastic, but effective. Mister O'Raedy would have liked your flair. Your number two problem is Mister Nando ... except that he has been walking the Flats for the past thirty minutes putting the fear of all that is Holy in the crew about crossing you or causing trouble. Unless, of course, they want him to pull their '*heaving lungs out through their mouths*' and force them to '*chew slowly*'."

Hans blinked. "He is saying that?"

"Aye, sir. He seems to like you. At least for now. The Deck Officer is a bit fickle at times, but he is comfortable here and you represent some stability, so he is all for that. A bit of a Blue Blood, he is ... he likes his chaos and murder nice and orderly, he does."

Hans shook his head with a laugh. "I will keep that in mind," he said amusedly. He sighed and paused for a moment. "What is the big worry right now, Chief?"

Bridges thought for a moment before answering. "Mostly that you are going to cock this up, Sir, and that either the Russians will kill us or the Allies will bugger us."

"Not unexpected. That is pretty much my big worry right now," Hans said with a bitter laugh.

"Just be yourself, sir; be the sort of man that had the brass balls to take a bunch of Gunner-Marines to go '*shoot pheasant in a hurricane*', and you will do fine. Mister O'Raedy often said that the hardest part he had to deal with was second guessing his gut. The second guess was always made with fear and doubt, and the gut always ran on that edge of the possible."

Hans sat in the chair at the desk and thought for a moment about how that felt. Like the coat, it really was not yet comfortable. However, that would change after a period of adjustment.

"How are we for money, Chief?"

"Well, I can get you the heap of big numbers later, but the real answer to your question is that even if the Allies do not pay us the balance of what they owe us, we have enough in our coffers to pay for the refit and sit idle for three months," Bridges replied.

"At what share price? That is what the boys live for ... that announcement," Hans said, thoughtfully.

"A keen eye, Captain, a very keen eye. Two and three-quarter pounds Stirling per share. That is five pounds a month for most of the crew, for doing nought more than drinking and whoring, Sir, and is considered acceptable for time alongside. We certainly will want a couple of plump birds to pluck as soon as we get off the dock, though, Sir. A lot of the lads will be pretty much broke by then and itchy for a five pound share again."

Hans thought about that. "Very well. If we bag an average merchantman before we make for Persia, do you think we can get that up to an even three pounds? We are going to need to recruit and atop that I do not want our crew thinking about jumping the gunwale for some other ship."

"That happens less often than you might think, Sir ... when you do that, you lose all your share seniority on the new ship, unless you can get at least three folks to in your new crew to vouch for you. So unless things are really miserable, your more senior bodies will stay where they are, and just hope for it to get better," Bridges explained.

"Interesting. Keep your ear to the deck, Mister Bridges ... let me know if you hear of anyone with more than six months seniority on this ship getting itchy feet," Hans said, leaning back in his chair, steepling his fingers as he thought.

"Of course, Sir. Anything else you need from me right away?"

"Yes. Make sure breakfast tomorrow is memorable for everyone and tell me where I fill my coffee flask now that I am sleeping here ... I expect I will be up for a while, tonight."

*****

The sunrise found the *Bloody Rose* passing Cairo at high altitude, heading for the Nile Delta. She was running on two motors with the red-golds of the sky above and the blue-green glory of one of the most historic rivers in the world below her.

Hans was shaving when the bells and whistles of the action alarm stared ringing. He cut himself as he started, and said something in German that his sister would have been shocked by. He went to a voicepipe that led to the Steering House and called up.

"Sau ... Blackheart here ... what is going on?" he questioned.

"Two military ships, ahead, high, starboard, closing, Captain," Jeffery Wilton replied. "They have their backs to the sun so we cannot make out flags, Sir ... But Miss Tillie and I both think it is very odd for anyone's military to be this close to Egypt, Sir, so we are coming to Stations."

"Good job, Mister Wilton. Take us on an opening course and cut speed one-third. Let us see if they are hunting or not. I will be right up," Hans replied.

"Aye-Aye, Sir," came the reply.

Hans looked at his lopsided shave and sighed. It would have to wait. He washed his face, towelled off, and got ready to head to the Steering House.

*****

"Captain-Gunner, what have we got?" Hans asked as he walked into the Steering House.

"Two Russian ships, frigate sized, closing steadily. I would guess they will be ready to fire in a few minutes with their bow guns," Annika replied.

"Miss Tillie, where are we?"

"Twenty miles inland west of Al Jiza, near Cairo, Captain. We are running a roughly north-northwesterly course; Alexandria is due north of us by about seventy miles," the Englishwoman answered.

Hans glanced at the airspeed and altitude indicators. "Bring us up to seventy knots, bring us port ten degrees heading. Take us up to two thousand feet, even. Have Propulsion get the lifters running if they have not already done so. Captain-Gunner?"

"*Kapitan*?" Annika questioned.

"My intention is to soften them up with rockets and mines, then reverse course on them. If we can, we will fly between the pair. Once we see what the results of our first attack are, I want you to load solid ball towards the least damaged of the two targets and cinderball towards most damaged. If all goes as I desire, the cinderball salvo will finish off the victim of the rocket and the solid ball will be a good start on the other. From there, we will see what we have left to work with. Does that sound viable?" Hans questioned.

Annika thought about it for a moment. "You intend to commit to a boarding, *Da*?"

"*Ja*. After a round of grapeshot or two," he nodded.

"It should work. I will make ready the guns," she responded and turned to her voicepipes.

The *Bloody Rose* accelerated, made a slight turn away from her pursuers and began to climb. A pair of Sargasso balloon-mines went over the back railing in rapid succession about a half-minute after she picked up speed. Those were followed by a second pair another half-minute afterwards.

The results were predictable; each frigate used a salvo of grapeshot from her bow guns to wipe the pairs of drifting menaces from their path. As soon as the blossom of smoke and shrapnel had cleared from the second pair, the *Bloody Rose* fired a Cudahawk airship-to-airship rocket from her stern rack. Both ships veered apart from each other, unable to use their now empty bow-guns to try and stop the onrushing weapon. This gave the entire broadside of each ship as a much easier to hit target to Hans, guiding the rocket from the Steering House on the privateer. The kerosene-propelled monster struck one of the vessels just forwards of midships and exploded.

It looked to Hans as through the Russian ship had been struck with a giant hammer. The vessel buckled visibly inwards and then upwards at the point of impact and explosion. The blast threw one of the cargo-sized deck hatches, plus several gun-doors, as well as innumerable planks and timbers into the air around the ship. The pieces began a long fall to the ground below even as billows of smoke and fire poured out of the torn-open wounds from which they originated.

The ship suddenly split and broke apart completely where it had buckled. The severed halves of the burning hull began plummeting to the earth, leaving long black trails of thick smoke to mark their trajectories.

The remaining Russian frigate, forced broadside to the stern of her intended prey, ran out her guns in an instant and fired a salvo of ball and chain out of her heaviest and longest-reaching guns. The *Bloody Rose* shook and shivered as the Russian gunners marked hits on their target. Smoke streamed from one of her wounds. The pirate wheeled over and fired in return, then reversed her track and fired again in the "S-Figure Advance" of which her Master-Gunner was so fond.

"Bloody Hell," Hans cursed. "No plan of battle survives contact with the enemy, indeed. A few hits with cinderball ... that is not what I wanted!"

"There is no other way to unload the guns safely, *Kapitan*," Annika countered. "There is little point just firing the load into empty air. That is a military ship; the cinderballs will give them something to distract them while they fight the fires, but it will not prevent us from boarding. We are loading for ball and chain to starboard and then grapeshot to port."

The two vessels traded broadsides as they closed on each other, striking hard. The Russian was firing for structural damage, using solid balls which dug deep into the *Bloody Rose*, shattering everything in their path. The Pirate, on the other hand, used its strikes to damage control surfaces, shred precious cables and conduits for power and communication, and kill or maim the Russian Gunner-Marines at their posts.

The *Bloody Rose* fired another broadside of grapeshot at the same time as the Russian fired again. An explosion of fire and smoke poured out of the Pirate's stern quarter at the same time one of her motor pods exploded in a rain of bearings, coiled wire and other parts. The Russian guns on that side of the ship fell silent and the *Bloody Rose* fired her harpoon grapples, snaring the other ship.

"Captain-Gunner, make bells and whistles for a boarding and then come with me. We have a boarding to lead," Hans ordered.

*****

"We keep on beating them, and they keep not learning!" Hans shouted to the crew as the two ships drew together. Bursts from the Gatling guns had prevented any of the Russian Marines from taking to their own weather deck in preparation of the boarding. The bow Gatling periodically streamed bullets at the Russian bridge, blowing out windows and keeping heads down.

"One at a time, two at a time, convoy at a time! It does not matter! We are the pirates of the *Bloody Rose* and we smell blood and plunder! Come on!" Hans roared as the two ships ground together. He was the first one over the railing, scimitar and pistol in hand. The doors and hatches of the Russian ship flew open and the Russian Marines poured out, firing pistols and shouting in defiance.

The pirates and Russians collided head-on like a pair of steam locomotives. Bullets, blood, bodies and sanity flew in all directions. Hans and Annika accounted for almost a dozen Russians between them in the initial seconds as they emptied their pistols. Swords crashed into skin, steel and timber once pistols were emptied and the range became too close.

The initial exchange of pistol fire had been in the Russian's favour, but the grapeshot and Gatling guns had exacted a horrible price from their target. The tide of battle pushed the pirates back to almost the gunwales of the two joined ships. Hans gave a bellow of "follow me!" and literally ran the man ahead of him over as he charged forward. The pirates rallied and what had been something akin to a conventional set of lines of battle was suddenly a sprawling melee that covered the weather deck of the Russian ship. It was ruthless brawl in a matter of moments.

Hans dropped the man he was fighting with an elbow across the face and looked around. He found what we was looking for a the same time as the Russian Captain saw him. They locked eyes, levelled weapons, and ran at each other shouting in their native tongues.

Their swords rang together at their furied meeting and they traded fist blows as well. The Russian captain knocked Hans sprawling only to have Sauder kick the legs out from under him. The pair rapidly regained their footing and clashed again. Hans narrowly dodged a pair of expert swings and it occurred to him he might have bitten off more than he could chew.

The Russian Captain was easily ten years Hans' senior and he had learned the lessons of its offered experience well. He was a superlative swordsman and was stubbornly refusing to fall for any of the tricks Hans threw at at him. Indeed, Hans fell into a couple of the Russian's offered traps, with narrow escapes that were made by speed alone. The other man was fighting hard and gaining ground, forcing his younger opponent more and more onto a defensive. That was until the tip of a cutlass was driven through his back and out his chest by the Scotsman, MacIssac.

"Not my Cap'ain, you dun't, Ivan!" he snarled as the Russian collapsed to the stained deck.

Within minutes, the battle turned to a rout with the fighting going on below the decks of the Russian frigate at close quarters. A few minutes after that, Hans learned that the engine room and bridge were under their control. They had won.

"Get us to five thousand and on a slow course for the Med. Lets see what we bought with our blood today," he ordered as he wiped his own bloodied nose.

*****

"Yes, Captain-Gunner?" Hans asked wearily as he sat in his chair behind his desk. The salvage and looting work were proceeding apace, two or three of the other crew aboard the Russian ship had jumped the gunwale, and initial estimates indicated she was essentially fresh out of port. Her holds, magazines and tanks were full, and her coffers had two months pay for her crew in them. Of course, the Devil's Shares would count nine more, with another dozen crew in their hammocks with red tags.

Annika should have been outside, supervising the work to be done, in conjunction with Nando. Instead, she had all but stormed into his Mess after Sauder had bade her enter. She was evidently in a mood for a fight, while he for his part was supremely disinterested in the notion.

"What were you trying to prove, Sauder?" she said, crossing her arms across her chest.

"What do you mean, Captain-Gunner? And the name is Blackheart, thank-you."

"I am Annika, you are Hans and I want to know what the salted-water Hell you thought you were doing in that boarding?" she demanded. "You are damn lucky none of those Russians knew to 'shoot the man in the black coat' or you would have been dead in the first ten seconds! What were you doing? Did you take leave of your senses?" she asked, clearly furious with him.

"The crew needed to see that I was unafraid to go in head on, Annika," he sighed. "They needed to be assured that Blackheart might have a different face, but it was going to be business as usual."

"They needed, or you needed?" she questioned with a snarl. "And if you think you were channelling Michael O'Raedy there, you are sorely mistaken. He always got the boys ramped up with a speech as you tried to do and then let a dozen of them or so go charging over before he followed. It gave the other side someone besides him at which to empty their pistols."

"Thank-you, Captain-Gunner. That is more than enough. We can discuss this later. Right now I need you doing your job, which is getting the holds moved as fast as we can before anyone else shows up looking for us. Otherwise, we will be fighting a very tough battle on only one motor pod."

She blinked at him, apparently surprised at her dismissal. Before she said anything in reply he raised a hand to cut her off. "Hans would very much like it if Annika happened by about an hour after evening rounds were done. Right now Captain Blackheart needs Captain-Gunner Nadezhda to return to the weather deck and work a miracle while he tries to figure out what to do in the next twenty four hours that will see us all safely through it. Okay?"

She pursed her lips a moment and he thought she might argue further with him. Then she nodded curtly and departed without further comment.

Hans leaned back in his chair, looked at the ceiling and exhaled loudly. "Please do not let me have just cocked this up, Lord," he asked aloud.

"Into The Wind"

Diary Entry For July 14th, 1888

I am glad for Michael O'Raedy's example of the "Moses Reverse"; fleeing into Egypt when things got too hot over Europe. I fear that without the knowledge today that even Captain O'Raedy would cut and run, the bones of the Bloody Rose and her crew might well have been scattered across the floor of the Mediterranean Ocean. We were nearly baited into chasing a independent-flagged merchant ship into the arms of a Russian flotilla. We narrowly escaped coming under heavy fire and turned our stern and ran. As it was, Russian aeroplanes lobbing rocket-propelled bombs did serious damage to us. We only made good our escape through the outside intervention of the Allied Air Navy.

After watching the awesome display of power as the Allied and Russian battle groups clashed, I am becoming more and more convinced that piracy as we practice it is unofficially tolerated. I have no other explanations for why the Allies have simply not turned some of their humbling firepower upon either us directly or upon the friendly ports that shelter us.

We will be in London in two days. At that time, it is my intention to collect the balance of our reward and immediately make a southward course through western Europe until Gibraltar, and then take an easterly heading along the Mediterranean towards Persia. With luck we will fatten our coffers with a merchantman's holds before we reach Istanbul. I firmly believe that the crew can collectively use the time to put aside some of our personal losses from the past three months.

At the supper meal this evening, it was discussed that the Bloody Rose's legend may be growing by leaps and bounds, but it has been at a terrible cost. Since the month before I first joined the crew, casualties from her adventures have left almost half the crew with less than six months seniority. Compared to less than quarter of the crew this time last year, and it can be easily seen that the Devil has been well paid.

I am told that reality of piracy is that if you can last your first six months on any ship, you are twice as likely to last to your first year on any ship thereafter. Once a pirate has survived their first year in this life, they are essentially above the reach of anything short of catastrophe.

The bitter truth is that as of this morning, the Bloody Rose has narrowly escaped catastrophe four times since I have met her. Each time, she sheds some more of the collective experience and expertise that allows her to cheat the Reaper. One *of these days, at this rate, we will come up short of both skill and luck.*

It is, in part, one of the reasons that Annika pushes her gunners so hard during their morning "gun runs". She knows very well that practice out of a fight makes for fewer mistakes in a fight. I am told that the Bloody Rose is rather odd that she conducts gunnery, boarding and engineering drills regularly. Most pirates and privateers do not, instead choosing to learn in the heat of the moment. Again, the name of Michael O'Raedy is to be found in the success of the Bloody Rose.

I plan to continue firmly in his footsteps.

*****

"Well, Chief? Any good news for me?" Hans asked Arietta as he looked out over the shining waters of the Mediterranean Ocean. To Hans, it currently seemed to be a dancing sea of fire and gold from the combination of the morning's sun rise and a steady westerly breeze. The Italian-Ethiope had just come into the Steering House clutching her coffee flask.

Hans had given the engineers an impossible task to achieve; scrap the two damaged motor pods in twelve hours while on the wing, without the benefits of a dock and come up with one jury-rigged mess that would work well enough to get them to seventy knots. Arietta and the other engineers had been working since sun down last night when they had cut the Russian frigate free at five thousand feet.

As was usual in such matters, the frigate's guns had been spiked, her tanks drained and the bags left bleeding.

She was a doomed ship, destined to drift with the wind to hopefully come down on dry land where her surviving crew might make for home on foot. Of course, walking to Russia from Southern Greece was no minor task, but at least they were alive.

She rubbed at her eyes, fatigued. "You are good for fifty knots cruising on two motors. We can come up to seventy for short periods ... say, thirty minutes every two hours. So we have some spit if we need to run, but otherwise we are motoring on caution, hope and baling wire," she said wearily.

"Good job, Chief," Sauder said in visible relief. "That is great news. Go get some sleep and I will talk to the Chief Steward to make sure that a bit of extra coffee and breakfast makes its way to the Propulsion Room."

Soon after, the Mediterranean Menace was furling her sails, streaming her two mostly working motor pods and turning her bow to a more north-easterly bearing. Free from the constraints of the wind, her pace picked up noticeably as she doubled her speed made good.

Chief Bridges was more than happy to ensure that a bit of extra rations made their way to those individuals – most of the ship's unwounded crew, in fact – that had burned midnight oil in trying to get the battered pirate ship into something akin to a fighting trim.

"A full belly makes most other ills and trials far more tolerable," the portly Bridges had said with a sagely nod.

*****

Mid-morning saw them crossing over mainland Greece at two thousand feet in the air. Ahead of them, a line of cloud was pushing down from the north, threatening messy weather in its wake. Almost immediately, a look-out rang in.

"Captain, Sir," Amram Nando began, "gypsy trader, ahead, port, far, above. We are at two thousand feet by both fix and altimeter, with the the freighter at approximately thirty two hundred. We are coming up on her quarter. She seems to be running parallel to the cloud line at about forty knots."

Hans put his spy glass up and found the "gypsy trader" easily. She was brightly painted, as most were, with a thin plume of steam and smoke from badly run engines marking her flight. "Gypsy traders" were owner-aboard airships that flew wherever fortune and business took them. One day might see them in Norway, the next in Normandy and then on to Naples. Popular fiction of the day had them making money as smugglers, espionage couriers and scenes of torrid romance as they flitted from one exotic port of chance to the next. Hans could never stand to read that sort of drivel; his sister loved them.

"The poor beggar is right on our track. Easy prey," Hans said ruefully. "Make bells and whistles for action, *Fräulein* Redsands and get us up to thirty-five hundred. *Hern* Nando, ask Propulsion for lifters and that fabled thirty minutes at seventy we were told about. We should over take them in ten minutes if all goes well. I do not want them veering into that weather front and forcing us to try to chase them through it."

In short order, the pirates of the *Bloody Rose* were again getting ready to practice their trade. Annika arrived on the bridge and Hans explained to her what was going on.

"She is rather gift-wrapped for us, is she not?" Annika laughed. "Some risk free loot will go over well. Finally some good luck."

"Let us try and be nice about this and fire a broadside of cinderball ahead of them from maximum range with the twelves and eights," Hans said. "The balls exploding in the air ahead of them will hopefully convince them to strike their colours and heave to. No reason to be more cruel about this than required," Hans said.

Annika snorted and gave a wry grin to him. "As you order, *Kapitan*," she replied with a wink and then turned to her range finder and voicepipes.

The *Bloody Rose* heeled over as soon as she was in range and fired. A few seconds later splatters of fire and smoke erupted in the flight path of the gypsy merchant, named the *Charming Prince*. Much to the surprise of the watching pirates, the merchant turned sharply to the north and suddenly accelerated leaving a smear of black smoke and billows of flame pouring out from her stern.

"What the hell?" Hans spat. "She is running for it!"

"She is not only running for it," the Spanish Deck Officer commented as he stared through his spy glass, "she is laying smoke and apparently running rocket motors or something for speed."

"A blockade runner or smuggler," the Russian Brunette said with a nod. "That is the only reason she would have that sort of behaviour."

"Rocket motors? How the hell?!" the German captain exclaimed. "Alright. She is slowing down again. I would say her rocket motors are not something she can run on indefinitely. She has wasted her chance for kindness. Captain-Gunner, hit her. Hard."

"We are going to have to take her at an angle ... the smoke plume she is leaving behind her is making getting a good range on her impossible," Annika announced.

"Helm, touch port five degrees. Planes, take us up to four thousand, stand by to roll on the Captain-Gunner's command," Hans ordered. Smoke screens were only going to be of value in one altitude band. By both climbing and changing course, it took them completely away from the obscuring effects of the smoke.

The *Charming Prince* immediately altered her course to the starboard by almost a quarter turn and began a steep dive. As the *Bloody Rose* turned to bring a broadside to bear, the Gypsy Merchant infuriatingly flattened out and ignited her rockets again and jumped ahead. The salvo of solid ball and chain shot passed harmlessly astern of her.

"Brilliant ship-handling," Nando commented.

"Bloody annoying is more like it. Mister Nando, get us to an intercept course and inform the Propulsion Room to get ready to cut lifters. Lets try an attack dive to cut the gap. This bitch is not getting away," Hans declared.

Five more minutes of chess were played out in the skies over Greece by the predator and her prey. The two ships were trying everything they could think of to outwit the other.   Hans rarely lost at chess, but this game was touching towards a stalemate.

"Captain, Sir," Sarah Redsands spoke up, "Propulsion asked me to remind you that you have at most fifteen minutes left at this speed. A quick guess says we will be getting into that weather up ahead in less than ten."

"We are not letting this little bitch go," Hans snarled in frustration. "We can cut the storm, if we have to. We have done it before ..." he suddenly trailed off, with a thoughtful look on his face. Annika and Amram looked at him. He had a sudden vivid recollection of Arietta telling him once as they chased a Swedish merchant through a storm that "...*If Blackheart has a fault, Signore Sauder, its that once he smells Prey to be taken, he will not give up.*"

"You were completely right, Captain-Gunner," Hans said suddenly. "She was gift-wrapped for us. She is bait for a trap. Helm, bring us around 180 degrees. Planes, take us to two thousand even," Hans ordered. "We are getting out of here before we stroll into what ever is in that weather line. *Fräulein* Redsands, have you been reading up on the manuals for the mines and rockets?"

"Yes, sir!"

"Good. You might well get to use them," Hans said sourly.

"Captain!" Annika called out excitedly. "Lookouts are reporting they think they saw something at the edge of the clouds, and the *Charming Prince* is now turning parallel to the weather line."

"Of course ... they are keeping us in sight. If they were really running, they would have keep going straight into the clouds," the Spaniard said thoughtfully. The pirate ship turned as sharply as she could and regained altitude that had been sacrificed early in the game of chase with the *Charming Prince*. A thin line of blue smoke trailed from the *Bloody Rose*'s motor pods.

A buzzer rang and then rang again as lookouts reported in. "Sir, aft-port and aft-starboard lookouts reporting several ships coming out of the weather line," the sandy-haired Amerindian announced. As one, all the officers in the Steering House turned around with their spyglasses.

"Oh, merciful Mother of God ..." Amram whispered. "I count twelve ... all ships of the line..."

"As do I ... that is a RIAN squadron we nearly flew into," Hans said, his mouth suddenly dry.

"Now fifteen ..." Annika reported, trying to sound far less worried than she was. "Take a look at that monster coming out of the clouds ... its bigger than any two others put together ... I think it is a carrier."

"A carrier?" Hans asked.

"For fighter planes, *Kapitan*," Annika replied. "Remember what I said about that company of troops we ambushed?"

"Oh good Lord," Hans said. "It is exactly as you said, Captain-Gunner ... '*expecting a much bigger interference than one little pirate ship*'. That is a squadron on a revenge mission looking for something big and mean to smash, and right now all it can see is us."

"They cannot possible know it was us that thwarted them," Redsands declared with a hint of fear in her voice.

"It does not matter. We already have a history with the RIAN and you may be sure they will declare us a target of opportunity," Annika countered.

"Even if they do not, they are over Allied territory. That could be considered an act of war. I will guess that they will not wish us escaping to tell anyone we saw them over Greece," the Spanish Deck Officer said mirthlessly.

"Mister Nando, plot us an escape course and get us the hell away from here," Hans ordered. "Get us towards the Ionian Sea and Italy. Hopefully we will encounter an Allied Frigate or something."

"We cannot outrun them, *Kapitan*," Annika said slowly as she lowered her spyglass. Her tone was grim as she continued speaking, "The slowest of them will have a top speed of sixty knots. The faster will have speeds to seventy-five. The fighters will be eighty or so."

"We run for as long as we can," Hans said, "to force them to string the squadron out a bit and hit them, starting with the closest threat, one ship at a time. If they stay in formation, then they will only move at the speed of the slowest ship and we will stay away from them. Eventually they will want to turn towards Egypt to go looking for their missing ground company. We just need to stay away from them. Captain-Gunner?"

"*Da, Kapitan*?"

"The four-pounders are to load nothing but grapeshot and fire at fighters and rockets only. Load the eights and twelves with solid shot, Captain-Gunner, and get the Gatlings mounted and crewed on the bow and stern for fighter defence. *Fräulein* Redsands, standby to put the Sargasso's and Cudahawks to good use. Ladies and gentlemen, we are in for the fight of our lives."

The *Bloody Rose* swung her bow towards the west-northwest as orders, bells and whistles rang throughout its interior. Even as cannons were crewed and loaded, preparing for the coming battle with the Russians, the Sickbay was being prepared for its own battle to come. In the Propulsion Room, the scramble was on to try and coax more time out of the battered and over-stressed systems that would keep them ahead of the hunters even a few minutes longer.

"Captain, Propulsion Room says you have another ten minutes at this speed ... they say they found an old bottle of miracle water and are putting it to good use," Redsands called out.

"Thank-you, *Fräulein* Redsands. Please tell them to go sparingly with it, we will likely need some later," Hans chuckled blackly.

"*Kapitan*, stern lookouts are reporting the carrier is dropping aerofighters!" Annika called. Hans turned and raised his spyglass.

The fighters seemed to drop from the belly of the massive airship as Hans and the other officers watched. It was an all-inside design, bullet-shaped, with the outer skin being just an armoured cover around a space frame that contained all the ship's systems. A huge area of her underbelly, possibly large enough to bring the *Bloody Rose* into, had slid open. From it, they could see a trio of fighters drop, line-astern, into the Greek skies every minute or so. In short order, a squadron of a dozen fighters were flying in a two-decked line-abreast formation below the carrier. As one, they all surged ahead.

"You can say what you want about the RIAN, but they build good ships and train good crews," Hans said, sounding impressed with what he was watching. "Tell the Gatlings to fire until they run out of bullets or targets. four-pounders stand by to fire ... no salvos, gunners fire at their own discretion, missiles and fighters only. Helm and Planes, stand by to start evasive flying ... as soon as the shooting starts, I do not care what you do so long as it is not fly straight and level. Deck Officer, make bells and whistles for heavy weather. Cut speed to sixty knots until the fighters overtake us and then bring us back up to seventy or whatever Propulsion can spare us."

"They are a different design than the last bunch we fought," Redsands announced as she watched the approaching bi-planes through her spyglass. "Dual pusher-prop with open-top canopies."

"That means no rocket-motor I would guess," Hans said in some relief. "So, Maxims and bombs, I would think. Still very dangerous, but easier for us to deal with. The fours have a chance at hitting them this time, unlike those last fiends. Get ready."

The *Bloody Rose* slowed noticeably and the fighters began rapidly gaining ground in the chase. Tension was high aboard the fleeing pirate ship, with the clear awareness that even one single error in what would be a protracted battle could possibly spell disaster.

The formation of fighters split into two groups, each of which then veered to attack their quarry from a different side. Four of the dozen bi-planes never got a chance to do anything as the *Bloody Rose*'s gunners brutally demonstrated their skill and accuracy. As soon as Annika called that each group was within six hundred yards, the eight four-pound guns each chose targets and fired. Shredded canvas and spruce began tumbling to the ground half a mile below.

The fighters attacked en-massed, with pairs of machine-guns streaming bullets towards the gunners on the weather decks of the *Bloody Rose*. The pirate ship heeled and pitched, its steering team having decided to pick a random fighter and follow it at all costs.

One fighter split from the group it was with and made a straight run at the fleeing pirate ship. A black cylinder, perhaps a yard long, dropped from the belly of the plane. There was a flash of flame, a puff of smoke and the cylinder flew straight toward the *Bloody Rose*. It sailed harmlessly past the ship as the targeted pirate suddenly intentionally reversed the lift assist of its EMPIALE, violently dragging it nearly a dozen feet straight down.

"'Thud' Bombs," Annika offered. "O'Raedy told me about them once ... they are for attacking ground targets, but the push the motor in the tail gives them makes them somewhat suited to attacking airships. We would do well to not get hit by too many of them."

"Noted," Hans replied dryly as he hung onto a handle, trying to keep both his feet and stomach down.

The pirate ship surged upwards, rolled and pitched to bring the fighter into the arc of the Gatling gun at the bow. An arm's length of flame and twice as much smoke spewed from the front of the gun as the crew fired a sustained six seconds of bullets at it. The Russian pilot escaped with several new holes in his wings and tails, but nothing that would stop him from continuing to fly for now.

The Russian fighters were now a cloud of angry hornets stinging at the *Bloody Rose*. The four-pounders were firing as fast as they could reload, given the wind across the deck and the violent maneuverings of their ship. A Thud Bomb hit the midships deck and exploded, shaking the ship from stem to stern.

A drama ensued at the nearest four-pounder as one man was hurled over the side by the blast and two of his crewmates struggled to pull him back aboard. While everyone on the weather deck was tethered to the ship by metal cables, that did not make hanging two-thousand feet in the air suspended by your waist belt above Greece while being violently beaten against the spruce timbers of an airship in an air battle a preferred condition.

Three more fighters went down in flames and the Russians marked two more hits with bombs, tearing ragged holes in the *Bloody Rose*. Then, one of the planes fired a red flare into the air. All of the fighters broke off the attack and regrouped. They all wheeled around in formation, and flew back towards the ever-closing Russian squadron.

Immediately, the *Bloody Rose* levelled and slowed briefly. Hatch doors opened and men moved out in the mere gale of forty knots to bring wounded men inside. Fresh crew, munitions and two replacement gun barrels were brought out as well, as the *Bloody Rose* readied for the next fight.

"How bad?" Hans asked.

"Propulsion reports we have lost twenty percent of lift gas and we are leaking water and kerosene. We can resume fifty knots as soon as you want, save seventy for when it counts. Deck reports three fires burning inside and being fought. Guns reports two four-pounders destroyed and replaced, one eight-pounder damaged and unusable, eight gunners wounded," Nando reported.

"We are still in this fight, *Kapitan*," Annika said with forced tone of confidence.

"Captain, looks like a Russian seventy-four is coming after us. The rest of the squadron is turning south," Sarah Redsands announced.

"*Fräulein* Redsands, your Cudahawks are good to two miles. As soon as that ship breaks two miles you are to fire as fast as the launcher reloads. Drop mines as soon as the math allows," Hans ordered.

A lookout buzzer rang and Annika answered, then turned pale. "*Kapitan*, starboard bow lookout reports another formation of ships ahead of us, wide on starboard bow, at level, far. Possibly a dozen. Or more."

There was a moment of silence in the Steering House, and Hans was painfully aware that all eyes were on him. "Helm, forty-five degrees port turn. Clear the weather deck so that we can make top speed. Tell Propulsion we need that seventy knots again. Also tell them not to bother with a timer; this fight will be over before it matters."

*****

The *Bloody Rose* turned again, trying to avoid being pressed between two groups of much bigger predators. Blue smoke and sparks were trailing from one of her motor pods. Smoke and steam streamed from holes in her hull where the deadly bombs had struck home. Uncharacteristic arcs of electrical energy flickered from around the EMIPALE's electromagnetic drums mounted in the hull. She was no longer leaking, having transferred most the precious fluids to undamaged tanks and voluntarily dropped the rest.

In the Steering House, Redsands watched the pursuing airship behind them through her spyglass. Annika was likewise intently gazing at the group of ships that were now off their starboard beam.

"Captain, that seventy-four is keeping steady range at about five miles. As long as we can keep this speed up, we can stay ahead of them," Redsands said.

"Unfortunate, then, that we do not have that option," Nando commented.

"Hans ... *Kapitan*! The formation ahead of us ... they are challenging us. They are Allied!"

"For Peter's Sake, answer them. Quickly! Helm, starboard turn ... steer us right at them! *Fräulein* Redsands, drop a pattern of four mines over our stern as soon as we have come to the new course ... set those fuses as long as you can."

"They will go off before the seventy-four reaches them, Captain," Sarah replied.

"That is quite alright, *Fräulein* Redsands. I want those Russian look outs obsessing about mines, not looking past us."

The dulled pop-thunk of the smoke candle launchers firing reached the ears of the Steering House crew. Hans prayed that the Allies could be trusted. If there was a time to double-cross the ship renowned as the Mediterranean Menace, now was that time. The Allies' dirty work was done, the Russians had a squadron that would be a fine excuse for an accident and no one in Europe would cry at the loss of the infamous pirate. Oddly, he briefly wondered what Camilla would think at the news of his demise.

"Captain, flashing light Morse code message ... it is Commodore Anton's flagship, the '*Vaillantes Étoiles*', sir," Amram Nando announced in a awe. "He is wondering if we might have seen a Russian ship or two around here."

Hans chuckled. "Tell him we would be happy to show him where to find a few."

*****

The Russian seventy-four gunned ship of the line that had been pursuing the *Bloody Rose* realized that the tables had been turned in time to haul herself around. The pirate, by comparison, cut her speed as soon as the Russian had turned and continued steadily onwards towards the Allied group. The *Bloody Rose* and the *Vaillantes Étoiles* communicated back and forth via flashed light. The pirates gave the Allied squadron a summary of what the Russian group composition was and roughly where they might find it. The Allies were not surprised; they had been homing in on the Marconi transmissions that one of the ships had been sending for the past few hours.

"We are going to remind them they are in Allied airspace. Care to join us?" came the message.

"Yes," was the reply from the privateer.

"I cannot believe we are doing this," Nando breathed. "We are going into battle along side an Allied squadron of ships of the line."

"It will make one hell of a story in the public houses in the Pirate Towns of Egypt and Persia, will it not?" Annika laughed.

"We are not going to get to fire a shot, I expect," Hans commented amusedly. "We cannot keep up. The Allied and Russian formations are moving at sixty or so knots. We are going to be cruising at fifty. We have been invited to watch the party, not dance at it."

"The *Bloody Rose* being left a wall-flower," Redsands snorted, "hardly seems proper."

"One of those things you learn in social circles such as the ones Mister Nando and I are familiar with," Hans replied, "is that if you are well behaved at the first party, you get invited to the next one. I do not aim to misbehave."

*****

The Russians and the Allies went to war over the Greek coast at three thousand feet. Airship-to-airship rockets were launched by both sides as they closed, and the Russians put their bow guns to good use before turning to fire broadsides. Hits were marked on both groups; fire and smoke filled the skies as ships four, five and six times the size of the *Bloody Rose* unleashed their formidable arsenals on each other. Both groups of airship deployed fighters and an intense dogfight churned in the airspace between the flotillas. The Russian carrier seemed to stream an inexhaustible supply of rockets towards the Allied airships. The *Vaillantes Étoiles*, for her part, in addition to her formidable heavy guns, periodically lashed out with a blazing arc of energy from some sort of either Hertz or Tesla weapon.

The *Bloody Rose* cruised parallel to the movement of the line of battle, keeping out of easy weapons range at a steady thirty knots. The guns were all manned and the pirates all stood ready in case one side or the other should decide to involve them.

The officers and crew watched in awestruck silence as the Russian Carrier focused her rocket barrage on a hundred-gun Allied first-rate airship of the line. The air around the besieged airship was filled with fire-hearted blossoms of black smoke as the defending gunners struggled to down the incoming fusillade of deadly munitions.

One missile, then a second, then a third and fourth slammed home into the Allied warship. Secondary explosions rippled through the hull, leaving it completely engulfed in flames. The ship began to fall, only to be struck twice more by missiles fired by other ships. It simply blew apart in a tremendous booming roar that was audible on the *Bloody Rose*, miles away. Hans could see members of the crew watching from the weather deck crossing themselves in hopes for mercy and in thanks it was not them.

The *Vaillantes Étoiles* avenged her fallen comrade with a searing blast from it's energy weapon. Even in broad daylight, the beam was brilliantly visible in the sky as it lashed out over two miles to strike a Russian man'o'war. It was a lance of stark white, tinged with a sharp blue-green that made it painful to look at. The whining scream of raw power reached Hans' ears even as he shielded his eyes. The beam did not so much strike the targeted Russian as erase the her from the skies. The airship seemed to be eroded away to a derelict as though it were made of sand before a rushing tide. The charred hulk dropped from the sky like a stone.

Hans looked at Annika, his face white. The expression of horror on her face told him she was thinking what he was. That could have been the *Bloody Rose* and there would be nothing any of them could do about it.

The pirates of the *Bloody Rose* continued to watch in a fascinated horror as the full power of the Allied and Russian air navies was put on display for them to see. If any of them had considered the notion of wishing to join the fray, they had all changed their minds after watching the ruthless technologic violence the two sides turned on their respective enemies.

After a half-hour of brutal fighting, the Russians broke off the battle and dropped white smoke behind them. The Allies were content to let them go. Seven airships and their brave crews would not be returning to their docks; four Russian, three Allied. From what Hans could see with his spyglass, no ship on either side had escaped being mauled by their enemy.

The Allies parted ways from the *Bloody Rose* with a message to the privateers of "*Let us do this again some time. Fair winds, favourable skies.*"

*****

Hans stood on the bow of the *Bloody Rose*, coffee flask in hand. The sun was close to setting and the "Dog's Supper" in what was now his Captain's Mess was being prepared for. As with every night, the officers would assemble for the evening meal together with the Captain at the head of the table.

This evening, as it had been for just the past couple of days, it would be he, Hans "Blackheart" Sauder that sat at the head of that table. He chuckled to himself. How improbable an outcome from his father's decision last winter to send him to Stockholm for a degree in airship engine design. He was the captain of a pirate ship, he had an argumentative and strong-willed woman that he loved dearly at his side, he had friends that respected and fought for him, and he was functionally a wealthy man of his own labours. What more could a man of twenty-one years of age ask for in this world?

The *Bloody Rose* was still making steady progress at fifty knots towards London. This time tomorrow, they would be arriving at the airship docks of that famous city.

At the point that they had not been summarily blown out of the sky by the Allies earlier in the day, he had every confidence that they would collect their reward and be allowed to depart English airspace without hassle. From there, they would quietly make their way to Persia and disappear from everyone's sight for three or four months. That would suit him just fine.

Then what, he wondered? He watched the vista of the European mountains around Sarajevo to his right and the brilliant glory of the Adriatic Sea to his left. He was haunted, after a fashion, by something Michael O'Raedy had said to him when Hans had Paid His Respects. "*A challenge is what keeps a man from getting complacent, Mister Sauder, or old before his time,*" the Englishman had said. Now that Galahad had put his eyes upon the Grail, what challenge was left to him?

This question had two urgencies about it. The first was his own need for challenge. The second was an understanding that bored pirates plot mischief. As the captain to those pirates, that would only mean grief for himself.

The obvious answer was a swift return to the stock and trade of pirates; raiding. The question became on whose terms? He was confident that the *Bloody Rose* could continue to be the well-paid "dirty little secret" of the Allied Empires. After a wildly successful privateering operation and then this business with preventing the Russians from having an ancient weather weapon at their disposal, it seemed plain to him that they would keep refilling the feed tray of their prized bird of war with kerosene and silver.

Ultimately, however, they were an expendable solution to the problems of the Allied Empires. There would be no daring rescue mission should the *Bloody Rose* bite off more than she could chew. They would be an unfortunate and completely deniable casualty in the ongoing tete-a-tete between the Allied Empires and the Russians.

Was the answer to bite the hand that fed them? To take the money and run, as it were, and then burn that bridge behind them? After all, they had been a very wanted ship before the Allies had sent Camilla to come talk to them one night near Brussels. By the stroke of a pen, all had been forgiven and they were the well-paid iron fist in the velvet glove of diplomacy. If the Allies needed the skills of the *Bloody Rose*, they had proven that the past was of no consequence. He chuckled aloud at the memory of Camilla's faux-drama declaration of "*Oh dear, you naughty pirates have been naughty*" but since the Pirates were doing the Allies dirty work, "*we will just have to forget about it.*"

Camilla. He wondered what she might think of her "handsome pirate" being a wanted man again. Of course, he might well wind up the next assignment for her little silver pistol, too. Never a dull moment, he chuckled to himself as he finished his coffee.

Well, it was time to head to the Mess. Bridges was doing his favorite dishes tonight; *Maultaschen*, *Herzoginkartoffeln* and *Semmelknödel* with gravy. He was hoping for a *Strudel* of some kind for desert, but the Chief Steward refused to confirm nor deny that. Either way, he was not going to be a minute late to his table.

His table. He chuckled. That was going to take some getting used to.

*****

"So, tell me, Sir," Jeremy Grumman asked as they enjoyed a delicious sour-cherry strudel for desert, "What was it that tipped you off that we might be flying into a trap?"

Hans dabbed at his chin with a napkin before he answered. "Well, I recalled something the Chief Engineer told me about *Kapitän* O'Raedy never being willing to give up prey. That was something I had read, long before I met Michael O'Raedy, in a *kaffehaus* press sheet about the *Bloody Rose*. She was famously unshakable once she had her eyes on you. The Russians would have known that about us. So, it stood to reason that if they knew we were involved in some way, they would have possibly wanted to use that to their advantage."

"... and I should have realized there was more to that Gypsy Merchant than met the eye as soon as she started ship handling like a minor miracle," Annika said sourly. "It was clear she had been trolling for us and once she saw we were on the hook made ready to reel us in."

"Nonsense," Alexi Koblinski said charitably, "it is human nature to get caught up in a hunt or become frustrated when a supposedly simple task defies you. Officially, that little merchant should have been a pure formality. To have her constantly thwart our capabilities, particularly given the recent daunting task we just accomplished, it would be expectable to have anyone become frustrated and single-minded about her pursuit."

"I shudder to think what would have become of the Amir's lands had that Russian flotilla arrived unscathed over his castle," Chief Bridges commented.

"I expect they would have pounded that delightful oasis castle of his to rubble," Amram Nando said blithely.

"Always such a display of humanitarian concern from you, Mister Nando," Jeffery Wilton joked.

"I am renowned for it," the Spaniard replied with an airy wave.

"Your legend lives on intact, Mister Nando," Onora Lynch snorted. There was a round of amused laughter and then a companionable silence fell over the room. The relative quiet was broken only by the contented noises of good food being eaten in good company. Eventually, the cigars, cigarettes and port wine were brought out, as were the card and dice games.

Hans sat back in his chair, staring at the rich liquid in his glass. Arietta Itala glanced over and smiled at him. "Tuppence for your thoughts, Captain?"

"I was just counting my Blessings, actually, Chief," Hans replied thoughtfully.

"Oh?" both the Propulsion Chief and Doretta Tillie said in simultaneous curiosity. A few chuckles went around at the synchronicity.

"Aye, I was specifically thinking what a remarkable group of people you are and what an honour it is to be your

Kapitän," Hans said, setting the glass down. Everyone stopped to look at the young German at the head of the table. "All of you are individuals from an astonishing width and breadth of walks of life. Criminals to nobles, runaways to hideaways, beggars and rich," he said, gesturing at nothing in particular as he spoke.

"I have met the best in every walk of life aboard merchant airships, through my father. Men with formal training, expensive schooling, regimented practice; men that my father was gleeful to pay well for their talents. I would bet on any one of you at this table," Hans declared, tapping on the table with a finger tip, "in a contest with any of them on any day of the week." Hans raised his glass in a toast to them. "I salute you all for what you have achieved in spite of incredible odds of to the contrary. With you as officers of this ship, I am convinced that there is very little we cannot achieve together."

A round of surprised but appreciative thanks was offered to him in return and everyone drained their glasses. The duty steward, a fellow named Barrimore, hastily made the rounds to refill the empty glasses. Hans had made sure he knew the chap's name before they had sat down to eat.

"You know, Captain, we must have been making quite a name for ourselves for the Allies to be getting us to do this sort of grey-sails work for them," Jeffery Wilton observed.

"Yes, I concur. Our collective Legend has made us a choice asset to the Allies, it would seem," Hans said with a nod. He drew and exhaled from the cigar he had in his hand.

"We can be sure that our latest success will only increase our reputation. On both sides of the Scorchlands," the green-eyed Irishwoman, Onora Lynch commented with a chuckle.

"That may be the case," Arietta said sharply, "but it has not been free. In fact, it has been damn expensive. In the past four or five months, we have been forced to roll up twenty or thirty hammocks at one point or another."

"Very true," the Russian brunette nodded. "It is a type of expense that causes long term problems, too. Over half the men on the guns of the *Bloody Rose* right now have less than six months time in as pirates. Not pirates aboard the *Bloody Rose*; I mean as pirates in general. We went all last winter without one injury due to a sooted barrel or a improperly tied carriage on the gun deck. These days, if we don't have at least one injury of some kind every third firing, we are doing well." Annika sighed in frustration. "Our accuracy is going down, our reload times are going up and more hammocks wind up with red tags on them after a boarding."

"How do we fix that?" Hans asked the room at large. "I can see us standing into a particular kind of danger here."

"Agreed," Nando said after a mouthful from the glass in his hand. "Our challenges increase, but the skills available to meet them decrease, meaning we eventually will find ourselves caught beyond our skill with no handy Allied flotilla to save us."

"At the risk of empire building," the bearded Polish doctor said, "one long term investment is figuring out a way to increase the size of the sickbay and perhaps add one more crew to work there during battle. Chief Bridges and the other few stewards do an excellent job of being medical runners and handling minor injuries in the crew mess, but in some of these fights, we are loosing men because we simply do not have the space in the medical bay to care for them in time."

Hans thought about that and then nodded. "*Döktor*, work with the Chief Engineer and the Chief Steward to try and determine how we can get you room for three more beds in your sickbay. We will be in a graving dock for a while, I am sure there must be something we can do to get you some more space." The trio looked at each other and nodded in acknowledgement. "What else?" Hans asked.

Amram Nando chuckled as he spoke. "We should stop taking work that requires Allied flotillas to save us," he said with an amused glint in his dark eyes. A ripple of laughter went around the room before he continued. "I would say we stick to our primary calling as pirates, which involves picking fights with poorly defended civilian merchants. At least for a few months until we rebuild the collective experience of the crew."

Hans nodded. "I had already been thinking along those lines, *Hern* Nando," he replied. "While I consider it a long term waste of our talents, in the short term, at least, I think you are right."

Arietta spoke up. "The work being done during our planned refit in Persia will increase our speed, our endurance and our hitting power," she said. "That will give us a sharper advantage over whatever we fight. The fact of the matter is, the *Bloody Rose* should have gotten this work done last winter. It will make a noticeable difference even just having the Plante chemical battery packs refurbished."

"That is good to know," Hans responded. "I want all of you to keep the question in the back of your minds about what we can do to improve things so that we do not find ourselves in the position of our Legend having written a draft that our skills cannot cover."

*****

"You seem pensive," Annika said, tracing her fingers over a couple of fresh marks on his chest, left overs from their recent love-making. They were curled together with his arm around her in his faux-poster double bed. The heavy curtains around the bed had been drawn closed when they had tumbled together onto its relatively luxurious expanse.

Annika had arrived at his door an hour after he had completed his last rounds of the day and left his night orders with the Steering House. He had just finished tiding up his desk from the day's concerns when she had knocked. Her lips had been upon his as soon as he had locked the door behind her. Their coupling had been urgent and needy leaving them both marked and breathless. They had dozed for a period in each others arms before waking at the sound of the bell marking the change of an hour. They were both happily sated now and had been enjoying the warmth of their togetherness before she had spoken. A single linen sheet covered them, the rest having been shoved to the foot of the bed early on.

"Do I?" he asked.

"*Ja*. It is in your eyes," she said softly. She shifted so that she was on an elbow, looking down at him. "What worries you, Hans?"

"If," he said quietly.

"Shhh. It is a dirty word, that," she said with a firm nod. "None of the 'ifs' happened. And by now, they never will." She kissed him. "You are likely the youngest *Kapitan* in the fleet, Hans ... but you are hardly the least skilled. We won, today ... because of you. Tomorrow evening, we will sail like William into London and claim what is ours. We will spend a few days spreading our story around, recruit a few young hot-heads to our gun deck and we make sail to Persia. There is nothing for you to fret over."

She kissed him again, and that one led to many more that precluded meaningful conversation for a time. Eventually, they settled against each other.

"So you have yet to answer my question, Annika," he said amusedly. "The one I asked you on that rooftop that the Dragon chased us off of."

"Which was?" she asked stiffly.

"Why did you not kill me when we first met? And why did you have me brought aboard?"

"Do you believe in love at first sight, Hans?" she asked, avoiding his gaze while adjusting the lay of the sheet upon them.

"Not entirely."

"Me neither. All I can tell you is that when I first saw you fighting aboard that passenger-merchant, I just stood and stared. I instantly knew you were someone I wanted to know. I knew that killing you would be a mistake in my life. I have made enough of those I can recognize them in advance now," she concluded sourly.

"You are blushing, Annika," he said, clearly amused.

"I am not," she snarled in spite of the heat in her cheeks.

"Yes, you are. It is rather fetching, in fact. And I love you, too, Annika."

"I am not ... what?" she blinked at him.

"I said, 'I love you, too', you little Russian witch. I am very, very glad to have you as my woman," he said quietly and then kissed her.

"Damn you, Sauder! You are a man! You are not supposed to be able to know what I am feeling for you!" she growled in frustration. "And if you propose, the *Bloody Rose* will need a new *Kapitan* in the morning," she threatened.

"Settling Accounts"

Diary Entry For 19th July, 1888

It has been a very busy few days. We arrived in London, as expected, mid-evening on Monday. Before we arrived, I ensured that Annika, Arietta and Amram would impress upon the crew that it was imperative that word of Michael O'Raedy's demise not become public knowledge too rapidly for fear that British Intelligence might choose to renege on our payment. While pirates will gossip like milk maids, I will note that few things will silence them faster than an implied danger to the value of their shares.

We emptied our holds of the spoils of our limited war with the Russian Imperial Air Navy the next morning. Where it had only been a few days since our last Pay and Party, I opted to hold our cash to coffers. While some grumbling passed around, it was generally understood that weak shares were bad news and it was better to Pay Out when there was real money. Of course, what we have plundered from the Russian military in the past week alone makes for reasonable Pay Out, but Chief Bridges agrees with my notion that spreading good news thin is a poor practice.

Things have taken a turn for the complicated, of course. I had hoped for simple, and thus our Lady Whitehall had another errand for us to run.

I met with her for a social and business evening and I believe she remains unaware of my new job description aboard the ship. For now that suits me fine. We declined to undertake the errand offered, making it plain that once the winds of Autumn had begun to blow, the Bloody Rose would be available for employment.

My day today began with further complications. Khadija al-Heshjukur, the Amir's daughter, has requested to remain aboard as regular crew until after our return to Europe from Persia. While I was initially opposed to the idea, my Chief Engineer championed the notion and made a good case for it. I will note for posterity that our newest "Engineering Secondary" later won the second of her Right of Passage fights, but lost the first and third. It was rather startling to see her sporting Marianna's much less conservative clothes later in the afternoon. I wryly note the Traditions have been respected, much to the delight of the male members of the crew.

My early evening was further complicated by Gunner-Marine Cemil Jabbar presenting himself to my mess just after the "Dog's Supper". The attractive daughter of the Amir has been paying him some attention of late and the poor sot is completely beside himself. I decided to call in an expert on the matter and had André Dubé piped to my cabin. We murdered a bottle of rum *between us and hopefully Cemil has a more clear notion of what to do when your heart suddenly becomes involved in piracy.*

I have decided that tomorrow we depart for Persia — by way of British North America. That will keep everyone guessing.

*****

The *Bloody Rose* reached the mouth of the Thames River about an hour before sunset. They had made better time than expected, much to everyone's pleasant surprise. They followed the river of kings to the airship docks on the inland side of the great city. Hans stood at the back of the Steering House, watching Officers Lynch and Grumman working together to bring the ship alongside. The last time he had made this flight, it had been he and Nando under O'Raedy's silent but watchful eye. Much had changed since the last time the notorious pirate ship had darkened these skies, less than a month ago.

Grumman, Hans noted, was a far better ship handler than he was a fighter. It had taken the Confederate-American some time to get used to the way European pirates operated, instead of the American privateers with which he was much more accustomed. Both he and Redsands were proving to be talented individuals and valued members of the crew. As far as Hans knew, neither of the Americans had any plans to leave.

The *Bloody Rose* was soon secured alongside. The pale-skinned and red-headed spitfire known to the crew as Onora "Cranky Bitch" Lynch turned to Hans.

"Captain, sir, we are now secured along side, gangway is aground and Propulsion reports all shutdown and running on batteries. They are clutching in ground hook-ups for electricity and steam," she reported.

"Well done, both of you. Expertly done. London is a busy place, even on a Monday night and the airship lanes are no exception," he said with a light gesture.

"Give me a good compass and an accurate chart, sir, I can land you in the Tzar's rose garden," she boasted with a wicked grin, wink and hand on her jauntily cocked hip.

"Careful, *Fräulein* Lynch ... you never know what British Intelligence might ask us to do next. I may have to put your claims to the test," Hans laughed.

*****

Given the lateness of the hour and recent events, Hans declared that unloading the ship would wait until the morning. That would delay the expected Pay and Party until tomorrow, for want of having the price of the goods in their holds negotiated and committed to. He called Chief Bridges to his cabin to discuss the matter.

"Chief," Hans said thoughtfully, "we lifted a fair pile of silver rubles off that Russian frigate, did we not?"

"Aye sir. They had pay aboard for the crew for two months, sir, and enough money for supplies. About the equivalent of five thousand pounds, I think," Bridges said casually.

Hans tried not to choke on the mouthful of coffee he had just taken. "So, you say we might be able to spare a hundred pounds or so?" he said dryly.

"Oh, I should think so, Sir. What do you have in mind?" the portly, auburn-haired Chief Steward said blandly. The only hint of humour about him was an unmistakable twinkle of amusement in his eyes.

"It seems a tad unseemly to send the lads and lasses ashore their first night in London dry, a Monday or not. I was thinking of buying them all a drink to congratulate them on a job well done. Is there anything that says I cannot have you pass a pound to each of them without it being Pay and Party?" Hans asked.

"Oh, not really, Sir. Just do keep in mind that it all works out the same. It comes out of the same pile of money as for shares to Pay Out," James Bridges replied.

"I am aware of that, yes, Chief. It is something my father does every once in a while," Hans said thoughtfully. "Out of the blue, he sends everyone home with enough extra in their pocket for a pint at the local public house. It generates an awful lot of good will."

"And good will with your men and women in any place of work is worth a lot in the long haul, Sir. Your father is a right clever man. I can see how you come by it, Sir. Shall I arrange that for you, then?"

"Please do, Chief. Thank-you."

"My pleasure, Sir."

*****

The next day was full of the work of unloading for everyone involved. Chief Bridges brought to Hans a list of everything they had looted and brought aboard. As well, he brought "Buy Offers" posted at the local dock brokers. Each sheet represented one offer for a particular type of cargo, in a particular quantity, at a particular price.

In many cases a single commodity might have many potential matches in terms of Buy Offers. However, in many cases, there were conditions that made the offer less attractive than the price alone might suggest. For example, one Buy Offer for three tons of furs had a very good price, but the deal would only go through if all three tons were delivered, and it was the seller's responsibility to get them to the factory in Manchester.

As well, there was a provision that payment would be made via bank note five days after the goods had been delivered. That made it essentially valueless, since they only had a half ton of those goods and little time or interest in organizing further transport. Atop all of that, as pirates, a bank note written five days after they wished to have left London was practically worthless to them.

Sauder and Bridges sat down together and began the tedious process of matching attractive offers to corresponding lots of cargo that the *Bloody Rose* had plundered along its way. By noon, they had reduced the options to one or two Buy Offers per lot of cargo. Now they would review the remaining options to ensure they had missed nothing. Then Hans would sign the Buy Orders to have them executed and then Chief Bridges would go about the job of contacting the local dock brokers to have the cargo picked up and the money delivered.

"Slaying paper dragons is hardly the sort of terrors I had expected to be confronted with as the dread pirate Blackheart," Hans snorted after he emptied his coffee flask. The Chief Steward chuckled and passed him another Buy Order to review.

*****

Hans strolled along the cobblestone side streets of Westminster around mid-morning of the next day. He was dressed in the attire of a middle-class gentleman of London. He had a *portmanteau* in his left hand and whistled to himself as he went. It was Wednesday, but well after morning rush and while most businesses were bustling in the district, this was a lull time. As such, he was largely alone on the side street he walked down.

He chuckled to himself with amusement. The last time he had been here, he had been Blackheart's errand boy. Today, he was Blackheart.

However, the errand was the same; find a telegraph call booth and contact Camilla Williams of British Intelligence. He wondered if she was spending a lazy day in bed with her sea-going husband. Then again, she could be at what ever office it was that the "Blue-Eyed Beauties Division" of British Intelligence reported to. Or, perhaps, she was out of the country entirely, on some clever mission for Queen and Country requiring an extensive costume closet and a panache for double *entendres*.

He found the same lobby of the business building that he had called her from before and made his way to the battery of call booths there. He once again paid the operator a few shillings for the call. He adjusted the mouth piece to his level and tapped the "attention" button while he took the ear piece off the hook.

The feminine voice of the operator requested the number he wished to be connected to, and he gave it to her. Her accent was not British; it sounded more northern, perhaps Swedish. There was a momentary pause and then a polite word of thanks. Shortly, Hans heard the ringing noise of the call being put through.

"Good morning, Camilla Williams speaking," came the familiar warm voice.

"Good morning, *Frau* Williams. It is Hans Sauder speaking. Is your husband in town, or may I temp you with breakfast and other distractions?"

There was a momentary pause of what Hans sincerely hoped was shock, followed by a rather feminine exclamation of delight. "Hans! My favourite pirate! Where are you, darling?"

"Westminster, London, my dear. We came in Monday night and yesterday was the chore of unloading the ship of its cargo," he replied, switching the receiver to the other ear.

"Oh, darling! I am so glad you are in town. No need to worry about Terry; he is out for another two weeks. Unfortunately, darling, I have prior arrangements for the morning ... I do not suppose you would be available to escort me this evening to a social?"

"Escort you to a social?" he repeated, somewhat surprised.

"Yes! I have two invitations to a private social this evening. The band will be very good; the music will be Waltzes, Polkas and Gallops – very modern, you know. The champagne and treats will be free, naturally. You would have to dress up, of course ... and as I recall, you dress up very nicely," she purred. There was a pause before she spoke again and her voice conveyed a feminine pout in its tone. "Oh, I suppose your sweetheart will not approve of that, will she?"

"She will not mind, Camilla. 'Realities of the modern world', as you have commented on in the past. I would be honoured to escort you, *Frau* Williams. What time should I be at your door?"

"Eight o'clock," came the reply. There was a brief pause that ended with a naughty giggle before she continued "... or six if your sweetheart is a truly modern thinker."

*****

Hans picked her up in a rented electric car just a few minutes after eight. While he had intentionally arrived just a bit late, she had still made him wait just long enough for appearances sake. He held her arm and helped her up into the seat of the car and closed the door. She was dressed in a distractingly flattering plum evening gown with mauveine accents that made glory of her Raphaelite figure. A mauveine shawl and gloves, with double strand of brilliant pearls completed the ensemble.

"A dazzling beauty, as always, *Frau* Williams," he said as he closed his own door.

"You are such a flatterer, Hans. Please, do continue," she said coyly, with a glance at him over her fan. "Oh, and please do call me Camilla, my handsome pirate. We know each other at least well enough for first names."

His own attire was a blend of English upper-middle-class fashion and rugged accents of a well-travelled airshipman. Camilla seemed to enjoy "her handsome pirate", so he had opted to pander to her somewhat.

They chatted insubstantially as they drove along through the streets of London on the way to one of the city's social districts. "So, how did your vacation in Scotland go?" she asked, apparently out of the blue.

Hans chuckled. "Oh, very well. I visited a historic castle up that way with some friends, said hello to the locals and took some nice souvenirs home with us."

"So you had a good time, then?" she inquired, giving him an approving smile and flutter of her eyes.

"It was everything that my friend had described to me," Hans said firmly. "I will have to be sure to come up with an appropriate way to thank my friend for their suggestion."

*****

They went up the stairs outside the party venue. It was the home of some well-to-do upper-middle class chap that Hans had never heard of. Camilla had explained he was rather well known as being quite busily spending his inheritance on lavish parties and pretty girls. The party was a suitably impressive affair with likely around one hundred guests. An ample area had been set aside for the band and the dancers.

Camilla was was in attendance to discover what new faces were gravitating to whom. She explained to him as they swirled around the dance floor together in a Waltz that it was believed the inheritance money was, in fact, funds from secret ties to Russia. The expectation was that these social parties were being used as a place for intelligence transactions, as well as potentially seditious political discourse. Given recent developments, this was the sort of thing that bore keeping tabs on. As such, she had gotten two invitations to the place arranged but until Hans had called this morning, had expected she was going alone.

"You have done me quite a favour, Hans," she purred softly in his ear as they walked off the dance floor with his arm around her waist and her hand on his shoulder. "Coming here with a Naval Captain as an escort makes it hard for me to plead wide-eyed innocence. You, on the other hand, my darling Hans, are just enough of a head-turner that it nearly does not matter who I am."

They spent time mixing and mingling with different groups. Camilla had an easy and beguiling charm about her that seemed to allow her to drift in and out of any group in a way that caused little offence or question. She always had the right turn of phrase, wave of fan or language of body to disarm any fellow that might be otherwise defensive at their arrival.

Hans noticed that her ease with charming the gentlemen was periodically causing some ire with the ladies alongside them. He appropriately opted to spend his time indulging in idle flattery and subtle suggestions until feathers were at least no longer ruffled.

Later on in the evening, as they were changing from a lively set of Polkas to a more relaxed Waltz, she broached the subject he had been trying to bring up since the phone call that morning. "Since you are back in London, I take it your last voyage was ultimately successful?" she asked in a low whisper.

"Very," he replied carefully. "I have a letter for you to take to your employers. It includes a description of the work that was done as well as an invoice for the services rendered."

She smiled at him and her vivid blue eyes glittered in delight. "Oh, Hans ... you do so know how to show a girl a good time!"

"I am very glad you think so, Camilla. Do let your employers know that while we very much appreciate their patronage, we will be taking a much needed change in routine until the fall. You know how it is ... change is the spice of life. We would not want this arrangement with your employers to become too much of a good thing."

Camilla gave a feminine pout and set a gloved hand to her cleavage. "But Hans ... when will we see each other if you run off like that? Whatever shall I do without your winsome charm at parties like this?" she said coyly.

"I am sure, Camilla, that a lady of your ... credentials ... should hardly be a wallflower if one airshipman is off visiting Prague or Istanbul for a month or two," Hans replied with a chuckle. He pressed her other hand to his lips and winked at her. "I promise you I will write."

"I look forward to the seeing the talented hand of your penmanship, then," she said, still somewhat rather in a pout. Hans was fairly sure she was making play, but he still found it interesting how much the expression on her face and the language of her body prompted a rather protective reflex in him. He would have to be very careful with his Lady Whitehall, he decided. She was a talented manipulator of men, and he was not exempt from her charm. He reminded himself that there was a significant personal danger in allowing the attractive blonde spy to convince him of anything that Annika would disapprove of either professionally or personally.

"Excuse me, my good man," a gentleman said in a quiet voice. Hans and Camilla both looked towards him in mild surprise at the intrusion. He was tall and somewhat thin, with angular cheeks, a sharp brow and a thin moustache. His hair was a mild brown, with similar eyes. He was dressed rather fashionably and yet did not look to be indulged in excess.

"Good evening, Sir, what can I help you with?" Hans replied.

The other man leaned forward and continued on in his low tone. "I got the impression that you might be a merchant captain for hire ... the sort of chap that chafes under all the restrictions, taxes and paperwork that our government heaps upon good, hard working men." He gave Hans an meaningful look, clearly testing the waters.

Hans swiftly recalled what Camilla had told him about both the host and the party. He gave an aggravated chuckle and rolled his eyes. "You could say that, aye. Make three pence, pay one in taxes and one in fees, and have to run a ship on what is left." Camilla made an approving noise beside him and she possessively pressed herself to his left side.

"My name is Walther Graham ... I am an honest, hard working businessman, much like yourself," the moustached man introduced himself and offering his hand to shake.

Hans shook the man's hand, leaving his left arm around Camilla's waist. "Klaus Drosselmeyer, merchant airship captain ... home port of Bremen, Germany."

"Well, that is wonderful news, Captain. I run an outfitters' shop for airships ... you might say we have mutual concerns with how the government treats the people that truly make the Empire great. People like you and I, Captain."

Hans chuckled. "What is to be done?" he asked casually. "We can be the 'economic heart' of 'Imperial power' all we like, but taxes, licenses and surcharges are not anything an honest working man can ignore. If he does not pay up, he does not work." He was opening the door to see if the other man would take the opportunity. It was a risky game, yet if the other man gave him a lead, then that would make Camilla's visit this evening a success. A small price to pay in exchange for a handful of crates of Tesla rifles that had so far already proven instrumental in their survival.

He could feel Camilla move against him slightly, not having said a word thus far. Both Hans and Walther were paying her little heed. Even in modern times like these, a woman could not be reasonably expected to have an opinion on the men's affairs of business and politics. Of course, Hans knew better now. Until Mr.Graham commented on her, however, Hans fully intended to pretend she was just arm candy. That little omission on Graham's part was Sauder's spare ace.

A servant passed by and Graham snagged two glasses of Irish whisky and passed one to Sauder. Hans took it as the other man spoke. "What if I told you that there were more than just you and I that felt that the way we were treated by the government was unjust ... and that a few of them had an interesting solution to the problem?"

Camilla stiffened against him, barely perceivable. Hans took a deliberately slow sip from the glass, allowing a frown of consideration to cross his features. Hans was having difficulty believing that the other man was so anxious to recruit him to their cause, what ever it was, that he would be so quick to strike at an apparently hot iron. Yet, that seemed to be exactly what was happening right now. Camilla doubtlessly realized what was going on as well. He presumed she would make some attempt to stop him from pressing to far forward if she needed to.

"You are worried it might be something illegal, Captain Drosselmeyer, are you not?" Graham pressed in a casual voice.

"Of course," Hans replied quietly, looking around them at who might be listening. "That ship is my life. I cannot afford to have it confiscated."

"I completely understand, Klaus," Walther said with a reassuring smile and gesture. "Allow me to personally assure you that what we are doing is perfectly legal. All of us have a great deal to loose; lives and investments we have built successfully in spite of the Imperial government." Walther gave another reassuring smile and then seemed to be suddenly aware of the attractive blonde woman hanging onto both Hans' arm as well as their every word. "My apologies for the poor manners, Klaus ... I failed to make the acquaintance of your escort this evening."

Hans made a dismissive gesture with the hand holding his drink, and then sipped at the glass he held. "Walther, this is Rachel White. *Fräulein* White and I have a social arrangement. She is very discreet when it comes to my business matters," Hans said smoothly. It was his time to do the reassuring; if the Englishman spooked, a very tantalizing opportunity for Camilla would evaporate. Camilla gave a polite curtsy and favoured the other man with a demure flutter of her eyes and then gave a doe-eyed look of appreciation to Hans.

"Captain Drosselmeyer is very kind to me in our arrangement," Camilla said shyly, as though unused to discussing the matter in public. "I would never do anything to make him unhappy with me." A 'social arrangement' was a polite turn of phrase that meant she was his paid mistress; she traded her body for a comfortable home and an expense account. It would make significant sense that she would wish to do nothing that might endanger that income from a man who presumably was away more than he was around to make demands of her.

The hawk-nosed Englishman seemed to take all of that at face value and gave Hans a look of knowing appreciation. "Klaus Drosselmeyer" was obviously a man of both ways and means if he was a merchant airship captain with a beautiful mistress and the sort of contacts that got him an invitation to this class of party.

Walther gave a polite bow as he spoke. "Captain Drosselmeyer is clearly a gentleman of great fortune to have so lovely a lady with him, Miss White," he said in a flattering yet polite tone. He then looked back to Hans and summarily forgot about Camilla as he spoke. "So, do I have your trust, Klaus? We could use a man of your skills and assets amongst us, you stand to profit handsomely, and none of it is any more illegal than anything you do normally."

Hans covered his mouth with his whisky glass and opted to direct his eyes for a moment towards Camilla's modestly revealed cleavage; he was fairly sure he would have laughed aloud at the other man's last phrase otherwise.

*****

"You, Hans darling, are turning out to be such a wonderful person to have in my life," Camilla purred at him as she leaned against his shoulder. They were motoring through the rainy streets of night-shrouded London. They were just killing time for a while, making sure that anyone following them from the party would eventually decide that following an apparent driving enthusiast and his mistress around London was a waste of their time.

"Oh? Do tell, Camilla dear," he chuckled as he guided the rented electric car down the narrow street.

"Well, presuming that you continue to stubbornly resist my attempts to seduce you into going to that meeting the night after tomorrow to find out what this is all about, I can still inform Whitehall that we have fish in the pond. It would seem that if we dangle a moderately well-to-do merchant airship captain in front of that gaggle, they will jump for the bait."

Hans nodded at her but said nothing, making a left turn down a thoroughfare that was busy even at this time of night. He glanced over his shoulder briefly and then looked ahead at the road.

Camilla idly traced her fingers along the lines of his left forearm as they drove along. She said nothing for a few minutes, leaving only sounds of the electric car and the city of London to keep a silence from descending uncomfortably. "You know, Hans, I rather like the idea of being your Mistress," she said suddenly, with an amused note in her voice. "Mmm, yes. The paid lady of an airship pirate. I imagine that if I was a more easily contented woman that could be a fine way to pass a few years," she said with a laugh. "... and who is 'Rachel White', really? That name rolled off your tongue with the ease of regular practice."

Hans glanced over at her, amusement and surprise visible on his features. "You do not miss a twitch, do you, Camilla? 'Rachel White' was the proverbial girl next door from our family home in the country. Chestnut hair and a lovely smile. I had quite a crush on her for most of the summer of my fifteenth year. I am not entirely convinced she ever knew I existed."

*****

Hans pinched the bridge of his nose and sighed heavily as he sat in the chair at his desk the next morning. "Ladies, please. Start over again, as I am apparently failing to understand something."

Khadija al-Heshjukur, the Amir's daughter, stood up straight beside Arietta Itala in spite of the bruises he had been told were on her most of her face. Hans had heard that she had also had a injuries to her upper legs. If she was in pain at all, she was hiding it well. The Italian-Ethiope gestured for the young Egyptian woman to speak.

"We have reached the British capital, London," Khadija said. "It was my Father's wish that I travel with you this far. He said I should see the city and then make my way home. I think I have not travelled enough yet to honour the spirit of my Father's wish."

"Khadija," Hans said patiently, "you got hit in the face with flying motor pod parts, had your left arm scalded to the point of scars by steam and nearly had both your legs broken by a collapsing strut." He paused and looked at the young woman. "How much further is it you think your Father's wishes extend?" he asked pointedly.

"Until I am capable of weathering that kind of a storm without being a burden. When I joined your crew, I thought that I knew something about the world and my place in it. I fancied myself an able fighter, since I knew how to strike with a sword. I felt myself a promising engineer, because I had watched my Father and Grandfather working on the Stirling engines and the windmills." She paused for a moment, clearly mustering her courage to say what needed to be said in spite of how it might taste as it passed her lips. "I ... I know nothing, Captain. I am a babe in a palm grove I did not even know existed. I am exactly the weak, ignorant and unskilled woman that my Father's men fear me to be. I will not return home until I am fit to rule, *Inshallah*. I swear it before Allah," she said in a determined voice.

Hans looked at Arietta. "Your thoughts, Chief? She will be staying in your Propulsion Room if she stays at all."

"Are you deaf as a post, *Signore Capitano*?" Chief Itala asked charitably, unfolding her arms from across her chest. "I say she stays, and she works as an Engineering Secondary while training with the Gunner-Marines under Annika."

"An 'Engineering Secondary'? What the hell is that?" Hans demanded crossly.

"Whatever the hell I want it to mean," Arietta replied. "I just invented it. Right now, it means she spends every first watch shadowing me in the Propulsion Room, and every second Watch shadowing Annika with the Gunner-Marines."

"Give me one reason why I should agree to that?"

"Because unlike you when you joined, at least she understands she is clueless, needs to put her ego aside, get down and dirty, and learn about the real world," Arietta growled at him.

"Get out of my Mess. Now," Hans snarled, rising from his chair. He was barely keeping his temper in check.

Arietta glared at him silently and then nodded. The two women turned to leave.

"Chief!" Hans barked as they opened the door. The Italian-Ethiope and the young Egyptian woman both turned and looked at him. Arietta's face was one of proud defiance, while Khadija's was one of disappointment.

"Get that damn pirate some real clothes to wear. If she is staying on board this scow, she had better start learning the Code and Traditions. All of them," he said gruffly.

*****

"Yes, Captain-Gunner?" Hans asked as he pulled a clean shirt on.

"The little bitch hits like an ox," Annika said, pressing gingerly at her bruised lip.

"Good. I was thinking after the first fight that she was going to be hopeless," Hans sighed.

"Why Grumman?" Annika asked, sitting on the corner of his desk. One leg dangled, while the other foot was set firmly on the deck.

"She has an inferiority complex with men. A learned one. But it is there. Grumman got his ass handed to him by a woman in his Right of Passage fights. I knew he would not hold back. Did he actually break her nose?"

"No, thankfully. Cemil tells me she would have been unmarriable at home if that chain left scars on her face or had broken her nose," Annika replied gesturing slightly.

"She did surprisingly well against Yvette," Hans noted as he brushed his hair.

"It was an amusing collision of style. Both acrobatic players at the '*jeu marseillais*'," Annika laughed. "I do not know if you could see, but the look on Yvette's face was priceless when she threw that first whip kick and had Khadija not only block it but use an Italian reverse on her."

"It would seem the Amir brought home more from France than just a taste for *Champagne*," Hans laughed. "He apparently learned their martial art, too." A few moments went by as he adjusted his collar in the mirror. "You went easy on her, I noted."

"For the first ten seconds, until she punched me in the face," Annika snorted. "Then the kid-gloves came off. Even then, she was a handful. She lasted as long as she did on her own merits."

"Is she a mistake?"

"No."

"Is that a 'conspiracy with Arietta' answer?" he asked suspiciously, eyeing her via the mirror he stood before.

"No."

"Would you tell me if it was?"

"No."

*****

She drifted into the restaurant with the sort of head-turning grace that Hans was not quite growing accustomed to, but certainly learning to expect from Camilla. In further testimony to the happiness of her clothier, she yet again wore an outfit which he had never before laid eyes on. She was dressed impeccably as one of those "to the manor, born" sorts that he was familiar with from social parties his father had arranged to get him invited to in the summers of his mid-teen years. Of course, watching a woman of her looks and figure drift across a restaurant to his table was hardly like work to Hans.

She was wearing a wine-colored ladies tea jacket of a rich velvet, atop a high-necked and ruffled white blouse, closed at the neck with a gold and ivory broach. As well, she wore a dark blue gathered and bustled skirt, whose waist was a wide satin band. On her feet were dark leather boots, largely hidden by her skirt. Her blonde curls were curiously dyed a chestnut brown and mostly covered by a narrow-brimmed ladies felt cap.

She smiled at him demurely as though his opinion of her looks carried import with her and he suddenly had to suppress a groan. She was dressed as a very likely Rachel White. Damn the woman; further evidence he had to be careful of anything he said around her.

"I am very sorry to have kept you waiting, *Herr* Drosselmeyer," she said in a soft and contrite voice.

He gestured to the chair beside him, resisting the urge to scowl at her in displeasure. "It is quite alright, *Fräulein* White. I know how difficult London can be to travel in some days. Particularly at this time of the day. Please, do sit with me, my dear."

They had lunch together and chatted pleasantly. It occurred to Hans that Camilla slipped into nearly any role she took with remarkable skill, both from a perspective of look and body language. He sourly noted that in fact his Lady Whitehall seemed to be a commensurate actress and gameswoman. He was beginning to doubt how much of her was real as it concerned him.

As that thought crossed his mind, she discreetly passed an envelope to him. He opened it and read it over. British Intelligence wished to pay him to continue the guise and deception he had started the night before, with an eye to aiding Camilla to infiltrate and uncover whatever conspiracy or plot they had glimpsed the entry way of. It was a generous sum of money, to be sure, including an amusing set of props to facilitate the deception, such as a flat for "Rachel White" and a modest sized merchant airship for "Captain Klaus Drosselmeyer of Bremen, Germany" to use. He flicked his eyes up to Camilla, who was looking uncharacteristically eager to hear his opinion. He shook his head.

"I am sure that it would be a fascinating set of social engagements, *Fräulein* White. However, by tomorrow evening, I fully intend for my ship and I to be eight hundred miles closer to Istanbul than London currently is. As I said last night, when I return in the Fall, I will be very happy to entertain these sorts of parties and guests."

*****

Hans leaned against the window at the back of his cabin on his right forearm, looking out into the city-lit darkness of London at night. He was allowing himself a few quiet minutes of solitude and relaxation. He was dressed in a pair of loose grey cotton pants, an over-sized white cotton shirt left unlaced and untucked, and a simple pair of brown leather deck shoes. He was interested in comfort, and there was no one here to impress with his fashion sense.

The "Dog's Supper" was done, his rounds were completed, and most of the "Ladies of the Rose" including Annika were off "educating" Khadija on a few of the finer points of the women's culture of piracy. Hans expected that would involve a risque level of drunkenness somewhere in a place with attractive young men missing their shirts as waiters. He hardly minded. While he loved her dearly, the incessant intensity at which she lived made Annika a tiring person to spend all his time with. Hans liked his solitary time a great deal. Even during his days in school abroad, he always was the sort to need a few hours to himself towards the end of a week to digest and make sense of all the events of the week and the interactions in his personal life.

He took a sip from the cut crystal glass of brandy in his left hand, enjoying the fire of the drink and the warmth of the recollection of seeing Khadija working on the weather deck in Marianna's clothes. The leggy Greek woman had been somewhat shorter in the waist and leaner overall than the Amir's daughter, and thus even with some bit of tailoring, the dead woman's clothes were rather tighter and more revealing on their new owner.

As the newest and seemingly most naive female member of the *Bloody Rose*, it was rather obvious to Hans that a number of the men of the crew were already trying to determine what she would find attractive enough to be interested in at least for a night. Hans found her physically attractive as well, but a touch mousy in her demeanour for his tastes. He was very content in his off-watch relationship with the Captain-Gunner, and was hardly interested in jeopardizing that.

Annika had made suggestion once or twice during their pillow-talk of the notion that he should at least take one other lover. If not, say, Arietta, then even an attractive ground-side lass for a weekend of sinful delights. He found it viscerally odd that she would encourage him to stray to any degree. Her observation had been that he would otherwise have no real basis for knowing if she really was the woman he wanted in his life.

In spite of that, Hans had little interest in adding such a level of complexity in his life right now. His life was tumultuous enough as it was without adding the confusion of another romantic interest to it. He took a sip from the brandy glass. An electric buzz broke the quiet of the dimly lit mess, followed by a few raps upon the cabin door.

"Come in. It is unlocked," Hans said loudly. He was rather surprised when a rather timid-looking Cemil entered the mess and closed the door behind him.

"*Masaa' Al-Kheir, Qaa'ed*," the Arab said as he entered.

"Pardon, Cemil?" Hans asked, having completely failed to understand the other man's greeting in Arabic.

"Oh ... sorry ... I said 'Good evening, my captain'," Cemil replied sheepishly.

"What brings you to my cabin door at this time of day, *mein Freund*?"

"I was hoping to get your advice," the young one-eyed man said carefully, glancing around.

"It is just you and I. Close the door, pull up a chair and relax. Care for some brandy?" Hans asked.

Cemil shook his head as he moved a chair over to be in front of Hans' desk. Hans gave a wordless shrug and then moved to the sideboard that had the crystal cut brandy bottle on it and he refilled his glass. He went to his desk, sat down in his chair, leaning back slightly and having a sip of the liquid fire. He eyed the Arab appraisingly across the top of the glass for a few moments. "What is on your mind, then?"

"*al-Lateefa* ... um ... I mean, a pretty girl, Captain..."

"Just call me Hans. No need to be formal right now ... we know each other well enough that we can use first names, Cemil. I am sure I can guess, but tell me anyway ... who?"

"Khadija al-Heshjukur," Cemil said, almost sounding guilty.

"I cannot fault your tastes, *mein Freund*. She is a pretty girl, to be sure ... particularly with her new outfit. A bare midriff suits her," Hans chuckled.

Cemil gave a momentarily jealous glance at Hans and then relaxed. "Yes, it does," he said with a sigh. "It is all I can do not to stare when she is around," he said in a tone of near complaint.

"The *Bloody Rose* is not a ship for men without a bit of self-control, to be sure. I do not know what it is about this ship, but is seems to attract the prettiest of the women in piratedom," Hans reflected aloud.

Cemil snorted. "The Ladies of the Rose are above the average, but it is a generally high average," he said with a laugh. "Visivald and Dolores both routinely complain that there are more plain looking men in piracy by proportion than plain looking women."

Hans laughed and then had a sip of his brandy. "So ... what is the advice you are looking for? You and I both know the Amir will be somewhat reluctant to agree to a one-eyed pirate romancing his daughter."

Cemil nodded "Which is why I need your advice, Sauder ... because she seems rather interested in the idea of romancing me!"

Han blinked at him. "Wait ... what? Hold on, do not answer that ... I am not the resident expert in 'attractive daughter has powerful father I need to placate'," he said with a grin. "However, that is exactly André Dubé's lot in life. Do you mind sharing your situation with him and perhaps he can shed some light?"

Cemil thought for a moment and shook his head. "I do not mind. Dubé is a good man, and I am sure he would keep his mouth shut."

Hans nodded at him. He got up and walked over to the voicepipes and called through the one leading to the quarterdeck area to verify that Dubé was still aboard. He was and so Hans had him summoned to his Mess.

A few minutes later the jovial Franco-Brit was sitting with Hans and Cemil. Hans gave a brief summary of the important matter at hand. The dark-haired Dubé looked scandalized for a moment and then thumped with his fist on the edge of Hans' desk as he spoke. "*Attendez une seconde, mon capitaine. Ce n'est pas adéquate!* You cannot have a discussion about women by pirates without rum! How can you imagine we will make any progress here?"

Hans blinked at André for a moment and then quite nearly fell out of his chair laughing. He made a great if mirthful show about begging off the impropriety and in short order a tall glass of rum was in each man's hands and they were chatting amicably for a few minutes.

"So, André ... your wisdom? What is our poor man Cemil to do here?" Hans asked.

The Franco-Brit and the Arab looked at each other for a moment and Dubé had a mouthful from his glass before speaking. "First, win her heart, man. Without love, you are wasting your time. If she truly desires you in her life ... she will wait, she will fight and she will defy to be with you. *Et-tu d'accord*, Hans?" Hans wondered if it was a cultural trait that allowed Frenchmen to gesture so grandly while speaking and yet never spill a drop of their liquor.

Hans had a sip of his rum and thought about Annika, then grinned and nodded. "My limited experience with women who take on piracy for a living and lifestyle is that they are all rather driven, rather fiery, and rather willing to start a fight to get what they want. That is not the sort of woman who is for the faint of heart or the weak of constitution. I will note ..." Hans was interrupted by the other two men bursting into laughter. They knew the Captain-Gunner well enough to guess at what Hans was suggesting. Hans joined in, as much from the mild inebriation as the sense of camaraderie.

"Well, I think that perhaps she has already made a decision to some degree," Cemil said after a mouthful from his glass. "She has been going out of her way to work with me on deck chores ... and a couple of nights, now, we have sat together talking ... she has told me she thinks I am handsome, even with the eye-patch."

Hans and André glanced at each other and then back to Cemil. It was clear from the tone of voice of the other man that he was entirely smitten with the Amir's daughter. Hans found it amusing that the sharp, irreverent, rough-and-tumble Arab would sound like an awed school-boy as soon as his heart was involved. Perhaps, Hans mused, that was a universal condition for young men. Dubé was the oldest in the room at 24.

"Do not worry about her father ... yet, at least ..." André said firmly.

"But ..."

"*Non*! Do not! Until she decides to return home to her father's lands, her father is irrelevant. All that matters is you and she," the dark-haired Franco-Brit said forcefully, thumping his glass down on the edge of the desk for effect. "If you truly love each other, her father will wish his daughter happy. If he does not, his daughter will tell him to stuff himself as any woman in love would. You will understand her culture best, Cemil ... treat her like she is a vision of love to you, and enjoy the time you have. We are pirates, all of us. A single musket ball from an enemy or snapping rope in a storm can take everything we have and dash it like a bowl of eggs. You and she are no different. Live every day as though it is your last, and love her as she allows you.

It is nothing less than a man should do ... and there is nothing more he can do"

"Amen," Hans said. The three men downed their drinks, momentarily separate in their thoughts, yet joined by a male ritual as old as the drink itself. "Well said, André. Exactly right."

"To Persia by way of Montréal"

Tuesday, the 24th of July

It has been a very busy few days. At the same time, we have been blessed to have celebrated in the good fortune of a crew member while ensuring that our treasury remained healthy. We left a muddled trail of honest piracy and dubious merchanting behind us, which should serve to confuse anyone trying to keep an eye on our movements. The crew is in good spirits and there is much talk of the rest period coming up when we finally arrive at the graving cradles in Persia.

We collected our goods and bullion as thanks from the English government and departed from London at noon on Friday, the 20th of July. Once we reached the mouth of the Thames, we steered south into the Channel and then took a north-westerly heading. As we passed the Irish city of Dublin, we took prey of a heavily loaded Sopwith-built freighter named the "Pride of Blackpool". I duly note that the public houses of the City of Blackpool were likely short on their stocks of Irish whisky this weekend as a result of our passage.

From there, we crossed the Atlantic including a particularly miserable storm near British Newfoundland. We arrived in Halifax, British North America, in the early hours of Sunday, the

22nd of July. It was there that I explained to the Master-Gunner André Dubé that our little detour was in fact to allow him the chance to return home to his sweetheart. I could see no point in flying all the way to Persia to have him bake in boredom for three months to simply return to Europe in the fall and then need to take leave of us and make his way home.

We unloaded a good portion of our haul of paid goods as well as our stolen whiskey in the busy seaport. An airship is a bit of a strange bird in these areas, let alone a heavily armed "merchant" brimming with fine European goods. As a result, the local traders and brokers asked few questions and paid reasonably well in spite of our haste. André and I then invested in a selection of goods he estimated that would do him well in British Montréal as both wealth and station. We had loaded and let slip by noon of the same day.

We chased the sun all the way across the mountains and up the great river valley to Montréal, arriving at about six o'clock at night that same Sunday. Our arrival caused a bit of a stir, requiring Dubé, Martel and LeBlanc to do a fair amount of talking and hand-waving to obtain us docking permission in the city. The next day, being a Monday, we unloaded and sold the balance of the goods in our holds from Europe.

We then Paid Out shares, resulting in a fine night in the French city for most of the crew.

Myself and a majority of the officers of the ship accompanied André to the door of his intended's home. After surprising the young lass to the point of a near faint, we then made great show of riding the young couple to the door of her father's business with a guarded supply train of rich goods. The French gentleman was nearly beside himself at the display. After some introductions and a few words from myself, the Father agreeably consented to the marriage, to the rousing cheer of all in ear shot.

This morning, André arrived at my cabin after breakfast to Pay His Respects. It was a rather sobering moment for me to see my friend make good his dream and walk out of this life I have so entirely adopted. He reminded me of our "Memorandum" and I grudgingly promised to make a point of seeing him in late spring.

Tomorrow, we set sail for New York on an errand. From there, the skies of Europe will be our gateway a much deserved rest in Persia.

*****

Amram Nando looked up at Hans from the navigational chart. "*Capitán*, by fix and by eye we are clear of the Thames River navigational zone, standing at six hundred feet with a speed over the ground of thirty knots. We are about to take starboard turn, course of one-three-five, speed fifty."

"*Nien*, *Hern* Nando, please take starboard turn to course one-eight-naught, speed fifty-five, run for thirty minutes, then take heading three-one-five at one thousand feet."

"That is ... a somewhat non-traditional course for Persia," Sarah Redsands replied, her voice somewhere between cautious and curious.

They had departed the airship docks of London just after the reverberations of Big Ben's noon bells had fallen away. They had made way out the Thames in the warm air of a Southwest English summer Friday. The clouds were high, the winds light, the sun a blessing and the spirits of the crew were high. The rumour and the plan were for a speedy flight to the Mediterranean coast, followed by taking a few targets of opportunity, and then on to a three-month paid vacation in a Pirate Town in Persia. It was thus somewhat understandable that Hans' orders for a flight in the opposite direction were met with confusion .

"We are going to Persia by way of British North America," Hans explained. "We just left the airship docks of the British Air Admiralty's home town, where the better part of a hundred pirates have spent the last few days telling every snitch with a turned-up skirt and a bottle in hand that we would be back in our old hunting grounds by tomorrow morning. Ergo, we are going to be anywhere but there. To quote our good Captain-Gunner, '*It is much easier to not be found if everyone is looking for you in the wrong place*'," the young German grinned.

The brilliant light of the noon-day sun lanced through the encompassing glass of the Steering House of the *Bloody*

Rose as the Spanish Deck Officer eyed the new pirate captain. There was a moment of dubious expression on his face, which was swept away by an impressed and amused grin. "*Muy ingenioso, el capitán.* Very smart of you. Helm, take starboard turn to course one-eight-naught. Set speed to fifty eight knots. Planes, steady as you ride."

The Amerindian officer glanced at a large scale navigation chart and used her pinkie and pointer fingers as a set of dividers as she rapidly worked out the flight track in her head. "That will put us in the Dublin area right around sixteen hundred hours ... thinking of scalping a whiskey boat, Captain?" she asked.

Hans gave a sincere moment of applause to her. "Very well done, *Fräulein* Redsands. Excellent deduction. If we get lucky, we will be able to take prey of a freighter just loaded and leaving. I suspect having a load of Irish Whisky in our holds to go with the rest of our amusing load of 'thank-you' boxes from the English government will make us very popular when we get to British North America."

A round of laughter filled the Steering House as the *Bloody Rose* steadily came around to her new course. She cruised along on her repaired center-line motor pod in the clear air over the English Channel. She made way, "Jack over Roger", over the historic waters below her as she tracked southward, and then back inland over the rolling greens of the English countryside. Within six hours, they had left Bristol and Cardiff to the south in their wake and were again over water.

She continued onwards over the shimmering blue-silver of the Irish Sea, chasing the sun to the West. Once they had determined they were about midway across the waters separating England and Ireland, the Union Jack was taken down from her flagstaff. While many pirates tended to run with Allied colours hoisted, changing to the airship Jolly Roger as they attacked a victim, the *Bloody Rose* always prowled with her true nature visible. It was part of her Legend, through two prior men named Blackheart, and Hans was not about to change that.

*****

An hour later, with the Irish coast in sight, the bow lookouts reported in. Hans was in his Mess, relaxing with a book prior to the Dog's Supper, when the bells and whistles for action began sounding. He called up the voicepipe to the Steering House to ask what was afoot.

"Grumman here, sir. We have a small freighter about eight miles ahead of us, starboard side, low. She is Eastbound, moving slowly. Three other ships in the area, none closer, none military. Per your orders, coming to stations and making to intercept based on opportunity."

"Very good, *Hern* Grumman. I will be right up. Cut speed by two thirds to give us time to think."

Shortly thereafter, Hans came into the Steering House. Annika was already there, eyeing the misfortuned merchantman through her range finder. "Captain-Gunner, what is on the menu for this evening?"

"Fresh Sopwith, *Kapitan*. She is a smaller design, good for local runs around the Isles and coastal France. Not moving too quickly; I am guessing she is on a regular run with more worries about the cost of fuel than the time of arrival. She is trailing black smoke from her stacks, so she is running choked."

"Simple enough. Cinderball ahead of her from our starboard guns, then wheel over. If she does anything but strike her colours and slow, hit her with a broadside of solid ball."

"No sign of a storm front or military flotilla lurking in the area, Captain," Onora Lynch announced dryly as she scanned around with her spyglass. Annika snorted and Hans chuckled.

"Excellent. I would hate to have to explain to our Deck Officer why we needed to be saved by Commodore Anton again," he returned.

The *Bloody Rose* picked up speed again, changed course and began a shallow dive. She was now steadily closing with the oncoming freighter, who seemed to have failed to notice her approach. At a fifteen hundred yards distance, the pirate swerved sharply to bring her broadside square to the bow of the merchant. The hidden gun doors on the *Bloody Rose* swiftly opened and the facing eight and twelve pound cannons roared a challenge. Moments later, the air in front of the merchant erupted with splattering blooms of smoke and fire.

It looked to Hans as though the merchant was having a panicked moment of indecision. She swerved hard over, as though trying to avoid running into the insubstantial cloud of smoke in the air ahead of her bow. She then suddenly picked up speed, resulting in a a muttered "oh really?" from Annika. Just as quickly as she sped up, she suddenly turned back to her original course and cut her speed to nearly nothing. A moment later, a pair of white smoke rockets launched into the air.

"Well, that is rather amusing, do you not agree, Captain?" the red-headed Watch Officer questioned as she watched through her spyglass.

"Very, *Fräulein* Lynch," Hans said. "Bring us alongside, load everything on that side with grapeshot and have the gatlings readied," he ordered. His brow was furrowed in consideration.

"I doubt we will need it, *Kapitan*," the Russian brunette said. "I would guess that there was a moment of panic on the bridge followed by cooler heads prevailing. Heaving to as she did is no way to make ready for a fight." The Confederate Watch Officer, Jeremy Grumman, nodded in agreement with Annika's assessment.

The *Bloody Rose* boarded the *Pride of Blackpool* with no opposition. The First Mate was standing alone on the deck with a white cloth in hand and shouting that the crew of the merchant would give no resistance. All they wanted was to escape with was their lives and enough ship to make for home with.

On the bridge of the *Pride of Blackpool*, Hans and Annika were amused to find the ship's master tied and gagged with a nasty lump on his head, his hair and shirt soaked, and smelling of freshly spilt whisky. The First Mate explained that the Captain had wanted to run for it, or perhaps even try to fight back. The First Mate, however, had heard of the *Bloody Rose* and decided the smartest thing to do was abort that entire line of logic in it's infancy.

Hans pulled the gag off the furious Irishman. "Shut up and listen," Hans barked before the *Pride of Blackpool*'s Captain could say anything. "Your First Mate just saved your life and the lives of your crew. My ship makes eighty knots and puts a hundred pounds of the iron in the air with a broadside. If there had been so much as a wiff of match smoke aboard this scow, we would have blown your ship to flotsam, renamed her 'HMMAS Example' and just looted someone more reasonable. If you have any brains at all, you will thank your First Mate profusely for saving your life, and avoiding the wives of your crew becoming widows because of your stupidity. When a pirate says stop, little man, you stop. Anything else is suicide."

Two hours later, the *Bloody Rose* and the *Pride of Blackpool* parted ways in the thin air of five thousand feet over Ireland. Aboard the departing pirate were twelve hogshead of assorted Irish whiskies and ales, as well as the First Mate of the *Pride of Blackpool*.

*****

"Well, *Fräulein* Lynch? Have you found our rose garden yet?" Sauder asked as the deck heaved violently beneath his feet. Rain hammered against the glass of the Steering House and the wail of the storm's winds prevented quiet speech. It was sometime after midnight, and all the lights in the Steering House were either doused, or shaded red to avoid ruining the crew's night vision. Hans was hanging on to a pitch-handle with all the strength he could manage. They had been caught in this foul weather for over an hour now, with no good way to see either stars above or the ocean below.

"*Ar bith, nach bhfuil fós*," she said in her native Irish as she finished her calculations and marked a point on the map. "By plot, Captain, we are about one hundred miles Northeast of Saint John's, in the British colony of Newfoundland. Our current altitude is four thousand feet by altimeter, with the correction for the low pressure system we are in. The weather layer extends from sea level up past our safe ceiling of five thousand feet, with visibility being kept to around two hundred yards maximum. Winds are from the Northeast, gusting to a gale."

"In other words, you are guessing by math where we are, but have not been able to get a fix in two hours?" Hans enquired.

There was a sour pause in the Steering House, in which the sound of the storm and the noises of the struggling airship prevented an unpleasant silence. The pause was broken by the sound of the Planesman wreching into the bucket between he and the Helmsman.

"That is correct, sir. I am sorry," the Irishwoman replied. Her usual air of fire and vinegar was entirely replaced by one of frustration and defeat. Grumman said nothing, keeping his eyes to the churning blackness of the night time storm ahead of the ship.

"You do not need to apologize, *Fräulein* Lynch. I am personally impressed that, given the beating we have been taking, you can work out enough of the factors affecting the ship to even estimate to within fifty miles of where we are. Armed with little more than a clock, a chart, and the collective intelligence and experience of yourself and Mister Grumman, you can still look me in the face and tell me where we ought to be right now."

The Irishwoman brightened noticeably at the praise from the German pirate captain. Grumman shook his head and spoke up.

"It is all her, Captain, Sir. I am too busy trying to keep the ship on course. I have worked with navigators that, starting on a clear day and three lead marks, could not tell me where we were after an hour of clouds. Miss Lynch is a pleasure to work with, sir," the Confederate officer said matter-of-factly.

"Noted, *Hern* Grumman. *Danke*," Hans replied. Hans made a mental note that the swaggering, brash Confederate-American had steadily become more and more open in his respect and praise for those he worked with. At first, Grumman had done little but brag and boast about himself. Since the return from Egypt, Hans had noticed a slow but steady wind-change in the man's attitude. This was a clear example of the "new Grumman".

*****

They had suffered at the power of the storm for almost another three hours before they finally found respite. It was another hour before they could get a proper fix; Hans was openly impressed that they were a mere fifty miles north and delayed of the intended track. After six hours of essentially flying blind in a North Atlantic gale and it's aftermath, Lynch and Redsands had between them essentially ensured they were where they should be.

The balance of the day had been rapidly clearing, warm and sunny weather with an advantageous wind helping them make up lost time. They saw nothing else in the air around them for the entire day, while the sea below regularly was dotted with schooners and tall-masted clippers slicing through the waves. The *Bloody Rose* cut her altitude to six hundred feet to take advantage of both the weather and the apparent lack of company.

Late in the afternoon, André Dubé arrived in Hans' cabin after being ordered to do so. He was somewhat surprised to find Annika and Nando there as well already seated in the chairs flanking the sole remaining unoccupied chair opposite the captain's desk. Hans gestured wordlessly for him to sit down.

"*Oui, mon capitaine*? Is there a problem?" the Master-Gunner asked carefully.

"*Nein*," Hans replied amiably. "You have, of course, no doubt heard that we are on our way for Halifax in British North America, *Ja*?"

"*Oui, monsieur*," Dubé nodded, glancing back and forth at the Captain-Gunner and the Deck Officer seated to either side of him.

"And what do you think?" Hans asked amusedly.

"Well, it is not quite what I had expected, of course, but the Captain-Gunner has explained it is to throw the authorities off our true plans so they relax somewhat."

Hans nodded and Annika spoke up. "You are missing one key component of this entire scheme, however, Master-Gunner," she said with an flip of a hand.

"Oh?"

"Yes," the Spanish Deck Officer stated. "We are throwing you overboard in Montréal," he concluded flatly.

André blinked. "*Pardonez-moi*?" he said, his head flipping back and forth in consternation as though trying to see all three officers at once.

"Oh, we will dock first, do not panic," Hans said with a laugh. There was a countenance of confusion on Dubé's features and Amram could hold himself no longer, and laughed aloud. Annika grinned in bemusement and Dubé relaxed somewhat, but still looked at the trio suspiciously.

"It makes no sense for you to come all the way to Persia, then back to Europe in the fall, only for you to then decide to Pay Your Respects, André," Annika with a broad smile. "After some discussion, if you are agreeable, we are specifically taking the ship to Montréal from Halifax so you can take your leave there," she explained.

"It also means that you can make a proper splash with your arrival," Nando said with a nod. "The officers of the *Bloody Rose* recognize you have been an outstanding crewman and we are losing a tremendous man. We would like to do what we can to ensure you are successful in relaunching your life."

André sat in shocked silence as Hans spoke up. "Bridges and I worked out a few options for a shopping list in Halifax as well as what is in our own holds. The idea would be that you convert a significant amount of that hoard of yours into material goods that you can use to demonstrate yourself as a man of means to your intended's father. A lump of money is impressive; a store's worth of goods even more so."

The Spanish Aristocrat-turned-pirate cleared his throat, his current uncharacteristic joviality replaced by his usual distance as he spoke. "I know a few things about setting up a home for newly weds as well as how to convince reluctant fathers, Mister Dubé. So, if you would like some assistance in your shopping list and how to go about your presentation, do let me know. I am sure that with proper preparation we might achieve your desires."

*****

It was a bit more than two hours after midnight of the following day when they reached the British port city of Halifax. She moored at one of a solitary pair of modest airship towers, located on the western slope of the "Citadel Hill", that protected the heart and harbour of the city. While there was an extensive oceanship port, they discovered that much as with New Orleans, the airship docks were a complete afterthought. In this case, they were located as part of the military facilities of the city. The *Bloody Rose* had flown in with only the Union Jack on her flagstaff and Hans had made a point of ensuring the local military knew that they still had a valid Letter. By next week, that luxury would be gone, but Hans intended to make good abuse of it in the mean time.

Where they had arrived at such an early hour, there was little they could do save make fast alongside, and wait until the merchants of the port city had woken up and had breakfast. A trio of merchants arrived at the gangway sharply on the hour of nine bells from the town clock, requesting to speak to the captain. Hans and Bridges met with the two men and a woman.

"What can I do for you lady and gentlemen?" Hans asked. They were on the weather deck, where the trio had been welcomed aboard.

"Well, good captain," one of the two men replied, "it was more a question of what we can do for you, sir? We heard rumour that you were a merchantman with full holds, fresh from Europe. We are dock brokers for the oceanship port, but we could see no reason we ought not to be able to perhaps offer you our Orders and see if we had fit between your supply and our customer's demands."

Hans chuckled. "Word travels fast in Halifax, I see."

"Only good words, Captain," the lady said with a charming smile. "In business, sometimes a bit of boldness pays well."

The group retired to Hans' cabin, and he had Bridges bring enough tea, coffee, and breakfast for the group as they sat down to the negotiations. They reviewed the cargo list of the *Bloody Rose* together, and Hans was given the impression that the trio of brokers were trying not to visibly salivate. Hans noted that they periodically glanced around the cabin at the various aspects of its decor. They also made compliment of quality the food they were served. It seemed obvious to Hans that while a certain amount of it was professional facade, there was also a genuine element to them.

"As you say, *Frau* Trevis, in business, sometimes a bit of boldness does pay well," Hans said at one point, leaning back in chair and sipping at his coffee. "I have an interesting problem that I am hoping you will help me solve."

"And what would that be, Captain Sauder?" the fellow named Nevil Spears asked. Spears was the one who had done the bulk of the talking when they first came aboard. He was a stout chap with dark hair and a beard, well dressed in a fashionable jacket, vest and cravat. Had Hans have encountered him on a street corner somewhere, he might have guessed him a banker.

"Well, my intention is sail from Halifax for Montréal. What I want to do is import a selection of goods to Montréal that are unique to British North America, and yet might not be common stock in Montréal," Hans replied, glancing out a window briefly.

"A bit of speculative trading interests you then, Captain?" the second man asked. His name was Goodwin Stark; if Spears was the numerical brains of the operation, then Stark was the schemer and schmoozer. He seemed to have a head for names and connections like few other Hans had met. Give the man a cargo and he could immediately quote three names in three different cities up and down the Atlantic coast he had spoken to in the past month that might well be interested. What Hans found amusing was that he evidently spent a good amount of time outside; the tall man's brown hair was sun glinted and his worked hands were as well tanned as Hans' own.

Hans shook his head. "Well, not exactly," he clarified. "One of my men his investing his life savings into heading home with enough splash to marry a lass somewhat above his station. So, the idea is to ensure that when we arrive and he puts his goods for market that we know he will have little trouble finding bidders and buyers."

Tabitha Trevis momentarily covered her clear smile of delight with her fan and politely cast her gaze aside. She was a charming woman with a medium figure and strawberry blonde hair. While she was dressed as well as the men were, in a fashionable ensemble with bustle and corset, she was much quieter in conversation. She took notes and constantly flipped through a pair of small books she carried. She seemed to be the logistics wizard of the trio, with careful records of when she individually expected a significant number of coastal oceanships to be in port with empty holds. In addition, she understood the North American rail network well and seemed to be able to rapidly derive the swiftest and least expensive way to get a load of anything to any customer that Stark might suggest.

Goodwin grinned. "Well, that is quite an occasion to be shopping for. Hmm. You know, you and your man just might be in luck ... we had a captain who was down on his fortune sell us a load of brand new Boston-styled applewood furniture for a very good price. Of course, there is no fast market for that here, and we were trying to sort out what to do with it."

Tabitha spoke up. "I know that it would be impractical to ship it to Montréal to make a profit. But ... if you are going there anyway, then you would be in a position to bring a very popular style of East Coast American upper middle classed furnishings into a market that seems to have a love affair with things from Boston and New York, but would nearly never see that sort of item. You could do very well with it."

Spears chuckled. "Goodwin, old boy, do you think you might get a hold of Blanchard in Montréal by telegraph before noon and see if we cannot arrange a good amount of this pre-sold before our good Captain even departs Halifax?"

Goodwin Stark grinned. "I am sure something can be arranged."

*****

It was a frantic job to move half a load of cargo to the ground and then nearly a like amount back aboard the *Bloody Rose* in a mere three hours. However, the crew had gotten wind that the idea was to aid the well-liked and well-respected Master-Gunner marry the girl that everyone knew he held a torch for. Pirate crews were an odd type of fraternity, Hans reflected. The day-to-day squabbles and aggravations about living and working together with a hundred other people, in a space not long enough to allow them all to stand shoulder to shoulder on it's deck, sometimes seemed like a titans' troubles or an abyssal divide. As soon as common threat or idea confronted them, however, they were suddenly unstoppably united in body and purpose.

So it was with the story of Dubé; some wit did a tally of how long Dubé had been with the ship, how much he drank and made party, and worked out likely how much money he had put aside. There was then apparently a consensus that this was not hardly enough money for a proper wedding party, and nearly everyone in the crew threw one or two Marks or Stirling into a passed hat that was then given to a stunned Franco-Brit at breakfast that morning.

One thing most sailors – air or sea – know how to do is sew, by need of maintaining their own clothes as well as repairing the various leather, silk, canvas and cotton applications around the ship. "Auntie Coline" organized a group of a dozen otherwise unoccupied hands into converting some old cotton flashing and similar material into a two sets of house linens. Koblinski commented to Hans in passing that if anyone had ever told him he would see a pirate sewing bee in the main mess, he would have thought them either a mad dog or an Englishman. Two of the hullwrights had even fashioned a solid spruce steamer trunk finished with a rich stain and brass trim for him to replace the battered boot and locker boxes André had been living out of.

By just afternoon the otherwise impossible task of a day's worth of cargo handling had been achieved. The brokerage trio of Spears, Stark and Travis had worked another minor miracle on a Sunday morning in having the ground-side arrangements managed so swiftly. That Hans had left three bottles of Cognac and a box of cigars in their possession likely had not hurt his cause at all, but it was still a remarkable achievement on their part.

The *Bloody Rose* let slip her lines and turned her bow to the west-northwest by the time the town clock was ringing the first bell of the afternoon. She cleared into the skies above the port of Halifax, and began the trip to Montréal. The course she ran took her into the massive valley of the Saint Laurence river. While only slightly more than a third the length of the American Mississippi river, the Saint Laurence had an equally profound effect on both history and geography. The *Bloody Rose* followed the river inland at a modest altitude.

As with her flight into Halifax, she was the only vessel in the air that her lookouts could see in any direction. The weather held good with a warm sun and wind, as well as high clouds. They ran after the sun to the West, watching it transform the far horizon into a glory of ruby and gold and then progressing to the dusk of a summer evening.

Once they were within sight of Montréal, a dragonfly-shaped "Forlanini Flyer" flew out to meet them. With its pair of counter-rotating propellers, one on each wing tip, spewing steam and its pair of bright electric lights on its nose, it was a very odd-looking craft. In addition to being remarkably noisy for its size, it was also rather conspicuous for the trail of sparks and embers it left behind in the sky as it flew. It had two crew, sitting one behind the other. The pilot seemed to have his hands full with the job of flying it, rarely looking up save to check his position relative to the *Bloody Rose* as the peculiar vehicle flew alongside them.

The aft-chaired crew signalled them with a flashing signal lamp using Morse's code. Unfortunately, no one on the bridge read French well enough to make heads over tails of what was being said. They rapidly got Chief Nurse Coline to the Steering House to translate for them.

After an initial bit of straightening out, it was learned that the Forlanini Flyer was actually owned by the Port of Montréal, and was informing them to stop flying towards the City or risk being shot down. The *Bloody Rose* came to an abrupt halt at Hans' barked command.

"What, exactly, is the problem, *Frau* Coline?" Hans asked while watching the Flyer currently hanging in mid-air a dozen yards from their port bow.

"It seems, *Capitainne*, that the Port is suspicious of unannounced airship traffic. They wish us to land about eight miles down the river where we will be met by Customs and Commerce officials. They say that if we approach the City without relayed permission, the garrison will fire on us with anti-airship guns," she replied, looking a touch overwhelmed at suddenly being the lynchpin in such vital communications.

"You know, I do not envy that pilot," Watch Officer Doretta Tillie said with an amused tone in her voice.

"Oh? Why is that, Miss Tillie?" Jeffery Wilton asked.

"Well, he is two hundred feet in the air, only being held up by steam, spruce and duraluminum with a Gatling gun squarely pointed at him. He must be quite aware that he is making threats while a mere two cranks of a handle would leave him with naught more than a chair and a control stick to ride on the way down," she replied with a merry laugh.

Hans chuckled, as did Annika. "I am sure he is also very aware that if we want to actually be able to get anywhere near Montréal again, it is not in our interest to crank that handle at all," Annika said. "But yes, I do see your point. It is such a fragile looking thing. No gas bags at all; just raw horsepower and ingenuity to keep it aloft."

"*Frau* Coline, please help the Signalman reply that we will make our way to the landing point," Hans ordered. "Ask them for proper latitude and longitude. Helm and planes, bring us around, speed ten, altitude two fifty. *Hern* Wilton, once you have the destination plotted on the map, take us there."

A few more rounds of flashing light were passed back and forth before the *Bloody Rose* was on her way to the meeting spot. The Forlanini Flyer droned along beside them for a few minutes, at one point flying sideways while pointing her nose lights at the side of airship. It then turned and flew off towards Montréal, a wake of sparks, smoke and embers marking its path.

Hans had the ship readied for action in case this highly unusual situation turned out to be a deception of some kind. However, they found the small airfield with minimal effort. Several dozen electric lights lit both the ground, the structures and the sky above it clearly, even in the mid-dusk. A small watermill to one side of the field was the likely source of the required electric power. One of the building roofs had "Port of Montréal" painted on it in both French and English.

"Hmmm. That is rather interesting, do you not agree, *Hern* Wilton?" Hans asked as they approached. "A very well laid out and manged facility from what we can see here by spyglass. We are the only airship we have seen in ... what, four days? And yet they have a protocol for air control over the city and a small dedicated dock for clearing visitors."

The young Englishman nodded. "It is surprising, to be sure. There must be a very interesting story about this. Perhaps British North America makes more common use of airships in the interior and north than the United States of America?"

The *Bloody Rose* took a ground mooring in the middle of the field only a dozen or so feet off the ground. A group of French soldiers and bureaucrats made their way across the field from one of the buildings to the parked pirate ship. A set of electric lights was switched on, illuminating both the *Bloody Rose* as well as the group walking to her in the slowly gather gloom of the summer evening.

Hans welcomed them aboard with André Dubé, Nicolas LeBlanc and Charles Martel – all native Frenchmen – to act as translators for he, and the other officers. The entourage from the Port were brusque and to the point; they wished to know why the *Bloody Rose* was here, how long she was staying, what she was carrying and then wanted to be shown around the cargo and tank holds to look for signs of pests.

Both Nando and Bridges took some umbrage at the notion that the *Bloody Rose* was being accused of being a rat's nest, but Hans managed to prevent that from becoming an incident. The Port Commission team clearly had little interest in accommodating the pirates in anyway and were set like cast-iron on doing their jobs meticulously.

It took nearly two hours before the Frenchmen seemed satisfied that all was in order, charged a modest sum for docking at the field for the next week and then gave them a list of "approved" dock, warehouse and broker companies that they might wish to deal with. Once the group had departed the ship, Hans summoned the officers to his cabin.

"Well, that was a genuine pleasure," Hans snorted as Bridges and another steward brought out coffee, tea and a few sweets. "What have we learned in all that?" he asked.

"Well," Annika replied, "the obvious thing is that they have this port screwed down tight against airship smugglers. If anything is going on, it is coming by water or land."

"They were somewhat surprised that we had a proper doctor and nurse aboard," Koblinski supplied.

"*Oui*," Coline said with a nod. "I spoke with one of *les soldats*, and they were much more worried about us bringing in pestilence or plague than illegal goods from what I could tell."

"LaRoche, the man in charge, told me that the city suffered greatly about ten years ago from an illness brought from Europe by airship that killed many cattle in the area," Nando said while taking a date square from a plate before him.

"Ah! Now I understand," the Polish doctor announced with a look of dawning comprehension about him.

"Oh? And what do you understand, *Herr Döktor*?" Hans asked.

"Well, a sickness like that develops over time, you see. On an oceanship, signs of disease or pestilence would be evident amongst the animals or the crew and passengers by the time a vessel arrived here from Europe," Koblinski stated.

"But with the speed an airship moves, we can cross the Atlantic in a quarter or a fifth the time as an oceanship," Sarah Whitesands said. "So that would mean that an imported problem may not have time to make itself known."

"Exactly, *Panna* Whitesands," Koblinski returned.

"And so, once bitten, twice shy, as it were," Arietta remarked with a light toss of a hand.

"So it seems," Hans nodded after a sip of his coffee. "So we are to remain here, and we will have to hire a shipping firm to take our goods to the town for us."

"That is an aggravation," Onora Lynch sighed.

"Only a minor one," Chief Bridges countered. "We just need to be smart so that we only pay to move it once. Twice if we decide to warehouse it first and then work from within the city."

"My intention is to pass the rest of the evening and night quietly here, and we will get about the business at hand tomorrow, it being Monday", Hans announced. "We will arrange a warehouse in the city and move our holds there in the morning. In the afternoon, we will see to Mister Dubé's little errand, and then we will Pay Out in the evening before the Dog's Supper. That will ensure that everyone has a cause to celebrate and pocketful of money to do it with."

*****

The next day started with the dawn, as James Bridges and three Gunner-Marines, including Yvette LaBelle, set off to make arrangements for warehouse and transportation.

The Chief Steward and Hans had already sorted out prices and the like together the night before, so that no time was wasted in the morning.

By mid-morning, Bridges was back with a wagon train and a folio full of Buy Orders as well as a warehouse contract. In the meantime, the pirates had already been busy moving goods and materials to the ground on the leeward side of the ship by steam-winch.

Nevil Spears in Halifax had been good to his word and almost the entire shipment of of furniture they had run from Halifax to Montréal was sold by the time they had arrived. That added nearly a third to Dubé's fortune by itself. The Franco-Brit was beginning to look a little awestruck when Hans gave him the news.

"Powder dry and sights sharp, Mister Dubé," Hans admonished the Master-Gunner jokingly. "Your lady will not think highly of you should you arrive at her door as a drooling nervous wreck. I suggest you find a fresh can of *panache* and apply it to yourself liberally."

Shortly after the noon meal, Hans and the other officers all met with André Dubé on the ground beneath the moored pirate ship. In addition, a dozen Gunner-Marines were there with them, carrying arms. All the officers were turned out in their best Governor's kit, as they had been for the visit to the "O-Room" in the Azores. The Gunner-Marines were turned out in the best clothes they had, looking rather colourful. A trio of electric-powered trucks fitted with benches waited near by.

Hans walked over to André and looked at him squarely. "Are you sure this is what you want, *mon ami*? In a few moments, you will be giving a shove to the flywheel of Fate and the gears will begin turning."

"*Absolutement, mon capitaine,*" the Franco-Brit replied with a steadfast nod. "This is the day I have dreamed of for three years."

"Then let us go speak to a father about a daughter, a son-in-law and happily ever after, *mein freund*," Hans grinned.

*****

They made quick travel to the city where they disembarked from the electric trucks. They had been told that it would be almost impossible to maneuver the vehicles in the part of town they were destined for. Instead, the officers took to rented horseback and the accompanying Gunner-Marines guiding open-topped and side-boarded horse wagons. The wagons were heaped with the material goods that André Dubé had acquired with Amram Nando's advice to give an impression of solid material wealth and means. The Franco-Brit was riding in a chauffeured and modestly appointed horse carriage and possibly feeling a bit conspicuous.

The procession of more than twenty pirates, plus horses, wagons and carriage wended its way to an upper middle-class neighbourhood of the town, attracting a certain amount of attention to itself as it did. They halted in front of a rather impressive looking home, the residence of an inarguably moneyed family. A low stone wall topped with a wrought iron fence surrounded a small but lush summer garden divided by a walkway leading to the door of the house. Lillies, ivies, roses, and cedars held the smells of the city at bay, while a small fountain routed the encroaching sounds.

André stepped down from the coach he rode in and simply stood in front of the metal gate for a moment, looking at the place. Hans sensed there was a feeling of *déjà vu* in this moment, a thing done before by the precursor to the man that stood here today. So much had changed about Hans in a mere handful of months, he could not imagine the changes that the Franco-Brit would have undergone in three years.

Dubé pushed the gate open, strode to the heavy door and knocked on it sharply. There was a pause and the door swung open. A tall, lean, stern-faced and hawk-nosed man looked down his beak at the evidently undesired visitor. Words were passed, and the tone sounded less than pleasant. This was accompanied by a good deal of grand gesturing. Blackheart – Micheal O'Ready, that is – had once commented the quickest way to silence a Frenchman was to handcuff him.

The butler pointed back toward the open gate and clearly made orders that Dubé should depart. When the Master-Gunner shook his head, the butler produced a short club not much bigger than MacIassac's murderous belaying pin. They stared at each other for a long moment, with the butler tapping the business end of the club on the palm of his free hand.

A sharp whistle split the tableaux, and all nearby eyes turned towards its source. Annika lowered the fingers from her mouth. She then snapped the same fingers twice and pointed at the butler. As one, the second man of each cart stepped down from the seat, undid his coat, and tossed it up on the empty seat beside the driver. They each then rolled up their sleeves and moved to stand in a line abreast behind their Master-Gunner.

Dubé turned his head and gave an amused smirk to the butler. The butler looked at the gentleman before him, the line of rough men standing behind him, and gave a half-bow and went into the house without a word.

The young woman who emerged a short time later was unmistakable to Hans as Caroline LeGros, the Franco-Brit's fond love. André had often spoken of her to Hans and between the strawberry-blonde of her hair tucked under a modest hat, the combined tallness and gentle curves of her figure, she was immediately recognizable.

The butler had apparently not seen fit to explain to the young woman who her caller might be. The moment she laid eyes on the well-dressed chap in the gentleman's suit before her, her gloved hands flew to her mouth in uncontrolled shock. Her eyes went wide and she just stood and stared at him in wordless surprise.

Hans barely heard André's assertion of "*Je vous ai donné mon mot que je reviendrais pour vous*," before anything else the Master-Gunner might have planned on saying was eclipsed by Caroline's shriek of delight. She fairly leapt into his arms with such force that both their hats went tumbling to the ground. A cheer went up from the pirates around them, echoed by those that had followed the procession thus far. She kissed him soundly to a cheer and another round of applause from the pirates. In a moment of bravado, Dubé swept his lady-love up into his arms and carried her to the waiting carriage.

*****

"*Je suis désolé, monsieur*," the Sub-Sergeant at the head of the dozen or so men said. "I cannot let you parade an armed column through the streets of Montréal."

They had managed to cover half the distance between the LeGros home and Caroline's father's shipping business in the river port district when a sizable detachment of peace officers, each with a gaff-hooked quarterstaff in hand, blocked their way. The Sub-Sergeant at their head was obviously none too enthused with the possibilities stemming from a contingent of armed foreign privateers with horses and carts in the middle of the city's port district. Much to Hans' relief, the Sub-Sergeant spoken English reasonably well.

"Well, you cannot expect me to parade a column of carts loaded with expensive European goods through the streets of Montréal without guards", Hans countered. "These are wedding gifts for the couple and assertions for the father of the bride, monsieur. It would be terrible to have them not arrive at the possibly reluctant father's door. It would crush the young couple."

The Sub-Sergeant looked from Hans and then Annika, and then to André Dubé and Caroline LeGros where they sat together. He scratched his forehead with a knuckle, lifting the peak of his cap as he did. "*Eh bien, je ne suis pas sûr ce que nous pouvons accepter* ... Love is important, *bien sur monsieur*, but it is my job to uphold the law." Hans could see the fellow was sympathetic to the cause, but felt his hands were tied on his duties.

"*Pardonnez-moi, monsieur gendarme*," Amram Nando said with a sudden smile. "Could you not guard us as we in turn guard the goods of the young couple? That way the law is satisfied. With your excellent men keeping an eye on us, I am sure there would be nothing ... *mechant* ... that would happen."

The Sub-Sergeant broke into a broad grin at the the Spanish aristocrat turned pirate and then glanced back at the men with him. A round of silent nods and smiles were passed. A few men went ahead on foot shouting for the street to be cleared, while the Sub-Sergeant and his second walked to either side of the young couple's carriage. The remaining men walked one to each side of a cart, and one officer behind. This brought the total of the procession to eight pirate officers on horseback, two engaged love birds in a carriage, twelve armed pirates driving six loaded wagons and eighteen peace officers on foot.

To say the group was conspicuous as it made its way from *Champ De Mars* towards the port district was somewhat of an understatement. People were looking out of first floor doors and second story windows trying to figure out what was going on. By the time the "armed column" had arrived at the dockside offices of Caroline's father, the total number had nearly tripled with curious onlookers. A very perplexed Jean-Francois LeGros came out of his office with two of his dockmen at his side at the sound of the commotion, halting up suddenly at the display before him.

He blinked, adjusted his spectacles and realized his daughter was in the middle of all of that in front of his door. "Marie Caroline! *Ca vas dire exactement quoi, tout ca*?" he demanded.

"*Mon bon monsieur*," Hans began as he swung down from the saddle of his horse. "I am *Kapitän* Hans Sauder of the Privateer Airship *Bloody Rose*. My man André Dubé is a Master-Gunner of my ship. He has come here to ask you for your daughter's hand in marriage. He brings with him the entire contents of these wagons as wealth and security in setting up his new home and his new business, so you may be sure your daughter will be well cared for. Might he come forward to have a word with you?"

Jean-Francois LeGros blinked at the English-speaking German gentleman. The Sub-Sergeant, now standing beside Hans, translated from English to French.

It was one of those moments where Hans had dearly wished they had one of those Kodak boxes with them, trained from a roof upon the scene. Two ladies in the crowd swooned. Several other on-lookers cheered, clapped and shouted encouragements to the father to let the young man speak his case. Jean-Francois, for his part, looked like he might well collapse in shock. He fumbled in his pockets for a moment, took a pinch of apricot snuff from a small silver box and inhaled. He shook his head, and then took a rather severe frown about him.

There was a spatter of rapid-fire French, coupled with its customary hand-waving and a sound of dismay came from the crowd. Even the Sub-Sergeant sounded somewhat disheartened as he translated.

"Monsieur LeGros says that the fellow Dubé is a low-born man of insufficient station and reputation to be considered for his daughter. Just as he was the last time he asked."

Hans' eyes narrowed. Annika muttered something nasty sounding in Russian and Hans raised a hand to silence her. "Good Sir, please explain to him that my ship sails on the written orders of the Queen of England, and the President of France. Surely, were I such a man to hire such a man as he describes, I would not have such a Letter. Redsands, the Letter, if you please?"

The sandy-haired Amerindian stepped down from her horse and brought a brass and leather tube to Hans. She gave a nod and salute to him, much to his barely concealed surprise, before returning to her horse and remounting. He took the paper from inside it and passed it to Jean-Francois LeGros as the Sub-Sergeant repeated what Hans had said.

Before LeGros could make comment, Hans continued. "It is clear by the Letter he holds that the *Bloody Rose* and her crew are all respected by the Allied Empires. Surely, he does not gainsay the President of the Republic? Men and times change. *Monsieur* André Dubé is a fine man with a good sense of loyalty, compassion and right. He has worked hard and made fame and fortune for himself, all in the name of the young lady. He is a better man than he was, last he and Monsieur LeGros met. I will have words with any who would call me a liar."

As the Sub-Sergeant translated Hans' declaration, the German pulled the right edge of his black greatcoat back, hooking it behind the scabbard of his sword. The sizable holster of the LeMatt was now also plainly in view. It was a plain and visible statement of intent and willingness to duel over the matter.

The reaction amongst the crowd was mixed. Some found the implied threat to be a strike against the groom-to-be's cause. Many others seemed even more impressed that the man's captain would implicitly put his honor and life on the line as guarantee to the claim.

Jean-Francois LeGros looked from the Sub-Sergeant, to Hans, to the parade of pirates and policemen, to the young couple in the carriage, to the assembled crowd, and then back to Hans. It was evident to Hans the man was both feeling out-foxed as well as supremely unappreciative of that fact. At the same time, there was a shrewd evaluation of the event taking place, and Hans was given the impression the man was cagily looking for a way to make sauce of it.

After another long moment of consideration, he beckoned André Dubé forward, to a great shout and cheer from the crowd. The Sub-Sergeant announced that LeGros could find no reason to doubt a Captain in possession of such a Letter, and so he was moved to hear out André's proposal. André made a great show of saluting Hans as he strode past and then bowing to LeGros.

He made further display of presenting a written letter detailing the contents of the carts, his plans for a sugar-maple plantation, plus his sincere and steady love for Caroline that had kept him alive and true to his course all this time in his travels. He went on to declare his wish to have a family with such an esteemed man as Jean-Francois LeGros as it's patriarch to their children, and finally his request – nay, heart-felt and delivered from one knee plea – for the young lady's hand in marriage.

It took several moments before Monsieur LeGros was able to reply from the cheering of men, weeping of women and general near pandemonium from the assembled crowd. Hans had a mild and amusing suspicion that if Jean-

Francois LeGros said anything but "yes", the ladies of the gathered crowd might well string him up.

LeGros adjusted his spectacles and eyed the man kneeling before him, and then looked back to his daughter, likely weighting his decisions. He raised his hand in a surprisingly effective gesture of command and the crowd fell silent, waiting to find out what the finale to this unfolding unique drama in this unique French city might be.

"*Je suis un homme*", Monsieur LeGros began in a lofty tone, "*qui a construit la richesse de la modestie à veiller à ce que ma famille est bien soigné. Vous, jeune homme, ont construit la richesse de la pauvreté pour assurer une famille, vous n'avez pas encore seront bien soignés. Promets-moi de vous tiendrai toujours ma fille comme votre plus grand trésor de toutes vos richesses et que vous êtes digne d'elle.*" He concluded with a stern and expectant look at the man who wished to be his son-in-law.

There was a moment where André simply stared in disbelief at what he had heard. The crowd exploded in cheering and applause as André nodded furiously.

"Monsieur LeGros said," the Sub-Sergeant translated, "that he is a man who has built wealth from modesty to ensure his family is well cared for. He says that your crewman has built wealth from poverty to ensure a family he does not yet even have will be well cared for. If your man promises Monsieur LeGros he will always hold the young lady as his greatest treasure in all his wealth then he will agree to the marriage."

Hans gave a shout of happiness and the remainder of the pirates of the *Bloody Rose* echoed it. The young woman that would be Caroline Dubé ran into André's arms and then hugged her father with such force that she all but knocked his spectacles off. After a great deal of handshaking and applause had passed, Jean-Francois

LeGros gestured for Hans and the Sub-Sergeant to approach him.

After a moment of listening, the Sub-Sergeant looked at Hans and explained "Monsieur LeGros wishes to discuss a 'favour' with you relating to the happiness of the young couple."

*****

"So the jerk is blackmailing us?" Annika snorted, sitting on the edge of Hans' desk in his cabin, her legs dangling. Her men's white shirt was unbuttoned to the waist, her pants, boots and belt had been tossed at the foot of Hans' liquor cabinet, and she had a cut-crystal glass of brandy cradled in her hands.

"Not exactly," Hans said with a chuckle. He was sitting in the chair at his desk, his socked feet propped up and crossed. His own shirt was hanging from one of the corners of the backrest of his chair. He scratched absently at the linen pants he still wore, and then raised his own brandy glass to his lips before speaking. "I think a more accurate description might be that he wants every advantage he can eek out of this. I do not think he would actively try and prevent the marriage at this point. André put on such a show that the social pages of Montréal will be chittering for weeks. However, given the grief I personally caused him in front of his own office, I think he figures this is fair recompense."

"So, where exactly, again?" she asked, trailing a finger down from his knee to his ankle.

Hans made a mild noise of appreciation and had another sip of his brandy. "New York. We run a load of high-demand goods down and unload them, which allows him to steal a march on a competitor in Toronto, apparently. LeGros' goods will be on the market while the other chap's goods are somewhere on a train."

"And then? Back to Europe?"

"Yes," Hans nodded. "Same route back as we took here, hopefully less the North Atlantic storm. Cross Ireland, veer up towards Belgium and then down the Carpathians towards Persia. With some good luck and good fortune, we will have a full hold when we arrive at our planned airshipyard. That will give the boys and girls some extra Marks in their purses while we get the upgrades and repairs done."

"Mmmm. Good plan, Hans. You, my handsome pirate, are good at this," she said, giving him a pleased looked over the rim of her glass.

"I had the fortune of learning from the best," Hans replied quietly.

"Do you miss him?" Annika asked, tilting her head and then leaning forward to rest her chin on the heel of her left hand.

"Yes," Hans said with a slow nod.   "It is almost surprising."

"We all do," Annika replied. "But ... as I told you some time ago ... there are no happy endings for pirates. Just sudden ones."

*****

"Come in," Hans ordered, leaning back in his chair. It was the next morning, and he was just sitting down at his desk. He had not been in his chair a minute after breakfast when knuckles sounded on the wood of his door at the same time as an electric buzzer sounded from the base of the lamp on his desk. "Come in, it is open," Hans repeated.

The door opened and André Dubé entered the Captain's Mess, removing his cap as he did.   "*Bonjour, Mon Capitaine*," he greeted with a polite nod.

"Ah, bonjour, André. Tous et bien, j'espere?" Hans replied in his stilted French.

"Oui," the Franco-Brit replied as he moved to stand in front of of Hans' desk. He paused for a moment. "I am here to Pay My Respects, *Capitaine.*"

Hans blinked in shock. "Pardon?" he asked blankly.

"I am leaving the ship, *Monsieur* Blackheart. By the Traditions, I am here to Pay My Respects," Dubé repeated. He took out a small leather bag and offered it to Hans.

For an instant, Hans was catapulted back in time to when it had been he standing before the desk of a man named Blackheart, a small sack of money in hand by way of thanks for everything a Captain did to ensure that at least a few of his crew got rich and learned enough to leave. He recalled his first conversation with André, back on a loading dock in an Egyptian port town, and how the man had been so sure of the mastery of his own destiny. Now, here is was, having made good on his plan and eighteen months of deadly work.

"Well," Hans said slowly, "this is hardly where I expected to be standing right now when we first met, André." Hans took the bag of money from the other man and sat it on his desk without a second glance.

André blinked and then laughed aloud. *"J'imagine pas!"* he chuckled. "It is interesting how the world, it turns all our lives, yes?"

"'It can be interesting where life leads you', as I sometimes say, yes," Hans grinned. "Now ... congratulations. I am proud to know you, *mon ami.* I wish more people were as focused and worked as hard as you do. I know that you will be a success in your new life with your new family."

André pulled out a folded letter and waived it at Hans. "I still have our agreement here, Hans. You have invested heavily in my business in the time I have known you. I work for what I have, Hans ... I will not call this charity. Promise me that I will see you come the middle of spring to collect your shares."

"André," Hans began with a shake of his head, "I gave you that money because it meant more to your dreams than to mine. And we were both more than a little drunk when we wrote that 'contract'; it still has a stain of a rum bottle on the page."

"That just adds to it's veracity," the Franco-Brit countered with a laugh. "How else can you prove it was signed between two pirates?"

Hans laughed aloud for a few moments before he could reply. "That does not change that I do not consider it binding upon you and your business."

"Hans ... this is important to me. When you first gave me your Duties, you barely knew me. I was just another pirate. You did not even particularly like pirates. And yet, you chose to help a complete stranger you had a reason to actively dislike to achieve his life's dream. That is a kindness I refuse to allow to be unrepaid. It is a point of honour to me."

The two men stared stubbornly at each other for a few long moments of silence. "Fine," Hans said sternly. "You had better at least be making me enough money to justify a bunker of coal for the trip from Europe to this backwater!"

"Backwater? Luddite!" André retorted in mock outrage. "Have you any idea how much BNA maple products sell for in Europe?"

"No! And neither do you! But ... we will find out come spring of next year." He paused for a moment and then continued, amused. "You have my word. I look forward to seeing your new plantation and home, André," Hans said with a quiet smile.

André nodded slowly. *"Je vous remercie encore une fois, mon capitaine* ... for everything you have done in the time we have known each other." He saluted Hans, turned and left.

"Transits"

Monday, the 30th of July

We departed Montréal early afternoon of the 25th of July. We had taken a load of goods aboard for André's father-in-law to be, with the agreement that we would ship them to the American city of New York for him. This essentially would allow him to steal a march from a hated competitor.

While I understand that trains are fine ways of slowly moving around in North America, the absolute utility that an airship brings to high-valued cargo suggests to me that a place like Montréal would benefit from having them regularly available. Perhaps I should send a letter to Karl to this effect. A few S1-3C3s, as light as they are, would make fine packet boats.

We arrived in New York that evening, unloaded, and departed the next morning with little incident. We set our course for Europe, crossing the Irish coast two mornings later, on the 28th of July. Almost immediately, we were able to again take prey of a fat little gypsy merchant. Unlike the Charming Prince, there were no hi-jinx involving pulse-rocket motors and lurking Russian flotillas, much to everyone's relief.

Later that evening, as night fell, we reached our favorite little town outside of Brussels. Cargo was *unloaded and an evening of carousing and indulgence was the order of the night for the crew. Annika and I took our leave of the festivities and went for a swim. It would seem I have come full circle in many regards.*

Tomorrow, we set our course for Persia. Three days later, the Bloody Rose will be conspicuously absent from the skies of Europe until the chill of autumn again takes hold.

*****

Hans eyed Annika and Khadija dubiously from the vantage point of his desk chair. Khadija's left eye was blacked shut, and her bottom lip was split. Annika had a bruised jaw and her left hand was swollen and taped. Between them was an equally battered-looking Cemil, with a line of stitches across his forehead and his off-hand taped to immobility. All three were intently not meeting his gaze.

"So, let me get this straight. We are in New York, and thus the Ladies of the Rose thought this would be an excellent 'cultural opportunity' for Khadija and so you lot showed up at a bar frequented by the local Marine garrison? And when one of the patrons seemed to think he was implicitly permitted to take public liberties with Arietta, she put him through a window?"

"From the second floor," Annika nodded.

"With a kick," Khadija added, sounding somewhat awed.

"... which resulted in a bar brawl?" Hans questioned politely, his fingers steepled before him.

"Yes," Cemil answered.

"... that you and fifteen other Gunner-Marines just happened to be walking by the building in time for?"

"That sounds like a good story, *Qaa'ed*, so I am happy to go with that," Cemil said with a winning smile.

Hans scowled at him and Annika snickered.

"So how did the bar catch fire, then?" Hans said, getting up from his chair, beginning to pace back and forth behind his desk.

"Would you believe me if ...?" Cemil started.

"No," Hans said, with a dismissive wave. "Annika, your turn?"

"One of the patrons swung a mostly full bottle of brandy at Khadija, and Cemil interfered..."

"... with a banister post ..." Cemil supplied.

"... and put both the patron and the bottle into the fire place. It got rather chaotic after that," the Captain-Gunner concluded.

"I see," Hans said with a patient sigh, rubbing the bridge of his nose, looking rather pained. "Tally?"

"No one in jail, five with broken limbs, two with cracked rib cages, one with a concussion, two with minor burns and everyone suffering from bruising, aches and pains," Annika rattled off, sounding less like a school girl in front of the headmaster and more like the Captain-Gunner of the *Bloody Rose*.

"Have they any God-given clue what ship's crew that was?" Hans asked.

"MacIssac carved '*For a rematch, visit*', the ship's name and our docking tower into the bar door before we retreated," Cemil laughed. Annika snickered, which in turn reduced Khadija into helpless nervous giggles, which resulted in the three of them erupting into riotous laughter with a patiently exasperated Hans watching them in silence. His arched brow and sigh of aggravation, further prolonged the laughter for another few moments.

"Gang-plank watch until we leave tomorrow night is two on the ground, three on the deck," Hans ordered, still rubbing the bridge of his nose. "And for some reason I cannot explain, I am compelled to say 'good job' to you all. No matter how ridiculous the situation, we all have to look out for each other. Well done in making sure that our Legend and reputation remains intact, even in America. Now get out while I find something for this sudden headache I have."

*****

The sun had given way to dusk as the *Bloody Rose* cruised a few dozen feet above the port city of New York's upper harbour, heading southward. She slowly curved eastward, following the Ambrose Channel and heading into the steadily freshening wind that heralded the Atlantic Ocean. Once she was roughly at the Bight, she began turning more towards the North East, and climbing lazily to a comfortable six hundred feet above the waves beneath her battery ribs.

On the bridge, Hans stared out the port windows, back towards the area the locals called Jamaica Bay.

"*Capitán?*" the Spanish Deck Officer repeated.

"I am sorry, *Hern* Nando. Again, if you please?" Hans asked, sounding somewhat sheepish.

"I said we are now on track for our Atlantic transit, with all information suggesting we should have good weather for the trip. At current course and speed, we should be approaching the Irish coast in two days, after dark."

"Good. Very good. Thank you, *Hern* Nando and *Fräulein* Whitesands. Excellent work, as always. You two are unduly dangerous to me," Hans said with a chuckle.

"Oh," the Amerindian woman said with an arched eyebrow. "And in what fashion is that, Captain?"

"You two reduce getting in and out of places like London and New York into such boringly text-book affairs that I doze off," the German pirate captain grinned.

"Well, *Capitán*, I can arrange for some excitement on the next passage, if you wish," Nando replied dryly. "I would hate to have you suffering from acute boredom."

*****

The next morning found Hans and Annika in the midst of their sparring practice. She held a center bossed buckler in her left hand in addition to her cutlass in her right hand. Hans had the LeMatt in his off hand, using its metallic heft to parry with.

A furious exchange of sword clashes left Hans on the defensive, and Annika pressed him backwards a few steps before he dodged and rolled to a side, then subsequently dove over a capstan and rope drum. She pursued, and they clashed again, resulting in Annika balancing atop the capstan for a moment as they battled. Steel sang, thuds of limbs colliding, and gasps of exhaled air were audible above the sound of the wind sweeping across the deck.

Hans disengaged and raised a hand to signal a stop. He stepped into the lee of a windscreen and pulled his breather mask down, gulping air. Annika joined him, doing the same.

"*Luchshe*, Hans," she gasped raggedly. "Much better. That gap I usually exploit on your left side ... you blocked everything I tried there."

"*Lieber Himmel, Weibsbild,*" Hans answered, in much the same manner. "You are a windmill when you get going. I am so busy defending that I can barely get a counter attack executed."

She grinned at him. "That is the idea, *Kapitan*. It does not matter how good a fighter your opponent is if you can drown them in a wave of attacks."

"Clever girl," he snorted. "What is the plan for your day?" he asked, opening and then tipping his coffee flask to his lips.

"If you do not mind, I was planning on breaking out the Tesla rifles and getting the Gunner-Marines up here in shifts, practising shooting pheasant in a hurricane. I figure it is a good trick to keep sharp," she replied, taking the coffee flask from him and gulping back a mouthful.

Hans nodded at her. "What are you thinking of using for targets? I doubt the Russians will loan us any of their rocket-fighters for the afternoon."

She laughed, her blue eyes glittering in amusement. "Parachute flares, I think. If we fire them off a bow, then fire at them from a beam, it will give the Gunners a chance to fire on a small, swift target."

"Very clever girl. Keep score. Anyone that puts the flare out gets a plate from the Dog's Supper tonight," Hans said with a nod.

"A bit of competition to keep everyone sharp, *Da*? I like," she said firmly with a nod, sheathing her cutlass. She eyed him up and down for a moment. "Will Hans be interested in some company after *Kapitan* Blackheart is done for the day?" she asked, adjusting one of her gauntlets.

"Very much so."

"Good," she said. She gave a sassy wink, pulled her breather mask up and her goggles back down, and then turned on a heel to depart.

Hans watched her stride confidently across the deck, the few Gunner-Marines that were already at work on the decks acknowledging her with a nod or bow. O'Raedy had once told him that that the Gunner-Marines "loved to hate" the wilful and sharp-spoken Russian that led them. Hans had learned that there was a tremendous respect shared between she and the men and women that were the "violence scientists" of the *Bloody Rose*.

Hans had laughed aloud when he had first heard Arietta use that term. However, there was a ring of truth to it. Annika refined everything she saw, heard, or did in a battle into an ever-expanding knowledge that she ensured everyone that fought with her learned and benefited from. It was part of how the Mediterranean Menace had earned her nickname.

Yet again, he reminded himself that it was his responsibility to ensure this extraordinary group of individuals had a Legend to rally behind. It might not have been a Legend of his making, but at the point he put on the Black Coat, he accepted the responsibility and the standard.

"I am quite fine with that," he said to himself as he adjusted one of his cuffs.

*****

"Captain, our target is confirmed as a medium-sized Gypsy Merchant at six hundred feet, port bow, far. We are at one thousand feet, just south of Dublin. Visibility is clear to at least twenty miles, bright stars, full moon, no other ships in the area."

"Thank-you. Make bells and whistles for action. I think it's time to take some Prey. Let the Propulsion Room know what we are about, and ensure we have lifters ready to go."

"Aye-aye, Captain." Jeffery Wilton replied.

It was a couple of hours before midnight when the *Bloody Rose* passed over the Irish coast. The ocean crossing had been a delight of warm and cloudy days, clear and cool nights, and winds that either favored them or at least were no severe hindrance. The crew's spirits were high, and Hans had decided to be in the Steering House personally in case just such an opportunity as this presented itself.

Annika came into the Steering House and Hans gestured at the cluster of lights in the air ahead of him. She nodded and wordlessly raised a spyglass to her eye, studying the misfortuned vessel. She scanned around the *Bloody Rose* in all directions for a moment.

"*Hern* Wilton assures me there isn't a weather front or Russian flotilla for fifty miles in any direction, Captain-Gunner. However, should that little duck suddenly use rocket engines, we are turning south-east and running for France," Hans laughed. A round of chuckles passed through the Steering House, and Annika snorted at him.

She took aim with her range-finder on the intended target, and then looked back at it again with her spyglass. She lowered the glass and looked over at Hans. "Well, I very much doubt bursting cinderball ahead of her will work. We are coming at her from behind and in the dark. Whatever passes for a lookout over there is unlikely to see them exploding," Annika said with a clear note of distaste in her voice.

"So what do you propose then, Captain-Gunner?" Hans questioned.

"Dive to her stern, light her up with a couple of electric search lights, and drive a couple of solid balls into the area around her propellers. Then pull alongside and board," she replied with a shrug.

"And if she tries to run?" Watch Officer Wilton asked.

"We blow her ass off with a point-blank broadside," Doretta Tillie said with a laugh.

"Exactly," Annika grinned.

*****

The merchant was a saucily painted, single propeller affair that looked like it had been assembled in someone's backyard by a bunch of drunken grandmothers. Named the *"Becca's Delight"*, Hans was not entirely sure how it was the dubious looking craft stayed aloft. A single eight-pound ball expertly driven into her propeller shaft by Master-Gunner Cortez had been enough to convince the Gypsy Merchant to give up without a fight.

The crew of six were waiting on the midships deck as the pirates came aboard. The vessel's master, a man of about Sauder's age named Colin McGregor, demanded to speak to Sauder immediately before the pirates touched anything.

"So you're Blackheart, then?" the lanky Scotsman asked.

"Yes, I am. What is it you want?" Hans asked, eyeing the other man.

"Look, I know you're a pirate and you don't owe me spit. But do me a favor... don't touch anything other than the cargo hold. This ship is all we've got. It's our home. The cargo I can replace. The stuff outside of the holds ... that's our lives. I can't replace that," McGregor said, meeting Hans' gaze directly.

"You do realize you are in no position to do anything but hope you are not taking a gliderchute home, yes?"

"Aye."

"And you do realize that I could strip this ship down to the timbers if it pleased me to do so?"

"Aye."

"Did you really expect that asking me to just loot your cargo would change anything?" Hans asked.

The Scottish captain shook his head. "Nay. But I had to try."

Hans looked at the Scot for a moment with a harsh look about him. "It is your lucky day," he announced with a hint of amusement in his voice. "Captain-Gunner, have the ship's Master show you his cargo manifest, take the best third of the lot, and touch nothing else aboard."

*****

"I was a bit surprised at your decision to go easy on that Gypsy Merchant," Annika commented over breakfast. Hans, Annika, Arietta, Gwendoline and Alexi were taking a few friendly minutes and having breakfast together in the Captain's Mess. It was out of the normal for O'Raedy, but Hans had started infrequently requesting three or four of the officers to have breakfast with him, to sit, chat and discuss whatever was on their minds without the more formal and larger gathering of the Dog's Supper.

"What ever did prompt you to that decision, *Capitaine*?" Chief Nurse Coline asked as she spread some blackberry jam on her toast.

Hans had a sip of his coffee, looking thoughtful before he spoke. "A combination of things, actually. The first is a conversation I had with Michael O'Raedy in the good *Döktor's* Medical Bay on the day I first met the *Bloody Rose* and the man that was Blackheart."

Koblinski laughed lightly. "I recall you being a very defiant and self-certain young man that morning. Particularly for a chap who had woken up in his pyjama's aboard a pirate ship."

A round of laughter went around the group and Hans tipped his glass towards the Polish doctor. "Indeed. It was a very interesting day for everyone, to be sure. In our discussion where he 'persuaded' me to join the crew, he told me it was '*...very rare that the entire ship is taken or lost... we do not have the room aboard or the crew so we only take the cream of the crop*'. It has been a while since we have had the luxury of practising that approach to piracy, and so I thought it was a good time to resume it."

Nods and affirmations went around the group. "What else, then?   You said it was a combination of things?" Arietta noted.

"Oh," Hans chuckled as he paused with a piece of sausage on his fork. "I liked his brass, as it were. There he is, standing in front of the 'infamous Captain Blackheart' of the *Bloody Rose*, with enough guts to look me in the eye and ask for some goodness and mercy. He was standing up for what he believed in and what he felt was worth fighting for, no matter his situation. I like that. I thought it would be worthwhile to reward it."

"Well, bravo to you, Hans," Koblinski said with a nod and a hoist of his glass. "A bit of kindness from time to time goes a long way to improve our world, such as it is." Smiles and murmurs of agreement came from the others.

"Do not think me so humanist, *Herr Döktor*," Hans said with a laugh. "You never know when a kindness done as a favor can yield a fine repayment."

"They were quite a colourful crew," Gwendoline commented.   "The engineer was a snow-haired Basque gentleman who was older than I was and using a cane to get around. He took a musket ball in the leg years ago and the bone was never set properly, so he needs the cane to walk. The Cabin Boy ... well, if he was fifteen, I would be surprised. All full of fire and wind; very ship-proud."

Hans looked from Gwendoline to Alexi and back. "Spent a few minutes socializing, did you?" he asked, amusedly.

"*Mais oui*," she replied firmly. "I am a Nurse, *mon Capitaine*, and at the point we were taking goods aboard from that dubious little airship, Alexi and I thought it prudent that we check for signs of illness or infestation, so we did not bring anything else aboard."

Hans was rather amused by her challenging tone. "Auntie Gwen", like the good doctor Koblinski, always put her calling as healer and care-giver first. "A wise decision," the German pirate captain said with a nod of agreement. "What else did you discover about them?"

"The navigator is the young woman that was at the Captain's side. She is from Poland, originally; Prague to be exact. Not too talkative, but apparently quite good at her work. The other two are a pair of brothers from Romania; they are general hands. Jacks of all trades, as it were. From chatting with the young Polish lady, it seems they cross the Scorchlands regularly ... not quite smuggling, but not quite with papers and licenses, either."

Hans cocked an eyebrow for a moment. "Oh really? Well. That is interesting. Very interesting. Any idea where they were bound next?"

"Paris, actually," Annika replied. "They have a small contract for a set of runs between Belfast and Paris."

Hans tapped a finger on the table for a moment. "So, tell me, Alexi. Do you feel like taking Gwen to Paris for a month or so?"

The bearded Pole nearly choked on his glass of juice. "Pardon, Captain?"

"Quietly finding out a bit more about the '*Becca's Delight*' and her crew might be an interesting line of inquiry in the long term.   If they are crossing the Scorchlands regularly, that means they have found a route that avoids the Allied and RIAN ships and authorities. That alone is very valuable to us, given recent history. I think you might well have the sort of skills that would lend itself to this sort of thing, Alexi. Take Gwen with you; we will not need you in Persia for the first month. I will ensure Bridges has some travel money for you both when we get to Brussels. Find out what you can. This amusing little crew has my interest."

*****

Later that morning the *Bloody Rose* was angling herself for an approach against stiff winds as she maneuvered to the airship docking tower at the edge of a small town nestled into the beauty of the country side just north of Brussels. Hans watched Lynch and Grumman working together to avoid the twin calamities of either loosing headway, or surging ahead in a moment of lighter wind.

The docking tower itself was hidden in what looked from a distance to be a large, abandoned and somewhat decrepit barn. Watching the middle of the roof open, and the hidden tower of bass, copper, aluminium and wood within slowly rise upwards, was no less impressive to Hans than the first time he had seen it. Electric lights flashed, gouts of steam billowed down from piston heads, and sparks sprayed from gear wheels and cogbars. Once fully raised, the tower had increased the height of the barn by a factor of two.

Through his spyglass, Hans watched as safety nets extended out around the platform head by themselves, even as a rope and stanchion guardrail raised itself. He did not recall those being present on the last visit, a hint that the facility had made improvements in the past few months. He chuckled softly at the recollection of Michael O'Raedy's explanation of 'Economics and the Need of Distribution', as managed by pirates. He wondered how many other little towns like this one dotted Europe, politely and quietly hiding one of their true sources of trade and revenue; piracy.

"Helms and planes, mind your gears as we get close to that tower," the Irishwoman admonished. "There will be vortexes around it and if you are not careful, we will get beaten against that tower before our lines are secure." The two crewmen at the controls nodded and confirmed they heard the warning as they fought with the ship.

"Almost like she does not want to go along side, hmm?" Hans asked as he watched the bridge crew.

"Aye, sir. I have docked in worse ... it is tricky, but we will not fail you," the Confederate-American replied, trying to sound more confident than he apparently felt.

"Oh, I have no reason to expect you to fail," Hans replied with a casual wave of his hand. "The *Bloody Rose* is blessed with some of the best ship drivers I have ever met, and that includes you two. Let us get her alongside so we can get unloaded and make ready for Pay and Party."

After a few more tense minutes, the bow crew succeeded in getting the forward line passed to the dock crew. Shortly thereafter, her stern line was secured and the ship was made fast.

"Well done, all," Hans said. "I knew you could do it. Damn difficult approach with that headwind, and done flawlessly. Get the last details squared away, ladies and gentlemen. I will be in my cabin working with Chief Bridges."

*****

"Well, sir, this is all very good news," Chief Bridges said, setting the sheaf of papers down beside him and then picking up his tea cup. "Very solid numbers from everything the local merchants have proposed."

"We are rather much the beggars at the hawkers, are we not?" Hans asked, leaning back in his chair and rubbing his eyes with the heels of his hands.

"Aye, that is a good way to put it, Sir. This is not like London where we just match common stock to common needs," the frazzle-haired Chief Steward said with a nod.

"Mmm. Essentially everything they are buying from us is for speculation," Hans said thoughtfully. "So while our eclectic selection of goods gives them something their competitors cannot easily get, it also means they have to work harder to find an actual market for it."

"Absolutely right, Mister Sauder, Sir. On the other hand, things like Irish whisky, English wool and American motor parts are not as challenging as other things to find markets for."

"Any reason not to Pay and Party now, before we get to the leisure of Persia?" Hans asked.

"None at all, Sir. In fact, I think it will be a good way to finish off the run from America. We are only a few days from Persia, here."

"Less than two days, actually, Chief, even at a very leisurely speed made good on a single propeller. Particularly if we do not go looking for trouble on the trip. We could be there in little more than a day if we wanted to burn the fuel with all three propellers streamed."

"Well, then, Sir, I would say Pay and Party tonight is the right answer. This particular town is much more friendly than the shipyards of Persia."

*****

It was much later in the evening when the pirate crew assembled on the midships weather deck before their new captain. A hot European summer day had left behind it a cool and still night. A waning moon was shining in a star-jeweled and velvet cloud-curtained sky. The mechanical sounds of the airship and the docking platform obscured all but the loudest noises of the natural world at night. The man the world knew as Blackheart stood at the front railing of the quarter deck, flanked by his officers. The gas lamps flickered softly as everyone waited expectantly for the news.

Everything had changed since Hans was last here, he thought as he looked at the faces of the pirates that were now his crew. The last time he was here, he had barely known anything about himself, his world, or his place in it. He had not yet met Camilla, he had not yet gone for the the swim with Annika where she made her intentions plain to him, Michael O'Raedy was very much still the captain of the *Bloody Rose*, and they had not yet become the hired guns of the British Empire and her Allies.

"*Bloody Rose*," Hans began with a grin, "here we are, back in our favourite roost on the edge of our favourite hunting grounds. The folk of the town and the merchants from all around are happy to see us again. They know, as you know, as I know, that the *Bloody Rose* in town here means two things … booty to be bought and sold … and a helluva Pay and Party!"

The crowd hooted, shouted and stomped their feet in approval, filling the air with their glee. Night birds in nearby trees were startled to flight at the sudden commotion. Hans waited until the din began to subside before resuming.

"We have been to Hell … and America … and back on this trip," he said with a wicked grin. A round of laughs circulated on the weather deck. "Both our mercenary's errand and our pirate's work have paid well. But, the Old Girl is in need of time and money in a graving cradle to make sure she can continue to uphold her Legend. So with all that said ," he recalled the words O'Raedy had used to make this announcement, and repeated them "... a single crew share is a gentleman pirate's sum of ..."

He trailed off, leaving everyone to hang for just a moment longer, as O'Raedy had.   "Three and a quarter pounds Stirling ... For tonight and every month we are in Persia!" There was a blink of pause followed by a burst of applause and cheers.   Everyone had been expecting perhaps three Pounds tonight and two for each month in Persia. These numbers meant that the party tonight and the idle time in Persia would want for little.

Hans glanced to his left and right, meeting the smiles and nods of Annika and Arietta. He looked back at his crew and shook his fist in the air in triumph.

*****

"We have not done much swimming," Hans noted dryly as he adjusted the blanket atop he and Annika that kept the chill of the evening breeze off their bared bodies. Annika gave a feral chuckle and nibbled at his neck for a moment.

They had spent a couple of hours in the town's public house with the rest of the crew, "Laughing at the Devil" together. It was a closing of a kind; the end of the arduous voyage that had begun a month ago at the behest of the Allied Empires.   Curses and colourful declarations were made against the ships and affairs of both the Allies and the Russians, should they chose to involve themselves in the *Bloody Rose*'s "honest piracy" by several members of the crew. Several bottles of rum, vodka and whiskey met their ends at the hands of the pirates and the townsfolk who joined them.

Eventually, Hans and Annika slipped away, making the walk back to the willow and oak-shrouded cove at the far end of the lake from the town. The plan had been to go swimming together, as they had the first time Annika had brought him here. The process of undressing for the swim had resulted in them both being in a tumble on the thick ferns beneath an ancient oak.

"You did not require much persuading to put off the swim, Hans," she reminded him.

"You pose entirely too convincing an argument at times," he replied, running a hand through her walnut hair. She murmured something in Russian that sounded very content. "It is a very different visit here, this time," he said thoughtfully.

"Stop that," she sighed.

"What?"

"You have done nothing but wax philosophical about all the change that has happened to you since the start of this last engagement by the Allied Empires," she said crossly, poking him in a bare shoulder.

"You say that like it is a bad thing?"

"It is. You are Blackheart. Who you were does not matter twice over. When you put on the clothes of a dead man, that was the end of your old life, whether you knew it or not. When you put on the Black Coat, who you were was doubly dead. There will be plenty of time to live in the past when you are old and grey. If you live that long. Pirates are not known for retiring to a life of *noblesse* and quiet old age."

"Annika," Hans began.

"Oh, shut-up, Hans," she sighed in exasperation. "None of it matters. Why is that so hard for you to understand? You are who you are, right now. Who you were an hour ago simply got you to here and now. It is nothing to dwell on. It is like trying to navigate an airship by taking your lead-marks astern! It tells you nothing about the mountain before you or the valley beside it."

"Annika, a person needs to remember who they were so they can continue to make smart decisions about who they wish to be," he countered, propping himself up on an elbow.   "Otherwise, you repeat your mistakes in an endlessly and uselessly stupid loop."

"*Eto takoye der'mo*," she said in a scathing tone. "You do not have to wallow in wistfulness at bygone echoes of yourself that did not know enough about the real world to not have sought out a pirate ship without me having to club you senseless when I first laid eyes on you. You can learn from your past choices and the lessons of the world without acting like you are pining for a deceased friend."

"Listen, my little Russian witch," Hans scowled, his eyes narrowed as he answered.   "It might be entirely blase for you at this point to have done the unimaginable, but please understand that where I am right now is so far from where I expected to be that it might well be a ocean outpost on Mars.   Please do excuse me if I periodically wonder just how in mercy I managed to get here from boarding a passenger ship in London for school in Sweden."

She snorted at him.   "Do you not understand, Hans? Your story is merely as remarkable as that of anyone else that is interesting aboard the *Bloody Rose*.   You, Michael, Me, Arietta, Alexi, Gwendoline, Amram, Khadija, Bridges... the list goes on.   That scow is a weirdness magnet," she gave a nearly bitter laugh.   "It attracts the finest of the rejects of a world that has no place for them, or is done using them.   We are all casualties of a war that never ended, that is never fought anymore, and will keep making people like you and I because it is better for the Kings, Queens, Presidents, Czars and Generals to have it that way."

"It that what you believe?" Hans asked quietly.

"Yes," she answered firmly.   "I do. I am very happy as a pirate, because it means I am free of what this broken excuse for a world tried to make of me. And you, Hans Sauder, should be equally happy."

"Conclusions"

Friday, the 3rd of August, 1888

It has thus come to an end. The Bloody Rose is secured in her graving dock, her gas bags evacuated, and her tanks and holds being emptied even as I write these words from a hotel overlooking the river that pursues it's lazy, winding course through the heart of this Persian town that will be our home for the next three months.

Michael O'Raedy had made his plans in impeccable detail, and while it does fall to me to execute them, I see no reason I should deviate from them. His plans for his beloved ship will be seen through, even though he will not be at her helm when she takes to the air again in the grey skies of November.

It will be a busy three months for myself, at least. While I am sure I will have time to spend with Annika enjoying this beautiful place, at the same time I would not feel right as either a Captain, an Engineer or a Sauder to not stay abreast of the work being done every day to my home in the skies.

I am looking forward to our time aground, the improvements in the capability of the Bloody Rose, and the chance to recruit new faces to our crew. Even so, a scant day out of the sky, and I *am already looking forward to the return to our hunting grounds and the life of a pirate.*

*****

"*Bueno, mi capitán*," Amram said as raised his spyglass to survey the airspace ahead of them, "you must be relieved. At this point, we are effectively vanished into thin air, from the perspective of the Allied and Russian air navies. The Persians are one of the few people that can remain without an alliance, entirely on the might of their very modern military. Even if the Allies knew where we were, the Persians would be very pleased to make it clear that Persian airspace is patrolled by Persia alone."

Hans chuckled from where he stood by the chart table at the back of the Steering House. The morning sun had only been above the horizon for a handful of minutes, and the band of hills and mountains that ran from Turkey to the Persian Gulf glowed in a glorious radiance, as though sandstone, sky and sunlight sought to bedazzle the onlooking pirates. In an hour or so, they would be at their destination, and the job of securing the ship for the three-month long refit would begin.

"The Persian government are more than happy to provide a safe haven for pirates to disappear to from time to time, or so Chief Bridges tells me. Having a ship our size spend several thousand Marks on a refit, plus supplies and living expenses for a quarter year at a time is hardly something they object to. Particularly since they know that the ensuing heavily armed and lightly coffered menace will be somebody else's problem afterwards," Hans laughed.

The Spanish Deck Officer grinned at him. "I am looking forward to a bit of horseback riding, walking the city and reading while enjoying a glass of fine wine," the Spaniard said. "It will be a pleasure to spend some money on life's true luxuries."

*****

"Cut speed one half," Hans ordered.

"Aye-Aye, cut speed one half," Watch-Officer Grumman repeated, and then relayed the order via the voicepipe to the Propulsion Room.

The *Bloody Rose* maneuvered in slowly, lining up with the graving dock ahead of her, floating in it's artificial lake. The town sported a total of seven of these graving docks, of a variety of sizes from half the size of the incoming pirate ship, to triple her size in length and width.

Each graving "dock" was in fact a massive floating covered shed. The floor, from the front of the shed to the back and most of it's width, could be pulled out of the shed like an opening matchbox. It held the cradle that the incoming airship would land upon and rest in while being worked on. Each shed floated independently of the others, anchored from the end opposite the doors, swinging freely in the wind. Thus any landing or take off would always be done with the ship nose into the wind, and sheltered by the bulk of the graving dock shed.

"One quarter mile to the dock," Annika called, eyeing the structure via her rangefinder.

"Very good, Captain-Gunner. *Fräulein* Lynch, decrease altitude two hundred feet, five degrees down angle," Hans ordered as he studied the graving dock through his spyglass. The Irish Watch Officer repeated his order and nodded at the helm and planesmen to carry it out.

The *Bloody Rose* slowly eased in directly above the wood and iron cradle, hovering a few dozen feet in the air. On each side of her bow, and each side of her stern, dock men with line throwing guns game out, blew whistles to announce their intentions and then fired a carrying line up to the motionless pirate. The crew aboard the *Bloody Rose* pulled the carrying line up, and attached it to steam-powered winches. These in turned pulled up much heavy hawsers, which in turn brought up heavy chains. The chains were made fast to the *Bloody Rose*'s deck fittings, and then the decks were cleared. The pirate airship's propellers spun to a stop and then the motor pods were slowly retracted into the hull. The motorwell doors slid closed.

A flare fired out the bridge door let the dock crew know that all was ready. Then, slowly and carefully, the pirate airship was winched down into the cradle and secured.

A horn sounded three tones, paused and then three additional shorter tones. Slowly, the platform began to move forward, carrying the *Bloody Rose* into the covered shed. This would be her home for the next three months.

"Rather spectacular a process, is it not?" Hans asked, impressed. "Exactly as they said it would be."

"*Da, Kapitan*. They make this look easy," Annika replied. "Of course, having the landing approach always head into the wind makes this all much easier for the visiting airship."

"Indeed it does," the Confederate Watch Officer commented. "And once they have got the lines aboard, its not like we can go anywhere."

"Captain, Propulsion reports all motors stowed and secure, one coal fire lit on minimum until ground-side hook-ups are complete," the red-headed Irish woman reported.

"*Danke, Fräulein* Lynch," Hans said with a nod. "And that, I suppose, is that. Now we begin the process of unloading the holds and draining the old girl dry of anything not absolutely necessary."

****

"Well, Chief?" Hans asked, leaning on a guardrail overlooking the weather deck. Dock worker and pirate alike were moving together to get the ship ready for her refit. The sun was low in the sky as the first day the *Bloody Rose* spent in the shed drew to a close. Hundreds of windows in the shed roof let light in through angled *louvres*, which kept extra heat out. Windmills on the roof provided some of the electricity required for mobile lights, while gas lamps provided fixed lighting in the cavernous interior.

"We are making progress. There is a lot to move aground. The Dockers were not too happy we had a full magazine of powder aboard, plus the rockets and mines. They prefer we come in empty of weapons. A lot less dangerous a storage problem for them, of course."

"Yes, well, I am not flying a pirate ship the from Brussels to Persia without powder aboard. That is just asking to be picked off," Hans snorted.

"Getting shot at is an occupational hazard of piracy," Bridges observed with a hint of humour in his voice. He dusted something invisible from a sleeve of his jacket as he continued speaking. "Not being able to shoot back, on the other hand ... well that sort of thing can take all the joy out of the job. Fairly much what one might call subfunular, aye, sir?"

Hans snorted. "Yes, you could call it that. So, what is left on the list before our part of the job is done?"

"Well, sir, we have a set of lines run into the Propulsion Room and hooked up for steam and electricity, so according to Chief Itala, that means we can start emptying the Tank Hold. The kerosene and water are going aground via those hoses over there," the Chief Steward said, pointing to indicate as he continued speaking, "and they are sorting out how to get the coal bunkers emptied and the drain the ether and ammonia tanks from the Perkins-Harrison ice-makers."

"Understood. I will talk in detail with the Chief Engineer later about the status of her world."

"Aye, sir. On my side of the bulkhead, the Number Two and Three Dry Goods stores are mostly emptied out, and we will work on Number one tomorrow. The Can and Bottle lockers will be tomorrow as well and then emptying the Cold Storage holds will be the day after. Of course, none of that is going to keep for three months, so it is all being sold to the Dock."

"... And we will have to buy fresh supplies of all of that before we leave?" Hans asked.

"Aye, sir. Naturally, it costs more to resupply that what we will make in selling off our Stores, but it is better than loosing the whole lot for naught."

Hans snorted and shook his head in amusement. "After that it is the job of emptying the ship of hammocks, linen and personal effects, correct?"

"That is correct, Sir. Once all the lads and lasses have moved aground, then the ship is in the hands of the Dockers and they start at their part of the job. It will take them a bit more than two months to get the work done, then a week or so where they make sure they have not cocked anything up, then a week where we do day trips with the old girl to make sure they have not cocked anything up, and then a week of moving back aboard and getting stores aboard."

"Europe will not know what hit them when we get back. Between the better guns, better motors and the rest ... we will have quite a set of tools for keeping up our end of the Legend."

"Indeed we will, Sir. Oh ... I am sure the Chief Engineer will have all the details, but we have gotten a very interesting proposal and price for that in-ship voice telegraph system you were interested in. The lads in

Turkey were very keen at the idea of selling us something like that. I think you will be pleased."

"Wonderful news. Voicepipes will always have a place, but I can see how that voice telegraph will help tremendously in some situations," Hans said thoughtfully.

*****

"Just put those ... well, just set the whole thing in a pile in the middle of the room and I will sort it out," Hans told the Porter. "I am here for a while, so I will be unpacking everything anyway." The Porter nodded, unloaded the baggage cart as requested and departed gratefully with a couple of guineas gratuity in his hand.

Hans stood in the middle of his room and looked around. The room was almost embarrassingly spacious, with a fourth-floor balconied view out over the roofs of the town to the blue-green band of the river. The room was a dozen shades of almost white, with dark and rich colours provided by the wood floor, the scattered carpets, trios of planters containing ferns and palms, and paintings hanging on the walls. The entire outside face of the room was a series of French-styled glass double doors which could be opened onto the balcony. Double thicknesses of thin cream curtains kept the heat of the sun out, but allowed sunlight and a breeze in.

The central space of the room was surrounded by three alcoves, one with the curtained bed, one with a bath and wash place, and the third was a smoking room or study done in small. A hookah, a selection of tobaccos, and a backgammon set were on a shelf beside the small table and chair in that alcove.

Each of the alcoves could be screened by the same type of curtains at the balcony doors. At the ceiling of the central area of the room was a pair of clock-work fans that spun slowly, keeping a pleasant breeze circulating.

Hans sighed. He grabbed a *portmanteau* off the pile of his things and took it to a chest of drawers and began transferring its contents. After a few minutes of that, there was a knock at the door.

Hans called for a moment of patience, closed the drawer he was filling, and then went to the door. Annika was waiting when he opened it.

"Well, I see you are sacrificing comfort in the name of budget, Hans. Ever the frugal spendthrift, I see!" she said with a laugh as she came in. She dropped a modest shoulder bag onto a chair.

Hans rolled his eyes at her as she strolled through and headed out into the sunset glory on the balcony. "A lovely view; you can almost see the Graving Docks from here."

"You can, actually," Hans said, joining her and slipping an arm around her waist. "With a spyglass. Not much to see, of course ... just the sheds swinging with the breeze on the lake. I note you did not bring much with you."

"Of course not; I am just here for a visit and to go to dinner with you as we discussed. I already have the rest of my things at my room," she answered, looking up and down the street below. Hans lofted a brow at her, and she glanced over and then scowled at him. "Hans, I told you ... I am not sharing a room with you. I wish my privacy, and my space; something which I do not have the luxury of aboard the *Bloody Rose*. I wish to be able to come and go as I please without having to worry about disturbing you. I do not wish to be constrained in my personal affairs, and I do not wish to be a source of constraint in yours."

"Yes, you did tell me all that. I still consider it a waste of your money to be paying for a room you have said yourself that will be empty four nights in seven." he countered.

"And those other three nights are well worth paying for, Hans Sauder. When I wish to be alone, or with other company, then I do not wish to be feeling like I am held hostage by your generosity. I am my own woman, your lover or not, and my freedom is hardly an expense I begrudge footing a bill for."

Hans shook his head and rolled his eyes in amusement. "Modern women. Why must my tastes run to such modern women?"

She gave him a playful shove and grinned at him. "Because women like your sister would bore you to tears, and we both know it. Now go get changed ... I am hungry for supper and then for dessert."

*****

The moon glowed over the artificial lake that held the floating sheds that served as the airship graving docks. Night birds floated on the water, even as thin ripples of breeze channelled by the local hills played at the water's surface. Stars glittered and were mirrored on its undulating brilliance.

Inside one of the sheds, a solitary shadowed figure climbed the triple switch-back stairs leading from the dock floor to the deck of the *Bloody Rose*. The figure moved quietly and slowly in the after-hours darkness, with the deliberation of someone that knew the route they took by heart. The only light in the shed was the muted glow of moon and stars above, leaving glowing lances that blocked the deck in patterns of dim and shadow.

The figure climbed the stairs to the quarter-deck beside the Steering House. They leaned on the railing looking out at the bared upper decks of the infamous pirate airship in the relative darkness of the Graving Dock shed. The figure patted at a pocket and took out a match and a cigarette case, and lit up.

Hans Sauder, the man the world knew as Captain Blackheart of the *Bloody Rose*, exhaled through his nose and sighed. "I do not know if you can hear me, *Herr Kapitän*," he said in a voice barely above a whisper, "... I do not know where you might be, or if one day we will meet again ... but you have my word I will take care of your ship and crew ... I will not give you reason to regret your faith in me. *Sie haben mein Wort. Sie können mir vertrauen.*"

He took another draw of his cigarette, its glowing tip a little point of cherry in the dim light. He continued to quietly watch the ship, in the shed, in the darkness.

~~~***~~~

"EPILOGUE"

(Morning, Sunday, August 12th, 1888)

The sound of church bells rang clearly through the early autumn chill of Moscow by morning. A flock of loitering doves were scattered by an arriving motor car in front of the headquarters of the Russian Imperial Air Navy. The driver disembarked and moved to open the rear passenger door. A somewhat tall and business-like looking man stepped out of the back of the car. The soldiers flanking the foot of the stairs leading up to the building and those flanking the impressive oak and brass doors all saluted in unison. The door was held open for him as he entered.

He made his way through the largely empty corridors, save for the time to doff his cap and coat, and to pick up a cup of hot drink and a few envelopes from a steward in a large and well appointed lounge area. He greeted a few men in uniform that passed him and he then went up a wide flight of stairs that curled upwards to the next floor. From there, he entered a room a short distance down the hall way.

"Ah, there you are, Maksimilian," a man at one side of a table said in his native Russian. He rose and shook Maksimilian's hand, and then gestured to the man also seated at the table as he spoke. "It is good to see you, my friend. Maksimilian Alkaev, this is Taras Fyodorov, from the Foreign Office. Taras, Maksimilian is our expert on 'Non-Traditional Threats' to Mother Russia."

"Vasya, my friend, you are always too kind. A pleasure to meet you, Mister Fyodorov. Anyone that Vasya Utkin entrusts with his reputation is a man I immediately respect."

The three men chatted insubstantially for a few moments as an Aide brought in a tray with snacks, tea and coffee. Once the Aide had left, and closed the door behind him, Vasya Utkin looked at Taras. "So you have news for us?"

"Yes, we found them in Istanbul ... and promptly lost them again," Taras answered sheepishly, as he removed his spectacles. "However, they are hardly the sort to remain invisible for long. We will find them again soon enough."

"I find it fascinating ... the problems they have caused for us," Vasya commented, tapping at a folder.

"Remarkably resourceful and certainly a surprisingly resilient group, to be sure," Taras Fyodorov replied. "Beyond where the Allied Air Navies have apparently gone the unusual route of providing them with military weapons, they have been very capable at improvising solutions to intractable problems."

"The Allied Empires gave them weapons because there is nothing in the Truce of Paris that says arming proxies that cross the border is illegal," Vasya Utkin said with a laugh, "It is expensive and provocative, but not illegal."

"The Vice-Marshal's grandson has done very well for himself, it would seem," Taras chuckled. "Being paid as a hero by the side he bedeviled for so long."

"There is word that the Vice-Marshal's grandson has had his command usurped," Vasya replied.

"Hmm. It is hard to appeal to the patriotism of a a dead man. I hope the new Captain can be approached."

"From what you describe, as well as the literature that you have provided, I believe they are exactly what we need," Maksimilian Alkaev commented, breaking his silence. "We cannot approach the Allies on this matter, for worry of it becoming a reality from a fearful reaction on the Allies' part. At the same time, we cannot continue to sit here and do nothing."

"I think we are all agreed on the last point," Taras said with a gesture. "The loss of the Book has simply pushed the clockworks of Fate into a slower gear; they continue to grind onwards. I do not wish to see our homeland left a wrecked mess in the results."

The three men nodded. "Very well," Vasya said firmly, "Taras, put your people to the job of tracking the *Bloody Rose*. Once you have them, inform Maksimilian and myself. From there, we will make the required arrangements. Now, obviously, discretion is our watch word. Panic within or without will do more harm than good."

###

Author's closing:

I hope you've enjoyed reading the continued adventures of Hans, Annika, Blackheart and the rest of the scoundrels of the *Bloody Rose*, and visiting their Steampunk world. If you'd like to stay in touch to hear about upcoming books, connect with other fans or let me know what you think, here are some useful links:

Facebook Sauder Diaries Community Page:

https://www.facebook.com/the.sauder.diaries

Twitter:

http://twitter.com/MichelV69

KindleGraph Signatures:

http://www.kindlegraph.com/authors/MichelV69

GoodReads Author Page

http://www.goodreads.com/michelv69

My blog:

http://michelrvaillancourt.com/

I hope you enjoyed the story...

Welcome back to the world of The Sauder Diaries!

Thanks so much for reading! I look forward to hearing from you.

Regards,

Michel R. Vaillancourt, Author

~~~***~~~

The Sauder Diaries

"By Any Other Name" - Released June 11th, 2012

"A Bloodier Rose" - Released October 26th, 2012